Feeling Lively

A Love is Awkward Novel

Beck Erixson

Aegir Haven

Published by Aegir Haven, LLC

ISBN NUMBER 979-8-9897638-0-1 (Paperback)
ISBN NUMBER 979-8-9897638-1-8 (Hardback)
ISBN NUMBER 979-8-9897638-2-5 (ebook)

Editor: Kristen Weber, www.kristenweber.com
Copy Editor: Penina Lopez, www.peninalopez.com
Proofreader: Elaini Caruso
Cover Art: Melody Jeffries Design, www.whimandjoy.com

Dedication

For the ones who know love is awkward and wonderful,
those who give themselves to others wholeheartedly,
and those who fall for themselves while welcoming their soul-
mate.

CHAPTER ONE

Hooray for summer! Only, it's not a celebration day, not really. While most of my colleagues in academia felt the weight of the semester lift to the skies after they handed in their final grades before summer break, I did not. I sling my gray suit jacket over the back of the barstool. Nico, the Greek-god-looking bartender and owner of my hideaway, pulls an amber IPA imported from a trendy brewery in Brooklyn, a short distance across the river. He passes the glass to me over the sandy white bar top. The way I've propped my head up with my elbows on either side of the glass makes it difficult to take a sip short of burying my face directly into the foamy head, but staring down at the bubbles is hypnotizing.

The last day of the academic year should be a day to breathe relief as I shed my sixty-five-hour-base workweeks. I've eyed this cranking down of work at the university since the super-packed spring semester started. Summer break means no longer teaching four courses a semester on top of doing research, service activities for the university, committee work, advising, or whatever other tasks I'm voluntold for. My overloaded schedule this semester was partially my fault. I'm only contracted to teach two courses a semester, but as usual, an adjunct canceled at the last minute, and my boss asked me to take on extra courses, knowing I'd say yes so students wouldn't lack a class they needed to graduate on time.

Between my university work as a tenured associate professor in economics and my side work consulting at big companies, plus my investment properties, which need attention, and my taking on interviews for various television and radio stations as their expert for whatever financial or economic questions they want to parade an expert out for, I'd estimate I work roughly eleven hours a day, seven days a week.

This afternoon, before I could make my escape from campus until September, Dr. Roger Howlett knocked on my office door and in his authoritative yet approachable supervisor tone asked me to teach two courses this summer. Rather than giving my usual instant yes, I felt my brain pounding in my skull, darkening the room.

My visible-only-to-me calendar smothered me to a point I'd never experienced before. The room spun while I silently gushed invisible tears of fatigue intermixed with a heavy serving of overwhelmed. Through a dark blur, I slammed a hand on the giant red eject button by telling him I quit. For the count of two entire heartbeats, I could see clearly. My body held a new-to-me sensation of lightness seasoned with a pinch of terror.

He told me no. Per him, the students need me too much, and they won't be able to fill my position by the fall. He said to go home and get some sleep. I said okay. Like a moron, I apologized for being an inconvenience and told him I'd sleep on quitting, but I physically couldn't take on the courses this summer. The rest of the meeting is as fuzzy as my recollection of how I ended up getting from my office at the university in Manhattan to here with Nico, around the corner from my apartment in Hoboken.

Clearly, the wiring on my red eject button is faulty. Instead of a magical release of my soul from the slow death I've inflicted on myself at the university, my stomach is lead.

"Can I get a hot tea instead?" I ask, rubbing circles on my jaw.

Nico reaches underneath the counter, surfacing with a glass mug filled with hot water and a packet of the Irish tea he keeps for me. He places the drink in front of me, dropping the tea bag into the steaming mug. The mid-May weather isn't too hot for a malty tea—not that there is such a thing as a day too hot for tea.

Empty aged wooden tables are scattered throughout the room. I'm too early for the happy hour crowd but too late for the lunch crowd. My gaze lands on the mirror between the freshly painted white columns on either side of the bar. The surface has the eight different types of love etched into it with *eros*—sexual passion—and *philautia*—love of the self—etched boldest in the center.

I'm not so in love with myself right now, so *philautia* is out. *Eros* requires time to meet a person. Not any person, but the one worth investing my whole self in. My best friend, Fiadh, has been with her boyfriend for nearly two years. It's only a matter of time before she gets married and I see her even less. I've yet to meet anyone worth shuffling my schedule for in the way she does for Gavin. I tuck a strand of my hair into my slicked ponytail and groan at my tea. Maybe I do need the fall to get here.

The ocean-blue walls do nothing to help the blandness inside me except to remind me it's been nearly six years since I've taken any kind of vacation. I suck in a long inhale to slow the free fall inside me. A trip to Milos might help me relax. Beautiful beaches and so much fresh seafood plucked from the ocean. Or I could go to Waterford, Ireland, to visit my granny's friends. I picture my calendar, overstuffed with article due dates, interviews, and expanded consulting projects and grimace. If I'm lucky, I'll slide time in for grocery shopping and an outing with Fiadh.

I pull the tea bag out of the water, placing it on the saucer. With tiny gold tongs, I plunk two sugar cubes into the dark liquid, waiting patiently for them to dissolve rather than stirring to rush the process.

I click on Fiadh's name on my phone to tell her about my attempt to resign and Dr. Howlett's rejection of the attempt before she hears about it from anyone else. A well-manicured hand with fingernails painted a deep purple rests on my shoulder. I turn and find myself face-to-face with the chief academic officer, the provost, Dr. Vera Sokolova. Vera, my boss's boss's boss, is in my hideaway-from-work bar. As I tap off the screen, a numbness settles into my spine.

"Are these seats taken?" a voice not from the provost asks. Vera holds out her phone. She has the president of my university on the call from a conference in Osaka on higher education.

I plaster on the *Life is wonderful; I'm terrific* mask. "Hey, Lisa." I wave at the camera.

"Don't 'hey' me," Lisa says. "I've been awake all night. First in trainings all day here, and then working straight through the night since a certain professor for whom it was daytime was ready to resign." She counts off on her fingers. "I can't calculate time zones when I'm exhausted. I'm thirteen hours ahead. You do the math."

"I see the university gossip train hit you." I take a deep sip of my tea.

"Your resignation is rejected," Lisa says.

"I've heard. But how did you know?" I pull the drinks closer, swallowing down the saliva filling my mouth.

"Vera called me after Roger called her in a panic, saying that you were not only ready to quit but tried to and then rescinded," Lisa says. "Now, I know you, and I'm a little confused here."

"I assume this is why you're violating my special no-work spot," I say.

"You should have picked up your phone," Lisa says. "Move to the round table so we can talk."

I shrug. There's no one else here but Nico, and he won't really care about this.

I oblige Lisa's request. Who am I to turn down the university president, after all? Leaving my suit coat on the chair, I sling my white leather backpack over my shoulder and carry the tea to the round table. I glance at the door and blow out a sigh of relief. Fiadh's not here for this conversation.

Vera, more formally referred to as the provost, or my first true academic mentor, has a little over fifteen years on me, putting her in her late forties. She's intelligent as hell, with an ability to cut through bullshit with kindness as her tool of choice.

I raise my finger for a round for the table. "Can I also get a rag?"

The deep blue leather seat cushions are damp, making it rough to slide over. I tug up on the blousing of my sleeveless white silk shirt to avoid unnecessary stains. My elbows stick to the mix of caked-in grease.

"This place is subtle sexy." Vera pulls her thick black hair up into a coiled bun, with strips of gray set to the left side of her face.

Nico sets the drinks out on the table, lingering when he catches Vera eyeing the open top button on his black shirt. I slide my extra beer over to prop the president up so she can be part of her ambush rather than stuck staring at the pipes on the ceiling.

"Let me know if you need anything else." Nico takes a dramatic slow walk to the bar. He whips the towel over a wet spot on his sleeve, leans against the mirror wall, and focuses on the far screen, where a soccer match runs highlights.

"What am I drinking"—Lisa checks her phone—"at four in the morning?"

"Not wine." Vera rolls up her suit sleeves, revealing an impressive pink-striped lining beneath the navy jacket.

"Four in the morning is much too early for a decent red." I pick up the rag, focusing on the section of the table directly in front of me. The bar has changed hands eight times since I was a kid. This most recent run as a Greek bar has held the longest title of eight years.

Vera rests her forearms on a flattened napkin.

"Bottom line," Lisa says. "What's wrong? If you're burned out, I'll put you on sabbatical."

I have zero desire to continue to feel like I've blinked and the day has ended or to fall asleep at the computer again while my body slowly decays. "Sabbatical isn't going to solve anything other than give me time to finish some of the research I've been working on. Quitting happens to be a permanent hiatus."

"I hear that." Vera nods. "This feels like burnout. I know your schedule and how much you're taking on. This is why you have a community to lean on. So you can scream for help. We've all been there."

I give a soft laugh. Community is what this town was when I was growing up. This block was full of close-knit Irish families like mine and Fiadh's before the mix of investors turned it into a landing pad for city transplants as a Manhattan alternative. After all the areas right around the PATH station were taken, the newcomers pushed farther into the neighborhoods. The block over was all Italian families, and people helped one another. I suppose that's why I bought this building forever ago, along with the one I grew up in. I wanted to own pieces of the city that raised my parents and then me. Only now I don't recognize the neighborhood and practically know no one except Fiadh.

"What other professor at the university would resign and then be encouraged to stay by her chair, the provost, and the president?" Vera asks.

I take a sip of my rapidly cooling tea.

Lisa eyes Vera.

"Only because this is the three of us am I going to be blunt. This isn't professor, provost, and president right now. This is Piper, Vera, and Lisa," Lisa says. "You've clearly burned yourself out, and we're worried about you. Every time I switch on the radio or the news, I catch your voice, be it six a.m. or eleven p. m., when I'm going to sleep. I love hearing your voice. Only—I say this as a friend—I want you out living life."

Vera picks up her beer, and the bubbles fizz up. "Quitting is out of character for you. You love the university. You've never once complained, raised a flag, or requested to reduce your teaching load. Do you know the nonsense we get as requests?" She takes a sip, then nods approvingly. "I have a brand-new assistant professor starting this fall already complaining he has to teach more than one class a semester. His contract says he teaches three classes per semester and does research. He has no grants, nothing except a few papers down. What he has is oversized testicles and an ego he hasn't earned."

"I know you enough to know this mushy we-care-about-you part will not persuade you to stay." Lisa's tone shifts from friendly to more formal. "I'm going to appeal to your business side, but please understand, I'm here for the human side, too."

I lean closer, my head propped on my fists, my elbows sticking to the table. And here it comes, the business argument.

"Enrollment is down. Three other universities like ours have closed in the past week. We need the help of professors who are out there. You're bringing in funding and opportunities for students. Hell, your social and academic statuses are hugely valuable for an institution having to cut budgets." Lisa pauses. "Your classes consistently have long wait lists to get in, and I don't know of another professor in your department who can handle half of what you do."

The lead in my belly grows heavier. The enrollment cliff, mixed with the current shifts in the economy, has become a guillotine for small colleges and universities that don't adjust. Colleges shutting down is an arrow in my heart. The university I went to for my doctorate was close to going under until they took drastic changes like selling off chunks of land that held a portion of their endowment. Donations poured in from people trying to preserve the forest-like vibe of the campus. If my alma mater was at risk, I know my job has an end date. Fiadh and I landed jobs there together when we finished very different doctorates, despite naysayers saying landing positions at the same institution would be impossible. Fiadh needs the university. So does every single person at this table.

I take a long sip of tea. "I'll train a junior faculty member. Give me a hungry assistant professor or a postdoc."

"You don't get it. There isn't another you," Vera says. "When you go, what's left in the business school are a bunch of people who don't know how to communicate in ways that aren't so stuffy."

"Vera!" Lisa covers her mouth. "You're not wrong."

I grip the side of my mug. I don't look like most of my colleagues, undercutting many of their ages by nearly twenty years and being a woman. Vera and Lisa were exceptions like me until they shot up the ranks and switched from teaching to administration.

Unlike my male counterparts, I didn't grow up with money. This is, in part, why I don't always get along with my colleagues. I'm tired of their comments about my looks paving the way for the television spots where I'm asked about topics in finance and economics, thanks to my forging the right contacts for years to earn a spot as a go-to expert. My colleagues don't share my pleasure in breaking down information to be digestible for nonacademics. I can't be blamed for being ambitious, hungry to grow. In the same way, I didn't choose my long dark hair or my physique. I'd like to thank genetics.

Vera's tone shifts to more of a caring aunt. "Can you give me a read on where your head is at?"

"Honestly? I don't have time to feel or process anything. I'm less fun, less all the things I once was, because academia always wants more." The words pour out like I'm in confession, confessing aloud what I've fought for years to push down and ignore.

Lisa grows silent. Vera shakes her head, buying time with a series of beer sips until she's a third of the way down the glass.

"When was the last time you took a break to hang out with friends?" Lisa asks.

Vera squints to read the mirror. "Or had a date and solid eros?"

My mouth goes dry. I grab for the beer and take an extra-long gulp. Tea and beer are not the right combination.

"You don't have to answer that one," Lisa says.

Vera plays with the gold Italian horn that belonged to her late husband around her neck. "Relationships are important. Making time for them is important." She and her college sweetheart did all the things we warn students against, including getting married while in graduate school. They carved moments for each other between demanding schedules of teaching and studying, all culminating in her with a wounded heart after twenty-three years together.

Now she sounds exactly like the tiny voice in my head that I try to drown out with more work. "I don't have time to date. I barely get to be with my friends." The words strangle in my throat. The plural on the word "friends" is pushing it. I have a lot of acquaintances, but true, deep, meaningful friendships remain limited. My circle has shrunk to a single best friend and a neighborhood of faded memories. My phone contact list is primarily coworkers and casual connections. In another world,

Vera and Lisa don't feel obligated to come check on me as mentors; we're simply friends.

"Took me three weeks to know I was going to marry my husband." Vera slides the horn on the chain.

"This has nothing to do with my resignation," I say.

"I disagree," Lisa says. "This has everything to do with your resignation."

Debating among academics is not uncommon, but being the topic of the debate makes me shift in the bench seat. The eight types of love stare down at me from the mirror. I have nothing to offer a partner right now. I want passion and playfulness. A person who will walk over to me, wrap his arms around me when I'm taking on too much, and hold me in place to slow the constant rush of "get everything done immediately" that never lets me settle.

"I'm not against making friends. But when? The chair wants me to teach in the summer. When am I supposed to engage in life? Or find eros?" I roll my eyes at the last word. "For me to give the commodity of my time to a person, he'd need to be wearing a blatantly obvious sign that he is the best man for me." Not that this thought hasn't gone through my head a thousand times.

My phone dings. I rudely stop to check my texts. Fiadh sent me a short message with a picture. I blow up the image on the screen. My heart races a thousand beats a minute. I need to get to Fiadh.

I gesture to the bartender. "Give me two gyros, an enormous order of fries, and a six-pack." I punch out a reply. My dilemma can wait. Fiadh needs me.

"Only one fry?" He gestures across the table.

"To go," I say. "One's for Fiadh."

"Is Fiadh okay?" Lisa asks, her concern genuine.

I shake my head. "She's had a pretty shit day."

"Invite her down," Vera adds.

I give Vera a half smile. "That's not a great idea."

"I'll text her and let her know we're down here," Vera says.

"She'll think she's in trouble if you send her a text message on the last day of classes," I say.

"I'll message her," Lisa says.

"That would be worse." My ears ring. "If you two would refrain from texting Fiadh about this conversation before I get a chance to talk to her, I'll accept the sabbatical offer." I don't need to think. "Unpaid."

"No deal," Lisa says. "You'll do the expert interviews you've already lined up for this summer, agree to be paid, and agree that you'll not take on more projects. Or you'll cut self-imposed deadlines to focus on what's important to you, and then, around mid–fall semester, we can talk again to see how you're doing. The university needs you. Consider this all the release time you should have had since you started."

I glance over at Nico. He gestures that I have five more minutes. The walls in the bar grow closer. My shirt sticks to the table, holding it as captive as the university has me right now.

I tug at the fabric only to have it stick over and over while we wait. Vera sips at her drink, her eyes to the ceiling as she thinks.

The bartender drops the bag on the table. When I go to pay, Vera snags the bill.

"I didn't give you an assignment yet," Vera says.

"I figured Lisa's was big enough," I say.

Vera shakes her head. "Go do what makes your pulse race, even if it's uncomfortable. I want the Piper I met when you started. Get the fuck out of what's comfortable."

I stare at her, my mouth open. "What are the parameters here?" I slide around the side of the table, the pressure of the day squeezing at my lungs.

"If it's not going to kill you, and it makes your pulse race in a good way, lean in." Vera fiddles with the chain, tucking it under her shirt.

"I have to go," I say, excusing myself. "I'll take the release under your terms. Both of your terms."

I rush up the block to find out what the hell happened to Fiadh today.

CHAPTER TWO

T HE BEST-KEPT SECRET TO not sweating profusely in the middle of the woods while hiking is to attach a cooling patch to your lower back. An entire nine days after I attempted to quit and was refused, I'm wonderfully minty and sweat-free for adventure number two with Fiadh. Only, I haven't told her about that part yet. The same day I was being strangled by the overscheduled lack-of-fun life I've been treading water in, her academic schmuck of a now ex dumped her in a letter the afternoon she found out she lost her funding for her dream cidery project. What dickhead dumps a person in a letter?

Mr. Snoozefest had the audacity to call her boring.

She is not boring. She's amazing. He's no more than a piece of popcorn kernel stuck between teeth that doesn't want to come out with brushing.

Fiadh and I both need the time out of the city. Last week was horseback riding. I don't think I've laughed so hard in years. The days couldn't pass fast enough to get to today's sun-scorching Twelve-Mile Saturday Refresher, aka the twelve-mile hike I scheduled us for after a few too many drinks. She was upset because her world was flipped over, and I knew if I didn't act immediately to sign us up for a series of summer adventures, I'd lose myself in stacks of research papers. To be fair, at the time my eyes were blurry from exhaustion, and I read "two-mile hike." Twelve miles can't be that bad, right?

I'm not going to apologize for signing us up for a summer of distractions. Vera and Lisa's point wasn't wrong: I need to reconnect with the version of me where I'm happiest. Doing stupid shit with Fiadh makes me happy. There's an unspoken comfort in being around my best friend since birth. Our grandmothers practically raised us together like sisters, and as the older one by five months, I do my best to look out for her.

I not-so-sneakily pull a crinkly bag of granola from my pack. Fiadh and our adorable broody guide, Maverick, stare at me while I wrestle the package open like a bear. They could offer to help, but Fiadh knows I'd say no. Granola spills onto the ground. I toss a handful of what's left in the bag into my mouth in an effort to appear like I'm ignoring the flirt-fight-gonna-screw banter happening between the two of them. They're either going to fuck or murder each other before the end of the summer.

The health store two blocks up from my apartment has the best granola. They skip the raisins for cranberries, which are the superior option. As a bonus, the cranberries are grown here in New Jersey, which means that despite the extra cost of the granola, each bite I'm taking helps support a local small business. In one day I'm contributing to three small businesses before two o'clock. Graves Outdoor Adventures for Maverick, the farmer who grew the cranberries, and the health food store that created my customized granola. I crunch slowly between insects buzzing, birds chirping, and the wind blowing through the leaves. I'm free from the ping of my phone, the constant requests for my time, and the pressure from everyone to work longer and longer hours since I "suddenly have time since I'm not teaching."

"Three miles!" Fiadh lets out a groan. The sides of her neck have beads of sweat cascading down.

Great. I only made it to mile three before my head went to basic economics. I crunch harder on the granola.

Fiadh was smart to sport a black racerback tank. My fear of bugs crawling into my bra led me to wear thick leggings under shorts, a tight athletic shirt, and a pair of pink hiking boots. I am not inviting the bugs to feast on me. The outfit choice made sense until the sun cranked itself up way too high for the end of the month.

"Yeah, only nine more to go." I battle the slowly failing cooling patch with a swig of water. If this patch dies out, my legs will be slick with sweat. If this hike had started earlier, we'd all be a little cooler. I'll give Maverick the suggestion later. If he's grumpy, I'll wait until the end of summer.

Fiadh stops walking, her natural pep obliterated. "Twelve miles? We go from a few city blocks to twelve miles in the woods?" Her voice echoes through the trees.

The group ahead of us stops. They're an adorable cluster of teammates and friends who are part of an indoor soccer league in northwestern Jersey out celebrating a joint bachelor and bachelorette party. Their particular area of the state is not to be mistaken with northeastern New Jersey, where my air conditioner is inside a window near my desk right now, keeping the place cool. Nor the super-northwestern New Jersey we are currently in. If I throw a rock hard enough, it'll hit the Pennsylvania border.

The groom-to-be is Hawk. He's loud but funny. Elin, the bride-to-be, exudes a grown-up version of the epitome of the girl next door. The one everyone wants to be friends with and is, from what I can tell at a distance, a ball of happiness. They're both athletic and a little offbeat. Hawk pulls Elin into him, tangling their bodies together, his forearm pushing up a patch on the sleeve that reads, The Bees. Given all the women have this patch on their sleeves, I'm guessing they are all Bees. I study Hawk and Elin, their dynamic, their flirtation. There's a pinch in my heart. I shove more granola in my mouth.

Maverick's giant furry Irish wolfhound, Brendan, noses my arm. I offer him ear scratches with my free hand. The apartment would be less quiet with a dog. My smile fades. My hours are too wonky for a dog.

"Come on, ladies. You registered for this." Maverick signals to the group to keep moving.

Brendan drifts from my hand, slowing his pace in the heat.

"I did not register for this," Fiadh says, a tinge of bite in her words. "Twelve miles?"

I point to where we came from. "We can turn around."

"Giving up?" Maverick's steps are like two of my strides at this point.

"No." Fiadh grimaces. "You owe me a pedicure and brunch, but we're finishing this so his smug face can't be all..."

A tiny wave of happiness pushes through me. She likes him. If she didn't, she wouldn't keep engaging with him or mean-mugging him. "Smuggish."

"Smuggish." She practically jogs to catch up to me. "I want an Epsom salt scrub and a calf massage with twilight nail polish. No, steel-toned. And a big brunch with smoked salmon Benedict at the diner on the way home."

I chuckle. "We do more than this shopping in the city. There are fewer rocks and trees in the way."

"Fewer bugs and smugness, too." Fiadh begins to hike funny, her right foot not completely hitting the ground, like there's a boulder in her sneaker. Her watch beeps, marking that another mile has passed, and then another. I watch as the group ahead of us kicks a soccer ball up the path. If I rush ahead, I could join them. I'm not so great with a ball, but they're not controlling the ball either. I squint to read the letters on the black-and-yellow jerseys ahead. Elin's says BRAVE BRIDE, and Hawk's reads FANTASTIC FUTURE GROOM. BEST MAN is emblazoned in big bold letters on a yellow jersey, smacking my heart, pausing everything around me.

I need to get a better look at him. He's labeled. But that's a coincidence. He's part of a wedding party. I jog ahead to kick the ball, my heart galloping. My foot makes contact with the ball, knocking it into the high grass. I scrunch my face. A woman with thick black curly hair, whose jersey reads BEST MATCHMAKER, throws a thumbs-up. Another woman in their group, whose yellow jersey reads AMAZING BRIDES-MAID, jogs off to the side to get the ball. She waves at me to join them. Me?

Making friends can't be this simple. I catch a glimpse of Best Man again, and my heart pounds hard. I need to see his face.

My heartbeat returns to normal when Fiadh catches up to me. Her chin-length wavy red hair grows wilder by each humid mile. I can't see Best Man anymore—he's too far ahead. Fiadh has her eyes on Maverick. She stumble-steps, not once but twice, without taking her gaze off him. I elbow her and wiggle my eyebrows.

"That's not an adventure I'd pick out for myself." She's not convincing.

"That's the point," I say. "And he's got no ring."

Fiadh nearly crosses her eyes at me, and I stifle a laugh.

"Why on earth are you checking whether he's wearing a ring?" she asks.

Her words were directed at me, but her sightline is squarely on him. I take three intentionally angled steps forward, guiding her straight into him. If she'd bothered looking up, she'd have seen it coming. Her face flushes red.

"Why is my relationship status important?" he grumbles, mid–head count. "Let's focus on the trail before someone gets hurt."

This is my cue to push ahead and search for Best Man again. I'm on a mission to see his face. This will reinforce the coincidence of him being labeled in the middle of the woods. He could be fifty. Not that there's anything wrong with fifty. I know some women are into older guys, but a nearly twenty-year age gap isn't my thing. He could be married. I can't see his hand.

My mission is to confirm what a little flicker in my heart is pulling me toward. I check behind me, and Fiadh is engrossed in her conversation with Maverick. They're catching up to me. I turn in time to see a soccer ball arc wickedly in the direction of Fiadh's head.

"Fiadh, duck!" I scream. She's not moving. Why isn't she moving? Without hesitation, I reach my hand out and lunge to catch the mini missile looking to take her out. The ball bangs hard off my fingertips. There's a loud pop.

I yelp. Pain floods my fingers. I check for Fiadh and see she has clasped her hand over her mouth.

She's okay. There'll be no concussion for her today. I huff a sigh of relief. The adrenaline is wearing off, and I feel every ounce of the throb in my fingertips. I grip my wrist in an effort to stabilize the shake in my arms.

Then *he* appears. I don't need to see the back of his jersey to know it's him. Through a beam of light, the best man rushes down the hill at me. I gasp. My heart stops. It doesn't resume beating until he looks up, locking eyes with me. His sun-kissed white skin glows with each stride he makes through the runway of sunshine leading straight to me. My heart decides it's time to beat so hard, it's in competition with the wind fluttering at his auburn hair, helping usher him to me like a gift from the forest.

I don't know what in the inadvertently manifested gorgeous human is happening, but if I'm actually knocked the hell out on the ground right now, no one better wake me up. I grip my hand, cringing at the sear of pain, which does, in fact, indicate I am not blacked out in the dirt, dreaming. He's unreal. A six-foot gorgeously sculpted marble statue come to life.

"Are you hurt?" His concern tickles at my ears, sending a sweet breeze down my spine.

The bright yellow jersey with black accents clinging to his sculpted athletic body is incredibly distracting. I hold my wrist, twisting into myself, unsure how to respond. Yes, I am hurt. Super-obvious nail bent toward finger issue is happening.

"No, I like my nail like this." The throbbing in my hand lessens when my eyes drop to his mouth. How is his mouth so perfect? Even the little dip in the middle of his top lip is symmetrical. "I'm thinking I can convince the manicurist to charge me for one less nail next time I go."

His eyes study mine. I am not a "read auras" type of person, or a person who can feel energy in any way. But being around him frees every part of me that was in strangled chaos, and there's a fresh feral sensation engulfing my body.

A flood of jerseys descends on us, infiltrating our little dome. I'm frozen in place. A dazed sensation crisscrosses throughout my body, urging me to touch his skin.

"Damn, girl. You went for it," Amazing Bridesmaid says.

"I've been there," the adorable bride-to-be says. "Keep your fingers up."

Their buzz around us muffles, and it's like the man with the glacial blue eyes and I are the only two here.

"Get her a jersey," a player with long red curly hair adds. "She's got Bee potential."

Maverick and Fiadh are off to the right, talking outside my sports huddle. Tears prick at my eyes with my dawning realization of how bad my natural nail bent.

"Oh shit," the man says. "I'm so sorry."

I flick my ponytail over my shoulder and let out a giggle while pinching my wrist. Yup, this is real all right. *Blink, move, close your eyes to release me from this hold. Pick me up and carry me off into the sunset.*

He doesn't.

This isn't like me.

"Here." Maverick rudely slices open our bubble with a white first aid kit.

"I'm Thad, by the way." Mr. Best Man, Thad, reaches for me. "Can I touch it?"

I swish my ponytail, taking an extra beat to study him.

"I'm Piper." I lean closer, distracted by hints of vanilla and fig. "You can touch anything you want."

When his cheeks flush, I ride the high of knowing I might not be alone in the little run-over-by-a-truck daze he's put me into. He takes the first aid kit and guides us from the group to a large rock.

The coolness of the rock helps redirect this weird little orb pulsing in my chest. I'm now acutely aware of the goose bumps covering my body and the ones traveling up his arms despite the heat.

"I have basic medical training, but we should get you checked out by a doctor," Best Man says.

My brain does not know how to function. I put my finger in front of my face to inspect the full damage.

"Mmm...they did not prep me for medical assessments in any of my coursework," I say. "Simply rude of them to leave out such an important element in life and stuff my head full of formulas. What do you suppose is the statute of limitations on a refund for a degree?"

The most amazing thing happens. The strain of concern on his sweet face is swept away, replaced with an adorable deep dimple.

"Mmm, you're, what...three years out of your degree?" He winks.

"Wow, that's some line," I say. "I'm fifty years from my doctoral program. I discovered the fountain of youth. The celebrity NDAs I hold would make you blush."

His eyes drop to my mouth and rake slowly up. "No, I'd say you're less than ten years from your last degree."

"Bang on. What's the giveaway?" My tongue is tingling. Why is my tongue tingling?

"Give me your hand," he says.

His touch is a defibrillator, jolting every inch of me high and shattering the orb before it pulls itself together again, replacing the sensation with a slow and steady once-familiar pulse just awoken from hibernation. I squeeze his forearm, checking once again that he is not a sleep-deprivation-induced hallucination. My body needs a solid night's sleep so badly that I don't trust it to not lure me into such a dream. The ever-present "get everything done immediately" energy in me is off. I didn't know it could turn off. And it's not just off, but a delicious low current streams between us that I don't want to ever end. Asking him to come home with me so we can simply sit together to forever prolong this sensation would come off too bananas. But that's what delicious inside thoughts are for.

Not that he can hear it, but my heart is talking to his, pleading for it to not ever be too far away from mine again. This man has the potential to destroy me in the worst way possible. My hearing goes sharp, and the clarity in my head is intoxicating.

He deftly wraps my finger with a bandage like I'm the puff of a dandelion about to blow away if he rushes. "Am I hurting you?"

I wince when he takes his hand off mine. I don't hate this. Except my head is latched on to a coincidence. Best Man.

The wall of yellow and black around us breaks open, and the ball is kicked up the trail.

"Keep!" Elin yells, rushing to get the ball, with her playful swarm following behind her.

I'm up for this. Maverick and Fiadh can use some time to play fight. Skipping past them, I give Fiadh a thumbs-up. An *I'll find you later. Do your thing, my friend* that I hope she picks up on. It does not take long for me to want to keep these newly opened sensations of joy spreading throughout my body. Instead of hyper-focusing on how fast the day is going, I want to make use of my cell phone being in my car, well detached from my hand. Maybe even learn a little more about Thad. Because tomorrow I'll return to my books with my phone plastered to my body, and this orb will disappear.

I rush ahead, extending a reach for Thad and practically floating when his arm hooks around me playfully, encouraging me to join.

CHAPTER THREE

F IADH HAD CALLED THE spa on Tuesday morning at
exactly 8:00 a.m., when they opened, and negotiated
our way into a Saturday session in the private room during
prime time for pedicures.

"We're going to be late." Fiadh hobble-walks on her heels
to the check-in desk.

"There's no way your feet can still be that bad from the
hike," I say.

She gestures down hard. "Uh, they are."

"How is that possible? That was last week." When I, like
a punk, chickened out of asking Thad for his number at the
end of the hike. I'm chalking his not asking for my number
up to him not being as infatuated as I was. Therefore, my
body was reading things wrong, and the dull, empty ache
that's returned has nothing to do with his disappearing
forever because the small circles of our lives touching was
a one-time fluke. He's a good, friendly guy. Super friendly
and handsome.

The receptionist in the front wraps his hand over the edge
of the black counter. Indifference oozes from his inattentive

posture. Behind him is a series of certificates in gold frames against a shimmering peacock-blue wall.

He clears his throat, adjusting the largest of his gold rings on his forefinger, ensuring the enormous diamonds are set to blind us. We reach the counter and he doesn't make an ounce of effort to greet us.

"Lovely day," I say, dripping with sweetness. I swap my rings to my forefinger.

"Lovely indeed," Fiadh says, her faux posh accent nearly does me in.

"Last name so we can get you all checked into the system?" He takes his time hitting each letter of the keyboard all the way down before moving to the next.

"O'Cleary and Yeats," Fiadh says. "I have a set of coupons that my beautiful, hardworking, complete pain-in-my-feet friend and I would like to use."

He plasters a *Why do I have to deal with humans?* smirk on his face. "All right, I didn't sleep and I have a headache. Let's get you two into robes and in the correct room."

"He wants us naked." I tug up on the collar of my shirt until his face turns a shade of exasperated.

"Did the coupons say anything about being naked?" Fiadh scrunches her face, scanning the details on her folded paper for words I know aren't there. "I've never had to put on a robe for a pedicure before."

"This package includes a calf and foot massage. You don't have to wear the robes, but people tend to like them." The man pinches the bridge of his nose. A wide gold band on his pinkie takes up nearly the whole phalanx. "Can I offer you cucumber mint water or an herbal tea?"

"Two robes sound great," Fiadh says, dropping the accent.

The dark shadows under his eyes may be hidden beneath concealer, but I know that heaviness in his eyelids. I'm the same way practically every night until I force myself to go to bed.

"Can I get you a coffee with extra shots delivered?" I ask, dropping the playfulness.

"I should be asking you that question." The man punches what I'm assuming are our names into the computer—or more deserved nicknames like Pain-in-the-Foot and Pain-in-My-Side. "The coupons are for an upgrade from the level you registered for. Get me that coffee, and I'll throw in a manicure."

I bite my lower lip, raising my hand to show him the wickedness of my fingernail. "I love the offer, but I punched a ball last week."

He cringes. "Oh, honey, don't ever punch a ball." The man holds out his palm, gesturing for my nail. "Yeah, you're going to lose this in a few weeks. Come in when you're ready for tips."

"Lose the nail?" A green tinge blooms on Fiadh's face.

He pulls out two new coupons from beneath the register. The cream paper is printed with gold lettering. He slides one to me and the other to Fiadh. She bounces on her heels, wincing on the last down.

What is wrong with her feet?

He hands us fresh plush peach robes that I swear were on a hidden heater under the counter. I want to snuggle in a pile of these and take a nap.

"Walk straight through the hallway to the changing rooms. Once you're ready, come out and your pedicurists will be waiting for you." He shoos us on our way.

We follow the directions, swiftly changing out of our clothes and emerging from the locker room to be taken to the private pedicure space. I open my phone on the way up the Gothic gray hallway. The walls are more of a gravestone gray, not exactly relaxing. An ornate black beaded sconce illuminates our pathway. Despite the vampire vibes, this place is pleasantly chill. I open the local delivery app to order from the coffee shop next door. The lengthy list of additional options drives a pulse in my temple.

Syrup? Foam? Creamer? I know none of this. I tap at the screen, lighting it without making a selection. What's his caffeine tolerance? Is he lactose intolerant? The safest bet is black—let him flavor it here.

I hit the little plus sign next to the extra shot of espresso. Do I want to add a note? Sure. Why not? *Deliver to the fabulous man half-asleep at the front desk so he has a better day.* I hit submit order, then stuff the phone deep into the pockets of the robe. The collar's soft sides brush against my cheek, releasing the scent of rose hips.

Fiadh taps the wall placard with our names. She tugs me through the open door, and the vibe changes. The same peacock-blue shimmer of the lobby area frames the room. I carefully maneuver around trays of equipment to sink into a plush leather chair.

Technically, the room fits four people, but I couldn't think of a third person, let alone a fourth, who would want to join us, nor who has our more flexible schedules. Fiadh's mom would have been an option, but then I'd be barring myself from the topic of Maverick. Vera and Lisa may have said yes, but given the situation with Fiadh's grant, along with the sabbatical I'm taking, they weren't the best options. Plus, Fiadh doesn't have the same relationship with them that I do.

The two outer seats now hold our bags, keeping them high off the floor. Mine is a camel leather with gold accents, hers, a canvas vintage green with leather straps.

"I can move the bags into a locker if you'd prefer," the pedicurist on her side of the room says, wrapping a black leather apron around his waist to cover his black shirt and pants. The man's deep blue fringe is impressive. The upkeep on that type of coloring is expensive.

On my side is a short, adorable woman who at best is about eighteen, leaving me to wonder how long she's been doing this. She pulls a gator clip off the base of her black shirt, pulling her old-money blond hair from the front of her face. I've always loved that hair color, but personality-wise, I emanate dark brunette way better than I could blond.

"We're fine unless it's a spa rule." Fiadh pushes the buttons on her remote until the chair makes a loud whirring noise. She lets out a weird grunt, grabbing for her shin. Her calves are imprisoned in the leg slots, with her feet on the small bench.

"The rule is whatever you're most comfortable with, and no calls in the rooms. The less you have with you, the more you can relax," the woman says. She picks up Fiadh's remote and presses a few buttons. The chair releases the calf stronghold.

Fiadh sinks her blistered feet into the basin in front of her. The pedicurist sits on a small stool. He lays a gold towel across his knees. Once he's done situating, he presses a series of buttons. The first makes the massage chair glow red, and the next causes an eruption of bubbles to rise to the surface of the water.

Fiadh grimaces. "This is what I'm talking about," she says, feigning positivity. She bites down on the upper part of the robe.

Steam rises with the exploding bubbles, the rate of their production growing intense like a hot tub with soap added. My pedicurist touches my feet, drawing my focus. She slips them carefully one at a time into my cauldron. The temperature is a degree above scalding. Rather than asking her to lower it to a point where we can't make soup from my skin, I clench my thighs together and hope to acclimate. The woman jabs a knuckle at the bubble button, redirecting my focus from the heat to the jets annihilating my feet. If there were any dead skin cells on my feet of any type, I guarantee they're now evaporated. Fiadh is practically dancing, picking her feet up and out of the water only to dip a toe in, her face scrunched, staring down at the water splashing over the sides.

"This is nice." Her voice is pitched high.

"I'm sorry we can't do the manicure too," I say, holding up my finger. The swelling has gone down, but it remains super sensitive when I touch anything.

"You will forever be my knight in shining armor." Fiadh leans forward, adjusting two of the dials at her feet.

Both people attending to us are now crouched low on stools in a puddle of water, frantically hitting uncooperative buttons.

The woman flicks her bangs from her eyes and places her hand on the steam rising from my foot.

"Yikes!" The woman lays the inside of her wrist on my arch like she's taking its temperature. "I'm so sorry. Damn it. The hoses were swapped again." She stands up, not seeming to mind the water on the floor, to crouch between Fiadh and me. She swaps out some tubes, grabs a floor squeegee, and pushes the water to the center floor drain.

The man swaddles each of Fiadh's feet with dry towels. I bite my lip to keep from laughing. Fiadh reaches her hand out for mine to hold. Her arm is shaking, and the vibration of her chair travels from her through my armpit. I burst out laughing at the disaster in front of us, unable to resist any longer. Fiadh's giggles fill the space.

"The coupons should have been a clue," she says.

"No. No. No. This is the building. I'm so sorry." The woman pats at my feet.

Fiadh's more-than-silent caretaker has returned to his bench, and the water is safely down the drain. He frowns at the malfunctioned foot soaking bins.

"I can call Jeremy and ask him to give you a refund." He brushes his thighs off. His dropped gaze gives him the appearance of a puppy who wants an ear scratch.

"Jeremy is the man out front?" I ask.

The pedicurist gives a quick nod.

"We don't need a refund." Let the poor man enjoy a coffee without interruption.

My pedicurist leans forward, practically between my thighs, to reach the tubes next to my chair. I swing my leg over to the other side like a contemporary dancer in her first competition to give her access to the right tubes.

"If you move to an outer chair, we should be all right," the woman says. "'Should be,' being the operative phrase."

The man rolls his pedicure station closer to the wall to set up in front of one of the two vacant chairs.

"Hit the buttons first, I want to confirm the water isn't going to shoot straight in the air," Fiadh says. "She's a lot faster on the no-refunds thing than I am."

The pedicurist obliges the request, and the machine pumps tiny bubbles throughout.

"The one for the chair, too," Fiadh pushes.

Once again, the pedicurist obliges, and there's a soft hum from the chair next to her. Fiadh releases my hand to switch chairs. I stand and pick up my bag, dropping it into the now-free center seat. A little buzz shakes inside my pocket.

The rest of the appointment goes off perfectly. My calves are exfoliated, my pressure points, hit and released. The techs dim the lights in the room. The woman puts cucumbers on my eyelids, letting them drag down to a relaxation I didn't know I needed. We settle into the quiet.

We can hear the door shut as the two employees leave the room, and Fiadh and I are alone. Tiny giggles from my best friend turn into a roar of contagious laughter.

"Shh, they'll hear us," I say.

"I'm thinking we should stop using spas with coupons," Fiadh says.

I drop the mask from my eyes. Fiadh is relaxed and laughing, letting go like when we were little, despite the swirl of stress we've been living in.

I lift my phone, taking a snapshot of Fiadh mid-giggle to memorialize the day. My finger hovers over the button, and a text comes through from a number I don't recognize. I study the 908 area code, scrolling through the list of names in my head that I don't have a phone number for. The adventure center is a 973, not a 908.

My heart hits a double beat, urging me to click open the text. I glance at Fiadh. Her knees are bent, with her feet on the front of her seat, while we wait for our toes to dry. Her whole body is draped comfortably in the chair.

"What?" she asks. "You're staring at me."

I snap three photos in a row.

"I get veto power on those." She lifts a cucumber from an eye.

I wave her off. "You look like a lady of leisure."

"I'm a stress factory pushing stress to later me—like when we leave here."

An infuser mists threads of vanilla into the air.

Vanilla. I close my eyes, giggling to myself while cradling my phone in my palm. The warmth of Thad's hand on my elbow traces into my memory, the orb in my chest pulsing, and the full shock to my system of being alive in the moment with him takes hold. Please?

Heart beating in my ears, I flick open the text, and there are three simple messages.

908: *Hey, this is Thad.*

Thad: *I hope you don't mind, but I found your office number. The office number left this as the number to message.*

Thad: *I wanted to check on you and your finger.*

I peek at Fiadh to ensure she can't hear the thunderous pounding of my heart. If she can, she's playing it very cool. I lick my lips, my finger shaking over each letter as I type.

Me: *Finger's great. I can do all the things one needs to with a finger.*

Thad: *I'd feel better if I could see that.*

Does he want to see a picture of my finger?

I snap a picture and hit send. Sending a finger picture is a new one for me, but this is better than being asked for a shot of my boobs. My finger is swollen like a tiny thick dick. I groan.

"What's wrong?" Fiadh asks.

"I..."—*wish I could erase that*—"I banged my finger."

"Gross," she says.

Thad: *I'm not sure the picture is doing it justice. How would you feel about showing me in person? Say, 3:00 next Saturday?*

Yes, both my vagina and I scream internally. I glance down at my lap, wondering when she decided to chime in.

Me: *My finger has plans to be super busy on Saturday.* Delete.

Before I can be stupid, I type a new message. Not the right vibe.

Me: *My finger and I would be happy to meet you on Saturday at three. Do we get any more details?*

The internal scream shifts to a full-out desire to do laps of excitement around the room.

Thad: *1 Evergreen Drive, Chester, NJ. Semiformal to Formal Attire.*

Me: *I need way more details with that dress code.*

Thad: *What's the fun in that? I promise you a good time.*

My calendar appears in front of my joy, looking to demolish the buzzing of the orb. Task after task I need to get through piles onto me, smothering my ability to form a response.

"Piper?" Fiadh's words carry a gentle concern.

"I'm okay," I say, too fast. She doesn't need to know about a single date. She needs to figure out the grant for the cidery mill and not get distracted by me saying yes to next Saturday with him. She needs to heal her heart first before worrying about mine. My agreeing is no big deal. The last date I went on was...When was it? Crap. I don't even remember. Yes, she'll make too huge a deal out of this.

I mentally shift each appointment and task on the list to different days and different times. Pushing into what I know will be late nights all week to be able to go on Saturday. One night to feel the orb like I did in the woods before I get buried under work again.

Me: *I'm in. Soccer uniform, 3:00 in Chester.*

Him: *Semiformal to formal for 3:00. If you really want to sport a soccer jersey, I can make arrangements for after.*

I give the message a soft smile he clearly can't see.

Me: *Did you invite me to sleep over so directly?*

Him: *Yeah...that was not my intention. I'm so sorry. I really meant I can get us onto a soccer field afterward if you want. But I see how that didn't come through well.*

Me: *3:00 in Chester, semiformal to formal. Anything I should bring?*

Him: *Yourself. All I need is you.*

I slide down the chair, allowing my body to become the jelly it wants to be.

Footsteps draw near our door. I slide my phone into my pocket. The low buzz of anticipation inside me intermixes with the cloud of anxiety I feel at falling behind. Worst case, I can always cancel.

Who am I trying to kid? I'm not canceling.

CHAPTER FOUR

THE STEEL COLOR OF the pedicure from last Saturday is holding strong even after Fiadh and I left the spa to walk—in her case, hobble—miles around the city. I went to bed at two last night to simply not sleep, thanks to my anticipation for today: the need to get everything done, to not be late, and prepping outfits for a date I know little about.

The limited information is liberating in a way. There were no hours of research outside of discovering that the address I'm to meet him at is a building on fifteen acres of heavily wooded property. Fifteen acres of property that is not a farm is unreal in this area of the state, and despite my ability to research in depth, I couldn't 100 percent confirm the owner. Given the attire request, I'm pretty sure we aren't headed out hiking. To counter the extreme vagueness of the instructions, I have three additional outfits plus accessories hidden in my trunk. Should I have insisted on clarification? Probably. But if I'm going to give my best friend the advice to take a leap of adventure, I, too, can take a leap of adventure in formal attire with Mr. Best Man for one night. One night is not a commitment of forever. If nothing else, I'll get to see if that pull toward him during the hike was real or if it was the woods, my lack of sleep, and whatever testosterone I was inhaling off him.

Why is it getting so hot all of a sudden? The car's temperature is a steady 68.

A blinking arrow from the GPS grows brighter, and I crank the wheel to the right off the windy road and through the small clearing between a slit in the trees. My tires crunch on white gravel as the car crawls up a long driveway flanked with perfectly manicured box trees and evergreens. I stop biting my lips to avoid ruining the red lipstick I've applied several times over.

At the end of the nearly quarter-mile drive, I slot the car into a space on the grass between a series of black SUVs to the left of a grand Tudor. There are multiple great peaks with wood accents over cream stucco. Ample space around the building makes the size appear much cozier until I home in on the enormous windows. The building and grounds belong in a magazine.

I tug up on the front of my silk bronze dress. Leaning formal was the right choice based on the grand landscaping alone. I place my hand on my stomach and twist a strap on my dress. I didn't tell Fiadh where I was going, which isn't standard for the two of us. But she's busy at the adventure center and dealing with her broken heart. I can go on a date without letting her know where I am.

To be safe, I turn on my location marker and throw a tracker tag under the seat of my car. I step out of my small black sports car and make my way to the back. One click of my remote opens the trunk, revealing three neatly arranged emergency outfits and accessories in plastic containers.

"I'd go with the green bow," a man's tender voice says politely from behind me. "How's your finger?"

His politeness takes a strong hold of me. Polite shouldn't be an attention grabber. Nor should it make my stomach swoop. Yet here I am plucking the long deep green satin bow from the container.

"Never better." *Remain calm.* There is only so long I can keep myself from turning, and man, do I want to turn. The giddiness I feel at being in his proximity again is heavenly. "To be safe, I'll avoid trying to save a ball tonight."

He gives a low chuckle.

I pivot to face him, stroking the long ends of the satin bow.

My heart skips. I stop touching the satin and find myself looking him up and down repeatedly. No, not in a weird way. In a *How is Thad even sexier since I last saw him? Are my heels stuck in the ground, or are my legs frozen in place?* type of way. He's in front of me in a slim-fitting evergreen suit with a deep green vest over a crisp white shirt. A dried boutonniere of yellow straw flower and billy buttons is fastened to the lapel of his buttoned jacket, and a white pocket square is tucked into his outer breast pocket. The accent of his brown belt and shoes isn't helping the fact that I can't stop staring at him intently. Last time I saw him, he was in a soccer jersey and shorts, fixing my finger, and now he's emanating a different level of sexiness, leaving zero clues to go off for me to figure out tonight's plans.

He shoves his hands deep in his pockets. There is a clear definition of his pecs peeking through his top buttons, and to avoid making things more awkward, I choose to lock my gaze on his. If I keep staring at his eyes, I won't ogle him. Not as openly or drool-laden.

Thad reaches his hand out to me, and I more than happily slip mine into his. He then reaches across to close my trunk. I'm fixated on his face. His sweet grin screams that he might be as happy to see me as I am to see him.

"Thanks." I smooth down the front of my dress. "Why do you have a boutonniere?"

He takes a step to give us space I don't need, gently fidgeting with our fingers.

"I'm going to give you a chance to run now, but I'd very much rather you stay." He bites his lower lip, seemingly buying time. "This is Hawk and Elin's wedding."

"No. They're getting married at a farm in a few months." Jazz music mingles with a low rumble of laughter and giggles from the other side of the house. This is a wedding. I'm already outside. Why can't I find air? *Lungs, work, damn it.*

He shakes his head. "After we were hiking, I got a text from Hawk asking if I'd help him move the wedding date up and to here since there was some fundraiser at the farm so they couldn't do it there this weekend."

Fundraiser? "Wait, it was at Amelia's farm?" As in Maverick's soon to be sister-in-law's farm? "Was she bummed out? She's a sweetheart." I gesture to the wedding venue. "This seems beyond best man duties."

"Amelia didn't mind moving everything, but I'm sure she's not going to be happy to miss the party. Unfortunately there was no way for her to get out of the fundraiser." He tilts his head, his eyebrows reaching like he's processing the question. "You do know they're cousins, right? Amelia and Elin. The farm space was a wedding gift, but all Amelia wants is for Elin to be happy and married to Hawk. Given their past, we—my friends and I—are of the collective mind that nothing is going to stop these two from getting married. For them, the sooner the better."

"I didn't know they were related. Not that I should know, but, wow, Amelia was gifting them a wedding venue." In my short list of friends, there's only one person I can imagine trying to shift the world for me. This location shift wasn't one person. It was friends, family, caterers, every employee here, from musicians to who knows what else will be in the yard. A familiar, lonely twinge hits me.

I'm not sure if Thad caught the split second my smile disappeared, but he rubs his forefinger against the side of mine, then straightens his posture. I mirror his body language, giving a soft wish that he keep comforting my nerves with the gentle thread of the side of his finger against mine over and over forever. Forever? Not forever.

"I realize this is a lot." He speaks softly, like he's afraid he's going to spook me. "But I in no way could think of a better first date than a wedding with you"—his face goes pale—"than bringing you as a date to a wedding."

I smirk. "Smooth. Let's see how the night goes before either of us proposes."

He bites his lip.

I slide my hand farther up his, clutching to his warmth to brace against the sudden need to sit. Either the architectural wonder next to us is bigger than when I first got here, or I'm shrinking.

"You're here to have dinner with me. Dance. So we can get to know each other. The ceremony is done. They did that in the garden early this morning. This is no different from any other date. Except that my best friend got married today."

"Except that I'm crashing a reception for people I don't know." My stomach knots. I can't do this.

"How would this be any different if we'd been dating for three months, six months, or even a year already? Please be my date." The sensitivity in his voice mixes with absolute vulnerability.

Well, there's no way I'm saying no. When our palms press tight, without being able to explain why, it's like we're supposed to be here together.

"If I'm going to essentially crash a wedding, at least I know I'll have the handsomest date," I say.

His cheeks pinken, and his grin shifts to a full smile I'm now declaring as mine. For the night.

We walk up the stone steps, past the bees busy buzzing about the clusters of hydrangeas.

He stops before opening the door. "Thank you. If you need to leave at any point, or want air, say the word—"

"Blueberry macaroon." *Blueberry macaroon? Why?* I place my free hand on my hip, owning my ridiculous declaration.

"Okay." He laughs. "'Blueberry macaroon.' If either of us wants to steal time with the other, can it be 'raspberry macaroon'? 'Blueberry' to get air solo and 'raspberry' to go together?"

My stomach rumbles. "I now inexplicably want an entire plate of cookies."

We enter the house together. The inside is as grand as the outside, much like I imagine Thad to be. The furniture is masculine, but the vibe is comfortable contemporary. We pass through the foyer into an enormous living room with two gigantic navy blue couches with squared sides and clean lines. There are a few staggered white chairs with the same sharp lines. An entire soccer team plus their partners could probably fit in here to watch games on the...There's no television. There's a huge fireplace and pale blue walls. Rich burgundy curtains that extend from the ceiling to the floor are swept to the side with a puddle of fabric at the base.

He ushers me through the house and out the door, where the melodious jazz and the vibrations of happiness and celebration grow louder. People laughing, smiling, and talking closely are spread through the boisterous crowd. There's a group of older women holding hands with one another as they dance in a circle, and people are feeding one another. In short, yes, this is a wedding, but not the kind where it feels as if you are in a room full of strangers and people are clustering off with only the little table they know. This is different. There's a meld here. They're all connected in some magical way. My stomach quivers, and the urge to scream "blueberry" shoots through me.

Rather than letting go, Thad leans in. "We can go back inside if you aren't ready."

Hawk strides over to the microphone. I watch as he scans the backyard until his eyes land on us. Hawk waves us over. "If you two don't come down here soon, I'm going to tell the chef to hold the food."

Thad swallows. He extends his elbow, and I slide my arm through it, letting him guide us down to the grass. He gives my arm a short squeeze as we hit the foot of the stairs. Hawk and Elin have made their way over.

Elin has the stunning glow of a fresh bride. Her hair is long and loose with a peony tucked behind her ear. Her dress is near Grecian, and I swear with her curves she looks like an absolute goddess. Hawk pulls her in tighter by the waist, and she kisses his neck. His eyes flick to the sky.

Thad clears his throat and receives a jab to his abs from Hawk. He doubles over with an embarrassed laugh, maintaining our linked arms.

"Here, these are so no one sinks in the mud." Elin slides a pair of rainbow smiley face slippers from a basket nestled between the peonies. "Your dress is stunning. The bronze makes you look like a statuesque queen."

"You look..." When I look down, she has no shoes on. None. Gorgeous dress, perfect pedicure and manicure, but no shoes.

"Yeah, I don't mind the ground. I lost my slippers earlier." She covers her cheeks with her palms.

"When we had sex in one of the bedrooms," Hawk says bluntly.

Thad sucks in his lips. "You couldn't wait until you got home?"

Elin tilts her chin up. "Nope. We're making up for lost time."

She takes my hand, and I don't know what to say at this point. A fleet of servers comes down the stairs carrying trays of salmon, lasagna, and roasted vegetables. The scents of dill and thyme waft over us. Thad and I move quickly to create space only to find ourselves horrifically split from each other.

My arm is now locked with Elin's. Thad is out of reach thanks to Hawk ushering him to the microphone.

"Come on, you're sitting with us." Elin strolls us through a path of tiki torches. The head table is covered with a violet table-cloth. The chairs are filled with women in pale yellow dresses and men in similar suits to Thad's.

Not only have I crashed a wedding reception, but I've been kidnapped from my date by the bride and sat at a table with her closest friends in the world, and I'm not certain of her last name and don't know much about her. All I know is she's not letting go of me. Like she thinks I'll run away. I study her features.

There is a bit of effortlessness to how she holds herself. She's comfortable in her skin. In her life.

Hawk sits on the other side of her to whisper in her ear.

Elin leans in close to me. "We owe Thad everything."

Thad takes the microphone. Three catcalls and a hoard of whistles of the *you're smoking hot* variety, and his face is bright red. A server hands him a glass of champagne, and the jazz slows to a stop.

He stands in front of nearly two hundred people without hesitation. "While I appreciate the whistles and attention—"

"Let the sexy man speak!" Hawk's voice cuts across the yard.

The whistles stop. Forks stop moving. The hush is palpable.

"Thank you, everyone. First, I'm not sure how Hawk decided I'd be his best man after all these years. I'm guessing because the only other person in the world he could have asked is Elin. From what the minister said this morning, you cannot be both the best man and the bride at the same time. And I will forever acknowledge I am okay with being a second best friend to the person Hawk chose forever ago to spend his life with. I'm going to let Hawk and Elin in on the secret we've all kept.

"We all knew. Everyone knew. Since you came into our lives and joined our soccer family, we knew you were two intelligent people who kept missing the obvious signs we all saw. We watched through your heartache and our own as your dating lives played out like a soap opera, complete with villains, and there were moments we wanted to lovingly scream at both of you to wake up. But we knew you had to find your own path to each other. We all knew neither of you was truly on the dating market. You two are what we hope to find in our lives. A partner who sees us immediately for who we are. Who does not judge us for our insecurities but worships them—complements them. What I've learned is that you two have the patience of fools or saints. I'll go with saints. I cannot fathom meeting the person I know I'm supposed to be with and not wanting the world to know immediately." Thad gestures at Elin.

Wait, his gaze is on me, not Elin. I let go of Elin's hand and gently pinch my lower lip. He rubs at his mouth, then lowers his hand.

"I can't imagine the frustration of waiting fifteen years to declare what you both knew the moment you met each other. Should you probably have gotten married immediately and saved each other—and us—from the 'will they just be together already roller coaster'?" Thad asks.

Hawk nods repeatedly.

"Yeah. I'm glad we agree there. I have this theory, despite that you two unknowingly chose each other as teenagers, and it took only fifteen years for you to admit that you both knew instantly you'd met your forever. The theory is this: When you have met the right person, you know. There's an inexplicable combination of comfort and fear that overtakes you, and you know that's who you are meant to be with. When this occurs, we all have choices to make. The choice you two made was to run, and yet you couldn't. Being teenagers when you met, this makes sense. Your lives were tethered from the second your souls met. My theory on love means the overall timeline for couples is individual, but the outcome ends up the same when love is entered into with pure intentions. This isn't a certain type of rush of hormones, but rather a piece of you that feels at home with the other."

Elin gives a fake cough. I turn to her, and she's staring at me. Thad's not talking about me. He's not. That's impossible.

"I was honored to play a part in you two having to face your feelings. Cheers to the amazing couple. May their forever be filled with laughter, love, and happiness."

Hawk wipes his eyes. Thad strolls toward us, never taking his focus off me. There's a hum in the air. Men in green suits are slapping Thad on the back. Hawk jumps up, throwing himself straight onto Thad. Thad catches him, and Hawk wraps his legs around my date.

"You're an absolute jerk for making me cry at my own wedding," Hawk says.

"You cried three times this morning during the ceremony." Thad pats him on the shoulder.

Hawk slides off Thad. "Can you blame me? She married me! Me! Of anyone in the world she could have picked, it was me."

Elin stands. She gracefully walks behind Hawk and wraps herself around him. He leans into her. I don't know if it's the buzz of the wedding or Thad's speech. I cross my arms over my stomach. His words boom in my head from earlier, *three months, six months, or even a year...* and *an inexplicable combination of comfort and fear.*

Dusk falls, and the tiki torches glow brighter. Thad's face is soft. He plays with the seam on the side of his pants, almost like he's fighting his hand from reaching out for me. I reach for him.

He nods and pulls me in closer.

I rise to my toes to whisper in his ear, "Raspberry Macaroon."

Thad places his palm against the small of my back.

"Please don't make me wait fifteen years," he whispers.

I'd never make you wait. Rather than remain emotionally numb, my body chooses to soar into positive after positive in emotional overdrive. Thoughts overlap one another, swirling so quickly I can't do anything but allow them to rocket through the galaxy above. My insides are in a state of full-blown geeked-out warp speed, taking my heart rate for a ride like I've never experienced in my life.

I stretch my legs straight to keep myself from leaping into the air. A leap would be far too much for this moment. "Raspberry macaroon." The words stumble out much too loudly.

His free hand lifts mine to his mouth, and he kisses my ring finger. "Raspberry macaroon."

My head goes fuzzy. He spins us to an empty area of the dance floor. The wedding around us is a blur. I press my hand to his heart, taking in how quickly each beat hits. Fireflies flicker across the yard. I pull his arms tightly around me and lean against his muscular stomach. His sweet words traipse through every nook in me on repeat. *Please don't make me wait fifteen years.* My pulse ignites, and I hope he can feel it against his skin.

I snuggle my body into his warmth, refusing to acknowledge that the end of the night will come and we'll need to split apart. I close my eyes, attempting to picture myself fifteen years from now. An uncontrollable flush of heat crashes over me. Fifteen years is a long time.

CHAPTER FIVE

T HERE WAS NO POSSIBLE way for me to get any sleep this past week after the confusing high of being with Thad. We were among the last of the guests to clear out of the wedding and ended up sitting on the front steps, staring up at the star-laden sky, saying nothing for hours. If it weren't for the stack of work I'm now buried under, I'd still be on that step with him. Hell, I'd stay until we both became wrinkled from old age and withered away. A hard beat in my throat emphasizes the thought. I tuck down into myself, my legs folded over each other, shrinking myself into a ball.

I'm a mess. In the short time since I've met Thad, the three-quarters-dead portion of myself has been chucked to the side and awakened with new, gentle rhythms. Like a tap dance of *hello, how are yous* that slowed to a soft shoe when we parted and I had to take the solo drive home after the wedding.

Today I'm back to assuming I have a pulse because I'm breathing. I could run around my block six times and not get the same jolt of life I had each time he touched my arm, said my name, or even brushed against my hand to let me know he was there.

I tap on the screen of my phone and huff a long sigh of tiredness. My colleagues tap their phones, and I get glimpses of their significant others, their pets, or even their kids. Their phones are tiny windows showing that the work version of themselves is a small portion of their whole. While mine is a purple lock screen followed by a pale-yellow background that makes the array of apps and my academic stats folder of doom easy to read. There are six new work emails and no texts.

There's nothing saying I can't message him to see if he had a good match. This is part of the new us routine. Text throughout the day and into the late hours of the morning. But I've been messaging him constantly, and I'm not sure if it's too much. I don't want to scare him off.

My thumb twitches over his name on the message screen, but I click on the email folder instead. There is no mental preparation for academic guilt or expectations.

I scroll down the emails on my laptop searching for the link to join my second radio interview of the night. I click to connect to the virtual recording session. The host, Heather, hasn't arrived yet. I stretch, relaxing the heaviness of my head against the tan leather back that arcs up and over, shielding any light from above. The high wooden sides are too tall for the natural height of my arms, leaving me cuddled in the enclave of my hug chair. Despite being over-the-top, the chair is versatile, blocking the rest of the room around me when I take any Zoom calls from home. Or when I need to talk to a student and don't want them to peek at my personal life.

The cushion of the headphones presses around my ears, sealing out the night noise. I shift my jaw, working to relieve the pressure of the cup I'm gripping that's digging the frame of my glasses into the side of my head. Light pollution pours in through the extra-long windows, thanks to the street-lights and stoplights that radiate through the full-corner window wrap in my living room. I hit a button on my phone, and the curtains draw themselves shut, ending the repetitive flashing of the stoplight.

The hold room screen is black, with host will join soon steady in the center. Ten after eight comes and goes. Quarter after. I check my phone for any type of message regarding cancellation, tech issues, or an asteroid that's delayed Heather considering she's normally punctual.

I click open my messages and stare down at Thad's name. A throb in my wrist grows faster and travels up my arm. I tap open our message chain and reread the chapter-length exchanges from the past two weeks.

The computer screen brightens. I sit up, crossing my arms one over the other on the table to ready myself for the interview. Tonight's topic isn't what I normally get called in for to give my opinion. My expertise gets tapped more regularly for being a go-to talking head for the always-clever associate professor of industrial economics. I get bonus points for being from a small private institution in New York. They leave out that I live in Jersey.

I sink into the cold chair, missing the warmth of Thad's arms wrapped around me. The stiff leather doesn't give the same quietness to my head that being near him brings. Come to think of it, this is not a great hug chair. The screen dims.

I adjust to sit cross-legged in my favorite gray sweatpants and university-branded sweatshirt. If anyone who didn't already know me saw my current state of being, the oversized glasses that belong in a 1960s chemistry lecture that only come out in my apartment, or the small pink teacup with an exact single serving of coffee at eight on a Saturday night, I don't think they'd have as much trust in my expert opinion. But I've done interviews for this station for years and I know they care more about my voice being smooth than how I'm dressed. I snatch my phone from the table. A wave of adrenaline crashes over me, and I punch in a text to Thad before I can think too much and stop myself.

Me: *My hug chair is not cutting it tonight.*

After hitting send, I stare at the phone. Nothing changes. I check the computer, and I'm still in the limbo of the waiting room with no host in sight. I reread my message, cringing at my stupid words. He's not going to respond to this. I tap on the text to edit it to something that might come across as less strange.

Thad: *Hey! I don't know what a hug chair is, but my arms are naggingly empty right now.*

I wrap my free arm across my stomach, laying it where his wrapped around me.

Me: *I know the feeling.*

Thad: *I've tripped on my own feet no less than eight times today trying to play soccer. How's your night?*

I snuggle the phone in.

Me: *I'm waiting to give an interview then go to bed.*

Me: *Last night a delicious man kept me up and kept sending me sweet messages until 2:00 AM.*

Thad: *Funny. A captivating woman did the same to me. Staying up was worth every tired second.*

Thad: *What's the interview topic? Where can I hear or see you?*

Me: *This won't air for two weeks. You should go to bed if you're tired.*

There's a coziness to talking with him. My eyes half-droop, and I picture him asleep on my velvet rose couch, shirt off and hand resting on his stomach above green silk boxers, with me safely between him and the inside of the couch. Close enough to touch his skin, wake him with gentle kisses...

My phone flashes brightly, pulling me from the sleepy daydream haze.

Thad: *Too bad. I'd like to see you right now.*

Rather than searching through my phone for an image that sets me in the best light imaginable, where I look extremely intelligent and fuckable, I flip my camera on and take a selfie of me, a glorious mess in my hug chair, and hit send. Glasses, sweatpants, all the things that don't show the work version of me are captured, complete with a scrunched nose and tilted head.

Me: *Can you believe they let me teach students?*

Thad: *I love this! This is now my favorite picture. I'm calling it "Intelligent Woman Needs Nap."*

Thad—Mr. Polite, quiet Thad—sends me a shirtless picture.

Only he's not on the couch as in my daydream. He's sitting in the middle of an empty indoor soccer field?

Me: *No fair. I send you me as a mess and you send a hot picture?*

Thad: *A cute mess. I am at work. I'm usually here, and that picture is me right now.*

He works there? He works there and his closest friends are there. Feels familiar.

Thad: *We should stop this whole working on a Saturday thing.*

I'm much more awake now, as is my lap. Like awake enough to function for this meeting that still hasn't started. Energized enough to not need coffee but to soar around on the fact that my night includes flirting.

Ryu from my department could have taken this interview. A person from University Relations may have been a better fit, but the news media relationships have been mine for over ten years now, and they are a bright spark in what can be an isolating job. A job in jeopardy of collapsing with the university.

Ugh. Buzzkill.

I was brave when I resigned—until I wasn't and rescinded my resignation and agreed to take a short break instead. None of that changes the fact that I can be brave now.

I check the clock. Heather is now forty-five minutes behind.

My phone lights up.

I click into a message from Fiadh.

Fiadh: *Go to bed. I saw your light was on during my walk home. We have an early-ass morning.*

Me: *Creeper.*

Me: *We only have an early-ass morning because you want food.*

Fiadh: *Are you working or relaxing?*

Me: *I'll go to bed, mom.*

Fiadh: *I'll make my mom call you if you don't. I'll meet you on your stoop at 7 for breakfast.*

I glance to my left at the stack of research left to annotate tonight. If I don't get to the stack, I'll be behind schedule. I look up, calculating how many hours I'll need before bed.

Fiadh: *New plan. I message Maverick and tell him your finger is magically unhealed.*

Me: *He's not giving you a refund.*

Tomorrow is too important to cancel. I need time with her, and as an extra bonus, I can give an update to Lisa and Vera that I'm following our agreement.

Me: *Make out with Maverick while you're there.*

I grin, knowing she's sneering at the phone.

Fiadh: *I'm not interested in Mr. Grumpy.*

Like hell she's not. I know her way too well. The more stubborn she gets with a man, the more she's about to fall head over heels for him. Fiadh is stuck like a donkey in concrete. She's bucking but not going anywhere.

Fiadh: *I'm going to find you a date so you will stop trying to match me with strangers.*

My arms have that low numbness in them again. I bury myself in the memory from the wedding, where I'm tucked into him.

Me: *That's right. Stay in denial.*

This woman belongs in nature despite her constant stance of believing she belongs in the city. The apple trees she wants don't grow in the city.

Me: *I have to get on a call.*

Fiadh: *Please do not work yourself into a grave. This request is purely for selfish reasons. I suck at making friends.*

Fiadh loves to date and be in relationships. Her last partner was a canker sore of a human. She deserves to be with a person who will worship her the way she deserves and will be a continual orgasm train.

The screen flicks white, and there's a microphone on the screen.

"Shit. Shit. Shit. I'm so sorry, Piper." Heather's smooth voice cuts the silence. "Alexa fried her laptop with her water bottle."

I glance at my phone. Alexa could have texted me. She does have my number.

"No problem. We can pick another time," I say. Looks as if I'll be getting through some of the annotations tonight after all.

"If you're up for it, Alexa asked if you're free in August for a segment she's working on," Heather says. "Can I tell her you said yes for a television interview?"

A heaviness drags at my upper body. I made the promise to Vera and Lisa to keep doing the interviews. Normally I love interviews. I'm in need of a deep recharge.

"Perfect. Send me an email with the time, date, and topic. I'll be there." I should not be this polite or chipper right now. Maybe Alexa really did drown her laptop with water. Perhaps she is as burned out as me with too many meetings and doused every electronic communications tool she owns to sever the work handcuffs that come with over-interconnectedness. I should have stayed on that step with Thad all week.

"I appreciate how understanding you are. I know your schedule is always tight, so I'll email the information later." Heather does not look tired. I squint. The blur on the background of the call doesn't look like she's alone.

"Where are you?" I ask, squinting harder, working futilely to pull their screen into focus.

She turns, and across the room, the fake screen drops on the side to reveal a swarm of people in the studio.

She focuses on me. "Alexa got engaged in the studio, and the place is a madhouse. Alexa really did fry her stuff."

My throat clenches. "That's wonderful. Weddings are...Good for Alexa. Send me the details for when we can reschedule."

I turn off the meeting without waiting for a reply. There's no reason for tears and snot to be creating a cyclone on my face. Alexa is a wonderful human who deserves all positive things.

I pick up my phone, and instead of texting, I call Thad.

The phone hits the third ring, and the chaotic moths flitting in my stomach are bumping into one another, searching for light. On the fourth ring, he picks up. The light comes on inside me, and the moths all crash together.

"Piper?" Thad asks, with what I imagine is the world's largest smile, which I can feel through the phone.

The moths in my belly sigh with me, tension from my over-scheduled mess of a self escaping with an exhale. His voice is magic. "Are you able to tell me more about this fantastic woman you messaged with last night?"

He chuckles. I cradle my phone under my ear like a teenager and snuggle into my chair.

"Can I see you tomorrow?" I ask.

"Yes," he says. "I thought you had work?"

I frown at the stack of paperwork on my desk. Lisa and Vera did tell me to figure out what makes my pulse beat, and right now my entire body is telling me to burn the stack of papers on my desk.

"I do, but what are you doing tomorrow night?" I ask, bracing in hope for the slightest hint of further invitation into his world.

"Come meet me at the field house. I'll bring you that soccer jersey we talked about," he says.

Less than twenty-four hours from now I'll touch him again. My whole body wants to float up and fly around my living room. My jerk of a calendar pings, crashing me to reality. I liked floating. Floating was good and soothing.

Calendar Reminder: Canopy Cruise Graves Adventures 10:00 AM

The floating portion of the night has absolutely concluded.

"I can do that. I'm at the adventure center with Fiadh in the morning." Adventures are usually all-day activities. I'm seeing *him*. One way or another, I'm going to fulfill more of the promise to my mentors, get work done, and run full speed to that field house tomorrow to see Thad. I'll sleep eventually.

Chapter Six

I F I'D KNOWN COMING early for an adventure Sunday would land Fiadh and me in the cobweb-laden, apple-musk-scented defunct apple mill of her dreams across the street from Graves Adventures, I'd have prepared myself with a handkerchief. Cracks of morning light cut between the deep wood of the beams above us onto the dirt that's settled deep into the floorboards. Her eyes are nearing the size of the sun and are locked on me, waiting for me to verbalize my thoughts. I place my palm on my cheek in full awe. Fiadh belongs here. Not in a makeshift old chemistry lab on campus, but here, living out her life's work in a way she deserves.

"Well?" Fiadh tugs on the wrist of my shirtsleeve. "Do you hate it?"

"How could I hate this? This room is possibility. It's promise." I gesture to the raised stone platform for grinding. "Smells gross like you after a cider-making bender."

"Right, because I'm the only one who hyper-focuses on projects." She smacks my shoulder.

Fiadh will genuinely thrive here. Do I share her absolute obsession with making cider? No. But as her friend, it is my sworn duty to celebrate and be enthusiastic about things I know are important to her. This is important to her. Cidery has ties to her nana, which in turn has ties to my granny, given they, too, were best friends. If I can help make her dream of a mill happen, I can't imagine it being anywhere but here. Not with that sparkle in her eyes.

"Will you give up your moonshine bathroom setup if this happens?" I ask.

"Never," she says.

"We need to get out of here to go meet Maverick," Fiadh says. The upward lilt as she says his name doesn't go unnoticed.

I take in the room for an extended moment, picturing the final product. Dust removed, machinery fixed up, and Fiadh in a brown leather apron over a maroon T-shirt and jeans with black muck boots proudly teaching at a chalkboard in the front. Knowing her, she'll have a giant silver butterfly clip taming her hair. There'll be flights of cider samples near a long bar and crowds of people huddled in here for not only the history but for how important Fiadh makes an apple sound.

She belongs here.

Fiadh turns and heads to the door. "Come on. We're going to be late."

"He'll wait," I say, not quite ready to deal with the fact that a portion of me knows once she's working from here instead of campus, I'll see her less.

We walk elbow to elbow to the door, continue on the path across the street, and head in the direction of the meeting place at the adventure center.

Fiadh twists at a low wave in her hair. "You'd tell me if you think I'm in over my head."

"I think you'd regret it every day if you didn't go for this," I say. "I'd be mad at you if you tried to substitute any other location for this one."

She huffs out a nervous sigh.

We approach the meeting spot to find Maverick standing next to an enormous pole with hammered-on steps to the sky. On the ground is a pile of equipment. His helmet is a brilliant white with a long scuff mark on the side. The reflectors on his silver holster refract light at us.

"I'll need your phones and any loose items you have on you." Maverick unzips the pouch on his black shirt. His full-length orange pants are the traffic cone equivalent for the woods, easy to spot among the vibrant green quilt of the trees and the deep brown of the limbs and trunks.

"Straight to the point. I like it." I lean on the pole, waiting for Fiadh to add a quip that doesn't come.

The stretchy material of his shirt clings to his torso, drawing Fiadh's fidgeting attention from him to the sky-high platform above us. I study the cargo shirt and Maverick. I don't blame Fiadh for avoiding engaging with him. In a different timeline, I don't think she'd be as quick to throw up emotional shields between them. Her ex, with whom I wish she and I could both be forever strangers, is a colleague we can't avoid. Maverick isn't my type, but whether she'll admit it or not, if she'd give this man the attention she's denying herself, she'd see his earthy edges match hers. That is, if the lilt earlier and her gaga gaze aren't screaming tells that she no longer wants to bite his head off.

"You're late," he says. "I'm making up for time."

"We weren't late. Fiadh was showing me the apple mill at the farm next door. In all technicality, we were early," I say. The tick of his jaw tells me he's not buying my story.

"I've had this since I was sixteen. Don't lose it." Fiadh snatches a red handkerchief from her hair and places it in his hand.

"I'll do my best." He shoves it deep into the pouch. "Have you washed it since you were sixteen?"

She scrunches her nose up, redirecting her attention to his cheeks. "I'll have you know that cost three entire dollars."

"I'll refund you the three dollars if it disintegrates before we land." Maverick stacks a helmet, a harness, and a pair of thick leather gloves in each of our arms.

"Don't forget to calculate for inflation over the past decade and a half," I say.

Fiadh shoves her hands inside her gloves. "Plus inflation." Her commitment to their staring contest is impressive.

Avoiding new connections is one way to deal with the fear of additional hurt. Her response confirms my intuition to not share about being a plus-one with Thad at Hawk's wedding. No one grieving a previous relationship needs to have a new relationship blatantly in their face. Relationship? I pull on the helmet to refocus from the direction my mind wants to wander in.

Relationships require time. I huff at the bubble of emotion seeking to rip out of me. Risk aversion, while helpful in certain instances, like the preservation of capital over the potential for a higher-than-average return, immediately rejects the potential of a straight-up crash and burn of a volatile investment. Relationships, be they friendship or romantic, hold risk. Fiadh's and mine holds decades of compound interest, which makes me confident in my decision to let her figure herself out this summer without strapping her into my own roller coaster. If I tell her about my struggles at work, she'll redirect her attention to me, and she'll put aside her focus on formalizing a new location for her cider mill to help me. Given the financial state of the university, she has to focus on the mill.

I close my eyes, letting the memory of Thad's first touch on my hands in the woods settle over me, the softness of his presence shutting down the worry of right and wrong decisions.

My gut can't escape the notion that Thad's and my undeniable spark points past a seemingly volatile investment of the heart toward the likelihood of a lifetime of emotional richness.

After canopy cruising, after work, I'll get to see Thad and curl into that place where the stress of my overscheduled world melts away. On an exhale, a thin stream of anxiety releases itself. I squeeze into the snug body harness, tugging it over my workout pants and long-sleeve gray university workout shirt. The instructions for today's adventure to avoid loose clothing make much more sense now. I pull the straps until they hug my skin tightly. With a hard click, the harness is so secure, it's now an extra set of muscles on my body.

"The phone, too," he says. "It's a distraction and dangerous. If it falls, you could wobble, or it can smash someone on the head at high speed and injure them."

I cringe. Death by cellphone isn't ideal. Nor is homicide by cellphone. I grip the textured plastic in my hand, not ready to hand it over.

"One text," I say.

Maverick grumbles. I don't catch all the words, but Fiadh snaps her eyebrows close to one another at whatever he said.

I punch out a text to Thad.

Piper: *Going on a canopy cruise. Maverick's taking my phone.*

My phone instantly buzzes, and Thad's name appears on the screen. Warmth blooms in my heart. The fact that we're standing dozens of feet under a weathered platform that can hold at most four people no longer matters.

Thad: *Tell Maverick to check your harness a thousand times.*

Piper: *Nervous?*

"What happened to one text?" Maverick grumps.

Fiadh slaps her phone into his hand. "Give her a second."

Thad: *Yes. Very much so. Have fun and be safe.*

Thad: *Will you text me when you're done?*

Piper: *I will confirm when we're safely on the ground.*

Thad: *You do understand I'll be checking my phone every two minutes until the text comes through. Go have fun. Please do not be surprised if I hug you for a very extended period of time tonight.*

I smile, refraining from sending anything else to him. The corner of my mouth twitches. He cares if I'm okay.

"Well that melty look on your face confirms the text wasn't for work," Fiadh says to me.

"Here ya go." I hand Maverick the phone, intentionally ignoring Fiadh's comment. I shift my stare to the nearly vertical staircase we need to climb to get to the upper landing.

Maverick clips a cord to my front, tugging on it and finally nodding in approval.

"Time to climb." He gestures for me to start heading to the top. "The cord will get tighter as you go up so that if you slip, there's a safety and you won't go splat."

"Splat, huh. Sounds like a technical term." I start to climb up to the top, avoiding looking down. The breeze grows stronger with fewer trees to cut through the higher I get. Thad's message sits in my skin, of him waiting to hear back from me, concerned for my safety. I'm not sure the last time anyone except Fiadh wanted to check in on me in that way. Maverick doesn't count since his check on my gear was more to keep me from, in his words, going "splat."

"Use those long spider legs to move faster," Fiadh shouts up at me. Her hands are on either side of my feet while she closes the gap between us on her rise.

"Are you planning on me carrying you like a backpack?" I ask. "I'll do it. If one of us goes down. We'll both go down."

"No one is going down," Maverick says, his voice encouraging instead of sharp.

I believe him, which makes me trust him for Fiadh a little more. "Hear that, Fiadh? No one is going down."

If I didn't know my best friend of forever so well, I wouldn't know she's sending eyeball daggers at my skull while I climb higher. I shake my harnessed butt, earning a smack on my right cheek. Yup, daggers.

I imagine Maverick's pouch receiving buzzing text after buzzing text while he follows after us. Half of mine are calendar reminders. I hesitate before finding my footing on the platform. No, they wouldn't be. With today scheduled for Fiadh, I'd rearranged my schedule. When Thad invited me to see him, I cleared meetings without a second thought. That damn warm orb reappears, growing and shrinking like it's got its own heartbeat. Only this one says *See-Thad. Th-ad. Th-ad.*

"The description for this was misleading." Fiadh grips the rough wooden platform pole of the launch site with her leather gloves like a koala holding on for dear life.

"Be mad at him, not me. I didn't know what a canopy cruise was until we showed up." I check my helmet, not once, not twice, but three times to make sure it's snug for the zip portion of this adventure.

A stick cracks off the tree next to us, and debris falls through the crisp greenery below. Rather than shake from nerves, I'm half-frozen in place but doing my best to play it chill. Zipping down the thin gray wire is happening. We're harnessed, and the climb to get to this upper platform took a toll on my biceps.

Maverick clicks an extra carabiner on to Fiadh, securing it with bare fingers. He triple-checks each of her straps. "This will be good. What did you think you signed up for?"

"I don't know, a helicopter tour? Drones? I didn't exactly think it through when I clicked away and hit 'add to cart.'" I check the tightness on my own carabiner, tugging at the line that secures the harness to me, then on the skinny-ass backup wire that attaches a second carabiner to the barely thicker wire I'll be gliding on shortly.

"Where did you think a helicopter was coming from?" He shakes his head. "Never mind. Ground rules."

"You like rules way too much," Fiadh says.

"Do not under any circumstances remove your gloves. Keep your hands on here, and use them for stopping or slowing down. If for any reason you need to stop, grip it tight like this." He raises his arms up, bringing his hands around Fiadh's to demonstrate. Her lips part, and I can see her eyes close in on his mouth.

"How's she supposed to do this with a hurt finger?" Fiadh asks, gripping him for balance. "We need to climb down and not go whizzing through the trees."

Her protest is lovely, but given Maverick's perma-grump cheeks, he's not buying her pitch. He nods his chin at my hand. "Are you healed?"

"My finger feels fabulous." Did I overenunciate the word finger to turn Fiadh's cheeks shades of her favorite Red Delicious apple? Yes, I did.

I raise the gloved finger for his inspection, but he eyes the latches on Fiadh's harness instead. He pulls the straps tighter, running his thumb under the strap on her hip, checking for a nonexistent gap. She leans into his touch, and I avert my gaze. I'm clearly not the only one withholding emotional details. What have I missed? This third-wheel thing wasn't on the itinerary he'd sent. Not that I'm a third wheel. Am I?

"Has anyone ever fallen from here?" I ask.

"Piper! Do not put that in my head," Fiadh shrieks.

"You aren't falling. I won't let you." Maverick's words are thick with promise, tangled with more meaning than I'm guessing he intended. Or, I'm reading too much into the flash of non-grump he let loose. "I tested every single line this morning before you all came out. Cleared any tree limbs that might get too close. Two other groups have already gone off with my sister and with her fiancée. I'd never put either of you at risk of getting hurt."

"Maybe you two should go tandem," I say, teasing them. Great. Now she's pulling at his straps to see if they're tight.

Given the amount of extra touching, maybe she is better off going on these visits solo. He's a good distraction from the shit show of her ex and from the explosion of her funding for a working cidery. The way he looks at her, she's his entire world. If only his body language were less rigid, less protective of himself. To be fair, my own movements are stiff, my muscles tight, keeping me from venturing too close to the edge. I'm harnessed, and he gave the "all good," but he's meticulously checked her.

"I'm making sure they're done the same way," Fiadh says.

Sure she is. And I'm going to fly like Peter Pan without worries, with fairies guiding the way.

"Check her one more time," Fiadh says, pointing to me.

That's two people checking on me. My legs buckle, and before Maverick can reach me, I'm rocketing down the line, letting out a long "Whee." I throw my hands up on the wire like he showed us, clamping my hands tight to stop twenty feet from the platform.

"Clamps work!" I turn to look back.

Fiadh's right behind me, her legs split open, ready to grab for me, her eyes wide in terror.

"Piper!" Her legs clamp around me, and we're wrapped together.

I laugh so hard, tears roll down my cheeks. "What was your plan?" I ask her, my whole body shaking from laughter.

"There was no plan," she says. "My brain stopped functioning, and I jumped."

A metal-on-metal noise grows louder, along with an orange fireball growing closer. I nod my chin toward Maverick, whose face is a nice shade of white by the time he stops behind Fiadh.

"Typically people tell me before they push off," he says, eyeing me up and down. He releases one hand from above, gripping the wire with his other hand to ensure he's stopped.

He slowly inspects my equipment, nearly squeezing a flustered Fiadh between us. "Uncoil your legs."

Fiadh shakes her head.

"You said I was fine!" We look at each other. I raise an eyebrow at him. "If you admit we are your most fun clients this summer, I will release my hands taking her across with me."

Maverick gnaws at his bottom lip, not answering.

Fiadh releases me, and I spin in the direction of the next platform.

"Time to fly!" I release the tension on the wire, slipping farther from the protection of Fiadh into the unknown ahead. She's safe with Maverick.

The rush of the air across my skin invigorates me. My heart hits again, pulsing Thad's name through my body. The magic of our first meeting rests deep in my core, the stolen moments at Hawk and Elin's wedding, the text message check-ins, all of it with him. My entire soul craves the confusing sensation of feeling grounded and soaring at the same time that being around him brings. He can't slip through my fingers. I can't lose the opportunity to spend every Saturday night with him. Wildness blooms inside me.

I stretch my feet out to land on the next platform. Then I shimmy over my wire, checking it, and take off on the next run without waiting for the other two to catch up. There's a freedom to moving ahead, to leaping to my next platform, that helps me think clearly. If Fiadh is taking this leap of trust in herself for her future, I'm going to do the same with mine.

By tonight I'll know for sure if Thad will share all of his Saturday nights with me.

CHAPTER SEVEN

PULSATIONS SHIFT TO PALPITATIONS between this
morning's ziplining activity and arriving at the field house
to talk to Thad. I'd initially planned to get work done in between, but my head was preoccupied with what I'd say once I
got here. The blunt approach I thought of is giving me pause.
But big and direct is the right path.

Be brave.

I rush through the front doors of the indoor soccer place. The
judder of energy in me grows stronger the closer I get.

The lobby has a series of high-end art shots in
black-and-white with red highlighting the gorgeous curves of a
faceless woman. They're well done and not at all what I'd have
imagined in here. The woman is muscular, and the entire set
of imagery is a highlight of an athletic woman, one who oozes
strength in her femininity. I stop in front of the welcome desk
and look at the rows of images on the wall: tournament win-
ners, friends hanging out, entire clusters of people suspended
in mid-laugh.

My circle has forever been intentionally small. My work life
would need a drastic reduction for me to be like these people. I

adore Fiadh. She has an easier time welcoming in the world. In part, I know I have high expectations for the people around me. Like, don't get me wrong, I want to be friends with everyone. But, then, when it comes time to solidifying friendships, my calendar rears its vicious head. In general, it's easier to not make the connections so as not to disappoint people when I have to cancel plans a thousand times over. And there's the fear that they'll eventually find me to be not worth waiting around for. My stomach churns.

Behind the desk, a teenage boy with grass-green headphones dangling around his neck is perched behind the counter. His attention is glued to the screen above, watching match highlights. "The bathroom is on the right if you want to change."

"I don't need to change." I drum my nails on the gray lacquer counter in the hopes of drawing his attention.

"What team are you looking for?" His face lights up when cheers come through the speakers on the screen.

I turn my gaze to the area past the entryway. The air is filled with whistles and buzzers. The muskiness of the space would take years to get out of the walls. I weigh my options. There are three doors to choose from. I could wander through, but I really don't want to get another ball to the finger, or worse, face. No balls to the face. Maybe Thad's under the right conditions. What is wrong with my head? We're about to have a serious conversation, and my brain went straight to thinking about his body.

"I'm looking for Thad." Only, the words don't flow out as though I'm the confident woman in the pale blue shorts suit she changed into after ziplining. No, they come out as though I'm thirteen with a crush. My cheeks burn.

The kid points at the center door. "He's working on the nets."

Nets? Goal nets? I straighten and channel the confidence necessary to act as though I'm not out of place here. No, I'm following Thad's lead from his speech at the wedding. I rub at the tightness in my neck, pushing ahead to find him to help move my insides from the constant hailstorm of tasks and ideas sputtering throughout to the slow, steady rumbling rolling quiet after a summer-evening thunderstorm. There's beauty there, wonder, and a combination of stillness I can't identify in any other way.

I open the massive door and walk through. There's a large white dome overhead with grand lights. Scanning yields no additional people or whistles on this field. I trudge forward. My heel wedges deep into the fake grass. When I go to push my foot forward a second time, I topple down. The netting so kindly described to me by the gentleman in the reception area is now wrapped around my ankles, turning me into a trapped mermaid caught in a puddle of commercial fishing net.

I look up in time to see Thad come out in adorable royal-blue shorts that do everything to highlight his muscular thighs. His shirt isn't a jersey, but he has on one of those perfect navy muscle shirts where the sleeves arc in on the traps to give room for the arms to move. In short, I'm ogling the shit out of Thad.

This man can wear anything and I'd want to drink him in. That wonderful circular buzz under my skin, excitement, happiness, the world stilling around us all rolled into one ball.

"I should have set up a gorgeous-woman trap in here forever ago." Thad bites his bottom lip. I swear he chuckles at me, but in a way that sounds as though I'm adorable. I'll take adorable. Bonus points if he helps untangle me from this mess.

Instead of coming to help me, he's staring at me with a pleased expression on his face. I push to stand, only my success is limited as my ankle and heel are wrapped tightly, making me a helpless sea turtle. The best and only response I can muster here to keep my dignity is to go over the top. As such, I flop on the ground.

This isn't so bad. The net is like a cushion over the scratchy grass beneath me.

There is a negative. This net, or the plastic grass poking through the holes in the net, smells of vile gym socks. Is there a way to shampoo fake grass?

"Well, this is nice," I say, squinting up at the blazing white bulbs above.

Thad lies next to me, leaving a polite gap between us. His knees are bent, and he's staring up at the ceiling with his back flat on the floor. He's not caught in the net.

"Do you have any idea what you're lying on?" Thad asks, smoothing his hair from blocking his beautifully symmetrical face.

A net. This question is silly. I crinkle my nose. Or does he mean the smell?

He folds the hand I can't reach over his stomach and leaves his free hand open. He's within reach. My palm throbs for connection. If he presses our flesh together, there's a solid chance I'll permanently fuse to him.

I wiggle to lower my leg. "Based on where we are, and the smell that is never going to wash out of this shorts suit, I'm going to go with a body decayed here." If I can't get out of this tangle, mine will too.

He belly laughs, shaking his whole body. How is he so content to lie here with me? Like lying in the fluids of others is perfectly fine. I strain to take a peek at the soft rise and fall of his chest without moving my head.

"No, there are no decaying bodies here. There has been a lot of sweat, blood, and anything else you can think of." He doesn't even flinch. The disgustingness of the sentence scrapes at my tongue.

"Do you use a mint to try to dampen the smell?" I ask with polite sincerity. "The net smells like gum."

"I'm the mint."

"You smell like a bad mojito," I say.

"This mint would make your tongue go numb," he says.

He continues, but my mind flashes to his mouth on mine. I wiggle closer to him, catching a whisper of vanilla. A tingle overtakes my mouth and travels straight down to...oh no.

"A lot of the players use a muscle cream with a similar scent to help calm any pain from games," he says.

He reaches over to trace a line from my wrist down my inner forearm to the divot in my elbow. Crap. I missed a big bit of whatever came between him talking about his tongue and cream. I close my eyes and work to ignore my nipples, which are turning into a distraction beneath my silk shirt. Why did I go with the thin bra and silk shirt combo? I knew the lightness in the air that happens when I'm near him would come. From now on I'll factor this into my wardrobe choices. I didn't expect words like "tongue," "tingle," or "cream" to turn my body into inappropriate and ridiculous mush.

Thad pulls out his phone from his pocket and runs his finger down the screen, dimming the light above us.

"Neat trick." I let my body relax, the best it can, into the net. My eyes soften. Simply being next to him calms my nerves. I place my palm on his, my fingers curled up in a gentle half-commitment.

He shakes his head. "Piper—"

"If you're about to propose again, I need to point out that I'm wrapped up like a fish," I whisper.

I turn my head to face him. He's already looking at me, his eyes flittering across my face. We lie like this, without talking, the giant clock on the wall ticking loudly with each minute that passes. Whistles blow in adjacent rooms, and though we are inside, there's an openness in this space. The ache of vulnerability grows heavier. He cups his hands so that his fingertips press against mine like we're holding an invisible circle between us.

"Are you not denying that's what happened at the wedding?" I ask.

He helps turn me onto my side, his hand steadying my hip so I don't roll.

His cheek turns up. "Did I ask you to marry me?"

My ears heat—hell, my whole body heats. "You made several comments that I don't think were accidents. When I pull them together, it spells subtle but-not-so-subtle marriage proposal," I say with full confidence. "If I'm wrong, I apologize."

He tickles my fingertips with his. "What exactly did I say that led you to believe I was proposing we get married?"

"Exact phrasing isn't necessary, is it? You haven't run out of here or rejected the statement." Unless he's amused by my analysis, but I don't think I'm wrong here. "If I told you I wouldn't make you wait fifteen years, what would you say?"

"I'd say I hated not being with you yesterday, and the day before, and the day before that..." He adjusts his grip on my waist.

I speak slowly so as not to spook him or come across as overly eager. "I'd wait the fifteen years for you, but my insides would be screaming every day to shorten the timeline."

We stare at each other. The dim lighting adds ambience, and the buzzers indicating time is up on games in a different wing of the field house drown out around us while I focus on him, on the possibility of a permanent us, and as if my heart was jumped, I can feel every nerve in my body waking up.

I turn onto my back, letting his hand settle on my stomach. The ceiling is safest to stare at while I organize my thoughts.

"I wish dating and life were easier. Where, when you meet the person your body is perpetually whispering is your partner, it was socially acceptable to say, I think you're fucking awesome. I want to take a chance with you, get married now, and we can figure everything else out later." I lick my lips, combating the dryness overtaking my mouth. "If one could do so, life would be so much easier."

"Piper," Thad says, so close to my ear, I turn my head and find his lips at my eye level. "I've felt your presence missing each time we parted since the hike. Texting is great, but it's a fraction of the sensation of being close to you. I'll take all the fractions, but I need you in my forever. Can we please skip to the part where we get married?"

My heart hits five slow beats. A deluge of clicks occurs all at once. My grandmother used to talk about this with my grandfather. When he died, part of her died too. Not that an outsider would ever know. She and I were close, so I knew. I knew each time her eyes dimmed when she would glance at his picture. The way they lit up when she talked about how they met and were instantly inseparable. Which means whatever this thing is here, if my grandparents knew, there's no reason to question the yes raging inside me.

I offer a half-hearted protest. "I could be an awful human. Per colleagues and others, I'm a terrible workaholic." When I swallow, it's like pebbles are filling my airway.

"You know nothing about me either," he says. "For all you know, I snore and lie in decay all day."

I place my palm over his heart. The beats practically leap from him into me.

"If this is a no," he says, "then please forgive the ask, and we'll take things slowly. But know this will not be the last time I ask."

"What on earth makes you think I'm saying no?" I ask, a tease in my voice.

"When a person asks if you want to get married and the answer doesn't fly from your mouth immediately, the fear is you are trying to politely find a way to decline," he says.

"You've asked many people to marry you before?" I ask, my heart loud in my ears.

"Never. I've never in my life met a person whose presence I find as intoxicating as yours. I can't explain how I know, not even to myself, but I know you're the part of my life that's missing."

"Let's get married," I say. "Soon."

He pulls me and the net on top of him. We're both now fully wrapped together in the wide black webbing. He pulls my mouth down to his and presses a tender kiss against my lips, leaving traces of vanilla. I let out a grunt, failing to separate my legs to steady myself on him. His arms wrap under my ass, and I lay my cheek on his muscular pecs.

"Do you want a small ceremony, or do you want a big wedding?" he asks.

A stitch of pain pricks my skin. Tiny wedding for my minuscule list. "Super-small wedding?"

He presses his eyes closed, and a trace of panic starts to slither through me.

"A big wedding is fine too." My voice falters midsentence. "Or eloping."

His quiet returns. A soft contemplation during which I'm frozen. He releases a slow exhale, lowering me evenly across his body.

"How do we get married?" he asks.

"We register at the courthouse and have a small private ceremony." Very small. Like nearly no one.

"My sisters will have my head if they don't know," he says. "My parents, too."

"You have sisters?" I ask. "I'm an only child. Unless you count Fiadh. She's like a sister."

"So we invite Fiadh, our parents, and my sisters?" he asks.

"No Fiadh. She's having a shit summer, and I don't want to slam this on top of the breakup she's going through." Only, I don't want to halt what I know is right.

He pauses too long.

"She can know eventually, but not yet. I don't want her to try to talk me out of it, or to upset her at all."

"I'm confused. If she is like a sister, won't she understand?" he asks.

"Not right now." No, this is outside of who I am. I'm not the impulsive person who runs off and gets married. This is not impulsive. This is right. I know this is right, and my not telling my best friend in the world is strategic. I'm also scared of how much yelling she'll do. Yelling out of love, but there would be yelling.

He's silent again. Shit.

"We can tell everyone eventually." I stretch my hand flat against his. Our heartbeats sync, and I fight the pull to curl into his side. "I want it to be small and intimate. Us and a person to marry us."

"Can we agree to this: People find out as they find out, but we aren't announcing anything openly for now?" he asks.

Hmm. This could work. I swallow at the pebbles-now-turned-boulders in my neck. "I like this option."

"Then we get married. You'll pick out a dress, we'll register at the courthouse, get married, and figure everything out as life happens."

As life happens? What does that even mean? Our hands clasp together like a subconscious handshake, agreeing to everything.

I'm getting married—to Thad. There is a quietness inside me like the world is happy and happening in the way it should. Tingles prickle on my tongue. I blink slowly at him, trying to drop a hint to seal the deal and kiss me.

Only he doesn't, and we remain in the haze of the room. We sit up, our hands clasped, the net farther up my leg than earlier.

He slides his palm from mine. I let out a faint whimper. He crawls over me, his knees on either side of my feet. His warm hands rest on my upper calf, sending a tingle straight to my lips. They are in desperate want of a proper kiss. Instead, his hands press and slide between me and the netting.

Never in my life did I imagine how sexy being freed from this knotted monstrosity could be. He slides my leg out from between the nylon knot trap, leaving my shoe in the folds of the pile. My brain wanders into the peace of our personal cosmos. In here, the decades of layered distractions I've orchestrated to keep myself from feeling anything for someone new disappear.

I slide closer to kiss his cheek. His hands grip my hips and hold me tight. This is not the sweet Thad who was lying next to me. There's an animalistic glint in his eyes, and warmth spreads frantically through my core.

He holds on and stares at my mouth. "I need to add a rule here. Once we're married, we take the physical slow. I want to know you before...before we..."

Against every current urge in my body, I nod in agreement. I close the gap between our mouths until his shallow breaths whisper against my lips.

"We can take things slow," I say.

"Fuck," he says, his voice gravelly, his eyes drunk with want.

I slide out from under him.

His gaze wanders to the ground and then up at me. "Marry me next week. We'll get the paperwork done, and then by next Saturday...we can be married. I want to come home to you every night. Even if we only go as far as we just were in the net, I'll be a happy man forever with you."

Oh. I blink at pooling tears. Odd emotional tears that shouldn't be appearing. I'm unsure whether I want to be held or fucked.

"Next weekend we get married," I agree.

I need to get a dress, to pick out shoes and accessories. We need to get registered. I need to avoid my best friend for a week in many, many, many ways.

I'm going to marry Thad in a week.

The hairs on my arms stand up. Something isn't right. My stomach sinks. I can't hide from Fiadh; we have a standing brunch already scheduled for Friday.

CHAPTER EIGHT

T HAD AND I DISCOVERED through a joint research session in the dimly lit field house that the state requires three days between applying for a marriage license and the official ceremony. Which has landed us at the courthouse early Monday morning to get married by the Saturday timeline. The fine print we missed was the necessity of a witness.

We stare at the sweet woman behind the counter. The one who, despite processing a million forms a day, is greeting us with the cheeriest disposition in her buttoned sunshine-yellow cardigan and black skirt.

"Is there anyone you can call at all? Family members love being part of this kind of thing." She pushes the form out to us, tapping on the line for a witness signature.

I shake my head. "Not much family on my side to speak of."

Thad pulls his phone out of his pocket. He scrolls down a list of names, landing on one very familiar if not completely outrageous option.

"It's not a family member," he says.

"Him? I've met him. You think he can keep a secret?" I chew on my lower lip.

Thad scrolls farther down his phone. "The other option is to find a stranger."

"You really should know the witness," the woman in the cardigan says.

Thad leans closer, his arm touching flat to the side of mine. "I trust him, and yes, he can keep a secret." Thad scrolls up to Hawk's name.

The touch on my skin is more than distracting. Since he's said we'll go slow, I've pictured a minimum of ten different places I want to drag my mouth across him. No less than twenty ways we could fit nicely together while we...get closer.

I check the time on his phone, sinking comfortably into him. I should be more stressed. That's the stereotype of a wife-to-be, but I'm not. Everything is going to work out. The only worry I have is knowing my late-afternoon schedule is going to slide off today's timeline and not wanting to miss any appointments.

"Text him," I say. If he trusts him, that's all I really need.

"Elin, too," he says.

"I'm imagining they don't go places without each other." I grin at him.

A group text pings in my phone.

Thad: *Hey! Can one of you get down to the courthouse to help me?*

Elin: *Sure.*

Hawk: *Are you in jail? I'll be right there.*

"Why is his first thought that you're in jail?" I tilt my chin up to get a clear view of his face.

"I'm not sure. If either of us were sending the other a jail text, I'm pretty sure I'd be getting it from him." Thad shrugs.

"Are you going to tell him you aren't in jail?" I ask.

Elin: *Who is the fourth number? You don't trust us to come bail you out?*

I pick up my phone to type.

Thad blocks my screen with his hand. "Don't respond. They'll get here faster and with fewer questions."

I chuckle. The woman in the yellow cardigan taps on the counter. She turns, walks to her desk, and sits, giving us some space.

"Aren't they at work?" I ask.

"They work in the same place. More importantly, they think I need to be bailed out," he says.

Curiosity hits me. "Have you ever been to jail?"

"Me personally? No. I've gone to a jail on a tour. I've bailed out more than one of my friends and a few fraternity brothers. But I'm not acquainted with the inside of a jail cell." He takes a step to lean against the wall.

He pulls me into his side, and I rest my head on him.

"Same question." He nudges me.

"Me? When between studying would you like me to have been in jail?" I ask. "I've been behind the bars of a kissing booth in college. If that counts, cuff me." I hold up my wrists to him.

He wraps his fingers over my wrists, loosely holding them in place. In my twisted brain, I imagine him sliding the bow from my hair to use it to wrap my wrists in place. Pushing them up over my head against a wall before his other hand makes its way up my thigh. His mouth hovers over mine right out of reach, driving me up a wall because I can't satisfy the urge to have his lips on mine, his tongue across mine.

"Tell me more about this kissing booth," he says.

"Not much to tell. I was asked to sign up for a kissing booth. I registered, and when guys came around, I'd pick up a puppy and let it lick their face."

The tension in his forearm relaxes. "I very much like hearing that you didn't break a kissing record that day."

"Nope. Not one person grumbled, and all the money went to charity."

"What happened to the puppy?" he asks.

There's a small pull in my heart. "The dog belonged to one of my classmates. She ended up dating one of the guys we met, who gave an extra donation when he found out it was a puppy."

His eyes lower to my mouth. He leans down, my wrists pressing between us, and kisses my cheekbone. The parts of me once able to stand, swoon. He drops my wrists and pulls me in, turning me so his arms wrap around the front of my waist.

"Thad!" Hawk's voice echoes up the hallway. "I'm coming, man!"

"We're coming," Elin's voice corrects. "Where's the jail?"

Quick footsteps pick up speed, growing louder in our direction.

"No one is in lock-up," Thad says, wrapping his arms around my stomach.

"Why are we here, then?" Hawk says.

"Because I need your discreet help." Thad's voice travels up the hallway to the yet-to-turn-the-corner Hawk.

"Discreet?" Elin's laugh draws closer. "You texted him for *discreet*?"

Their beautiful faces appear around the corner. Hawk in a lab coat and Elin in a pair of jeans with a black T-shirt and blazer. The calm of Thad's arms around me is heightened by the current dancing between us. We're doing this. We have witnesses.

Elin looks at the sign above us. She grabs Hawk's sleeve and screeches.

"What? What?" He looks up.

She points at the two of us, a huge knowing smile growing across her face.

Thad pumps his hands in a *calm down, be cool manner*, but she screeches again.

She covers her mouth, her eyes open as wide as possible. "No way."

"What?" Hawk says.

Thad remains still. It's like he's waiting for all the signals to click in Hawk's head rather than saying anything.

"Hawk, where are we?" Elin says.

"Not jail," Hawk says.

He looks at the two of us, then at Elin. His mouth forms the letter *O*. The boisterous man I've met several times now appears to be at a loss for words.

"We need to ask a favor. Well, a few favors," Thad says.

"How did you two get here so fast?" I ask.

"When Thad texts you to meet him here, you leave work." Hawk says it like it's everyday knowledge.

"He'd meet anyone here," Thad says.

"Not true," he says. "There are definitely people I'd let sit in a jail cell."

"No, there aren't," Elin says. "Your heart is too big. Regardless, what is this? What's happening? Please let this be what I think is happening."

"We need a witness, but we also need you two to keep this a secret until we're ready to tell people." I pull Thad's arms tighter around me.

"How is this a secret?" Hawk emphasizes every word, waving open palms.

Elin gets closer to the window, where the marriage application sits with a pen on top, waiting. "Secret baby?"

"What? No," Thad says. "We haven't even...Never mind."

"Oh, that's hot," Hawk says.

Elin shakes her head at him.

"Parental pressure? Tired of being single?" Hawk presses.

I shake my head. I'm pretty sure I feel Thad doing the same.

"It's not an inheritance thing," Elin says. "And there's no bad-boy image to repair."

"Rude, I could be a bad boy," Thad says.

"No, you couldn't, and that's not a bad thing," Hawk says. "Piper, are you running for political office? He'd make a great first husband of any kind."

"First husband?" Thad asks.

"First husband. Only husband," I confirm. "No, I'm not running for political office. What do you two do all day when you're not making up for lost time?"

"Watch romantic comedies." Elin inches closer to the paper.

Thad lets out a chortle.

"Cinematic masterpieces." Hawk's attention turns to the paper on the counter. "Every single one of them."

Elin snatches the pen. Hawk rushes over to take the piece of paper. They're now in a standoff with each other as to who gets to be our witness.

I blink rapidly. "We really need you to not tell anyone else."

The two turn to me with the sincerest of faces.

"It took me fifteen years to tell him how I felt," Elin says, gently taking the paper from Hawk.

"When it's public, we will scream to everyone that we were the witnesses." Hawk clears his throat. "We know what we should have been doing the whole time we've known each other. I should have been shouting louder. What you two are doing is exactly what we should have done."

"It's not that we aren't going to tell people," I say. "As people find out, they find out, but—"

Elin cuts me off. "You want to live your life without a bunch of people interjecting why things might not work."

The words hit with a thud. Yes, because I know some of the comments already. This is too fast. We don't know each other well enough. Waiting won't hurt. My invisible-to-them calendar page with all the tasks I have for today opens in front of me. Each fifteen-minute time block filled. Page after page scrolling by, and I'm left with a hole in my heart at the end of the calendar when I'm at my funeral with no attendees because I was too afraid to grab for happiness, for wholeness, over obligation. Being with Thad makes me want to chuck the entire calendar. I'm grabbing for him with two hands and my heart.

Elin motions for Hawk to turn around. He pivots on his heels, bending at the waist. She places the paper on his butt and signs on the witness line.

"Joy should be shared," Elin says. "Thank you for trusting us with your joy."

"How long do we have to keep this a secret?" Hawk asks, still bent despite Elin's waving over the woman to hand her the paper.

"I'm not sure." Thad releases me, taking a step out from behind me to Hawk. He pulls his friend into a hug, patting him on the back. When he lets go, Hawk turns to me.

My ears burn, and my nerves are tight bundles. Do I want to tell the world right now? Yes. But deep down I want to revel in the newness of this all.

"The goal is organic. But organic isn't screaming it to everyone. It's slow, and we aren't ready to tell our families we're eloping."

"That would pretty heavily defeat the point of eloping," Hawk says. "Who are the witnesses for the ceremony?"

"Us," Elin says. "If we're the only two who know right now, it makes the most sense."

Hawk begins mini jumps in place. He's a puppy who has a giant juicy piece of bacon in front of him.

"Are you two free on Saturday?" I ask, hesitancy in my voice.

Thad walks over, standing between me and the counter.

The woman presses the notary stamp. "Come pick this up on Thursday. You then have thirty days to file everything to make it official. If you have any questions between now and then, give a call."

"Thank you," I say to the woman.

She slides the glass door shut, giving us a modicum of privacy in the hallway.

My stomach churns. "Elin, please don't tell Amelia."

"Amelia?" Elin asks. "Why would I tell my cousin?"

"Do you know that game where there are short degrees of separation between an actor and another actor?" Thad asks. "In this case, the actor is Piper, and the connection is Amelia. Piper's best friend is seeing Maverick."

"Oh damn. Maverick has a girlfriend?" Elin's face perks up.

"Girlfriend" is a heavy term. One not confirmed yet by Fiadh.

"They have a love-hate thing going on," I say. "I'm less concerned about your soccer team than I am her."

"I can keep it chill and organic," Elin says, her tone way too happy. "So can my teammates, the Bees."

"I'm not sure what organic means in this situation," Hawk says. "Like, I shouldn't go tell someone 'Thad's off the market.'

But if they find out due to extenuating circumstances, we can't be blamed."

"Right. Don't take out a TV commercial or a newspaper ad. If my parents—or worse, my sisters—find out before I tell them personally, I'm going to take it out on you." Thad slips his hand protectively around my waist. "On the field."

"Got it." Hawk dips down like he's going to rush Thad.

Elin, completely not chill, bounces on her heels with her fingers hooked together. These two are so going to blow the secret.

She tilts her head to the side, looking me over from head to toe. "Are you getting a wedding dress?"

I suck in my lips. If I didn't miss the appointment I'd booked for fifteen minutes ago while we waited for witnesses I was too excited to realize we needed, I'd say yes. Hopefully. Probably.

"I'm going from here to look at dresses," I say, itching to pull my phone from my pocket to check my appointment hasn't gone up in flames.

She lights up like the ball on New Year's Eve at midnight. "I'd be happy to help you if you'd like."

My insides scream yes. But that other little voice in my head, the one where Fiadh is crying, keeps me from letting the word come out. I swallow down the urge. "Oh, that's all right. It'll be a surprise for everyone." Including myself.

"There has to be an errand Hawk and I can help with." Elin looks down at the sweet sapphire engagement ring on her hand with the newly acquired thin black hammered band snuggled below. "How about rings? Will you two wear rings?"

Thad and I look at each other, his eyes pulling me in and softening the stress that was building. Eloping is meant to eliminate stress, not add to it.

"Yes," Thad and I say at the same time.

"We're..." I lose myself in the hopefulness of his gaze.

"We're...picking them out for each other."

"We are." I like this idea.

Hawk's mouth tilts in a smirk. "What kind of band do you think he should have?"

"I, um..." I straighten, pulling in confidence. "A strong band, but not flashy. Fashionable, but classic at the same time. No diamonds or other stones, and given the amount of soccer you all play, I'm guessing durable."

Hawk nods. "And hockey."

"You play hockey?" I ask. "That's sexy."

Elin giggles. "He owns—"

"Soccer wasn't sexy?" Thad says, cutting her off.

"I'm growing a new appreciation for soccer players." Like, one where, after the game, when everyone else has left, he pulls me onto the field, and we let our voices echo in ecstasy as loudly as humanly possible. No. I change my mind. In his office, where fewer people have likely spit or bled. The soccer grass is much less sexy when you realize how much sweat is intermixed in the fake grass.

Hawk's band is a thicker version of the one Elin has. The ring suits him, suits them. I stare down at my fingers, unable to picture anything beyond the rose-gold rings I've been wearing for most of my adult life. The ones that let me fidget.

I slide the three bands onto my ring finger and smile.

"I like that a lot." Thad squeezes me in comfort.

"Is it wrong to use these?" I ask.

"They're beautiful," Elin says.

"Use them, then," Thad says. "We can pick out bands together after the ceremony so you get exactly what you want."

I blow a slow stream of relief at the statement. A vibration from my pocket snaps my attention. My phone's alarm is alerting me to a client call. I suck in a hard inhale, coating my mouth with dryness.

"I have to get this," I say.

Thad kisses my cheek with the lightest brush of his lips. If a kiss could be a whisper that lingers after the person has pulled away, this is the kiss now settling on me. Held on to my cheek with the sensation of needing more.

Leaving to take this call is abrupt, but this is part of my job. I turn to walk down the hall for the call.

"Piper, I'll see you Saturday?" Thad calls to me.

I turn to face him. "Thursday to pick up the form. Then Saturday."

"This will be my third-favorite Saturday ever," he says.

"Mine too," I say.

I pull my phone from my pocket and click the number in my email to join a teleconference. I slide into my car in time to put on a background where it looks as though I'm in my office at the university, not outside a records office where a change to so much of my life is under way.

CHAPTER NINE

T HIS IS FINE. BY this, I mean everything. Eight in the morning on a Friday in the summer means a ghost of a building. I woke up at six to get here. Part of me wishes I'd turned toward Thad's instead of the office.

Should I be getting ready right now for a fancy brunch with Fiadh as we'd scheduled? Yes. Is she thrilled to meet on campus at ten instead? No.

She didn't seem surprised when I texted her at seven this morning to adjust our schedule. The woman who thrives on long-range solid plans to make her life tick went with the schedule rearrangement without a second of protest. The whoosh of her instant yes released the vise on my nerves, nearly toppling me over. Our calendars are where we're different. She is a planner, a scheduler. That's part of who she's always been. She functions better when everything is all laid out for her years in advance. Whereas my calendar packs itself.

"Damn it, Lisa! That was my coin." Vera tilts the steering wheel with the entirety of her upper body while transfixed on the humongous screen on the far white wall of my office. Sure, the screen is meant for video conferencing and presentations, but who looks at a giant monitor and doesn't think it'd be amazing to play video games on it occasionally?

Vera leans back against the gray mesh of the white-framed ergonomic chair she is seated in, the sleeves of her pale gray jacket falling across the table. The comfortable high of the air-conditioning in my office saves us from the sweltering humidity that sits in the New York summer air.

"Get better at the game," Lisa shrieks mid-lift of the controller in a useless attempt to get her duckie motorcycle to jump.

Vera places her heels flat to make way for Lisa to reach across and grab her coffee thermos off the poured-concrete conference table. The centerpiece of my office, the portion that brings the *oohs* and *aahs* more so than the giant gaming screen, was a student project between an interior design and a product design class. The students factored in everything but the weight of the gorgeous steel and concrete masterpiece, which now permanently belongs to this office. They didn't stop at the table, picking out a brilliant pearl-colored desk that glimmers when the sun hits it just right. To suit the geek in me, they went with an option that can go from sitting to standing in seconds with a flick of a button. Standing up from the white gaming chair I chose for my desk helps keep me from getting distracted during meetings. The design students weren't as thrilled with the chair, but it's more comfortable than most office chairs.

"You know, I'd bet they could set you up with a straight IV of that coffee so you wouldn't have to lug around the thermos."

Lisa pushes her sneakers off and settles her white ankle socks into the dark gray carpet.

Unlike Vera, who is overdressed for a summer Friday, Lisa is in designer jeans and a deep purple university-branded polo.

"Ankle socks show your age," Vera says, her body now twisted to the opposite side, while her avatar's car makes a wide left turn.

"Oh no, I'm Gen X, take away my socks," Lisa says with a sense of false horror. "But don't because my extra ones are all the way in my office."

"Two floors up," Vera says. "You can walk two floors without them."

"I think you two are missing the finer art of trash talk," I say. "Too much coffee and sock-ageism is a little weak."

I press my thumb hard on the X button to make the car go. They are so focused on the screen, it wouldn't hurt to check my phone. I fumble my phone with my free hand, tapping the screen to peek at an image of the white cotton dress with eyelets throughout I'd found while scrolling at five this morning. The straps are thick, and the whole look is pretty. An unfussy number to go with a discreet wedding ceremony. It'd look great—on a picnic with a yellow sweater. Is this a wedding dress? No, I suppose it's not. But anything can be a wedding outfit if that's what you show up in. I click off the ankle-length dress. The screen blurs, and squinting brings nothing into focus.

"Earth to Piper," Lisa says.

"I'm sorry, I was playing." I wasn't, and they know that. "When did the race end?"

"When you got distracted by your screen," Vera says. "Turn off your work."

"It's not work." Protesting is dumb. My track record isn't going to help me at all in proving I'm not doing work.

My stomach gurgles, demanding attention. I lick my lips, willing moisture to combat the dryness in my mouth.

"First order of business," Lisa says. "You're not supposed to be on campus. I'm going to forgive you because I love seeing you."

"Face it. Summer has been too quiet, and I have nowhere to vent after stupid meetings." Vera's character chucks a beach umbrella. The spinning rainbow monstrosity hits Lisa's car, causing it to go to the side of the screen to tan for a few seconds, pushing her farther behind.

I tap my thumb on the gas pedal, revving the engine unintentionally. "Consider this a check-in as to how my assignment was going."

"Bullshit," Lisa says. "With respect and love, of course." Her avatar chucks a teapot, hitting my character and transitioning my car from a lime green furry monster shoe to a teacup on wheels. "Why else are we meeting?"

"Is there a chance you might share an unofficial financials update with me?" I bite my lips, stopping myself from talking further.

Lisa stretches, dropping her controller on the table. "Straight to business."

"Off the record? I'd say less than five years until the doors close. The more the internal auditors dig, the more garbage we're finding. One department was so low in students, and instead of laying off a few professors to save the program, they falsified who was teaching which courses. Essentially, a long-range shell game where millions are now gone. That's just selfish!" Vera scrunches her nose. "I don't know if it was incompetence, denial, or jack-holeness that the head of the department didn't come forward, but I'm unearthing more and more of this. What might have been preventable five years ago if it'd been caught is irreversible now and rampant. So yes, there's an enrollment cliff because fewer people are going to universities, so we have to fight to get every student we can, but also bad financial habits that compounded the issue." She's gripping the edge of the desk so hard, I'm half expecting blood.

"How many programs would need to go to save the university?" I ask, my attention locked on the screen.

Lisa blows out a huge huff of air. "More than I want to think about right now. All those faces. We've looked into selling off buildings, but that only extends the timeline so much. It doesn't fix the gusher we're in."

My body grows heavy, quicksand taking hold of my limbs. "Is that why the university didn't agree to the terms of Fiadh's grant?" I ask, knowing I'm pushing the boundaries on this one. But it's for Fiadh.

"What grant?" Lisa straightens in her seat, her head snapping to find my face.

"The one to set up a cider mill on behalf of the university to also use as a makeshift lab for the students," I say. "The agreement between the university and the funders didn't happen. Fiadh's been a mess trying to get everything up and running again." I'm skating too close to the line of talking to them as president and provost.

"She wants to set up a cider mill?" Vera asks, dropping her controller to her lap. "I can see her doing that."

This shouldn't be as much of a surprise as it is coming across as. Which means the blockage is from either the dean's office or her department head and has nothing to do with the financials of the overall university.

"We aren't eyeing any of the sciences to shut down in the first round, if that's what you're asking," Vera reassures me. "Besides, Fiadh's program is a surprisingly popular niche for us. No one around offers the cidery or brewing program. I'll look into the funding issue for the grant because that part is curious. You're a great person, Yeats, always looking out for your friends."

My brain fails me, forgetting how to properly process oxygen. As in, no more inhales. No exhales. Self-doubt slips up my neck until my ears prick with heat. Tomorrow I'm putting myself first. Is that fair considering Fiadh and the university need my attention? Sciences aren't being cut in the first round, but that doesn't mean it won't occur sooner rather than later.

My phone buzzes on the table. Thad's name flashes on my screen, and I can't click the message open fast enough.

Thad: *Morning, beautiful. Let me know if I can help prep anything you need for tomorrow.*

Thad's voice in my head while I read his message waves away the ball of nerves tightening at the base of my spine, replacing it with the safe quietness we shared last night.

Me: *Happy day before our wedding.*

"Knock, knock," Fiadh sings through my office. "I've got grub."

No. No. No. Crap. Fiadh's early by thirty minutes.

"I...I...I...," Fiadh stutters, strolling in with two armfuls of brown bags. "Piper," she very unsubtly whisper-shouts into the office. "The president and provost are in your office. Thought you should know."

I raise an eyebrow at Vera, hoping she'll read the apology in my eyes. She raises a hand at me and shakes her head.

I playfully open my eyes as wide as possible. "You never told me you're the president and provost. Should I curtsy? Bow? Kiss a ring?"

"Let's pretend I'm not the provost today." Vera turns to face my very confused friend. "For fun, I'm going to pretend that all day. Less getting yelled at by angry people."

I snap the pink controller into a pinker kitty cat racing wheel to hand to Fiadh. "They prefer to leave the provost and president titles at the door."

"Do I get fired if I beat them? Seriously. I'm a menace at this game," Fiadh says.

"Yes," Lisa says sweetly. "But you're not going to win, so it doesn't matter."

"Lisa, you suck at trash talk," I say. "It's more like, I'm going to stomp your car into the road like rotting apples and drive over them until they're applesauce."

"Whoa, whoa, whoa." Fiadh raises her hands in surrender. "What did the poor apples do to any of you?"

"You're right, that is better," Vera says.

I accidentally hit the right flippy ear on the wheel, which ends the game. The screen shuts off, and my phone overrides the Bluetooth, leaving the white dress in full view on the screen. Spikes form in my rib cage, and I grab for my keyboard to close the photo.

"If you were afraid to lose, you could have simply said so," Fiadh says.

"Oh, I like that headband. The twist of the white into the blue would look cute on you," Lisa says. "Are you switching out of bows to headbands?"

"Never. I love my bows." Why is the screen not clicking off? "Maybe. That one is cute."

"Click down into the recently viewed. Are you getting that white dress?" Fiadh spreads out two huge bags on the conference table near the windows in my office.

I click open the eyelet dress, the spikes thickening between my ribs.

"It didn't feel right," I say.

"That's too long for you. I'd go with a shorter option."

I look over at her. Her short-sleeve red silk top is dressed down with a pair of wide-leg jeans. She smooths a floral clip that's struggling to keep her hair in place. Is it wrong that I can picture her in a cap-sleeved A-line lace gown that hugs her gorgeous curves in a delicate ivory—no, champagne. A green ribbon threaded around her waist. Her nails golden and bright, shiny red lips. Her imaginary future wedding dress I can picture without a second thought.

Why is it so hard to picture my own?

"Is it for a date with Thad?" she asks.

"Thad? Who's Thad? Are you following my directions and living life?" Lisa asks.

"Hot guy from a bachelor party she met in the woods who was instantly smitten with her." Fiadh doesn't hesitate to fill in my blanks.

"There are no details ready to share other than he makes my pulse race in a good way." I rest my elbows on my desk. "If I give you details, you're going to internet stalk him and turn him into a research project with findings and conclusions."

"What makes you think I didn't already do that?" Fiadh asks. "Please. He was gaga over you the second he saw you. Of course I already did a dive into who he is. Everyone wants a piece of you, and that man wants a whole Piper pie. I had to make sure he wasn't a creeper or a murderous convicted felon on the run. Which he's not, so good job, you."

Vera absently touches her necklace.

Fiadh narrows her focus on me. "Now, tell me more about the dress we want. What kind of date is this for?"

I can't swallow or move. The air is strangling my brain functions. The logical part of me says this is my opportunity to tell her, to tell all of them I'm eloping. But it's also not the right time whatsoever.

"Is it a sweet picnic? Or a—what is Thad into besides soccer?" Fiadh asks earnestly.

I study the office, the one that's part of the university currently teetering in financial ruin, where I know both my mentors will go down with the ship, fighting for the students and faculty. Fiadh unpacks the brown paper bags on the table. The sparkle of curiosity in her eyes doesn't hide the stress twists she's dug into her hair from trying her darndest to get her grant settled this summer and rebuild her social life. Acid rises in my throat.

"It's...a...casual day date." I hate myself a little. "The dress didn't feel like me."

Meeting here was a mistake.

"Let us pick out a date outfit for you," she says, motioning for my keyboard. "Open a new tab."

I click open a tab on my phone. The university financials pulsate on the screen like a beacon.

"Are these crepes?" Vera's voice cracks as she grabs Fiadh's arm, freezing my friend in place.

I tap the *X* to close out all the evidence of my early-morning searches, primarily of the university finances intermixed with a sprinkling of the marry Thad variety.

"Yes! I brought them from the place around the corner. I can't help myself there. I picked up pear, raspberry, and apple toppings." Fiadh frees herself, jumping to get a plate to fill for Vera.

Vera takes the plate from her and gestures for her to sit in one of the open chairs.

"I physically can't do that," Fiadh says.

"I told you to forget I'm the provost." Vera waves her off.

"It's not that. Our grannies taught us to serve guests first. She brought the food, which makes her host," I say.

Vera softens into her seat and watches as Fiadh prepares plate after plate for the room.

"I also happen to like feeding people." Fiadh carefully places a dish down in front of each of us to avoid spilling an ounce of the sweet sugary goodness wafting up. "If I'd known it was the four of us—"

"We'd have food for twelve instead of six," I say, cutting her off.

I hit a few keys on my laptop, and the shared screen switches to fresh tabs. "What do I wear to a casual"—*informal wedding*—"event in the middle of the day?"

The search bar blinks at us while I wait for search terms from the group. My phone buzzes. Thad's name flashes across my phone screen. I swallow in relief that his name didn't show on the big screen for prying eyes.

Thad: *How's New York?*

Me: *I'm in a last-minute meeting on campus. Then food. Then shopping.*

Thad: *What happened to brunch?*

"Is that him?" Fiadh makes doe eyes at me.

"Give me a search term." I gesture at the screen. "Yes, it's him."

Me: *Fiadh says hi.*

Thad: *Fiadh's in your meeting?*

Me: *No. She's early.*

Me: *Picture three women talking shop while playing a racing game interrupted by food.*

Thad: *Sounds fun.*

"Search for a *hot bang me* dress in silver," Fiadh says.

My thumbs stop moving over my phone. "Say what?"

"What does that even look like?" Lisa asks.

"Spaghetti straps, to the knee with a slit, in silver or a blush tone because they look good on her. Maybe some lace." Fiadh shimmies. "Plus cleavage."

"This is for a daytime date," I say.

Vera snorts. "Who is to say you can't get dressier in the middle of the day? Maybe not the lace, but the rest sounds wonderful."

Me: *My boss, her boss, and Fiadh are trying to get me to wear a slutty dress. Thoughts?*

Thad: *I'm not saying no to that ever. But do they know what they're recommending this for?*

Me: *Negative.*

Thad: *If you find the dress they're describing, please feel free to use my credit card.*

I smile as if he can see me.

"Definitely talking to Thad," Fiadh says.

Thad: *Buy the dress.*

Me: *I cannot wear their suggested outfit in front of Hawk or Elin.*

Thad: *Ha. Have fun with your friends at your brunch bachelorette party.*

Me: *This isn't a brunch bachelorette party.*

I flip my phone over to keep prying eyes from catching any new incoming texts. My heart is happy and light. I punch in the keywords Piper suggested, and an immediate warning screen comes up.

Lisa laughs with her whole body. "Looks like the university doesn't want the words 'lace' and 'cleavage' as a search string."

"Piper, you did a porn search," Fiadh says flatly. "I'm proud, but you're absolutely on IT's list now."

With a quick flip off of my friend, I shift to place my fingers on the keyboard. I delete the word "cleavage," and a litany of images comes up. I swap the word "silver" for "navy," and the cutest dresses come up. They're preppy but professional. Not too edgy, with a slight sophistication to them. They'd be great for everyday wear, but not for tomorrow. Which is where my head is stuck. I need help, but I'm not ready for a conversation about the wedding with this group.

"Searching online is a waste of time." Lisa gestures to the door.

Vera shoves a crepe into her mouth mid-nod, powdered sugar fluttering down to the plate.

"Get up. We're going shopping for your date," Lisa says.

Fiadh hesitates. "All four of us?"

"Of course all four of us," Vera says, picking up her bag from atop the table. "We're in the city. There's no reason to do an online search when the stores are a short subway ride away. If this encourages Piper to live life off her calendar a little more, we can shop all day."

Oh damn. This really is a bachelorette party for me. One where I'm the only one clued in. I grab my leather backpack.

"I'm taking a raspberry one with me." I roll the crepe carefully in leftover foil. Fiadh and the others are already halfway out my office door. I sprint to join them. Vera and Lisa are chattering about where to go first. Fiadh is looking at me with a twist of confusion on her face, undoubtedly related to the less-than-scheduled morning we're having.

Tomorrow is the start of forever with Thad, but today I'm going shopping for a dress with these three guests of my inadvertent bachelorette party.

The thick spikes retreat, and my lungs inflate. Albeit not perfectly.

"I'll tell you one thing, you're not getting that white eyelet dress." Fiadh tugs her phone from her pocket and shoots out a text. "You need something hotter."

"We're going to need a tray or two of mimosas for lunch." There's no way to pick a wedding outfit for tomorrow without being too obvious. Hot-girl outfit, sure, but I don't know that I'd consider myself a hot bride. Not that I've ever truly thought about the perfect dress outside of when I was ten and playing dress-up with Fiadh. At this point I've grown past my initial declaration to wear a pink fairy princess dress with a full veil on my wedding day. The important part isn't the outfit. It's marrying Thad tomorrow. My heart thumps. He's going to look dashing.

CHAPTER TEN

TODAY I'M OPENLY, CONFIDENTLY, and wholly ready to shift my new status from Thad's wife-to-be to Thad's wife. I get the arguments other people might make to rationalize today. But this isn't a rebellious act against how overly focused my life is. This isn't because I'm at the right age and should settle down with a respectable man. I don't settle, not for anything, which is why I know this decision is right. The softness that penetrates me when he places a hand on my skin, erasing the world around us, is a sensation designed especially for me, for us. Yesterday's dress shopping during my bachelorette but not a bachelorette brunch helped the day fly by, and I can't imagine not having spent the day before the ceremony with anyone but Fiadh. Even if she didn't know what we were shopping for.

In full déjà vu, I'm at the house in Chester where Hawk and Elin were married. Only this time, the front door is wide open, and I know to go ahead and make myself comfortable in the living room. He'll be here soon enough. Only, I can't flop on a chair. I want him to see me. To rake his eyes over me and pull me close the minute we are within proximity of each other.

I lift the front of my white cashmere shirt, letting a cooling puff of air enter through the buttons. Turns out giving carte blanche to my mentors and Fiadh on a date dress was not the worst idea in the world. They picked out wonderful outfits, but none that felt right for today. Especially not the seafoam-green lace number with a silk underlay that Lisa picked.

I'd change nothing about how yesterday went. The point of the wedding isn't the dress. The point is not only promising your whole self to the person you are marrying but giving your whole self to them.

After combing through my closet, I found a pair of designer khaki pants that flow loosely around my legs. The top is a favorite of mine that I rarely get to wear, and the combination, while simple, is comfortable.

Thad rounds the corner from the kitchen into the living room, shrugging on his white blazer. He's wearing khaki pants not too dissimilar to my own. Only his are topped off with a pair of sea-blue dress shoes. His eyes sweep up and down my form, hovering on my face long enough for me to feel the heat fill my cheeks.

"You're beautiful..." He rubs his hand across the back of his neck. His eyes are glassy. His smile is soft.

I twist my fingers together. Flashes of excitement are scampering throughout my body. If he's experiencing even an ounce of what I am, I'm surprised he's still standing.

His shirt has a button undone, and he is oh so perfect. Only, when I picture what we'd look like side by side, I'd say we look more ready to go on a sailboat than to get married.

His light auburn hair is meticulously styled. "This is not the dress you described in your text."

"Don't you worry. Lisa found one I think you'll like." I'm talking much too fast for this situation. "You look handsome."

He rakes his fingers through his hair, eyeing me up and down, a soft smile settling on his face.

I shift my weight.

"I know I already said it, but I'm saying it again. You're beautiful." Thad pauses. He reaches inside his jacket and pulls out a simple long box. "I saw this and thought you might like it." He walks to me, holding out the golden box. "If you don't like it, I understand."

Whatever it is isn't moving around enough to be a necklace. I open the box and grin. Inside is a long white satin ribbon. The shade is close to that of a fluffy cloud.

"This is amazing." I hand him the box. His thoughtfulness adds a sweet sting to my eyes. "Can you help put it on me?"

This interaction is awkward, like we're each not saying a piece of what we want. My gut is happy to be here with him. This is nerves, and nerves are completely normal.

He places his hand on my hip. Flutters zoom up my spine, and his full lips part. He turns me to face the fireplace. With the ribbon between his knuckles, he drags it up the curve of my biceps, the ends awakening goose bumps. I tilt my head down, exposing my neck, hoping he'll take a hint to kiss the exposed skin.

Instead, he ties the ribbon in a simple knot around my ponytail, leaving the ends long. I turn around, and his mouth is close enough to my temple that his fresh shave brushes softly against my skin. My pulse bangs hard in my ears, and I forget how to move.

"There's no way I get to be this lucky," he says so low I'm not positive he meant to speak aloud. His words settle into my skin, warming me to the core.

Ping. Ping. Ping. Ping. Ping. His phone goes off like crazy. *Ping. Ping. Ping.* The moment is broken. None of these pings is helping the lurch in my stomach.

He checks his phone. "We needed an officiant, and I messaged Hawk for the name of his."

"Makes sense," I say, grateful that he handled the speed-bump, taking the anxiety an MIA officiant would have caused to my brain today.

"Well, we have an officiant now, but it's Hawk."

I rub my eyebrows. "I'm not understanding why your face is suddenly pale. Hawk is ordained?"

"He is. I asked him when, and he said to not ask questions." Thad shifts his jaw. "We will also have Elin, but we need one more witness."

"Your sisters?" I ask.

He shakes his head. "Fiadh?"

My stomach turns into an angry acid field. "She's at the adventure center." This should be an easy yes. Only, it's not. Plus, she knows nothing about how quickly we got serious, which is on me. Yesterday could have been the right time to tell her, only it wasn't. I could tell by just looking at her when we were out that she's stressed. My eloping would have added more stress to her life.

Gravel crunches outside. The hum of an engine—engines, there's more than one—ceases. One door closes. Another door. The third one shuts with such confidence, it echoes.

Thad grimaces. I take his hands in mine, and we walk to the door. My eyes grow as wide as saucers. This isn't Hawk and Elin. Well, it is. Out the great front window are three large black SUVs. Hawk and Elin, and three additional women piling out of what has to be the most expensive trio of soccer mom cars I've ever seen. Each of them are dressed in full formal attire, and they are headed toward us.

"Shit. Hawk. Damn it, Hawk." Thad tugs me to the center of the room. "I know you wanted a small, intimate..."

I run my hand down the side of his face. His eyes are big, concerned.

I laugh nervously. "You have a fan club."

"This isn't what you wanted," he says.

"I want you. I'm getting you." And a few strangers.

He shakes his head at Hawk. "Hawk, you had explicit directions."

"In his defense, it wasn't his fault," Elin says, the words rushing from her mouth. "I called Liv to see if we could borrow an SUV so we could take you all out for a nice night. No one had to know what was happening. I said it was for Piper's birthday. But then Liv wanted to get her a penis cake. I told her I didn't know if she'd appreciate a penis cake, and I know Thad would not appreciate a penis wedding cake. I told her a penis cake wasn't a good idea for a birthday, so she was going to opt for a breast cake because she's Liv and she's great but she likes pushing Thad's buttons to make him get all gentlemanly awkward."

"Oh, I like Liv already. She sounds fantastic." I rack my brain, trying to recall which one was Liv. Had their jerseys been labeled with their real names, this would be much easier.

"How did she land on 'wedding'?" Thad asks so gently, I'd swear he's an anxiety whisperer.

Elin covers her face with her fingers. "We needed another witness since Hawk is doing the ceremony. I knew this would nix the penis cake. Only, I didn't know she was in the car with two other Bees. I made Liv, Rose, and Margaret swear on so many things to not say a word. They've agreed when we go out that it's a 'birthday party.'" She uses air quotes on the last two words. "I'm sorry. She'd have gotten you a giant penis cake, and you needed a witness. I could not let that be your wedding cake. You cannot start your marriage feeding each other a cock cake."

"You're right. A cream pie is a much better way to go," I say, reveling in the blush on Thad's cheeks.

"Does the entire league know?" Thad asks, sweat pricking at his temples. He doesn't break his gaze from mine.

"No. They think there is a birthday party for Piper, and people in the league invited themselves to the bar later. There are a lot of questions. It would help if you weren't consistently single. But instead, everyone wants to know who Piper is." Elin looks at me. "Thad's amazing, and this isn't exactly the kind of thing you can hide when the league is like a giant nosy family. A family that loves Thad."

Guilt scrapes a hollow into my stomach. His family is here. Not his sisters or his parents, but his soccer family, nonetheless.

"Out of curiosity, when did you text Hawk about the officiant?" I ask.

"This morning when the call came in that the judge in the league was busy," he says.

He pulls my hand up and presses his lips to my wrist. Hawk and the thick noise around us no longer exist. Thad's lips on my wrist make my head swim.

"I didn't think he could do this much in a few hours," Thad says. "I'm sorry."

"Are we having a wedding today or what?" Hawk, dressed in his wedding suit from barely a few weeks ago, saunters into the lush green yard. "Meet us in the greenhouse!"

We move en masse to the greenhouse. Thad holds my arm in his, steadying the earthquake inside me.

We're the last to enter the space. The room contains strangers and my soon-to-be husband, who in reality is a stranger my heart seems to think I've known my entire life. My heart beats erratically through a free fall of emotions, creating a cluster of anxiety that I can't parse whether it's a warning or a celebration. The air grows thick, swallowing the inhalations in the room. This many people exhaling in a glass room is shockingly loud.

Hands grab my hips and turn me to face Thad. I study him. There's not an ounce of tension on his face or his body. He's so calm, so sure.

We don't have to do this right now, he mouths to me.

I want to, I mouth without hesitation. Then, like that same spark from when his fingertips first touched my busted finger, he touches my wrist, causing a shock that sets my body to a steady rhythm. The rhythm where I'm fully myself, with an extra dose of confidence.

"Lay it on us, Hawk," I say.

Hawk leans between us. "Do you have middle names I should use?"

"Anne," I say.

Thad chuckles. "As in Anne Yeats?"

"My parents were very into literature," I say. "Family lore is we're related, but I've never seen a family tree that proves the relation to William."

"Piper Anne Yeats." Thad says my full name, drawing butterflies on my skin.

Hawk shifts onto his heels. "Thad, I'm waiting."

There's an eagerness to Hawk with this question.

"Is your middle name a big secret?" I ask. "Or is it strange?"

"Thaddeus Angelus Cosimo," Hawk says, with a thick accent and a flourish of his wrists.

I giggle softly. "This is how I shall forever say your full name from now on. Thaddeus Angelus Cosimo." My flourish is nowhere near as fancy as Hawk's, but I also have no desire to stop touching Thad while I replay his full name over and over in my head. Dr. and Mr. Thaddeus Angelus Cosimo has a beautiful chime. No, I'll keep my name too. Dr. Piper Anne—my brain freezes. Do I keep my last name? Take his? Does he take my last name? One step at a time.

"Let's do this!" Hawk shrieks with excitement. "Do you have the rings?"

I slide two of the rose bands off my fingers, dropping them into Hawk's hand.

Thad runs his thick fingers through his hair, staring down at the tiny rings. We're going to need to get him a huge ring.

The room hushes, like a collective breath is being held.

"Do you, Piper Anne Yeats," Hawk booms, "promise today to take the best man I know, Thaddeus Angelus Cosimo, to be your wedded husband throughout sickness and health, old age, for richer, for poorer, for the eternity of your time on this earth?"

"I do." I attempt to slide the band from my thumb up his ring finger, and it stops at his first knuckle.

Honestly, who knew how giant his hands were? I certainly didn't.

"Do you, Thaddeus Angelus Cosimo"—there's no sparkle flourish from Hawk this time; instead, there's a seriousness to his tone—"take Piper Anne Yeats to walk with you through this life as your forever partner in this world and the next?"

My head spins, a familiarity in the words stitching my heart. That's the feeling I haven't been able to identify. My body's known from the minute we were within proximity of each other in the woods that we would end up here. If I allow myself to delve further, I'd say my heart knew before the rest of me.

"Without reservation, with my entire soul, I do," he says.

He removes each of my bands, and the one on his ring finger, stacks them, and slides them onto my ring finger in one swift move. The confidence, the promise, everything in the push of the rings against my flesh.

A damn breaks inside me. Tears roll down my face, while my entire body shakes with a tornado of emotions ready to explode. I grip his hands in mine, and we hold each other up, the room no longer as quiet as it was earlier. Replaced with claps, whistles, and pure joy.

"By the power invested in me by the great state of New Jersey and the website I registered with, I pronounce you two married," Hawk says.

"Kiss!" a woman's voice rings out.

I rise on the balls of my feet, a great grin cutting through the tears. He sweeps a grip under my ass, lifting me up to him, kissing me deeply. Respectfully, demurely, before placing me gently to stand on the floor.

I want less demure and more kissing. Given the way his eyes are on me right now, I'm imagining he's in the same boat.

He tugs me closer.

"Did you just claim me, Thad Yeats?" I ask.

"I did." He kisses my finger, sealing the stack in place, giving no objection to the use of my last name.

An awe settles into me, where the words Hawk said at his wedding sink in further. Of all the people Thad could choose to marry, he chose me to be his family. My eyes well up again, and he pulls me close.

His chest heaves high against my cheek. I'm not the only one wrestling with a deluge of emotions right now. I wipe the drops at the base of my eyes before tears can fall, smiling my way through the release my body needs. I look up, wiping a tear, and then another, off Thad's cheeks.

"Ha! Now you understand." Hawk gives a playful pinch to Thad's shoulder.

"I didn't not understand. I've always known what Elin means to you," Thad says. "I just didn't think I'd ever have a person who makes my heart explode."

Hawk pulls at his ear. "I know what you're going for, but that description is more horror film than you might be intending."

I laugh into Thad's side, not a small, dainty laugh, but enough to make the room reverberate. Elin and Hawk join in the laughter. Thad tips his head down with an embarrassed groan.

"Remind me to never share my feelings with Hawk again," he says to me.

The action is small and is the emotional equivalent of having three thousand pounds of feathers dropped on me. There's a lightness, it tickles, but the weight is still the weight. His unknowing signal to confirm I'm his person to giggle with, to talk through wants, dreams, desires, ridiculous moments, and one day, sorrow.

"I hear there's a cake to try," I say.

"To the fleet!" Hawk motions with his hands to the door for people to funnel out to the SUVs.

Multiple hands grab at me and then Thad and tug us out the door. I grip Thad's hand, ensuring we aren't separated while people pile into the rides. He pulls me with him into the third row, and before I can click my seat belt, Liv is behind the wheel, peeling us out of the long driveway.

Thad grabs my buckle and clicks it into place. I turn to grab for his buckle, Liv takes a wavy turn, and I slide the buckle between his legs, grazing his penis. He snaps his legs shut and emits a high yelp. We both freeze, my hands between his thighs with the buckle in hand. Elin and Hawk turn from their seats in front of us to see what's wrong. Elin pulls her lips in, biting in a smile, while Hawk stares down at Thad's lap, then up at him. Their stares shift like we're specimens for study.

"Sorry! I hate driving this thing," Liv says from the front. Given the tone she's using, I do not believe any of that was an accident.

If I pull up too hard, I'll hurt him. Too slow, and well, I'm not super keen on the idea of fondling him in front of his friends.

"For the love of God, please turn around." Thad's tone is gentle, but there's no mistaking that he isn't up for any jokes from Hawk right now.

His friends oblige, leaving us to sort out the issue. I leave the buckle where it is, pulling my hands out slowly, then stop when his eyes flicker from the graze of the side of his shaft. He opens his legs, freeing my hands. I adjust in my seat, unsure where to put my hands. He pulls the buckle out from between his legs, clicking it into place on the other side of his hip.

"I'm so sorry," I whisper.

He slips his hand to the inside of my knee, sending a *hello, vagina* jolt through me. Despite leaving a respectful amount of room between my knee and my groin, I'm squirming, wishing he were closer. When did the knee become so erogenous?

If my pulse drums any harder, we will be experiencing the heart explosion mentioned earlier. The car pulls up in front of an old Irish bar that looks like a thatched-roof home in Ireland. I smile. Granny would approve of the style.

"Get behind me." Liv pushes in front of the rest of us.

Thad wraps his arm around my waist, a move I didn't know how much I needed until we met. Especially now, when I'm walking into a room full of strangers he knows. Those who love him and will be sizing me up. The cool air isn't soothing the spike of fire growing on my skin.

CHAPTER ELEVEN

LIV AND ELIN LEAD us through the doorway. Inside the Irish bar, a live band is set up in the corner next to a white brick fireplace large enough to fit a cauldron. The fiddle player pours his body into his instrument, while the members of his band sing out the folk songs Granny taught me forever ago. A light warms my skin, like a sign she's here. Like she was at the ceremony this afternoon and then came to the bar with me. That her best friend, Fiadh's grandmother, the woman she grew up with and then immigrated to New Jersey with, is here. Even my parents and Fiadh feel present. I am not going to get these damn tears to knock it off.

Over the mahogany paneling is a stripe of green frames, followed by white, and finally orange from ceiling to floor. A not-so-subtle abstract Irish flag. When we get closer, I squint to make out the black-and-white images in the photos. There are soccer players, including some of the Bees, men holding something that looks like a hybrid of a lacrosse stick and a field hockey stick. Hurling maybe? There's a sweet shot in one of the green frames of Thad embracing a few of the men in the room with us right now. His face beaming like that of a proud parent.

Liv's voice booms out. "Per the text chain, this is a social-media-free event. Elin, Hawk, and I are the only ones with phones. Your phones go in a bucket. If you post anything, it better be for birthday wishes, or I'm going to slide tackle the shit out of your ankles."

"What's a slide tackle?" I ask Thad.

"In her case? She's explained that she's going to make it so they can't walk for a long time."

"She threatened to break their ankles?" I ask.

"That's Liv. Well, honestly, that's all the Bees. They protect each other," he says like this is an everyday occurrence.

"Why would they do that for me?" I clear the disbelief from my throat.

"Because they're the Bees," he says. "They don't really need an explanation for why. They trust and support one another."

"I'm not a Bee," I say.

"I'd say they're not-so-subtly courting you." He wags his eyebrows, then leans down to take my mouth in his. The kiss my body wanted earlier is here. His lips over mine, he nips my lower lip with his teeth. His hands press down on my sides. I straighten as high as I can to be taller, the pressure of his palms on my hips pulling me closer to him.

"Thad!" Liv says, interrupting us and bringing us ramrod straight.

The bartender, a giant man with gorgeous flowing raven hair sculpted into a low ponytail, holds out a tray of drinks. "These are for you two."

I gulp down air. There is no way I'm drinking all of these. "While I appreciate everyone wanting to see us fall on our faces halfway out the door, I'd much prefer a toast to all of you."

Before I can grab my own drink of choice, we're swarmed with hands coming from every which way. Thad's hand, or a hand, smooths across my hip.

The tray is wonderfully empty.

"In the simplest of ways, I'd like to say thank you for joining us. For celebrating Piper's birthday with us," Thad says.

Thad throws a finger in the air, gesturing a large circle for the bar.

The room erupts. The bartender lines glasses three rows deep on the bar.

"Sláinte!" I say.

The bartender passes around the glasses. There are four left with what could be vodka, rum, or any other dangerous clear liquid.

"The two on the left are water." The bartender shoves the tray between us. "The two on the right are straight-up vodka."

"What are you up for?" I ask Thad.

"Water. I don't want tonight to end." He picks up the shot glass of water.

I choose the same. "To forever."

"To forever." Rather than taking the shot immediately, he lets his eyes linger on me.

"Sláinte." I gulp down the shot of water, placing the glass in Thad's.

With the shot of confidence, I hop onto one foot, bringing my other foot up behind my knee, then stepping my back foot up and repeating two more times. Am I an excellent Irish dancer? Absolutely not. Rose, the woman with the deep red curls from the hike and who witnessed the wedding, does the step with me. Joining her is Liv, and flanked on their other side is Elin, who does her best but manages to stumble on her own heel.

Thad leans forward and kisses me mid-hop. He waits for the combination to repeat and kisses me again at the top of the hop. The women all around me are laughing, holding one another up.

Song after song plays and the room gets thicker with crowds of people who all seem to know one another on a deeper level. Each one of them saying hi and wishing me a happy birthday. I let go of the women on either side of me, take one more high hop, and let myself crash into Thad.

The bartender yells, "Last call."

Reality spins down. Despite the fact that I want to keep dancing straight through to tomorrow, I knew today would end. I stumble over the winding down of energy.

My tongue is obnoxiously large in my mouth. "We haven't decided where we are sleeping tonight."

Thad stares at the door, then timidly at me, his body language shifting to match mine. "No, we have not. My house is close. There are plenty of bedrooms, or—"

He stopped himself? Finish the sentence. Finish the line. Or, *There's a tire swing to play on. A giant tree house. A roommate named Olaf he forgot to disclose.*

Before he can continue the sentence, the microphone makes a shrill sound, deafening the room. A swarm of Bees now holds the microphone, belting out "Happy birthday" to me. I can't stop laughing, enjoying their wonderfully timed cut into the decision at hand.

Time slips faster without a way to add more or hit pause. I want to stay suspended in the purr of the room.

The last rendition of "Happy Birthday" for the night completes with a round of birthday shots from the handful of Thad's teammates who refused to be outdone by the Bees. The bartender passes Liv the bill, and I reach for the paper. The woman spins on her heel to go join her teammates in the corner, where they all start to pull out credit cards.

"We can't let them pay for everything," I say to Thad.

"They believe, as do I, that among the truest of friends, everything comes back around." He looks at me like I'm the brightest star in the universe. "If we go to pay, we'll be insulting their kindness. Hawk will make a dramatic scene to distract us, and then they'll end up paying anyway."

I turn to find the bartender sliding card after card while Liv strokes his biceps.

"If it makes you feel any better, that is Liv's boyfriend, who I'm guessing gave them a heavy discount for the night," he assures me.

"I've done nothing for them." I stare up at him in a haze.

"You have." His eyes have that faint slickness again, like he's still going through each internal strike of emotional shrapnel like I am. While many of the pieces are rounded and soft, others are spikes of worry and anxiety.

The feeling like I want to belt out songs of happiness boomerangs into an overwhelming twist in my heart of *Please don't let him be screwing with me. My soul could not take his rejection.* Old wounds like to rear their stupid heads up at all the wrong times.

Elin leans into Liv, and they walk to us elbow in elbow.

"Know what I love?" Elin asks.

Thad tips his chin up. "Hawk, the Bees, jazz, not wearing shoes."

"Besides that," she says, swaying side to side from one bare foot to the other.

"Where are your damn shoes this time?" Liv asks.

Elin waves them off. "No, besides all that. I love that you two saw each other and were like, hell yeah, that's my other half. Let's fucking do this shit right now."

"I love that I wasn't the one who hurt your finger," Liv adds.

"Happy birthday," Elin says, raising a glass of end-of-the-night water.

"I don't think I've ever seen her this drunk," Thad says to me. Then he turns to Elin. "Who is driving you home?"

"She's exhausted, not drunk. It's eons past her bedtime." Liv raises her hand, pledging her life. "I'm your driver. I asked Steve to make everything he puts in me virgin tonight."

"Pfft, he can't make you a virgin." Elin snorts.

Liv spins her in several circles. Elin wobbles, reaching out to steady herself.

"Okay, okay. Too far." Elin laughs and falls full body onto Liv.

"As your humble driver, where am I taking you home to?" she asks.

I drop my arms, staring up at him, neither of us responding to the question. This silly little conversation again. If we simply party until the sun comes up, then no one has to decide, until tomorrow.

"Er..." Thad says.

"Uh..." I add.

"Oh...oh...Liv, I need more water," Elin says, dragging her to the bar.

"Well, that was obvious." My apartment maybe? His place? The list of things we should have talked through is growing immensely. Enough so that the club soda and lime I grab off the high top is very heavy. My stomach churns.

He looks to the floor. Like he is having a similar conversation in his own head.

"I..." We've never shared a bed or done much of anything beyond kissing. He's never been to my apartment, and I don't even know his address. Does he have a house? The room grows stupidly fuzzy.

"Piper, take a sip," he says. "There is no wrong answer here."

I oblige, because this makes sense. I can take a sip.

Hyperventilating makes it super hard to think.

He leans practically inside my ear. "I will play this however you want." He's not loud enough for anyone else to hear, at least I don't think so. "We can go to our own places, you can come to my house since it's close to here, we can go to Hoboken, or I can get us a hotel. We'll do whatever you are most comfortable with. I will never rush anything."

I let out a wheezing laugh.

"Unless you feel we rushed this. I don't think we did. But, oh God, are you okay?" he asks, his own anxiousness flooding out.

I take a sip of my drink, buying time to think. Then I place my palm on his heart, his muscles melting against me.

A hotel is way too much pressure. My house, or his? "I don't want to start our marriage in two different apartments. Though, I do appreciate the offer."

He bites his lower lip.

My apartment is far, and everyone is exhausted. I can't ask Liv to drive us to Hoboken, and my car is at the wedding site. I 1,000 percent cannot drive us to my house from there because of exhaustion and having had a few drinks.

I pull in a long, slow stream of air, studying the hopefulness on his face. "You said you live closer, so your place makes sense."

The dimple in his chin peeks through. "I will sleep anywhere in the house. You don't have to share…"

I raise a finger to his lips. "We'll figure it out when we get there."

He kisses my finger, then tenderly presses his lips against my wrist. If he keeps doing that, I will be the one who has to worry about rushing things.

He lifts his chin to Liv. She skips to us, leaving a half-asleep Elin at the bar leaning on Hawk.

"My house," Thad says.

Liv waves over to the bartender. He walks to Hawk and bangs his knuckles on the bar. As much as I strain to hear their conversation, it's too loud to grab a single word. Elin curls into Hawk, and he helps guide her to the door. The five of us go outside. The night air is gorgeous, with the stars above to welcome us. Not as many as at the farm, but a crap ton more than in Hoboken.

Liv leaves us to grab the car.

The car ride is quiet. Hawk and Elin are on the bench seat in front of us. Elin's head is resting sweetly on the stillest version of Hawk, one I didn't know was humanly possible for a man with his energy levels.

I lean into Thad, letting my arm fall across his stomach. He kisses the top of my head. His arm wraps over my shoulders, making room for me to snuggle closer.

Thad taps Hawk's shoulder with his elbow. Hawk turns his head but not so far as to shift and cause him to wake Elin.

"Do you two want to stay at the house tonight?" Thad's voice is tender.

"I'd love to. She's exhausted, but..." Hawk changes the direction he's looking to try to catch my attention. "I don't want to interrupt your first night married."

My ears perk up. Pretending to be half-asleep is harder when my body is involuntarily tightening every muscle I have.

"I'm not inviting you to share a bed with us," Thad says. "You're both exhausted, and we have the room."

We. He definitely said "*we* have the room." I relax deeper into his side, the adrenaline from the day wearing off. I walk my fingers across his stomach. He flexes his abs low against my touch.

"Please stay. You're both exhausted. There's no sense in picking up your car and then driving home if you're tired. You can get your car in the morning," I say, picking up the smooth cue from Thad. The two of them sleeping over takes the pressure off staying together on our first night. It alleviates the pressure of being alone in his dark room beneath his comforter. I'm imagining a comforter. He doesn't seem like a guy who has a stack of quilts. I'd guess a full matching bed set.

The car turns up the driveway to the place where we got married.

"Welcome home," Thad says.

My heart beats rapidly. "Home?"

"Home." He opens the car door and slides out, while I sit inside with my mouth open.

Why—no, how—did I not realize this place with the elegant tree-lined driveway was his house? Maybe it was the lack of photos everywhere, or that he didn't call it his home at all. But there was his ability to move his best friend's entire wedding to this gorgeous venue in an instant.

"I thought you worked at the field house?" I say quietly.

"I do," he says.

Elin yawns next to me. "He owns the field house. A small detail he didn't share with anyone until the end of this past April."

Thad shrugs. "I didn't want people to be weird around me."

I tug on his sleeve. "Are there any more surprises you'd like to share?"

"A lifetime of them." Thad unlocks the front door to the well-lit living room.

In a swift motion, my feet are above the ground, and I'm safely in his arms. As we cross the threshold, I can't take my eyes off the softness of his face in the pale light. I put my finger under his chin, gently guiding his mouth to mine for a soft, flutter-filled kiss. He pulls me in for an exploratory graze of his lips across mine.

"Fuck," I wheeze.

Tiny bursts of want pop like bubbles throughout my entranced body.

"Liv can drive us." Hawk's voice cuts through my haze.

"No," Thad and I say simultaneously.

I take a step from Thad to let my body cool down.

Thad snags a pillow off the couch on his walk to the hallway. "You two can stay in this wing."

"Thanks, man," Hawk says. "I'm pretty sure Liv's halfway home already. She was yawning half the drive here."

"Night, Thad," Elin's sleepy voice adds. "She's super lucky."

I am. I'm too nervous to sit, too floaty from the entire day itself. There's a ton of questions to dive into, but they are for tomorrow us.

Thad comes back into the living room and gestures up a different hallway. I follow him in outward silence while my heart is practically playing rounds of ska music with an enthusiastic trumpet solo.

His bedroom, like I'd predicted, has a fully matched bed set. The summer comforter is a crisp light blue. He stands by my side, both of us staring at the bed. I relax my jaw to pull in air. His shirtsleeve brushes against my skin, sending warmth up my neck.

"I probably should have told you this was my house." Thad rubs the back of his neck, mussing his hair.

"Yup," I say. "Rather small detail you left out."

The boom of his heart shows on his neck. "There's another bedroom I can take."

I slip my shoes off, walk to the bed, and place them evenly in front of the carved maple footboard. "Can you help me?" I ask, pointing to the ribbon I can easily take out.

The polite gap he leaves when he comes up behind me only adds a wanting from my body to pull his skin flat against mine.

He gives a soft tug, releasing the bow from my hair. I swallow at the tension in the air, the polite heat growing in my body. He holds the top of my ponytail, slipping the thick elastic from my hair and letting the brown strands cascade down. He lets out a choked moan.

His forehead rests gently against the top of my shoulder. "If I told you all I want to do tonight is sleep in this bed with you—sleep, not anything more—will you join me?"

A tingle sweeps my lower body. I want the same soft touches he's giving me now, but everywhere. I walk to the bed, tugging open the corner on the right side. The sheets are silky, calling me to slide into them. Reaching across the intimate queen-size bed is what I imagine moving on a cloud to be. I pull down the corner on the left side.

Thad takes his shoes off, lining them near mine. His eyes dart from the left side to the right side of the bed.

"I usually sleep on the right," he says.

"Not anymore." I climb into the bed and pull up the sheet, hoping to hide the nervous bouncing of my ankle.

Thad slides in on the left side, far from the edge, close enough to leave space. Given we're both still wearing our wedding clothes to go to sleep, I'm guessing I'm not the only one unsure how to navigate this moment. He's close enough for me to want to roll into him to shut the gap between us, that damn orb sending waves of want through me. He traces my jawline, pulling in for a soft kiss good night. The pressure is a sweet whisper. A promise.

I press a second kiss, my promise that this is the start of everything.

"Pipes," he says. The sweetness in the way he says my name clears my head.

"Yeah," I say, my mouth millimeters from his.

"We need to talk about a few things tomorrow." He chuckles. "Nothing bad, but we really need to talk."

Shots of concern dig at my skin. "You can't say that and let it linger. My head isn't going to shut up."

He repeats the sweet kiss, erasing the flash of panic in me. His hand slips over the dip in my waist, grounding me comfortably. His arm twitches, and his breaths slow. He's asleep. My body grows heavy, fighting the need to know what the conversation is about. The irregular rhythm of my pulse keeps buzzing me awake, while my head replays, *we really need to talk.* That is not how you go to sleep. We talk and then go to sleep. Or, in my case, not sleep.

Chapter Twelve

M Y INTERNAL CLOCK GENTLY pushes me awake at seven a.m. For the first time in my adult life—hell, my post-tweens existence—I'm well rested. I slide out from under Thad's arm and stare at his sweet face. I can't remember the last time I didn't wake up at five a.m., anxious to get moving on the day to make the world go faster. Not wanting to wake him, I get up slowly from the bed, grab my work backpack, and walk softly across the steel-gray rug to his side. My wedding clothes from last night are as wrinkled as his. His angelic face is peaceful in this light, and the tight lines of his jaw are blissfully relaxed. I reach out to stroke down his cheek, stopping myself before I make contact. He needs sleep.

I tiptoe to the doorway, scrunching my stomach with each tentative step, unsure of where the squeaky boards are. There's a rustle. I turn and catch him repositioning himself, drawing the pillow into the spot with my first body imprint in our bed. An imprint that cradled me in the best night's sleep I've had since I was a child.

"Pipes," Thad mumbles.

I glance over at him, but he's asleep again. I grab my phone from my bag. With a click, I take a picture of him, turning it into my background image. The boring screen-saver image protecting his first light vulnerability for my eyes only.

The chair in the corner of the living room is big enough to settle into. I drop my bag next to it on the way to the curtains to let light into the room. My first attempt at pulling them manually to the side is an utter failure. They're much too heavy. I walk over to the far end, to the light switches. I begin to flick switches. The first turns on the overhead fan. The second turns on the fan's lights. On the third switch, an overhead light comes on above the chair in the corner. Seriously? How many switches can a single room have? I strike a fourth switch, and a screen drops down from the ceiling, covering an ornate oil painting easily as tall as I am. I reverse the switch and watch as the ceiling pulls it away like magic. Great, there are no more switches. I move the corner of the curtain and find a button to press on the wall tucked behind a pullback.

When I press the button, the blinds open, and the curtains draw back. This experience is more cinematic than the projector screen the ceiling practically birthed. Glued to each other out the window are Hawk and Elin, headed to their car.

I inhale deeply, and that silly orb reappears, beating melodically. Thad and I are alone.

With the sun pouring into the room, I flick the overhead light off. I walk to the fluffy white chair and slide in with my legs crisscrossed. A series of sweet little birds sing in chorus at the feeders outside. There is a hummingbird among them. Its energy and the rapidness of its movements have my full attention. I slide my laptop from my bag and onto the wide arm of the chair. Several goldfinches find their own feeders, followed by another bird with a red spot on its wing. No idea what the bird is.

The laptop chimes, and I swear it echoes through the house. I smash down on the mute button. Please don't let him have woken up.

There's no stirring from the bedroom, but it could be too far away for me to hear. Crap. This thing wants a password for the wireless. I shut the lid, switching to the browser on my phone.

I open a fresh search and punch in "Thaddeus Angelus Cosimo." This is simply to prepare for the conversation he wants to have today. Thad Cosimo comes up with multiple pages. The first is a picture of him surrounded by kids at the field house. I click into the article. "Thaddeus Angelus Cosimo, grandson of the late former professional soccer player Angelus Cosimo and his wife, the late heiress Caterina Cosimo, has stepped up to take over Angelus and Caterina's nonprofit training program." My body clenches. The program is designed for youth who otherwise would not have the opportunity to afford travel camps, helping to even out the playing field when it comes to athletics.

Heiress? Former professional soccer player? I click through the next three articles. Each offers more information on the Cosimo family, their ties to massive soccer stardom, and the grandmother whose family essentially makes most of the soccer balls used across the globe at the professional level. Not to mention clothing and accessories I didn't know were needed in the sport.

Thad had left details of his life out—way out. We've got to get him a prenup. Postnup? Either way, we need to protect him.

Fresh coffee wafts in from the kitchen. I look to the left of the chair and let out a yelp. Crouched next to me, holding out a cup of coffee equal to twice what I'd normally take in the morning, is Thad.

"Did you fly here, or do you have the ability to teleport?" I ask, my whole body settling from the jump scare that woke me better than caffeine ever could.

His eyes are fixed on my phone, and his smile fades. "I was hoping I could tell you first."

"We need to get you a postnup." The words tumble out.

He sits, stretches his legs out, and holds his cup up to his mouth. "We don't need a postnup." He takes a long sip, only I need him to keep talking.

I lean in. "I have a great lawyer. We can get a document written up."

"My lawyer already looked you up," he says.

The room grows smaller. "Your lawyer?"

He points and flexes his feet over and over. "She's a trusted friend."

Now, I'm not a jealous person, but the "she's" in his sentence does a twisting sensation to my confidence that I don't like.

"Rose, the woman with the long curly red hair," he says with a knowing smirk at the little rush of jealousy that had to have traced itself across my face.

I work hard to relax the creases in my forehead. Play it cool. "I like her. She seems great."

"When she found out she was headed to our wedding, she did some digging into you," he says.

"Did I pass with flying colors?" I ask. What the hell was she digging into? I fold my arms across my stomach.

He flexes both feet up at the same time, seemingly stretching his calves. He shrugs and holds the cup up to his mouth again.

"Do you even know how much you have in assets?" he asks. "Because I'm curious as to why, without knowing about me, you didn't ask for a prenup for yourself."

I stare at him, my eyes growing wider by the minute. For as much as I do in investing, I know exactly what I have in retirement, in my bank account, and in several other portfolios. I know what additional items I have that I could sell off in a pinch if I ever needed to. I know what buildings I own, about what they're worth, but I don't ever look at the final number. Which is stupid and the opposite of what I'd tell anyone else. But it pushes me to go harder and to keep going. To not take anything for granted.

Think. Think. Think. "Granny said in marriage and friendships, you give all of yourself. If either side withholds, the friendship and marriage risk breaking." I trace the piping on the edge of the chair cushion. "I own a few buildings."

"I also own buildings," he says. "Your granny sounds smart."

I shift in my seat. "She was."

This isn't the conversation I was expecting when he said he wanted to talk today. I don't totally know what I was expecting the conversation to be, but assets and finances weren't top of the list.

"Help me wrap my head around the scale difference in our investments here," I say.

His gaze drifts up to the ceiling fan. "Not billions, but each of my sisters and I, as well as my parents, has enough that we'll never have to go without. Nor will our families, or grandkids. My sisters and I wanted to take it further, so we started investing together and bought out the entire building complex around the field house prior to the pharma companies moving in. We went in together after my grandparents passed. The field house and an ice rink are both mine."

"That complex must have fifteen humongous buildings," I say. "How do you keep up with everything?"

"We have a property manager." His brows furrow with confusion. "Do you manage all of your properties by yourself?" This feels super rhetorical.

I don't answer. Instead, I look outside for the now-gone hummingbird.

"You manage them by yourself." The astonishment in his voice isn't necessary. "And you work full-time at the university?"

"Yes." I'm thinking this question may have been rhetorical, too. "But you work at the field house."

"I work because I like working. I've always liked working. My sisters each have their own jobs that make them happy. My grandparents put no rules or restrictions on the funds." He follows my line of sight outside to the hummingbird. "I call the little guy Marty."

"Marty is gorgeous," I say, my attention now squarely on him again.

"Pipes," Thad asks. "Did you marry me thinking I worked at the field house?"

Yes. "Did you agree to marry me thinking I was a stressed-out professor at a small university?"

"I said yes to the stressed-out professor." Thad places his mug next to him on the ground. "But Rose messaged the rest." He strums the lines in the hardwood floor. "But I also feel like I'd heard your name and your voice a thousand times before we met."

My cheeks grow warm. "I'm on the radio a lot, and television, and quoted pretty often in print."

"No," he says. "Well, yes, because Rose sent me link after link to check out. But no, I can't explain it. Wait. How often is a lot?"

I slide my laptop into my bag, then slip from the chair to the floor to sit next to him. When I stretch my legs out along with his, my feet don't come anywhere near even with his, while we're hip to hip.

"I work a lot," I say.

He lengthens his neck. From here our heights are right. I prefer this angle where his head is tilted down and he's looking at me with admiration. He takes my chin and carefully pulls my mouth to his, delivering the same softness from last night. I lean into him wholeheartedly. His free hand supports my waist in a manner that says I can trust him with forever.

"Pipes." My name rolls off his lips, inviting me into him further. "Are you sure you have time for this? Us?"

A zap hits like a bee sting inside my heart. "Absolutely."

He takes another sip of his coffee, letting the liquid linger in his mouth before swallowing.

"Do you know that question the guidance counselor in school asks you before they pressure you into picking a college or university and a major to determine the rest of your life when you're fifteen?" he asks.

"Yeah," I say. "I wanted to be a professor."

"At fifteen you wanted to be a professor." He places his cup on the floor between his legs. "I told mine I wanted to be a footballer. She informed me I'd need to change sports if I wanted to do that, and most kids start when they're young. That was when I learned she had no idea how to help me."

"Did you take out a dry-erase marker and show her the difference in the balls?" I ask.

He gives me a playful groan. "I did not. I listened to her lecture and took a stack of pamphlets she felt might be a good match, given, in her words, how behind in training for my sport of choice I was."

"Oof. Did you ever correct her?" I ask.

"No, but I did show her my acceptance letters." His mouth grows so close to mine, I catch a tiny whiff of cinnamon. "Don't think you're off the hook for my questions. I see what you're doing."

Me? I mouth, pressing my wrist against my forehead and feigning insult.

He lowers my wrist, giving me a better view of the relaxed version of himself. "She asked me the same question, about money being no object, and I can fully acknowledge my life is a privilege. Less than six months ago, I quit the job that was stressing me out and making my life miserable to build up the field house to where it is now. I'll happily pass on the post-nuptial offer to ensure you understand you will forever have the same opportunity to always do what makes you joyful. Not that you need me for that."

This man has done what seems impossible, choosing to say *fuck off* to a job to prioritize happiness over stress.

"Money isn't an obstacle for you with what you've accomplished on your own, or with what's ours," he says, lifting an eyebrow. "With that knowledge, do you still choose to be a professor? There's no wrong answer here."

I lean closer to him, taking his mouth against mine, sweeping my tongue across his bottom lip. He delicately cups my cheeks, feeding off the tender kisses, not rushing or pushing, but letting me get lost in his supple lips.

"You don't have to be so gentle," I say into his mouth.

"I want to," he says. "I'm going to take my sweet time."

He opens his mouth more, allowing us to explore further. The pads on his fingertips tickle down my arms. I suck in a breath, fighting the desire to push this further, but pacing myself because while we have a forever of firsts ahead, I don't want to rush a single one. His mouth moves, carefully pressing kisses down the side of my neck. My nipples grow firmer with each kiss. I whimper when his teeth scrape away from the side of my neck.

He bends his knees up, clasping his hands around his legs. I grin, nudging my elbow to push his knee open, pressing in, laying a kiss on his mouth. I repeat his efforts, returning sensations in kind down to the dip in his collarbone. His body twitches. He bites his lip, dampening the groan I've rightfully earned.

He leaps up from sitting, shifting his hips to unsuccessfully hide the bulge in his pants. "Let me take you on a tour of the sports complex and the other buildings."

I glance down at his groin. "I'm going on the record first as saying I'll sign anything to protect you."

"And I, you," he says. "Only right now, I want to take things slow, and if we don't leave now, I don't know how well I'll be able to maintain not ripping your clothes off."

"I'm happy to check out your assets," I say, emphasizing the intentional double entendre. I reach out a hand, inviting him to pull me up. When he pulls me up, we're toe to toe, our bodies radiating hot energy in need of release.

He sucks in an extended inhalation. "Do you, uh...? Do you need to borrow an outfit?"

I check out my clothes. "I have a few outfits I brought with me." The makeshift wedding outfit from yesterday, wrinkles and all, is getting worse for wear by the minute. "Let's get changed and meet in ten minutes?"

"Five?" he asks.

Five works. Five is much less time to be apart. I pull a sundress from my backpack. He rubs his hair on his entire walk up the hallway until he disappears into his bedroom. I lean over the chair for balance, my vagina practically screaming at me to disappear for a while and touch myself, but there's no time. Relief will have to wait until after the tour. After a full day with him. I can do this even though the carnal sensation in me isn't as supportive of the decision to wait.

I pull off the outfit from yesterday and slip the lemon sundress over my head. I cap it with a short-sleeve green cardigan for our excursion. Thad reenters the living room wearing salmon dress pants topped with a fresh white polo.

He lifts my ring finger to his lips, pressing a kiss to the rose-gold rings. His eyes lock on my face, and he playfully nips at the sensitive dip between each finger, an erogenous area I was unaware of until this moment. This slowness, this living for extending sensations, is addictive. Spending time with him is addictive.

CHAPTER THIRTEEN

O N MONDAY, BETTER MARKED as "fully married morning two," I'm already poured into the white chair before
the sun has fully risen. Our outing yesterday didn't end until
nine p.m., when we came home and rolled into bed. Except this
time I didn't wake up in the same clothes. The focus of the
conversation yesterday was economics and finances, not exactly
bedroom talk for most people. Laying out our investments was
weirdly fun. I'd go so far as to compare it to the nerdy equivalent
of throwing open a trench coat while wearing nothing else.

There aren't many people outside of academia that I can
have a conversation with that isn't solely focused on work. Only
now, I want to push through the work that's piled up over the
weekend so I can get more time with Thad.

I settle into the chair in the corner, opening my laptop on the
flat arm. The past few marvelous days have been a blur, but I
need to stay on top of all the inquiries coming in so as to keep
my promise to Lisa and Vera about continuing my interviews
and media appearances.

A sticky note is on top of my backpack with a note: *Try
"Gioia Ru Me Core."* What is this mess of letters? I yank out

the stack of binders and folders from my bag, laying them out in piles around me. The ring creates a little cave to curl into. I punch the letters into the space for a password, and my email refreshes. Elation fizzles as fast as it starts. I cover my mouth, swallowing against the hyperventilating I'm edging toward. Coffee will be a great reward after I knock out a couple dozen emails.

A lead weight hits my stomach. Not only are there over three hundred emails, but several are marked as urgent by the senders. Subject lines read "follow-up to previous message," "deadline approaching," and the always lovely "urgent response required." I can do this before Thad wakes up. My throat dries at the knowledge that I'm lying to myself. This will take a full day, if not two, to clear out.

I open the first message, scanning the contents to assess the scale of urgency. An email, or rather a long chain of repetitive emails growing in desperate intensity, is from a student wishing to challenge their grade. I squint at the date of the request. The email has no personal information, isn't an official university email, with something that might prove helpful, like a last name. No ID number, nor the course or year. I punch out a chipper email requesting further information, adding a link to the email with the form to be completed. My stomach gurgles when I hit send.

I clear through thirty emails before responses begin to ping my inbox. Marty zips into focus outside the window. The sun is up, beaming glorious midmorning light into the room. A presence next to me draws my focus. Thad places a cup of coffee down to my right on a small table that wasn't there when I sat down.

"Hitting the emails early?" he asks, keeping a polite distance from my screen.

"Only a few. This shouldn't take too long." I hope. Until I open the emails, there's no way of knowing the follow-up necessary.

A pleasant smile that says, *Yeah, right,* is plastered on his face. He gestures as if to say, *Carry on,* shuffling his feet across the floor toward the bathroom.

I grab for the coffee, swallowing down the steaming French vanilla with a kick of espresso. The gray porcelain cup is daintier than the one yesterday and is the exact amount of what I drank on Sunday. On the table is a corn muffin with a smear of whipped butter on the side. A treat for later so I don't end up with muffin bits all in my keyboard or on the papers I'm reviewing.

With the caffeine rush, I narrow my focus on the screen, determined to blast through a clip of the emails. No need to hit all three hundred. Getting through at least a hundred and fifty will inch me closer to being less behind. An email pings in from the student I redirected earlier. I hover the mouse over it, clicking it open to what must equate to a six-page explanation of why I'm wrong about how to do the grade challenge. Close email. Mark as unread. That is a later problem. This is going to be an energy and time suck that I'm not prepared for right now. I go to the beginning of the bolded emails, back a few days to the last clear out I did. Answering in the order the emails came in is a better system. Plus, if I'm lucky, I'll clear out some of the ones who sent several reminders in the process.

With swiftness, I respond to email after email. The battery drains from my laptop. I root in my bag, hunting for a cord, coming up victorious. Plugging in brightens the laptop, and I'm good to keep going.

I let out a yelp when the bottom of the laptop sears my skin. I peek up from my screen, and Thad's standing in front of me with two glasses of water. This man walks with the grace of a ballerina for me not to have noticed the food change. That or the tunnel vision that comes with engrossing myself in work is functioning at high capacity. If he heard the cry of pain, he's ignoring it.

"I have to run to the field house for a while to let some people in to repair a damaged part of the wall." He sets the drinks down on the table next to me. "Per the front desk, no one knows what happened, but there's a body-sized print in the drywall."

"How would no one see that? Don't you have cameras?" I ask, horrified at how hard a body would have to hit the wall to cause that much damage.

"I'm going to have to review the tapes, but last time this happened, it was a celebration gone wrong." He crouches next to me. "I don't mind celebrations." He runs his thumb over the bands on my ring finger.

"I'll stay out of your way," I say, not sure whether he was inviting me or giving me a pass on shifting out of what I'm working on.

"You wouldn't be in the way, but I can see the stress on your face while you stare at your work laptop," he says.

"I fell a little behind the past few days," I say.

Thad eyes my screen, his smile hesitant when he sees the number of unread messages. "Stay home and knock out some work. I'll take care of dinner tonight, and we'll eat in the greenhouse."

Take me with you is what I should say. Instead, "Sounds great" escapes my lips.

"I'm a text away if you need me." He kisses my wrist and heads to the front door. "Ciao, gioia ru me core."

I sit up straight, papers falling to the floor. "What is that?"

"You didn't look it up?" He winks at me, closing the door behind him.

I open a fresh browser on my laptop, punching in each letter on the paper he'd left with the password. His car works its way up the driveway before I can hit enter. Before I can respond to whatever he's said.

Per not one, not two, but three different search pages, he called me the joy of his heart. I sit stunned, in his chair in our house, looking at the empty driveway, alone. Stupidly wishing I'd shut my laptop and gone with him. Only, I'd be useless in repairing a body indent in a wall. What I can do is focus on parsing through the requests in my email to carve out time for us later. The more I dive into the emails and work, the faster time will go, and the sooner I'll see him.

I clear a series of emails from various requests to take on additional work and sort through more grade challenges from very optimistic students, whom I'd love to give the benefit of the doubt. Only, I don't think they showed up to more than the first day of class, skipping the remaining fifteen weeks. The excuses are truly excellent this round. My favorite is the one who thought their twin was attending classes for them. That student almost had the world figured out. Too bad their twin wasn't on the same page in this case.

The emails are half-cleared. A victory considering the speed at which they come in. There's no way I can keep up with the replies coming in right now. I rest the laptop on the arm of the chair to pull out a brown binder from my bag.

I flip through to the middle tab and read through an article submission. I begin to mark the paper in purple ink, getting lost in the words while time ticks.

Midsentence, two lips press against my forehead. Their warmth stills the urgent desire to push through the work in front of me. Thad squats down, making us eye level.

"Have you moved since seven this morning? Taken a bathroom break? I need to know your secret." He rests his elbows on my knees. "Did you diaper up like New Year's Eve in New York City? Or are you simply a camel?"

"Chamber pot." I close the binder on my lap, clearing room for his hands by placing it on the arm of the chair. "Only, I couldn't find a regular one, so I borrowed a huge mixing bowl and hollowed out the chair." I tug up my mess of hair, noting another important grooming step I missed this morning. "I can move if you need to borrow the pot." I catch the clock on the wall. It's five forty-five. Goal accomplished; I made time move quickly. "Or, I'm a professor and we learn how to not go to the bathroom for long periods of time thanks to meetings and teaching."

"Ah, so the dishes are safe." He bobs his chin. "Good. I have dinner ready."

My stomach answers in a low-pitched growl. Stacks of folders waterfall from my lap. I bend forward to pick them up, leaning my cheek against his, the soft sweep of his five-o'clock shadow teasing my skin. Hungry, I turn to kiss him, missing, and lay my open lips against the throb below his ear. He slides his hands up the sides of my thighs, pressing against the soreness from sitting too long in the same position. The two of us pause here, my entire body suspended between strong pulses to not lose the sensation of floating in the early flicker of heat that comes before I need more of his skin on mine.

He releases a shaky stream of air. "Dinner. Made. Fuck."

My head wanders in and out of a hormone haze. He's wearing a pale brown leather apron over a pair of gray dress pants. The sleeves of his crisp white button-down are unbuttoned and rolled to his elbows. Another growl releases from my stomach. I wrap my arm across myself, hoping to shush the angry little demon. Unfortunately, not eating throughout the day is now coming back to haunt me. From here, I could slide down, spreading my knees and straddling him, to see how he feels, get the press of our bodies together.

He digs his fingers in further, shooting an electric jolt to my center. I suck my stomach, curling into him. Decidedly better than the shrieky belly.

Thad takes in two short inhales and then exhales down into his lap. "I made dinner."

Then the satisfaction of completing work to snag more time with him later bursts. It's replaced with a desire to fold into myself in the same way an embarrassed child might. I should have helped with dinner. We should have been doing whatever it is people do who said "I do" only two days ago.

"I'm starving," I say to him sweetly while internally berating myself. We had imbalanced priorities today, and I can admit mine sucked worse than falling on black ice.

My hands shake while I slide the binders and papers into my backpack. I didn't even hear him come in. I catch the glint in his sweet eyes as I shove my laptop into my bag and close it.

I go to stand, and he releases his hands, switching instead to looking at the ground.

"Give me a minute," he says, placing one finger in the air.

Confused, I stand, my center square with his face.

Thad lifts his head, his eyes rolling up to meet mine. He stands tall, leaving a sliver of space between our bodies. Instead of closing the space like my body wants, I listen to the small voice in my head saying, *Eat.*

Moving from the chair becomes a clumsy dance of turning into each other, each of us apologizing for inconveniencing the other. He steps up, guiding me in front of him by my hip. I let my forearm drop, trapping his touch in place.

We stroll through the kitchen, where there's not a single dish in the sink. He leads me out to the greenhouse, where there is a table set for two.

I grab at my knee-length T-shirt, the sleeves hanging down to my wrists. "I'm not dressed for this level of dinner."

The table is an old oak kitchen table complete with pulled-out leaves to accommodate the emerald-green glass plates and vintage crystal cups in a deep blue. The night paints the sky above the pitched green-tinted glass ceiling. A half-moon is freckled with glimmering stars. If I were in my apartment, there'd be no stars. But here, in this room, it's like the night sky was waiting for me to appreciate its beauty.

Golden flatware and serving utensils are laid out in perfect settings. Black stone plates are topped with gold domed lids, keeping the food warm.

He did this for me. I clear my throat, sucking down any emotion before it can break past my lips.

Thad comes around to my chair and pulls it out. When I sit, he pushes the chair in. A rage of hunger hits me with the mix of spices wafting through the room. I place the green satin napkin on my lap. There's a blush-toned fainting chair in the far corner that wasn't there the day we got married. A perfect spot for reading. On the other side of the chair there is a table with a gold-and-green Tiffany lamp.

"Did you bring this in here?" I gesture to the table.

"I did." He takes his seat and lifts the first lid, releasing the trapped steam. "We have a mouthwatering pasta con le sarde. Which is kind of a rustic comfort food for me. Translated, it's pasta with sardines."

I give a mini round of applause.

He grabs for the next dome. "An arugula salad with walnuts, dried cherries, and crumbled soft cheese. I kept it simple because we haven't discussed allergies or food we like or dislike."

"Fun fact about me. I have zero allergies to food." If he'd kindly push the pasta dish in front of me, I'd go to town.

He's super adorable. He tips the lid of the final dome up enough for steam to escape. The lid slips down, wafting lemon and grilled fish. If my stomach had teeth right now, I'd be in danger of it boring through my skin to get to the main course.

"That was a tongue tease," I say. "Take it off!"

He wags his eyebrows, revealing the last dish. A pair of grilled branzino. I married a man who can cook. Life is so good right now. For a final reveal, he lifts the corner of the napkin that's resting over a bowl on the table and whips it off like a magician.

"Okay, there's not a chance I'd have missed the smell of you baking bread," I say, the delicious yeasty scent of fresh rolls rising to join the symphony of the feast.

"I can guarantee I did not make the bread. I can cook fine, but baking is a whole different art. I have a friend who owns a bakery in the area that specializes in bread." He passes the basket across the table.

The rolls are pillow soft, perfect to go as a side with the pasta. "When did you do all of this?" A prick of missed opportunity stabs at my heart. I'd have loved to be in the kitchen cooking with him.

He bites his lower lip. "When I finished up at the field house, I went to Hawk's and borrowed his kitchen so I wouldn't disturb you. I hadn't heard from you, so I figured you were still deep in work. The rolls were delivered to his house. Wine?"

"Wine would be perfect," I say.

He stands up and disappears into the house.

I pound my fist against my forehead in frustration. "I'm an asshole." One basic text and he'd have been home sooner.

"Please don't call my beautiful wife an asshole." He walks through the doorway into the green room holding a bottle of red and a bottle of white. "You had work to do."

I nod to the red, unsure of which to actually pick with this meal. He proceeds to effortlessly pop the bottle open. Rather than a short pour, he lets the liquid flow, filling the glass appropriately high. He stops at his own glass, pouring the same amount.

He raises his glass to me. "Cheers to our second full day of being married."

I raise my glass and take a sip, then several gulps. The liquid filling my mouth keeps me from crying about choosing work over seeing whether he minded me tagging along today. I will

not be a selfish partner. I can balance a relationship, a marriage—a somewhat secret marriage—with everything else.

Another sip of wine helps me clear the emotional blockage
in my throat. "Can we have a redo, where I'm not working all
day?"

"You had work to do," he reiterates, like saying it again will
make a difference in the ridiculousness of what I've done today.

"What's one thing you've wanted to do that you haven't
done?" Give me a hint, a large neon banner of what would make
him happy.

He bites a forkful of pasta, taking time to chew slowly. "I'd
like to put a desk and bookcases in here for you, so you can
spread out and be more comfortable. Being a pretzel all day isn't
good for your body."

My eyes widen in excitement. "I can have an office in here?
That's like working outside but without the bugs. I might be the
first academic in my department to get a tan before the school
year restarts."

"Is that what you want to do? Go back in the classroom?" he
asks.

I spin the wineglass in front of my face, blocking him from
any readable facial shifts. The liquid swirls, leaving a pink hue
behind as it settles to the bottom.

"Not ready to talk about it yet," he says.

Now it's my turn to take a long chew of the pasta before
responding. The delicious tomato coats my tongue. I moan,
taking a bite large enough for three forkfuls.

"I propose," I say.

"No need. We're married," he teases.

"I propose"—I wait for him to cut me off again—"we go on a date where neither of us touches anything work related. I want a full day of asking questions, learning about each other, with no question being too ridiculous."

He studies me, that damn grin sweeping up the side of his face. "Do you prefer popcorn or ice cream?"

"We're starting this now?" I wave my fork across the table.

He twirls his fork through his fingers in a manner I've only ever seen a magician do with a quarter. This man and his agile fingers have my full attention.

"All I want to do is sit on the couch with you, put a movie in we've both watched before, and talk until we fall asleep." He lifts his glass of wine to his mouth. "I do draw the line at horror films. I've never been a fan."

"I like ice cream and I like popcorn, but not together. My mood dictates my snack choice, though those are both my favorites."

He tips the wineglass to his lips.

"My favorite ice cream is mint chocolate chip with crushed Oreos ground in." I mimic his lean. "In relation to popcorn, I like it buttered with Old Bay seasoning."

He crinkles his nose. "I was following you with the ice cream, but the popcorn is horrifying with the celery salt."

"We'll have to do both," I say. "I can run out and get some when we're done with dinner."

He shakes his head. "Everything is in the house. I picked up snacks earlier to maximize couch night. Only because I wasn't sure what flavor you liked, I have Neapolitan ice cream. I'll get mint chip next time. There are Oreos in the cabinet that I'd be happy to crush on any of the flavors."

I take a bite of a roll. The fluffy center practically melts in my mouth, leaving hints of basil and sun-dried tomato on my tongue. I may not be able to resist the impulse to shove the entire roll at once in my mouth.

"Returning to this date suggestion you gave. I want to take you out next Saturday." The gears in my head churn on how little I know about him. "Is there anything I should avoid choosing?"

Thad picks up a roll, inspecting each crevice before answering. "No, but can I make a request?"

Please ask for what you want. Give me any type of hint possible here.

"Nothing soccer or university related," he says, limiting my initial thoughts.

Then it dawns on me, like a halo from above. "How do you feel about giraffe tongue?"

Best Poker Face Award goes to Thad, who crosses his arms over each other, leaning forward. "Piper, please tell me you aren't taking me to a place to eat giraffe tongue."

"Block off from eleven a.m. on—you, me, and a giraffe tongue," I say.

CHAPTER FOURTEEN

EIGHTY-FIVE DEGREES IS ROUGH weather to be engaging in outdoor activities on a devastatingly high-sun Saturday. Adding in hills, hordes of people from infants to grannies, and a loaded backpack give it an extra layer of challenge.

"Straight to the giraffes," Thad says.

I motion for him to turn around before we venture past the entrance. When I untuck his shirt, his lower back muscles jump at my touch.

"What on earth are you doing?" He pulls up the linen fabric, giving me more access.

I pull two cooling patches from my bag and adhere them to his spine so he'll be more comfortable. He shimmies when the coolness touches his skin.

"I'm taking care of you." I tuck his shirt back in.

"This is fantastic. Why did I not know about these?" he asks.

"I found them when I was on a trip once, after many internet searches. They have become a staple when the sun decides it's time to scorch New Jersey."

He pulls a map off the kiosk next to us, scanning with his finger until it lands on a picture of a giraffe.

I take the map from him, tucking it into the pocket of my white khaki shorts. "Coming to the zoo is part one. Part two is a game."

He raises both eyebrows at me. "Hide-and-seek?"

"No, but that's a good guess." I press my fingers together in a steeple. "Ten points to you for creativity."

With my ankles tight together, I waddle in a circle, catching his low chuckle while his eyes rake over me in this glorious unsexy penguin moment.

He runs his palm over his mouth, presumably bemused by my commitment to acting.

"Not a giraffe tongue, that's for sure," he says. "Penguin with hot feet from the blacktop?"

I flap my hands in pleasure and steer us in the direction of the penguins. In return, Thad does a strange thing with his tongue, where he pushes it forward from his mouth and then rolls it like a damn taco.

"Giraffes cannot do that with their tongues, can they?" Can I? I try to roll my tongue inside my mouth.

He stretches his torso high, his neck practically straining in the air.

"Giraffes are last. I booked us a time to feed them." Which is now no longer a surprise.

He walks in stride with me, once again playing with his tongue, reaching it toward his nose. "Tell me you aren't the least bit curious about what a giraffe's tongue feels like," he says. "I have fallen down the horrible web search rabbit hole trying to figure this out."

I stop waddling, staring at the weird taco tongue now contorting into a three-leaf clover. "They certainly cannot do whatever tongue origami you just did," I say, fascinated by the fact that his tongue has tricks. My attempt leads me to bite mine, demonstrating my dexterity is not equal to his in this manner. "Is it slobbery like a dog? Thick like a human? I'd imagine slobbery like a dog, only ridiculously long."

"We'll find out. Prepare for more like scratchy with tongue saliva that's thick like glue," he says.

I tilt my gaze up, admiring the wonderment on his face. When my mind switches his tongue out for a giraffe tongue, it adds a further lightness to the situation.

We push ahead, landing at the grand wooden entrance to the penguin house. The space is crowded with sweaty bodies pressed in an uncomfortable ick type of warmth. Not to mention there's an odor I'm fighting from gagging on, thanks to the heat. Birds in tanks do not smell wonderful. Inside their glassed-in area, complete with a dive pool that looks much too small and shallow for the number of little cuties sharing the space, is a pelican hamming it up for the crowd. The pelican throws water about, diving down deep, coming between the penguins. He's flashy, as if he wants people to acknowledge how fantastic he is when we've all come for his formally dressed friends.

Thad slips his arm around my waist, pulling me in so more parts of us touch. We stand there together, not talking but connecting. The thing we should have done the Monday after we were married, but instead I didn't speak up and was stupidly working. There's a sweetness in our quiet. Like a permission to exist as we are.

He peeks down at me, catching me looking up at him. I raise two fake paws and nudge at him with claws in to be respectful.

"Lions or puma?" he whispers loudly, to be heard over the shrieks of the crowded room.

"All the big cats," I confirm, not breaking the glue holding us together on the exit to the pathway.

He sticks his tongue out at me, reiterating his desire to get closer to the graceful giants a short distance from us. In return, I playfully stick the tip of my tongue out. He grabs hold of my chin, lowers his face to mine, and takes my tongue into his mouth, kissing me deeply and melting every organ in my body to puddles.

When our mouths part, I want to press them back together, but his gaze hovers over mine, sweeping me to a different plane.

"I love your playfulness," he says into my mouth.

A whole different set of visions sweeps into my head, redefining his words and turning my mind to filth. In one, we're in the living room at the house, and he's pressing the muscle in his tongue deep into the space between my neck and collarbones, which sends streams of desire directly to my clit, rendering me unable to think straight.

Thad tugs at my finger, drawing me from the marvelous place in my head, where I'm daydreaming of future foreplay.

"I'd like to be playful with your tongue," I say, the words sliding out in a half-dazed pressure-building way that is not appropriate for the situation. "I mean your taco tongue." Screw it. That slick little grin on his face is enough to accept that he knew exactly where my head went. If giving permission for your husband's tongue to play with you is wrong, I refuse to be right. The husband I still haven't had intercourse with. How is it that being married makes touching him in sexually intimate ways intimidating?

"Can you teach me how to make the taco tongue?" This was not a recovery in any format.

He pulls us off to the side of the path. His confidence is a gravitational pull. He points to his tongue, sticks it out, and folds it in half. I try to mimic him and fail. The soft, wet, pink invitation shape-shifts into a three-leaf clover.

This has moved from sexual to a highly instructional fascination on my part. I've never in my life seen a tongue make this shape before. I stick my tongue out and use my fingers to try to force it unsuccessfully into the same position.

He pushes my jaw up, leaning in close to me. "It's a gene. Either you have the gene and can do it, or you don't."

"I want the gene!" Stomping is not going to get me the gene. "My parents really let me down on this one."

"They did bless you with incredible streaks of gold in your eyes." His forehead is seriously close to making my heart skip the beats it is well accustomed to hitting. "It's hidden in the deep green."

I nod, thwacking my forehead on his in the inelegant manner that breaks the tension between us, replacing it with a mini throb.

"My grandmother said I have Irish eyes like hers." I hold the bump I've given myself while he holds his.

"I forgot to let you know how incredibly smooth I am," he says.

"I can guarantee it was my fault on that one." I take his hand, tugging him onto the path to get to the next exhibit. "Why is your arm all wet?"

Thad gestures to the water mister he'd been standing within range of.

"Why didn't you tell me you were getting soaked?" I ask, scanning myself and confirming I'm a little wet, but not soaked. "I'm such a jerk. I didn't feel anything." The entire sky could have opened and I wouldn't have noticed in that moment.

"I needed to cool off." He tugs at his collar, giving me a wink like I shouldn't worry. Only, I do worry. Is it possible he didn't notice? Or was he simply being too nice?

Thad shortens his steps, but he's not breaking a sweat despite the constant up and down of the old glacier hills all over the zoo. This must be from the accidental cooling off at the mister. Or maybe from his sculpted soccer legs, which are much different from my city legs. The city, and Hoboken—at least where I tend to go—are much flatter.

We've been through most of the zoo at this point. An ache in my hamstrings grows from the hills we've been climbing and descending. We hoot at a sleeping owl, crouch in front of the grand tortoises, waiting to see them move around their enclosure like little old men. Instead, they sleep soundly. Both of us retreat when a playful jaguar crashes his side against the glass enclosure and shows his belly.

"How far do you run in a day?" I ask, adding a real question to the list of random ones from this past week.

Thad scratches the side of his neck. "I don't know that I've ever counted. But figure I run up and down the field a few nights a week, plus repairing everything in the field house."

"I'm sticking a pedometer on you," I say.

"We can sit if you're tired." His gaze drifts to the line at our final goal.

"If this park closes before you get to feed them, I'm breaking us in here so you can feed them." I gesture to the giraffes.

"I'm happy to have had today with you. The tongue thing is simple curiosity," he says.

"A curiosity I now have, too. You cannot describe their giant purple tongues and the texture without seeing this through. This will remain in my head as an unfinished date until we can complete it," I say.

He pulls me to sit on a bench with him, taking my legs up on his. I grab for a water, and he looks out over the zoo. Cool refreshment coats my mouth, quenching the dryness that comes with walking. My feet are achy, tiny throbs shouting at me for making the wrong choice in footwear today. The day I met him, we did twelve miles. How is it that the zoo is making me sore? The heat is higher, thicker, and these sneakers are thinner than what I wore that day. Today I mistakenly chose cute over comfort.

He pulls the calf of my left leg closer to him, kneading at the tightness. A glint of searing pain freezes me in place. After a second the pain passes, and he continues to work the muscle with his forefinger and middle finger. I rest against the arm of the bench, unfrozen and able to move but not wanting to.

"Am I hurting you?" He slows his movements down, and it's like he's inside my skin.

"If you stop, you'll be hurting me." I bat my eyelashes at him.

Rather than instantly restarting the heavenly pressure, releasing the stress from my calf, he leans in and gives me a tender kiss on the cheek. He sits up straight, working my calf and releasing the built-up toxins that deposited themselves deep in me through years of stress. I'm no stranger to a massage, but this is different. Like he wants to be touching me, to help me, to take care of me.

With this realization, I tense. I'm not the greatest at taking care of myself, let alone other people. Since we met, this is what he's done. This is what marriage is, though. I've seen my parents and grandparents all with healthy relationships. Ones that ended in funeral homes with the greatest sorrows I've ever witnessed.

"Piper." He says my name sweetly, like a tap into the panic my brain is treading toward.

A knot of tension releases, old memories dragging up from deep in the tissue. "Wow, that spot hit some things."

He raises an eyebrow at me, taking my other calf in his hands. "Anything you'd like to share? You went pale and distant."

I shake my head too long to hide the fact that I should share. Instead of pushing me to talk, he works on my other calf. We sit with the world moving around us. The adorable red panda in front of us climbs about in her enclosure while onlookers rudely tap the glass.

"That panda is waving at you," Thad says.

"There's no way the red panda can see us." I look up at the little creature, high in the enclosure, staring at us. Waving, like, *Hey, get me out of here so we can cuddle.* The gorgeous red tones in the fur flitting with little twitches. "Nope, you're right. Think we could heist it so it can live at your house in a much bigger space?"

"Our house," Thad says, the words coming out like a two-word open-armed hug.

"Our house," I repeat, a softness settling into me.

"You've now recommended we do two illegal things on this date," he says. "We're still learning each other, but I'd bet if I said yes, I wouldn't have to worry because there's no way you'd do either."

"Keep massaging," I say.

Thad's right. I'd never do either. I'd never intentionally break a rule without the fear of immediately being caught and all the worst things in the world raining down. I don't like not finishing projects for the same reason. I especially dislike hiding information like I am right now from Fiadh. Closer to the end of summer, after she's figured out her plans for the fall, would be better timing than now to tell her. I peek up at the red panda that we will not be heisting.

"I don't think we can heist the panda," I say.

"Do tell," he says.

"I want to spend time with you. I can't add a panda to the list right now," I say.

He studies the red panda like it's the most important puzzle in the universe. "What if we left a donation for the care of the panda before we left instead?"

I go to move my legs off his lap like some kind of imaginary timer has gone off. He tugs them back, resting his forearms on my shins.

"We can leave a small one today, say ten thousand dollars," he says. "A small fraction of what a larger wedding would have cost."

"Only if we both contribute." I love this.

"However you'd like to do it is fine," he says. "Here's the rest of what I've been thinking about. I know my family. You haven't really experienced them yet, nor the extended family from soccer. What's going to happen when everyone finds out we got married is they are going to want to send us gifts."

"My circle isn't that large"—*or that well off*—"that I'd expect anything other than a *you did what?*"

"My friends are among the most generous people I know," he says.

I flash to Hawk and Elin's wedding. To the people who moved mountains to see them happy together, including her cousin Amelia focusing on wanting to see Elin happy.

"What if, when people want to celebrate us, we ask them to donate to our friend over there?" Thad says.

"To the zoo itself, or to our new best friend?" The red panda prances up high, tilting her head with curiosity.

"To the red panda. The more specific the donation, the more parameters you can put."

The panda leaps from the top branch to a lower one before scurrying down the rest of the tree, passing from the top circular window to the lower one. "Do you think ten thousand is going to do much to help?"

"The ten thousand is a start," he says.

He reaches for my water, and I, in my things I know are weird about me, pull my water bottle away. I do not share my water. There's a blocker in my head regarding germs and things that get passed into the water. Beer, I'll share. Other drinks you can't see through are fair game. But water, no.

"Water thief!" I tease, gripping my bottle and handing him a fresh one from the bag.

He chugs down the bottle without coming up for air. I grab for another. His jaw moves with each gulp. He shakes his head.

"How heavy is that bag?" he asks. "Or better question, how many bottles of water did you pack?"

"I packed four…each." Plus a stack of snacks and sandwiches. "There's a small first aid kit."

He takes the bag from me, lowering it to his side. "Why didn't you tell me you were carrying thirty-eight pounds all day?"

"Did you weigh that with your thumb?" My mouth is open in shock.

"I did. I can also measure with my knuckles." He zips the bag and effortlessly slings it on.

I open my arms wide and do a large circle, enjoying the air hugging my body. "I am lighter and less overheated."

"Are you averse to requesting help?" he asks quietly, like he knows it's a delicate spot in my soul.

A pebble lodges in my esophagus, but I push the pain down. "Hey, let's go for our appointment to feed the giraffes before the zoo closes!"

I tug him to the long-necked beauties. He doesn't push the question further. We wait in a small crowd for our turn to hold up the lettuce.

"If you were to grade today's date on a scale of A through F—mind you, I'll be forced to try way harder on our next date if you give me below a C minus—where does today land for you?" I ask, pushing enthusiasm past that damn painful stone growing, knowing he didn't mean the question in the way it's hitting. I'm not averse to help. I can do everything. I can. Doing so gets tiring.

"Solid D," he says.

My attention shoots straight to his mischievous eyes.

He puts a hand on each of my arms, steadying me. "D for delightful. You said anything under a C minus—a grade I imagine you've never earned in your life—means I get another date."

"I didn't say...Oh. I see what you did there." I close the space between us, resting my chin on his chest.

He squeezes me into the best encapsulating hug possible. "Piper..." My name shakes from his mouth. "You don't have to answer right now, but can we talk about going to your apartment and getting whatever you want for the house?"

My feet are planted firmly in place. But what about my apartment? The inquiry makes sense, but I don't know how to answer. I can hear my blood pumping in my toes at this point.

A throat clearing saves me from an immediate answer. We're each presented with two partial heads of lettuce. I can't concentrate on the buildup of the day because my head is in my apartment. The giant tongue sticks to my hand, wrapping around it with a saliva sap unlike what I'd imagined. It pulls at my arm, a giant set of lips wrapping over my hand. The creature is tugging me up. I'm about to belong to the giraffes.

Chapter Fifteen

I N ANY OTHER SITUATION, bringing a person I met less than two months ago to my apartment, be it friend or other, would not be on the list of possibilities. In the last decade only two people besides me have been inside, my housekeeper of twelve years and Fiadh.

Thad bounces on his heels, his eyes lasered on the key while I unlock the door.

"You are more hyper than I get on Christmas," I say, holding the doorknob in my hand. Maintaining an effortless smile is a strain on my nerves, thanks to the current choke hold on my confidence. The stiffness of my body highlights how carefree I'm not.

"Come on, come on, come on." The typically chill man is not afraid of letting out his enthusiasm.

Once the giraffe released me from the snack she assumed I was and the zookeepers checked both her and me out, I agreed to make coming here our next Saturday date. After an entire week of mentally scrubbing the rough texture of the giraffe's tongue from my body, I'm enjoying a bouncing Thad, whose delicious tongue is far from sandpaper.

"Why are you so excited?" I ask, the handle firmly in my palm.

He stops bouncing and leans against the wall, facing me head-on. "I've been trying to picture what makes you comfortable so I can incorporate it into the house. The awful temptation to take your key and break in to sneak all your things into our house since I can't ask Fiadh—or anyone else—about your style has been overwhelming."

"Why didn't you?" I ask, appreciating that he didn't call Fiadh, who would have sniffed out so quickly what was happening.

"I'm a gentleman, not a pirate. Doing so would have been a rude invasion of your privacy." His voice drops. "Plus, there was a tiny concern that I would find something an ex may have left behind, like pictures or anything else."

"No worries on the ex front. I've never had much time to date," I say.

He doesn't need all the details of my dating history—the way I found excuses to say no, where with him, the only words my mouth and body wanted to do then, still does, and I'm positive always will, is say yes.

He puts his hands in his pockets and waits patiently while I avoid catching his supportive gaze. I open the door, leaving room so he can pass me, but he doesn't.

"Is this a vampire thing where you need to be invited in?" I joke. "Mr. Vampire, please enter my humble apartment."

He kisses my cheek on his way across the threshold. I touch my skin where the sensation of his lips on my skin still lingers and let the door smack me on the ass.

"Welcome to my first-ever investment," I say.

He spins in a circle, his smile nearly reaching his temples as he takes in the room, which is flooded with enough light coming through the windows that I never need to turn on lamps or overhead lights. I picture it from his eyes: the white wallpaper with shiny little patterns of white roses, my bookcases filled with shelf after shelf of every book I've acquired since my first semester of college that isn't in my office at work, the silver shelves up high with my collectible plastic figurines outside their boxes, not blending into the rest of the motif. He crosses the room, putting his hands on my grandmother's antique desk. I walk to him, taking a seat in my hugging chair.

With his fingers, he frames a rectangle around me in the chair. "Hold that pose."

I lean my elbows on my desk, propping my chin up, cheesing. I like him here.

Thad slides his phone from his pocket, swipes the screen, and holds it up to snap a photo. "This is my background picture. That chair is coming home with us."

A stack of rainbow sticky notepaper draws his attention. "Let's mark everything to pack." He pulls off the first paper and sticks it to my forehead, then another to the desk, and one to the chair. "You can take everything, including the wallpaper, or leave everything, but you, the desk, and the chair are very much needed in our house." He places another Post-it Note on my arm, my stomach, my cheeks, until I'm a rainbow of Post-it Notes.

He pulls me up and takes the seat in the hug chair. I sit on his lap, draping my legs over either side of him, letting his arm support me from falling.

"Absolutely coming to Chester." I kiss him playfully, nipping at his lower lip. The sticky notes shuffle between the two of us, a few pieces transferring to him.

I pull the stack from him and add more, covering him in the way he did me. When I stick one on his heart, that spot on his jaw jumps with pleasure.

"I'm ready," I say.

He shifts his hips. "I'm going to need more specifics."

"Let's figure out what's moving." I let my arm drop to his lap, discovering the potential alternative particularly ready for discussion. Rather than getting up, I stroke his groin. He tucks his head down amid a muffled groan. Flames of want ignite in me. I want to make him feel good. I want to find the little places that make him squirm. I split my fingers on either side of his shaft, pushing harder. His mouth opens, his eyes rolling white. His responses only make me want to take him over the edge. I slow my strokes long enough for him to grab my hips and pull me closer to him. The tiny sticky rainbow squares we claimed each other with fall to the floor, while the heat of our bodies rises. He tucks his hands under my ass, pulling me closer to grind on him, pressing against the soft ache of my center.

His thumbs work the silk of my blouse, my nipples becoming hard nubs as he teases at them. His firm press slides up my shirt, and I pitch forward, closing our bodies tightly together. I need his skin on me.

Rocking my hips slowly left and then right earns me a gasp. There's vulnerability, trust in his eyes, the ones simultaneously pleading for me to not stop touching him.

I tug my skirt higher, guiding his hands to my inner thighs, giving permission for him to explore. We're in this rhythm, the one where desire and awe of the moment hang in the air together. The *I can't believe I get to do this* in heavy combination with *Fuck yes, let's do this.*

He presses my thighs apart, his fingers slipping directly into my wetness. I gasp, my spine working to stay up and not curl over onto him.

"Piper, have you been walking around like this all day?" His voice quivers.

"I'm not a huge fan of panties unless I—" I don't get to finish the thought. His thumb sweeps a circle over my clit, and the words are gone. His mouth is just barely open, and my eyelids are heavy from pleasure while my hips rock him deeper into me before he slides another finger in. He strokes his forefinger down inside me ever so slowly before making rhythmic thrusts, taking away any ability I have to think.

I paw at his zipper, whimpering in displeasure when he shifts me off the thickness I want more of—only inside of me rather than pressed against me. The hand not currently driving me to the edge pushes my shirt up higher, and he takes my nipple into his mouth. The swirl of his tongue over it scrambles my thoughts. He scrapes his teeth across it before teasing at it again, the sensation bridging between my center and his mouth.

"I need you inside me," I plead, my hips grinding on his hand.

"Not until you come," he says. "Harder, or softer?"

"Har—" I can't get the word out, and he's slowed the rhythm. My body is lunging, screaming for him to go harder.

"Harder it is then." He thrusts his fingers deep inside me, rhythmically gaining momentum and depth.

If he didn't have his pants on, I'd swear his cock was deep in my core. My muscles start twitching, grabbing for him to stay inside. He sucks my breast into his mouth, his tongue folding in a manner unexplainable outside of the suction, the wetness. The entire crescendo comes together, and my chin tips up and my legs grip him to me while I come apart in his arms.

I can't move. There's a haze floating around me. Around the way he's holding me, kissing my flesh, pulling me to him in a protective hug. That he won't let me fall from the chair, and he won't push any further despite the obvious bulge pressing on my leg. One I would not mind alleviating for him.

"I'm thirsty," I say, stroking between my thighs and his desire.

He narrows his eyes at me. "Do I need to keep a cup of water nearby for whenever you orgasm so I can keep you on me?"

Biting my lip, I stare down at his lap.

"I'm okay." He pulls my chin up. "The way you move, the suspension of your body mid-pleasure...I want to make you do that again."

"I want to touch you," I say, shifting onto his legs, giving us enough separation to notice how wet I've made his pants.

"So touch me," he says.

I push him to splay his legs in the chair, then lift the front of his shirt, revealing the six-pack I've been dying to learn every groove of. I reposition my body between his legs, my breasts falling to either side of his cock.

He swallows so loudly, I swear his own nervousness is spread through the room. Or anticipation?

"Before I choose where to start"—I blow at the happy trail from his navel to his pants line, his muscles twitching as they follow the sensation down—"is there anything you don't like?"

"I'll let you know," he says in a choked whisper.

I lick my lips, then brush them down the ridges of his muscles, landing at his lower abs. I scrape my teeth down. His hips buck up in reflex. I giggle, move to the other side, and repeat the movement. He twists in the chair. I brace myself, ready to take charge. With torturously slow movements, I undo his buckle and unzip his pants. Blowing a gentleness onto his skin, I watch as he works to maintain composure. I lick down to the start of his shaft, taking him in my hands, swallowing at the new thought of how do I tackle this with my mouth? Granted, my experience is limited, but I understand the law of averages, and in all definitions of the words, this man is a high achiever.

"Hands are fine," he says, his hands moving down like he's going to rudely hide this challenge from me.

I work my hands in two circles, one on top of the other at his base, and glide him into my mouth. He is much too large for this angle. I'm barely past the tip. He lets out a raw grunt when I press him in farther. His stomach trembles like he's already about to lose his mind.

I start to get into a rhythm, enjoying the moans and pleading coming from him, my body already needing him inside me again.

A giant bang from the other side of the chair jostles me from my focus. I squeeze my hands hard at the base, and he comes flying over me.

"Piper! Your phone says you're home!" Fiadh's voice rings out while his dick is halfway down my throat.

Stunned, I catch a ball of air, while he comes out of my mouth with a loud pop. I scramble to pull my shirt down, while he's already sitting hunched over his lap. His face is so white, he looks like he's seen a ghost.

"Fiadh! Turn around," I say.

Fiadh spins on her heel to face the closed door. "I've seen you naked before. What is the issue?"

Thad clears his throat to cover the clank of the metal when he threads the leather of his belt through the buckle. Fiadh has her hands on her hips, her focus now aimed at the wallpaper above the door while she taps her foot. Given the mess of her short red hair, I'd guess she's been deep in her work. Her choice of a distressed dress with cutoff sleeves leans toward drafting recipes or researching and not pressing cider in her apartment.

"I'm going to turn around in three..." She does a strange jerking dance, taming the wildness of the waves in the process. "Two..."

Thad gives me a hard nod, like he's ready to face her. I'm not sure if I am. My stomach sours, bitterness taking hold of my mouth.

"One," Thad says.

Fiadh doesn't spin in a circle to face us. No, she bounces up and down. "Pipes, did you know there's a man in your apartment? One who doesn't know how to properly put a shirt on."

My best friend has so many fantastic qualities, ones I know better than to expect right now. "I am so incredibly sorry. I wouldn't have busted in if I knew you were getting ready to bust together."

Thad's face goes redder than the cherry tones of Fiadh's dress.

"I'd ask what's up, but I can guess," Fiadh says.

"Fiadh...I..." No, when she walks in mid–blow job is not the right moment to tell her we're married. "Do you want to give Thad a tour?"

Fiadh beams in a manner that lets me know I'm fucked. She skips over, extending her hand and then pulling it away like she's thought through more of what we had been doing. Or that she noticed the dark wet mark on his pants.

"Follow me," she says. "How much has she shown you?"

My best friend has composed herself. I let out a relaxed sigh, grateful that she is not paying me back for some of the pranks I've pulled on her.

"The living room?" Thad sheepishly slides his hands into his pockets. He follows her lead around the apartment.

Fiadh turns to me, winks, and eyes the door with a fingerprint lock.

Fuck. Fuck. Fuck. Fuck. Fuck.

I tap my chin. "Start with the kitchen or the bedroom. Possibly the bathroom."

She puts her middle finger up behind her, faking scratching at her bra. Damn it.

Fiadh points with her other hand. "Kitchen's over there. Bathroom is behind the closed door in front of us." She's beelining for what should be a second bedroom, and my heart is pumping so hard, it wants to rip from my chest. The truth is, he's in the apartment. Which means she knows I trust him and he's important. This also means she's going to challenge the fuck out of him.

"Fiadh, he isn't going to be interested in the second bedroom." It's not a bedroom. It's a private room that I don't share with people, except her.

I move fast to hide the fingerprint lock behind me.

"Bedroom is the door behind you," Fiadh says, coming nose to nose with me at the door. "This is the impressive room."

Thad rocks on his heels. "Am I allowed to see the impressive room?"

"Don't worry. It's not a sex dungeon." Fiadh blows me a kiss.

"How's Maverick?" I shoot her a look of warning.

"He's great." She makes a shooing motion for me to move.

I stand my ground, opening my arms for a hug. She's doing this out of love. I know this. She's the person who knows all my buttons and will slash every tire on Thad's car if she feels he wronged me. Which is another solid reason she's not ready to know Thad's my husband yet.

Fiadh is the sister neither of us has ever had, my forever best friend. My platonic soul mate. With Maverick in the picture, she's more herself again. She's more playful, motivated, alive. In this current moment, without needing words, she's a thousand percent right about showing him the room.

She charges into the hug, knocking me into the wall. Thad pulls his hands from his pockets to intervene, stopping when he sees me wrestle her forward from the door.

"Are you going to help me here?" I ask Thad.

He shakes his head. "That's a hard pass. I have four sisters. If I go to help, this turns on me."

"Smart man." Fiadh peels off me, her hands on her hips. She is winded from wrestling me. "You told me to give him a tour. I'm giving him a tour."

Thad stares at the door behind us.

"Don't worry. It's just a taxidermy room. She has all the mummification tools in there and a big table." Fiadh tilts her head, laughing herself through the clear lie.

"Now if I don't show him, he's going to assume I do surgery in here," I say.

Thad's eyebrows reach for each other, crinkles growing on his forehead. "There's a fingerprint lock on a door in your apartment that only three people have a key to."

"Two after today," I growl at Fiadh. Argh. "Fiadh, do it. I can't." I cover my eyes, bracing for teasing.

Fiadh gently takes my arm, pulling my thumb out and pressing it against the scanner instead of her own. The mechanism says, "Welcome, Piper", and my phone dings with a notification.

She rises to her tiptoes to get closer to seeing him eye to eye. "Thad." Her voice is calm, serious. She has the strong short-girl energy happening. "This room contains the insides of the best person in the whole world. Outside her business facade, the internationally renowned academic, her put-together style, and her impressive-as-hell résumé hides the true Piper. She is the biggest nerd I've ever known, with the biggest heart."

That huge heart aches with the words coming out. I rub at my ring finger, the idiocy of my selfishness kicking in, but I stand by this not being the right time to tell her. There will be a right time.

I can't get a read on Thad in any manner, except he's also rubbing his empty ring finger. I push the door open and brace for his response.

CHAPTER SIXTEEN

T HAD TAKES OUT THE elastic from my ponytail, rustling my hair loose across his lap. I cross my feet over each other on the lower arm of the pink fainting couch, my head settling into his lap in the stillness that hovers within the gloaming. The release of the ponytail does not exorcise the stress pulling at my skull from not being forthcoming with Fiadh earlier in the day. The glee on her face when she opened the door to my closet of collectibles. Rare comic books, various fandom figurines, the hidden parts of me that are cataloged and kept safe, are all on full display after she used my own thumb to open the door.

Her excitement at Thad's awe and my relief combined into her holding me up on the sly while I trembled. My closet of pride and shame is out in public. Everything about her showing up was that balance of *oh crap* and *thank God*.

His fingers thread across my scalp, weaving the dark brown strands between them. I hug a box of items from the closet to my lower stomach. We left everything in my apartment except a painting from the closet, including the hugging chair, so as to avoid suspicion if Fiadh saw me moving any piece of furniture out.

"Oh, we fucked up," Thad says.

"Now do you understand my request?" I ask.

"I never questioned the request," he says. "That woman loves everything about you. We should have invited her to the wedding."

"She's going through too much." And I'm scared to let her down. "Losing funding on a major project in academia has massive spiral potential. One that I can see her teetering on. Academics pour countless hours into their research. It's a huge part of their identity. Her losing the funding is more than a shift of work. Cidery is part of her DNA. I'd guess that her actual blood is apple juice."

Thad leans against the upper arch of the couch, careful not to disturb my laid-out position. He tips his head up, looking at the open sky through the glass ceiling.

"From where I sit, Fiadh is going to hate me forever for taking her out of being your maid of honor, even though I am the person you married. There's no way that woman hasn't been planning your wedding since you were small children."

There's the numbness again. "A double wedding. In her dream we got married at the same time in matching dresses to brothers so we could be related by blood. I did explain that our kids would be related by blood, but we were nine, so I think we can let go of some of the confusion."

"I'll remind you that you two have done everything you've planned from childhood. I'm the wrecking ball in those plans." His voice is strangled on the last words.

"No. Marrying brothers is very different from making plans to work at the same university, live in the same town forever so she can be the cool aunt..." I scrunch my toes, fighting the swell of tears wanting to rush from my face.

Thad twists at my hair slowly, a frown crossing his features.

I reach up, stroking the side of his cheek, drawing his attention down to me. "I don't know how to explain to her that the minute you touched my hand, I felt whole. I'm still trying to understand it myself, but I know that I'd do it again in the same way all over."

His face softens, the moonlight illuminating the hushed smile on his face, the concentration of his eyes on mine. "When you figure it out, can you help me understand why I've felt weak when you're not around since that first day? Because I've been racking my brain trying to figure out what I'm going to do if you ever change your mind."

His chest pounds rapidly against my spine. His arms slide over mine, holding me closer. I tap the side of the box.

"What if you kept the apartment?" he asks.

"Are we moving into the apartment?" I ask.

"I'll live wherever you want. I don't care if it's this house, the apartment, or a new place. All I want is that wherever we pick, we come home to each other." He relaxes the hug but doesn't fully let go.

All the images I'd conjured as a kid of Fiadh and I being two little old ladies with walkers making it to the corner store flicker. Replaced with Thad and me sitting in the yard while our imaginary kids play with our nieces and nephews, them all running through the Tudor playing flashlight tag, game nights on the giant couch, complete with family sleepovers and brunches with mountains of food in the morning. Fiadh's here too, with her other half, who looks suspiciously like an older Maverick.

The images change again, only now it's my grandmother at her desk in the apartment. My parents waving goodbye on the front steps before leaving on their permanent trip to London. Sitting with my grandmother, followed by Fiadh's, after their husbands passed, drinking spiked tea and watching the neighborhood start to change. Then Fiadh leaving me behind while she went to Ireland for adventure. Buying my grandmother's building and then the bar to protect it from investors. To protect the plans.

Plans can change—they can. "I want to live here, but I don't need a new room for everything. I can keep my clothes and jewelry, what's in this box, the painting leaning against the wall, and I'm happy."

"Hawk and I will figure out a date to pick up your desk and chair when you're ready," he says. "You could keep the apartment as an office, and keep your magic nerd room."

"Investments. Everything in that room is an investment." I lift my head from his lap.

He shifts his legs, slouching lower in the chair. I settle my head on the relaxed muscles of his lower stomach.

"I've never been into memorabilia," he says.

"They are not memorabilia." I sit up, resituating myself. "There are original paintings from artists long gone in the comic book world. Do you know what those things are worth? I have prototypes for anime characters no longer in circulation. There's one in the apartment worth more than my car."

He crosses his hands over his stomach, his lip twitching with amusement. "I married the queen nerd. Sexy, sexy nerd."

I put the box down on the couch between us, readying my hands for a lecture on investing in the collectible market. He sits up, takes my hands in one of his, and I no longer know how to dive into my lesson without the ability to use my hands to make points. Very valid points that emphasize growth, demand, and the meticulous records I've kept over the years on each item.

"What is your favorite item in the room?" he asks.

"An original piece by Todd McFarlane," I say.

"Who?" he teases.

"Artist for *Amazing Spider-Man*. Did you really not read comic books? What did you do growing up? What did you escape into?" Comic books were my life.

"Balls. Pucks. Mainly a lot of balls." He shrugs. "I was in sport after sport. If there was a gap of time, Mom filled it with me in a one-on-one training or travel sports. There wasn't a lot of time for comic books."

"I learned about trading and investing from comic books," I say. "What can you learn from balls?"

He tilts his head down. "That was on purpose."

"Absolutely was—I guess I should have realized you were a full jock." I wave my hands open like *I give up.*

"Being a jock didn't pay for my education," he says.

I chew my lip, working to cover the frustration that sets in on the completely unfair gift athletes so often get. I paid on my own, busting my ass and trading my skills for tuition waivers to go with my scholarships. "Did your parents pay for you to go to school?"

"Not a dime. I didn't want their money. They gave me a short list of universities I was approved to attend; I chose one not on the approved list, and my parents weren't happy. The one I picked was outside their one-hundred-mile radius, so I had to pay on my own. My grandmother offered to pay, but I landed an academic scholarship, so it changed the rules for me."

"Were they upset?" I ask, much less frustrated as a sense of pride fills my chest.

"They weren't at all. I ended up making the soccer team as a walk-on tryout. I'm not sure if my making it as a walk-on was my family name or coaches remembering me from when they were initially recruiting me but it worked out. Mom went to every game she could, screaming at me from the sidelines of the soccer field like when I was a kid. My sisters in tow for weekend games. Grandma gave a scholarship to a classmate who needed help." He changes his attention to the sky. "She always pushed for us to choose happiness."

We sit in the darkness, the night air settling over us, leaving nothing between us and the stars. Crickets chirp. A warm glow frames the moon. I could fall asleep here so easily.

Thad's hand inches toward my stomach. I shift my shoulders, settling higher up on him. He traces figure eights on the exposed flesh near my navel. Gentle exploration moves down to the edge of my pants, and I tip my hips down, giving him access. Only, he doesn't move my clothes. Tickles trace over to my side, up my ribs, over my collarbone. An erotic sensation mixes with a confused appreciation for the gentleness of it all. In kind, I return the sweet sensation up the side of his neck, down each arm I can reach from my laid-out position. I want more, but tonight I'll revel in this silent flirtation, the confidence in his touch. Our series of hesitant first everythings unfolding in our developing relationship timeline. I want this—him—so badly, but part of my head is stuck on what to do about the collectors room at the apartment.

Chapter Seventeen

A WEEK OF SOFT touches between meetings, sweet whispers of intimacy late at night, and today there's an inexplicable excitement sparkling through me. We are on a date.
A real date. The circumstances to get to today's adventuring
outing turned date sucks ass, but when Fiadh needs space, the
best option is to give it to her. Based on her text late last night,
I can't totally understand whether it was the investors or the
university who said no to the location shift to the mill across
from the adventure center. The spiral I'd been worrying about
her having, the one where her identity is wrapped up in her
research, finally hit, and she closed herself off in her apartment.
This is also the reason I haven't told her about the garbage
finances at the university, because I don't know how I'd lift her
from that level of an emotional implosion.

Maverick, bless him, was so panicked when Thad showed up
with me instead of Fiadh for rafting, he was eight shades of
awful. I told him she closes herself off from the world when she's
sad because she gets really self-destructive, but that can't undo
the garbage-sack-sized bags under his eyes. Maverick's jittery
to the point where he disappeared to his truck and headed to

her apartment, leaving us down a guide for today's two-guide adventure.

Maverick's sister, Shea, hums to herself in the driver's seat of the van on the way to the sunniest spot on the Delaware River following Amelia's van up a narrow bumpy path in need of a fresh pave. Shea shares a lot of features with Maverick. They have the same pale skin with tan lines from hours of working at either the farm or the adventure center. The same dark wavy hair, hers a little longer than his. The Graves siblings are both ridiculously tall. Shea is lean but muscular. She's more chatty than he is. The thing I like about Maverick is how clear it is that he would tear apart a mountain if he thought Fiadh was in danger.

Amelia beeps a horn at us and pulls over to the side of the road to park her van for our rafting end point. Shea glides up next to Amelia's van and waves for her to jump in on the way to the launch site. Amelia's all levels of kindness, with a *let's have fun right now* attitude, bottled into a gorgeous human. Seriously, I work at my ponytail, but I can't fight the waves that form by midday without a heavy amount of product. Her hair, every strand of the dark blond, remains in place, lying flat together. She and Elin have the same smile and nearly identical laughs. I don't know that I've ever not seen her grin when she's with Shea. I pull an extra dark blue bow from my bag and show Amelia.

"This would be super cute with your outfit," I say.

"Will it work in my hair?" Shea says, flicking her head left and right, her hair falling over her ears.

"Accessories are about confidence. Wear anything you want with confidence and it fits you," I say.

Amelia takes the bow from me, slides the clip above her ponytail, the two long ribbons falling to either side. "Can I get this wet?"

"How do you look more adorable?" Shea wags her eyebrows at Amelia. "Where can I get her more of those?"

"I'll text you some links. There's a set of super-cute clips that I think would work well for your hair." I rifle through my bag looking for my phone.

"What about mine?" Thad says.

I stop digging and look over at him. "I can absolutely get a mini ponytail into your hair if you let me. It will keep the wind from smacking your hair into your eyeballs."

He leans forward, letting the longer top of his hair sweep across his forehead. "I have four sisters. I'm rather used to having my hair done."

"If you have an extra hair elastic, I'll take one. I forgot mine." Shea flicks her hair back from her eyes. "Maverick used to let me do his hair, too. Now he'd get growly if I tried. Speaking of, any idea if Fiadh's okay?"

I snort. Worst segue ever. "Eh, she's going through a lot. She'll be okay." Hopefully without breaking anyone's heart. I thread my fingers into Thad's and give him a gentle squeeze.

"Is there anything we can do to help her?" Amelia asks.

"Love her. She'll fight it, but she needs to be reminded she's loved." As vague as the statement is, it's the truth.

"Sounds familiar." Amelia turns around to face us. "I think it's always good to remind people they're loved. What about you? When you're upset, what do you tend to do?"

"Work more." I bite the inside of my lip, the words coming out more like a confession than intended.

Thad squeezes my hand.

"Well, you're not working today." Shea checks the mirror, her dark brown eyes looking right at me. "If you get upset, you can push me off the raft. Much more fun."

The van hits bumps as we round the corner and pull onto a grassy parking area next to the river. Now, one thing to take into account, while the description for today is white-water rafting, we are in fact nowhere near heavy white water. The river is at a standard pace for summer, which means we'll get a day of leisure and sunshine.

"I hope everyone is excited," Shea says.

We unload from the van, grabbing bags and life jackets and heading down the thick tree line to a clearing. Amelia drags a cooler large enough to fit a body, kicking up sand and loose gravel, to the silver raft waiting at the water's edge.

A group of six tubers launches from the grassy area at the bank of the river. They bob up and down a few little rock pools before the river ushers them downstream until their orange life jackets are out of view. This is going to be a blast.

"A small housekeeping item," Shea says, sounding surprisingly like she's channeling her brother. "The water does have a few small rapids. Nothing major. Should you get dumped from the raft, hug your knees and let the water bring you to safety. One of us will come get you."

Amelia opens the cooler, checks what's inside, and closes the lid. I can't hear her over the gust of wind rustling the trees, but she's pointing in the direction the rapids are heading. She goes in up to her knees. A strong arm wraps around my hips, and Thad tugs me close, his warm torso flat against my skin.

The four of us hoist the cooler into the raft. We encircle the raft, bending and shoving with all our might into the water. Another gust of wind releases the raft from the shallow water, pushing it farther into the rapids. Shea grabs hold of the safety rope, reining it in as one would a wild animal.

Amelia strips off her black shorts down to a pink floral bikini bottom. She grabs the life jacket, zipping it up over her Graves Adventure tank top. Thad and I follow her lead, me shedding a swimsuit cover down to a white-and-blue-striped one-piece. Thad blinks rapidly at the suit, changing his focus from my face to my waist. He mouths, *Damn*, but I'm pretty certain he wasn't expecting me to notice. His cheeks flush when I smirk at him.

He opts to remove his shirt to go straight-up skin to life jacket. The life vest rudely blocks my view of his abs. Not to mention, hides the gorgeous V from where his navy blue swim shorts sit on his hips.

"Jump in," Shea yells.

Amelia launches herself into the raft in the way a gymnast launches from a pommel horse. I less gracefully swing my leg over and roll into the center of the raft, into the cooler, then crawl across the raft to sit on the edge behind Amelia. The pull of the current is much more intense than it looked from the river's edge. Shea wraps the rope around her wrist, steadying us. I grab a paddle and put it into the muck to help anchor us in place.

Thad pushes up with two arms and swings his legs over the side in one motion to get into the raft.

"Where's the pizzazz?" I ask.

"Did you want me to roll into you on the raft?" He reaches out to help Shea on. The moment her feet are inside safely, Amelia picks up her paddle, and the water ushers us in the direction of the tubers. Tiny slaps of the ribbon hit next to my ear around the first bend.

The rapids pick up, forcing me to grip the side of the raft with my thighs and paddle harder. I listen and move with each call behind us from Shea. Three more bumps.

"This is awesome!" Amelia says, the muscles in her biceps becoming more defined with each stroke.

Exhilaration fills my chest. Each corner we cut offers a shot of adrenaline mixed with the exact right amount of fear. We pass tree after tree, weaving toward rapids to pick up speed. A man launches himself high from a tire swing, landing in the center of a group of guys. They all cheer. We watch as three more people swing into the river.

"Lean left," Shea calls out.

We follow instructions, but the raft doesn't adjust fast enough. My side of the raft catches across a large rock, tipping the raft up. I tumble into the center. When I starfish out in the middle, I see two feet go over the opposite side of the raft.

Shit. Shit. Shit. Thad's in the water.

"Fetal position!" Shea yells. She uses her paddle to slow our speed and turn us 180 degrees.

I'm gripping the inside of the raft. My eyes dart across the water. Where is he?

"Grab your legs!" Amelia shouts.

I grab my legs, then let myself tumble off the raft. I'm getting him.

I kick over to the rocky area and stand up. The water rushes around me. I see a bright red jacket coming up the river. Thad! The river works to push me in the opposite direction, but I fight it with every muscle in my body.

Shea is now in the river, walking on an angle toward me, extending the paddle out. I grab the edge of the paddle and follow her lead. We stand on either side and lower the bar. Thad comes bobbing up the river as if he didn't get flung from the raft or carried up a rapid on his ass. He's hugging his knees. Then I hear it. He's laughing so hard. I'm here worried, determined to get him out safely, and he thinks this is hilarious.

I follow Shea's stance, putting one foot ahead of the other, bracing for Thad to grab the paddle. He grabs it, and his legs float forward.

"My heroes," he says.

The tension on Shea's face floats away. "I had no idea how I was going to explain this to my brother."

We walk the paddle to the raft. Thad happily floats with us.

"Piper, are you okay?" He hoists himself up on the raft. There's a stream of blood going down the side of his leg into the water.

I touch my temple, and a wooziness splashes over me. Shea and I shove him up and into the raft, bleeding leg and all.

"I'm not the one bleeding." I grab the emergency backpack. "What happened to fetal position?"

"Better to have a bloody leg or butt than head." Shea inspects his leg. "The water will keep you up, but flailing gets you more hurt. This isn't too bad. The water cleaned it out. I have a first aid kit in the van to disinfect the cuts."

"My wife will be happy to help you," he says. He throws his hand over his mouth. "I..."

My wife. The happiness I feel from hearing those words does not have time to set in before it clicks what he's done.

Amelia and Shea look at each other and then at the two of us.

"What do you mean, *my wife*?" asks Shea.

"Figuratively." I twist at the center of my jacket in a failed attempt to wring out water.

She shakes her head. "I'm not buying it."

"Slip of the wishful tongue," Thad says so unconvincingly, we deserve the callout.

Shea tucks herself next to me on the raft and inspects my hands. She tilts my chin up with her nail. I look everywhere but at her, which doesn't help any of this situation. My best friend is dating her brother. She's here because her brother is going to see whether my best friend is okay, and if my best friend knew the truth about me getting married without her there, she would shove me in the water. Multiple times.

Thad grabs a paddle.

Amelia takes the paddle away from him. "I'll ask Elin, and we both know she won't lie to me."

How is everyone connected to everyone else here? When did this happen? I close my eyes.

"Please don't tell Fiadh or your brother. We aren't ready yet." The wind blows on either side of me, sending a chill up my spine.

"I will sign up for every adventure you have for the next five years if you let us have this for now and don't ask more questions," Thad says.

"What do I care if you sign up for the adventure center?" Amelia says. "You'll do it anyway because Fiadh and Piper are a package deal. Plus, Elin will sign you all up."

"Name your price," Thad says.

"Oooh, this is good." Amelia readies her paddle in the water. "I need time to think."

"Piper, I do have one question." Shea places her paddle in the water, launching us into the natural rapids. "Fiadh would walk on glass to save you while a volcano erupted and ash fell. Would she do the same for my brother?"

This is not the question I was expecting. I nod vigorously. "She likes him. She can be thickheaded—we both can be…" Fiadh would find a way to adjust time itself for the people she loves—for me. "I'm sorry, what was the question again?"

"Does she love him?" Thad asks, the question stirring a sensation in my chest like it was meant for me in a different way.

My shoulders grow numb. "I think so. She hasn't flatly said it, but she wouldn't have shut down in the way she has if it were just about losing the location for the cidery," I say.

The rapids slow, leaving us in a gentle rock downstream, growing closer to where Amelia left the second van. Thad steers on the far left side in a half straddle. Each pump of his arms works hard to keep us moving forward. Beads of sweat gather on his brow. The glow of his skin beneath the sun is near angelic. I don't want to know a time when he doesn't exist in my life.

CHAPTER EIGHTEEN

I'M OUT OF PLACE. The rafting trip was much easier than a Wednesday night at the field house. A soccer ball whooshes toward the black net of doom. I squeak like a squirrel getting their tail stepped on. I shift my weight side to side, pretending I know what I'm doing. Thad rushes over to me, looking simply adorable in his black shorts and black soccer shirt with shiny dark stripes. I make a mental note to ask him to not change immediately after his game. Even the black socks up to his knees are cute. My husband has slamming calves.

I want to sink my teeth into those calves. After the close call at my apartment, we slowed everything down to a crawl physically. Yes to sweet kisses, gentle touches on the hips, tucking into each other on the couch at night or waking up draped over each other. But any inkling of knocking me over and throwing my ankles behind my head is top of my imagination rather than happening all over the place. He's got to be aching in the same way, but I don't know that I'd be able to restrain myself to going slow if the flame goes high again. The man is kind, intelligent, and damn gorgeous.

A few women in yellow jerseys with black lettering filter in.

The one closest to me, Rose—the woman who did a background check on me for Thad—was at Hawk and Elin's wedding. Her deep red hair is swept up in a high ponytail. Her shorts come down to her knees, more like basketball shorts than soccer. The teammates she's wandered over with have on much shorter shorts, which look easier to run in.

Rose grips the net. Her indoor soccer shoes are black with yellow flourishes on the sides. The other two women are busy fixing their hair while they yell at players on the field.

"Get your head up!" Liv pushes a wraparound headband on to keep her thick black hair off her face. "He's going to stuff you." She points to another player. "Are you parking a bus over there?"

The player waves her off with a wrist flip.

There's no bus on the field. I squint to search for a toy, a sign, anything. The bulb above me heats my body in a way that puts me on display. I don't belong here. They know the game. I mean, know, know. There is no bus on the field. They have their own language. A knot forms in my stomach.

I can make a mean spreadsheet. I'll talk your ear off about policies, economic growth, the trendy places people are investing, but soccer is a mystery.

Rose nods to the left. "That's Ariana."

Ariana gives an adorable wave. She's a sweet blonde, shorter than the others. She has a *come hug me* vibe. I'm here for this. I can relate to Ariana.

"Are you the wife?" Ariana's voice is like a whistle on a train. The words come out loud and long. "I was hoping you'd start to come to games. Thad's amazing. Kindest man I've ever known. Many here have tried and failed to get his attention."

"The man was created to be a husband," Liv says.

The words sit weird. "What does that mean? Created to be a husband?"

She shrugs.

Another woman walks over in a yellow jersey. She's the kicker. No, that's the wrong sport. She's the striker...or is she defense? Her name is on the tip of my tongue. *Come on, brain.* I smile, pretending I remember her name.

"The entire time most of us have known him, he's wanted a wife." The woman, like Thad, has the hair of a goddess. Her thick black curls cascade from a high ponytail. She pulls out small clips to keep everything off her face. "I'm Margaret. I know there were a lot of us that night."

Margaret! Yes! I liked her. She's a personable CFO with a love of numbers that makes her easy to bond with.

I swallow down as a ridiculous tinge of doubt creeps across my shoulders. "Did any of you date him?" My attempt at nonchalance fails. I'm not cool, I sound like a worried moron.

Margaret laughs. "Mr. Polite? No. We thought he had a thing for Elin at one point, but the man is so polite, it can be hard to tell. The big artsy pictures in the hallway are her."

The ball boob pictures of the sculpted woman with no head are Elin. I need to pick up a sport. Those are fantastic.

"He wanted to date to be married." Margaret clicks a rogue curl into place.

"Elin didn't want to be married?" I ask. Much better, more controlled, totally not with any nerves vibrating out of my mouth, either. I swallow them down. Thad is mine. I'm being stupid. The past is the past.

Margaret smirks. "Elin wanted to be married to Hawk. We all knew it for years. Hawk and Elin have forever been a package deal. It doesn't mean people here don't hook up or date. But Thad has *never* been into random hookups." She narrows her focus to the field. "Get off the ground! I don't think I've ever seen him with a girlfriend. He's always tended to be more private about his personal life."

She glances at her teammates. There are now seven yellow jerseys down the line of the net. They confer and shake their heads.

"He went from first date, skipped the girlfriend stage, and went right to wife." Liv chimes in with a sultry voice. "I need a list of notes from you on how you accomplished this. I've been seeing my boyfriend for almost a year."

I freeze. We skipped the boyfriend-girlfriend stage. I play with my empty ring finger in a search for comfort.

"You met him. He's the Poseidon-looking bartender from the fake birthday party." Margaret fills in the details. "She's never allowed to break up with him."

"Poseidon is impressive," I say.

A series of phones beep. The women turn to the bench, fishing out their phones one by one.

"Oh fuck," Liv says. "They better not be skipping for another fuck session."

Margaret's mouth curls up. "Liv's the goalie tonight."

"The fuck, you say?" Liv says. "I vote Ariana."

"I can't dive." Ariana points to her back with a pout.

"Liv, get your ass in goal." Margaret pulls a set of goalie gloves from her bag. "Put these on."

"I hate goal. Who is going to score if I'm in goal?" Liv pushes the gloves to Margaret. "I have no one to help me defend when they strip the ball from you."

All I hear is fucking, stripping, and gloves. I start to giggle.

The group goes quiet. I look up to find their entire team staring at me.

"I'm an excellent cheerleader." I move to the bench. "Watch."

I scan the men running up and down the field. Thad has the ball. This is good.

"Go Thad!" I yell with my whole heart. "Go black!" I pull an old star jump from my cheer days, adding in as much exuberance as I can. I leap a little too far forward, ending up with my face hugging the net. There really should be more room between these two items.

Thad whips his head to the side in time to run into a player from the orange team. The player takes the ball from him, running toward the black team's goal. I cover the lower part of my face with my hands. The orange player, number seven, winds his leg to his ass and takes the shot on goal. The ball goes in.

A hand, I'm assuming Liv's or Margaret's, helps me to my feet. This stupid net has it out for me. I mentally threaten the net, *Next time I bring scissors.*

Thad jumps to his feet. He blows a kiss on his stroll to the center to reset. I release the tight cringe on my face.

"I think I cheer-failed," I say.

Liv belly laughs. "That was amazing. Please be sure to do that to him more often."

A whistle blows. Orange and black jerseys scatter, and Thad has the ball. I will not cheer to the point of distraction.

"Another night maybe?" Ariana asks in that sweet *let's go adopt all the puppies* kind of way. Seriously, this woman must go home to piles of snuggly kittens.

I shake my head. "I have zero clue how to play."

"Perfect," Liv says. "That means we can train you. I love when people don't bring bad habits to the field."

"Did you play before this?" I ask.

"Division one in college," Margaret answers for her.

"College was eons ago," Liv says, downplaying the skill I can't imagine she's lost. "What do you know about playing soccer?"

I stare out at the field. Thad's passing the ball to another player. He runs backward to the net. He grips the netting, no longer watching the game he's currently in. I'm a distraction.

His goalie yells, but I can't make out the words. Thad takes a step toward me and wags his eyebrows.

"Can you distract me with a kiss instead?" he asks.

I step straight into him, the net separating us, and lean to give him a kiss. A loud bang hits near us, followed by laughter.

He bites his lower lip while his eyes track my face. I lean in and press a full-bodied kiss to his mouth. He releases the net, skipping over to the ball.

"Who nailed my ass with the ball?" he shouts.

One of the players in black raises their hand. "Get your head and ass in the game."

"Can you blame me?" he says to the goalie.

They reset the ball. I'm on cloud ten thousand. Nine would be too low. I calculated this in my head. Ten thousand is the perfect number in this situation.

Margaret's jaw drops. "I've never in my life seen him act so—"

"That was hot," Liv says. "He's hot in general, but that move. He didn't even flinch when the ball hit him. He looked like he wanted to drag you from the field and have his way with you."

No. This was just a kiss. A fuck-the-world-around-us kiss, but not one intended to disappear into his office to see how sexually charged we could make each other. More like the type of kiss that helps turn my brain to mush and erase the world around us.

"Is he like this all the time?" Margaret asks. "I need that. Not him, but that."

Rose blows Margaret a kiss.

"I'll take that too," Margaret says. "He's like a new person. Whatever you two are doing, keep doing it. Then give us notes. Then buy a set of indoor soccer shoes and join us on the field."

"The only part of soccer I know is to kick the ball up the field to the goal." I pause to watch a flash of orange go by with the ball. "To not use my hands and to keep the other team from having the ball."

"Do you want the balls in your hands?" Ariana asks, not so innocently. Minx.

"Ariana!" Rose chuckles.

"I'm saying, she could fill in when Elin is out." Ariana gives herself a mini halo.

Two men collide. One in a black jersey and one in an orange jersey. I clutch my stomach. *Please don't be Thad on the ground.* They are too far away to make out who is who. Everyone on and around the field is silent.

Thad rushes from the other side of the field. My whole body tenses.

The two start moving. The one in orange screams at the referee. He's a stocky guy with blond hair. He grabs his shin mid-yell.

Margaret rolls her eyes. "Drama king can't take a damn night off."

The referee waves his arms like he's dancing. Three remaining minutes show on the clock while the players reset on the field.

"I have an extra uniform in my bag," Margaret whispers. "I promise, no one will care if you are good or bad. We come to play and blow off steam."

I'm not ready. Stepping onto the field into a game I don't know with people who have played forever is an enormous risk. Not that I haven't taken risks lately, but I should kick a ball around with Thad first. Maybe go watch a professional match. Study the rules. Then I'll think about touching the turf after a few practices with the Bees so we get used to each other. "Not tonight. I promise, next time I will."

Why? I should do this. I pushed my best friend out of her comfort zone. Hello, canopy cruising. We've done incredible things together that aren't part of our everyday life. Why is this so different? Because I'm exhausted. Every inch of me needs a nap, and I'm doing my best to keep pushing forward in the way I've always done.

The buzzer goes off. The men on the field shake hands. I couldn't tell you who won because I was so engrossed in how fast the players swooped across the field while play changed, I forgot to keep track of how many times the teams scored. The control of the ball and the gorgeous muscle tone on the field are mesmerizing. I was busy watching the man I didn't date but leapt into marriage with, and hearing about his past, or non-past as it were. Tremors spread through my body. Am I a wife of convenience?

CHAPTER NINETEEN

I FLIP THROUGH THE stack of papers on the desk, half reading them, half distracted by Thad hovering in the doorway. He stares at the mass of work next to me. For the last two weeks I've buried myself in this mess of paperwork in order to meet the agreement I made with Vera and Lisa. I'm not technically taking on too much more work, but I do need to complete what I'd already committed to for the summer in order to free up time. The interviews have slowed down, and by not teaching courses this summer, I have more time to polish a new article for submission. I like interviews in part because my articles will be read by so few people, but the interviews reach a wider audience. I get to teach a broader audience.

"Do you have much more to go for today?" he asks, his arms crossed in a deep lean against the doorway.

His standard athletic pants are gone. Instead, his long legs are poured into a pair of tapered linen suit trousers, topped with a white cotton polo shirt. He's effortlessly stylish.

I'm very not matching his level of dress in a bright pink T-shirt with the white outline of a puppy in combination with dark blue sleep shorts.

"I'm happy to shift plans." I turn in the chair to face him fully. "What do you have in mind?"

The camel-tone leather shoes capping off his outfit are perfection.

"I have tickets for us to attend a lecture." He walks over to the desk with his thumb tucked into his pocket. His focus on me sends sparks of giddiness through me. His gaze says I'm the entire world.

The entire world, hiding in my work, not knowing what or how to act.

"A lecture. You've been studying how to woo a nerd." I unfold my legs from the chair, placing my feet on the ground in front of his. I glance down at the mound of papers on the desk. There's no time to finish reading another article today.

He squats lower so we are eye to eye. "I went to grad school with the guy. He's brilliant. Weird, but brilliant. He can be a little unpredictable, but at his core, he's genuinely a good guy."

"You do understand that inviting me to a lecture is the equivalent of academic flirting?" I reach out and run my finger down his jawline. I freeze at his chin.

His lips part. He takes my hand and gives a half nip, half kiss.

I'm not sure if it's the fluttering in my chest, the invitation from his mouth for mine to come closer, or how long he's stayed in a squat to make us equals in this conversation, but I'd like to immediately consummate our marriage. I'm halfway to a nerd-gasm.

"I'd like more academic dirty talk, please," I say, dropping my voice to what I thought would be sexy but ends up more like I'm chewing my words.

He moves his hands to my knees, letting his thumbs glide down the insides of my thighs, gripping me for balance. I watch him swallow, as if he's trying to compose whatever is going through his head. A piece I wish he'd say aloud. Given the brushing of his thumbs on the insides of my knees, I'm pretty sure if he knew he was making my nipples too sensitive for my shirt, he'd share what's in his head.

"The lecture is on soccer and economics." He tilts his chin up, his eyes locked on mine. "The guy giving it is working on his next book on the economics and finance of soccer in the business world."

I close my eyes, imagining Thad's hands traveling up the center of my thighs slowly, parting them with one swift movement when he reaches my wetness. His needing to change his entirely innocent-appearing outfit from making me drip all over his face and then undoing his pants to—

"Are you interested?" he asks.

"Yes." I heave out in a half moan. When we hit the gas physically, I imagine we'll be in a bedroom-bound bender for three weeks straight. No leaving except for hydration and bathroom breaks. Much like telling people we're married organically, I want this part of us to be organic, too. The wait is a little sexy.

He smirks and drags his thumbs in large circles on the insides of my thighs.

He's doing this on purpose. "I'd very much like to go to the lecture with you." I bite my bottom lip.

I stand up. The top of my shorts is less than an inch from his face.

"We leave in fifteen minutes," he says. "Unless you'd rather stay here hidden inside your books."

He stands up, too, his hands running up the sides of my legs. The muscles working to hold me up begin to wobble. This is fine.

I strut out of the room to get changed. I hear his shoes hitting the floor in the living room with slow steps. In ten minutes, I've changed my outfit to a cap-sleeved formfitting lilac dress. Shit. My calendar. I pull out my phone, hitting cancel on a block of time I'd set aside for working on reviewer two's feedback. I'll email them tomorrow with my data points. A move that will take ten minutes. I don't need this publication. I want time with Thad. I tug out a light gray cropped jacket to cap off the outfit.

His eyes rake me from my ponytail to the matching white leather backpack and boat shoes I've opted for in the name of relaxed fashion. There is an inviting sense of confidence in these shoes. Thad laces his fingers through mine and opens the door for me, shutting my paperwork away inside the house.

During the half-hour drive, I'm not sure where to put my hands. I move them from my lap to my side, hoping he'll take my hand. Only he doesn't. Possibly because I keep catching him staring at the road and peeking over at me. There's no way he saw my hand down low. I suck up the confidence to rest my hand on his thigh. As soon as I make contact, his muscles tighten and he straightens his posture. He places both his hands on the wheel, adjusting his hips in the seat.

"How much farther is it to the college?" I ask.

"We passed it three times already," he says. "Four."

"Good." I stroke my thumb down his knee and up his thigh like he did to me earlier.

When he adjusts his neck, I slide my hand a couple of inches higher.

"Are you distracting me on purpose?" He raises an eyebrow.

I take my fingers off his leg. "I can stop."

"Every nerve in my body is awake right now." He takes my hand, placing it on his thick soccer quads.

"Mine too," I say, likely too bluntly.

He pulls into the institution and parks. Rather than jumping out of the car to open my door so we can go to the lecture, he unbuckles his seat belt. He then unbuckles mine and cups my chin with his hands. I let him draw me in further. My lips pulse desperately to be against his. The kiss isn't soft. It's hungry. His mouth parts mine, and I lock into the kiss. He sweeps his tongue over mine, and I want more. More of the kiss, of his playfulness, of his desire to openly want me. His free hand slides down under my ass, squeezing gently.

The longer he kisses me, the more the vision from earlier shifts. I want him to lay me on our bed. To explore me, so I can explore what parts of him he most likes kissed, fondled, pressed, sucked.

I close my lips, breaking the seal of our mouths.

"Piper, you are ridiculously irresistible," he says.

He kisses the inside of my wrist, a new favorite spot, as I had no idea how immediately this spot could connect to my slit.

There's little chance I'm paying attention tonight to anything other than Thad. He holds his arm out for me to grab. We walk past the statue of a man on a horse, up a set of gray steps to a grand brick building. Inside is cozy, like we've been invited into the dining room of a university president's home. The walls are a dark wood paneling, and there are oil paintings displayed on them, each easily over 150 years old. There's a long table in the front with a man close in age to the two of us. I tug on Thad's sleeve.

"Did you say you did your MBA with him?" I ask, creases rise up my forehead.

"We went to Wharton," Thad says. "Do you know him?"

I give a soft confirmation squeeze on Thad's biceps. The problem is I can't pinpoint where or why. The man is the same age as us, but much stockier than Thad. His head is shaved tightly, with unkempt eyebrows that nearly touch the rim of his glasses. He dashes from behind the desk in a manner that doesn't fit the polished academia vibe of the room. Nor does it match the standard blue academia suit he's wearing.

"Thad!" The gentleman reaches his hand across me to shake hands. "I'm so glad you came!" He opens his arms to me for a hug. "How do you know Dr. Yeats?"

I hug him and mouth, *I forget his name*, to Thad.

Thad unhelpfully covers the smirk breaking out on his face. I let go of the hug and stand awkwardly.

"She's my w—Piper" Thad tugs me closer to him, wrapping his arm around my waist, not fully recovering from his near verbal blunder. "How do you know her, Brent?"

"I was at her last two signing events, and I've attended several lectures." Brent looks over at the podium. "Last time I saw her, I acted like a fool and practically begged her to do a book with me."

Thad runs his thumb up and down my spine in a soothing manner.

"I can understand why. I make a fool of myself for her attention, too," Thad says.

If I weren't already going home with him, I would be after that line.

Brent rubs his palms together. "Do you have anything new coming out?" His focus drops to my left hand, to the ring finger I can't help but touch. He squints, and I slide my arm behind Thad. The corner of Brent's mouth pulls back, and he tilts his head as if he's deep in thought.

"Tonight's your night, not mine." I really don't want to talk about my research. Mainly because while I have the giant pile on my desk, I've been so distracted that I've spent a good deal of time running internet search queries.

How to be a successful partner. New wife. How to tell your best friend a big secret.

I don't think Brent would be interested in my current internet searches.

How to be a great wife. Thad Cosimo. Power couple. Soccer terms. University corporate donations. Enrollment cliff. Sexy soccer talk. Thad Cosimo; Chester, New Jersey. Thad Cosimo soccer. Hot soccer players. Enrollment cliff and financial decimation of universities. Projected university closings.

If I had to pump out an article by tomorrow, it would contain historical details of Thad's life that I could find online. Thinking further about this, I realize the searches might be creepy.

"Drinks afterward at the reception, then. I want to hear everything there is about you two." He presses his palms together, his eyes narrowing at me with a curiosity I hope stays academic and doesn't lead to questions about Thad's near verbal accident. "I still can't believe you got Dr. Piper Yeats to come tonight. Do you know how impossible it is to get on her calendar? I've tried for years with her department assistant."

I blush. I peek around to see if any beverages have been placed out yet. The bartenders are still setting up in the hallway. I'll have to wait.

Thad leans in close to my ear. "Am I going to need to worry about academic groupies?"

"I'm smart and amazing." I flip my hair. "My legion of three fans out there contains bragging rights."

He pulls me closer to him. "You have many more than three fans."

My brain and mouth quit working. The only part I can now comprehend is how closely he's holding me. Minus the hug from Brent, I don't know that we'd have come apart at all, and I like it this way.

I press my hand down his backside while we walk to our seats. Thad pulls to go to the front, and I tug us to the tenth row.

"If we sit up front, I'm going to make him too nervous." Plus, I want to keep my hand on Thad's thigh, which would be more distracting in the front row.

I guide us to seats, and Brent taps on the microphone. He fidgets with the remote to get a presentation loaded on the screen.

"Welcome, everyone," Brent says. "Bear with me one minute." He turns, lifts his camera up, and snaps a photo of himself with the audience. The people around us chuckle at his antics. Meanwhile, Thad's hand is draped over my knee. Each time he laughs, the tips of his fingers brush against the inside of my bare thigh. I drop the cross of my legs to ground my feet to the floor. Instead of feeling grounded, I nearly melt off my chair when the brush turns to a steady press of his hand. All parts of my brain fire at his touch. He's so close to the hem of my skirt. It looks innocent enough, but the tiny little grips are far from innocent. He presses his forefinger down, followed in turn by his middle and then his pinkie, at which point I swallow down a squeak.

I force my focus to Brent. He's facing the audience again, his hands on either side of the podium, hugging it like an old friend. "This is one of those capture forever moments for me. I do not want to forget anything about tonight. I'm excited to see so many familiar faces. Whenever I agree to go to a place to speak, there's always an enormous fear that no one will come. That I'll let down the institution that's invited me to share my research. Tonight I get to go home and remind myself that so many of you came to attend, including a close friend from graduate school, who could tell you some amazing stories about when we played intramural soccer between study sessions. Then about when we sat in his living room and remapped his future. I'll also get to go home and tell my wife, who is home with our son, that the esteemed Dr. Yeats found time in her demanding schedule to join us tonight."

"Have you completely underplayed your academic standing?" Thad whispers.

I give a single, confident nod.

"Why does that make you even sexier?" Thad presses the side of his leg against mine.

"You've got a kink for nerds?" I flagrantly check him out.

"Intelligent women are a weakness of mine," he says.

"Remind me to not bring you to work," I say. "I don't need to be fighting off a swarm of horny professors."

His eyes drop to my mouth. "Do you know how much I want to kiss you right now?"

My lips part. This is academic foreplay, and I need his mouth on mine now. I need his skin pressed against me, with sweat coming down the two of us. Only we're in a room full of people on a campus that I don't know well enough to know where to duck into a classroom to rip off his clothes.

Brent's laughing at himself during a talking point. He's on slide seven of forty. This is fine. On a scale of one to fuck me now, I'm at a fuck me soon. Why are we still on slide seven? I cross my legs. Thad pushes them apart with his knuckles. I fight my instinct to grab his hand and walk out of the lecture. Brent would notice. He'd then probably invite us up to add to the conversation. I don't want to crush Brent, but I need to mount Thad. This is ridiculous.

The slide changes. This is more of a show than a deep analysis. His book is mainstream, so maybe that's the point. Thad moves his touch from my thighs, wrapping his arm around my waist and letting his long fingers dangle across my hip. Two can play at this shift to a less-than-gentle torment game.

I press my side against his, settling into him. He straightens. Good old side boob for the win.

Brent's hands are flying about while he points to a soccer ball and a row of men I've never seen in my life. There are countries on the slide with numbers. I sit up, squinting at the data. Thad pulls his glasses from his pocket and hands them to me. I slide them on, and while they aren't my prescription, they help enough to make the numbers clearer. The amount of money that goes into this sport could feed the hungry several times over. The money that changes hands for top matches, the influence of the teams over major political deals and historical events is...soccer and the economy of soccer is so engrossed in GDP for certain countries, it may as well have its own line.

Now I'm horny and fascinated.

I peek at Thad, checking on his interest level. He's focused on the screen. I hand him the distance glasses and smile at the nerd next to me. This right here is what I thought we missed out on. The flirting, the connection, the buildup of the unknown.

Brent's talk finishes. Thad stands, eyeing a path to the exit. My over-the-top ravenous need for his dick has shifted to a desire to touch and discover him.

Brent rushes over. "Can I get a photo with you two? Maybe a drink?"

Thad shakes his head. "We really need to head out. Piper's schedule is packed tomorrow."

I don't have anything to do tomorrow except for more of the same from today. Did I forget appointments?

"I'm happy to take a picture if you'll take one of Thad and me first," I say.

Brent takes my phone and snaps a photo of me in mid-laugh while Thad adjusts his hair.

"One more," I say, straightening myself against Thad.

Brent retakes the photo. My eyes are full of a familiar old sparkle in the still on the screen. Brent turns and holds the phone high for a selfie, leaning in to split Thad and me.

"If you post that anywhere, can you tag me in the photo?" Brent says, like he's cool. "If not, you can text the photo to me."

He doesn't seem that weird, at least not for academia. He certainly doesn't come across as unpredictable. What is Thad talking about?

"I'll text the photo over," Thad says.

Thank you. Thank you. Thank you, I repeat in my head.

"I'll send an invite to one of the open play nights at the field house. It'd be great to play together again." Thad gives my ass a small push to the door.

I oblige the nudge and make my way through a throng of people chattering about the presentation. The cheap cheese and budget academic wine will wait for another day.

The moment we are outside, Thad pushes us forward in more of a sprint to the car. At the door, he pushes my hair from my face, his palm cupping the back of my head, and pulls me in for a deep, long kiss. His tongue sweeps my mouth, and I hungrily step into his space. I like this version of him, the goes-for-his-desires version. The teasing version is nice too, but this one is self-possessed.

He pulls the door open behind me. I break the kiss and slide into the passenger seat. He shuts the door, makes his way around the car, and slides in. With set concentration, he turns the car on, and drives us from the parking lot to the road home in minutes. He's not wasting any time getting us back to the house. He slides his hand up my leg less than an inch from where my leg transitions to my softness. The buzz of earlier, the heat and desire return. I tap my knee. His hand brushes the fabric of my skirt against my slit.

"Pull over," I pant.

"Not yet." His grin is pure mischief. He continues to tease me with each tight corner.

I untuck the side of his shirt, exploring the skin above his waistband. He shifts his legs.

"I need to concentrate." He gulps down air.

Neither of us backs down for the next ten minutes. We pull into the driveway of the house. I break from him to get out of the car. By the time I round the corner, he's already out. He drops low while I run to him, scoops me up by the center of my legs, and places me on the hood of my car with my legs open and my skirt covering my skin.

I shift to hop down. His hands press on either side of me, and he leans forward, taking a nip out of my neck. I groan, lengthening my spine. He grips each of my thighs, holding them apart.

Mid-kiss, he hovers, staring up at me. "Lean back. I need to taste you."

"Here?" Only this doesn't come out sexy.

He lifts my skirt up, then brushes that damn knuckle over my slit.

"Here," he says.

"Yes. Yes. I—" Before I can get another word out, he's flipped the skirt up.

"I like the no-panties option on you." He slips his fingers into his mouth, then touches my wetness. I give a whimper. My stomach trembles at the graze. He parts my legs further and wastes no time in sliding his tongue across my clit. I pound a fist onto the hood of the car. The trees around us leave us hidden under the dark night sky. The gentle suck of his mouth turns hungry, like he can't get enough. He nibbles and sucks the wetness while I writhe with pleasure on the metal bed that is my car. I sink my hands into his hair, pulling him tighter against my center, my hips moving with his mouth.

"I need you in me." The night sky starts to swirl above me. I move to climb onto him.

"I'm not done." Each word vibrates against me. He stops me with his forearm, adding pressure to my hips. "Give me all of you. Trust me and let go." He then inserts two curled fingers, and I can no longer control any portion of my body. He increases the pressure of his kisses, his tongue vehemently transforming me into a toy for our pleasure.

My hips grind against his open mouth, and when all the parts of me squeeze around him, he wraps his arms around me, encasing me in a layer of safety. I follow his request, letting go, falling with the sensation rocketing through me.

CHAPTER TWENTY

THAD GETS A 100 out of 10 for surprises last night. I hadn't imagined the scene on the car, nor what he deemed midnight snacks three more times that night, each time leaving me more spent than the last. I've practically flown around the house all morning. The idea of walking around with no pants on until he dives face first into me for another round is tempting. But I do have the ability to restrain myself. Especially since we'd initially agreed to take everything slowly. Except for him savoring me like candy after one of the best foreplay—dates—of my life. That was a pleasant bonus. I didn't know it was possible to thoroughly tickle my brain and clit in the same night.

During the second round, he'd declared the night "worship Piper evening." For him, this meant I lay out on the bed with my arms up, not allowed to touch him. In all my years I didn't know this was a thing. I was ill prepared for how hard it would be to not put my hands on him, to let myself be taken care of without the ability to immediately reciprocate or solely focus on taking care of him. This man needs to lose himself in my mouth, for both our pleasure. I'll be slow and methodical when the opportunity presents itself. I've got plans for every damn inch of his body.

Thad's phone buzzes next to us on the couch. He puts his e-reader down and picks up his cell to check the texts that have come through. He wipes his hand down his face, leaving it hovering on his chin. His face is a tinge of green.

This is a vomit face. "I'm a sympathy vomiter." I take the phone from him, reading the message.

"Is this Gianna, as in your sister?" I ask, a rise of bitter fluid in my throat.

Thad grips either side of his head, messing his hair.

Gianna: *Rumor is my only brother got married and didn't introduce us to the woman beforehand. He also didn't invite his favorite sister to his wedding.*

Gianna: *I told Mom.*

She told Thad's mom. My mother-in-law. I have a mother-in-law. My cheeks turn pink. This is not the way to start off with in-laws.

Thad's phone pings. A photo of an older woman with chin-length hair the same tone as his pops up on the screen with a message.

Mom (my mother-in-law): *My heart is breaking. We're on our way to your house. I must meet my daughter-in-law.*

This is bad. They hate me before they know me. "How close does your family live?"

"We have less than fifteen minutes, assuming they aren't already driving," he says, still mussing with his hair.

I flop into his side. He wraps his arm around my waist, hugging me like a teddy bear.

"They're going to love me." I hope. "I'm great with people."

Thad raises an eyebrow. "My family is a lot."

"It'll be fine. Give me a highlight reel of what to be prepared for when it happens." I play with the sleeve of his shirt.

"There are topics we haven't covered." Thad pulls me into him on the couch. He stretches his long legs out. His right foot taps about as fast as my heart is beating. "Piper, we have—"

We hear a key in the front door lock. We immediately detangle from each other like we've been caught making out on the couch. We are sitting too close.

The door opens, and not one but all four sisters pile inside. They have stern looks plastered on their faces. Oof. My skirt is growing smaller, locking my legs in place. Next comes his mom, who stands in the same way as her girls, and then his dad. His dad is a very short, stocky man, while his mom could grace the cover of any magazine.

They glower at us. *Do not squirm.* I swallow, keeping my professor face on, the way I do when a student tells me they didn't have time to finish an assignment that was given the first week of the course, when we are in week fifteen. I refuse to be intimidated.

The shortest one—I'm going to need name tags—cracks a fast smile before she returns to the glower. Oh, she's an ally.

Without hesitation, I get up and break through the strangle of my skirt to walk straight to his mom and wrap my arms around her. She's the second to break.

"I am beyond excited to meet you." I'm not going to be the first to release the hug. "I know pretty much nothing about you except for the fact that your son is an incredible human." That's right, I can do this. I'll be the best daughter-in-law she didn't even know she had.

She's still hugging me. Only now it's tighter. I didn't know a hug would make my insides mushy. The short one who cracked the smile comes to join our hug, followed by all three of the others and his father.

We are now in the largest hug I've ever been in. I gasp from being squished in the middle.

"She hugs!" one of the sets of arms says.

The mass of arms around me lets go, minus his mother, who guides us to the couch. We sit. Thad stands. He rubs the back of his neck, looking at the space next to me on the couch, the other side of the couch, then the white chairs.

"Thad, I have things in the car. Come help me," his father says.

I cross my ankles while working to plead with him telepathically. *No! Stay with me!* If the hug was a trick, he's leaving me to be devoured.

"One way or another we're going to spend time with her solo. Go help Dad, or we'll kidnap her for the rest of the day," the short one chimes in.

She must be the youngest. Thad follows his dad out the door, leaving me with the rest of his family—my new family.

"Introductions first. I have a good feeling my brother hasn't said much about us." She gestures to the tallest of the women.

The tallest of the sisters has long straight mousy-blond hair. Her nails are a shade of ballet pink, and her outfit is simple: basic jeans and a white shirt topped with a cropped blue blazer. All of his sisters dress a little higher end.

"I'm Antonia." She gestures to the shortest. "That's Gianna. She has two very loud boys who are at home with their dad."

"When Mom said we were coming here to meet you, I jumped in Antonia's car and ordered them delivery for lunch." The rings on her finger are massive. The oval diamond on her engagement ring alone has to be three carats on platinum, accompanied by a wide band of square diamonds. She has a stack of thin sparkly rings on her other hand, which catch the light. "Their dad is taking them to the field house later for a foot skills training private session."

I'm not sure if it's the head tilt or the dazed look on my face, but Gianna starts giggling.

"You aren't into soccer?" Antonia claps her hands together.

"I'm not, not into it, I didn't grow up playing at all." This is a fair enough reply. "I cheered in high school, but soccer was never part of the Yeats repertoire. Besides cheering, I survived an awful short-lived stint in Irish dance with my best friend. I'm not coordinated enough to get across the floor with a group of other people in step and without running into people."

"Good news, in soccer, you can run into people if the ref isn't looking." Thad comes through the door, and the anvil on my nerves lessens.

He and his dad are carrying bags in each hand.

"I brought panelle, which is similar to a chickpea fritter. We have rice balls, but they have meat in them, and I didn't know if you like meat or not." His mother—I need to pick a name for what to call her—gets up from the couch.

Thad motions for her to sit. His father follows him into the kitchen, where a series of cabinets open and close. They're talking, but I can't make out the conversation.

"Tell me about you. Tell me about your family," his mother says. "What is it that your parents do?"

Silverware is clanking in the kitchen onto the counter. *Prep faster.*

I pull in an uncomfortable stream of air. There are few questions that can ruin a moment more than this one, but not answering would be rude.

"They were university professors," I say in the same manner I've said countless times before.

Noise from the kitchen ceases. For the number of people in the house right now, the silence is thick. Past tense was heard. Dead parents are inherently a conversation killer when meeting new people, no matter how long the deceased have been gone. A glance around the room and they are frozen statues.

"Ah, like you." His mom thankfully breaks the silence with her sweet tone.

"Well, sort of. They were literature professors at a private college in Hoboken. I'm in the College of Business."

"The business school? How wonderful," his father's voice chimes from the kitchen, acknowledging that they can hear every word of our conversation.

His mom brushes a hand through her hair in the same manner as Thad. She waves her daughters over.

"I'm Lucia." This sister takes a seat next to her mother and holds her free hand. "There's a basket of cheeses and breads in the kitchen, and I brought wine."

"Which leaves me. I'm Isabella, and I also brought lots of wine." This one looks more like her dad with the dark brown hair and light brown eyes. "I also brought sparkling cider in case you were pregnant."

My mouth goes dry. A plate or bowl or whatever was being held smashes across the floor in the other room. This is the second time the assumption has been made that we married quickly due to pregnancy.

Their thoughts included vegetarianism and pregnancy.

Thad rushes into the room, puts his hand on his hip, and leans forward.

"Can you not walk in assuming the only reason a person might marry me is that they are pregnant?" Thad gestures wildly with his hand. This is a different him. "That is not a question that is okay to spout out at anyone."

His dad walks in with a fistful of glasses and two bottles of wine tucked under his arm. He passes out the glasses. "Who would like some wine?"

Every hand in the room goes up.

"I don't see what the problem is. I'm asking if she wants kids." Her mother shrugs like this is a normal, everyday first conversation with a brand-new family member.

"Mom." Thad lets out a strangled laugh.

"No, Thad, it's fine. We needed to discuss this eventually." I grab the bottle of wine from his father. Family history and kids within ten minutes of meeting.

Thad holds out two glasses. I oblige, filling well past the polite line to the top. I put the bottle to the side. Rather than taking the first glass for myself, I hand his mother the generous helping.

"Well, Mom..." My tongue tastes of rubber. "Mom" is not going to work as a name for me to call her. Placing my hand on her knee earns me a pitying look I've seen before. Not pity. That's not the right word. I've hit an emotion that's overwhelmed her, knowing my background. Honor maybe? But mixed with what I imagine are bubbling feelings she also doesn't know how to discern right now.

Until she selects beaming instead of a quaking chin. She takes the tiniest, most polite sip I've ever witnessed.

"I love that you'd call me Mom." The beam turns into the molten sun, but there's a devilishness in the rise of her cheek. "Thad and the girls call me Mama. How's that sound?"

Thad clutches the other glass high, like it's going to stop the unfiltered exchange pouring forward. Antonia grabs the bottle, turning from my grandbaby-hungry mother-in-law and filling each of the glasses high.

"Drat. The bottle's empty. I'll grab more." His father begins heading to the kitchen but is blocked by two of his daughters.

Lucia taps her ring finger on the outside of her glass, her eyes fixed on her mother.

"You have a lovely family, Mrs. Cosimo," I say.

"I liked Ma better." These tiny sips can't be real. She's never going to finish that glass.

"Why did you stop at five? Surely you can have more than five. I heard about a woman in her midfifties who recently had a child. You can't possibly be much older than her." I touch my hand to my chest. "The magic of medicine has shown there are ways to continue to have kids even once our cycles have declared that egg production has dried up."

Antonia takes a swig straight from the bottle. Thad clutches his glass, not intervening. Does he want kids? Growing up with so many siblings, he must have an inkling or desire one way or another. My stomach wobbles like a top falling from a full spin.

"I've heard about this." His mother nods. "I'd need to borrow an egg or two. Riso, you want to have more babies?"

Thad's father gives each of his kids a full once-over, nodding between the inspection of each child. His sweet eyes land on his wife, giving her an even larger head-to-toe rake. I immediately understand why there are five children.

"With you? I would make a thousand babies," Riso says. "Let's go try."

With that, I break into whole-hearted laughter. Thad wags his eyebrows at me, takes a sip of the wine, then offers the glass to me. His mother licks her lips before pulling her wine to her face. She reaches an arm out to her husband, inviting him to sit on the couch with her.

"Piper, you can have a hundred babies or no babies. If you treat my baby with love, I promise to be the best mother-in-law you've ever had." She clinks her glass against mine.

The room settles while we all take a short sip together.

"I like her," Gianna says. "She's not afraid to speak up."

With those words from Gianna, the nerves I've felt since they walked in are gone.

"Are there any other questions I can answer?" I inhale deeply, taking in the warm herbs wafting from the kitchen into the living room.

Thad holds up a hand. "I'm more than ready to answer one question before we bring the food out here."

Lucia gives a deep throat clear. "I've got one. How long did it take before you knew she was the one for you?"

Thad looks me dead in the eyes. "The moment she got on the trail with her friend, crunching granola and lost in her thoughts. I kicked that ball over her head three times, and she didn't notice."

"Prior to the finger ball incident?" Gianna says.

Thad groans. "Ball finger incident, and yes." His voice turns dreamy. "She didn't notice me until one of the Bees kicked a wild shot. She didn't even hesitate. She protected her friends who weren't paying attention."

"Are you saying if I'd let the ball hit Fiadh, we wouldn't be married right now?" I playfully pout my lip out.

"No, I'm pretty sure we'd still be married. I'd been thinking of ways to break the ice to say hi. Elin inadvertently makes everything happen." Thad's sincerity washes over my skin. A blanket of foam bubbles tickles my nerves, causing a sensation I've never felt before. Love, but different. Comfort, but more. Safety, but excitement for what's to come. I don't know if I'll ever be able to repay Elin or the magic of the woods. For granting the random wish I'd made before the hike in jest, for delivering Thad into my life.

Thad lays a soft kiss on my mouth in front of his family. The touch melts the room to a universe of us. When he stands, I want to grab him to help halt time.

Instead, food is being laid all over the immaculate coffee table. His sisters are taking seats on the floor, passing dishes, teasing one another. This is the noise he grew up with. The noise of a big family sharing food. There's no isolation here, no burying my head in a book to get lost or find a fact or two to share for conversation. This is like having a roomful of people like Fiadh who want to exist with me without pretense. I get to exist in this, with him.

I home in on the conversation between Thad and Riso. They are within earshot. I slowly sip my wine and fake being engrossed in all the food before me.

"Your mother and I want to throw you a proper party," Riso says.

"We don't need a reception," Thad says. "Consider this the reception."

Riso shakes his hand, his thumb against his other fingers forming a circle. "You marry a smart, beautiful woman and don't want to show her off? Introduce her to everyone?"

Thad's quiet. My heart pounds in my ears.

"She wanted a small, intimate wedding," he says. "I want a happy, intimate life."

The thrumming in my eardrums picks up.

"Your mother wants a reception. She wants to meet Piper's family. She wants to show off your wife." Riso chews while he speaks. "She's so proud of you. She wants to announce you both to our circles."

Thad doesn't answer. I want to peek over, but it will be too obvious I'm listening in.

"Not right now," Thad says. "Our family is overwhelming in one shot. Let her get used to everyone here, and then we'll talk. The goal was to keep this all quiet."

"A secret? Marriage is beautiful and to be celebrated! But, we'll keep whatever secret you want. The whole family will. Let us do dinner." Riso is impressively insistent.

Thad's voice grows softer. "The whole family is over two hundred people. I'm sorry, but there's no way two hundred people can keep a secret like this."

Two hundred people? For immediate family? That has to be extended family. Who has two hundred aunts, uncles, and cousins? I'm an only child. Our family get-togethers were fewer than ten people growing up, and that includes my best friend, her parents, and her grandmother. There could have been more extended cousins, but they lived in Ireland. Two hundred aunts, siblings, cousins...I try to do many forms of math to parse out the makeup of his family.

Night one with his family is a combination of them learning about my family history and whether they'll get grandbabies. Then wanting to introduce us to the world. Too many people know about our marriage. Fiadh's going to find out. Worry spans my body as I tick through each person excited to congratulate him—us—and think about how small my list of people close to me is.

Chapter Twenty-One

WITH A FISTFUL OF popcorn in my mouth, I grab for the purple marker to begin marking up the clear portable board I usually use to solve large problems. I could have used it eight days ago when Thad's family showed up and practically gave us a "we're your family and happy for you" intervention. At this point I need a running list of all the people who know and when they found out.

Fiadh settles into my hug chair, a bowl of popcorn on her lap, her hair half-up to keep her bangs from becoming a nuisance.

"Rule number one, you have to believe this plan is going to work," I say.

Fiadh's in crisis mode, a solvable crisis she's come to me for help with. Her asking for help is a solid distraction from the fact that too many people know about me and Thad before she does.

"You can't know that." She angrily chomps a mouthful of popcorn. "I thought the first plan with the grant committee was going to work. I was wrong. The second plan, of moving the location to a historic mill, was also a bust. I'm a failure."

"No. Your petty dick of an ex intervened and was a part of the equation you hadn't counted on." I write "cider mill" on the upper-left corner of the board and Mav's name on the upper-right corner. Tonight requires notes, diagrams, and every ounce of the cheerleader in me I can conjure.

"I need a blanket," she grumbles, tucking her knees up higher, refusing to turn her head to read the right side of the board.

I grab a blush-pink quilt from under my desk, hugging it to my stomach on my walk to her. "Do you want me to call Amelia? Shea? Perhaps Maverick?"

She shakes her head vehemently. My lovely best friend, with all the best intentions in the world, did the equivalent of lighting her potential happiness on fire with a man who loves her in the way she deserves to be loved for all the wonderfulness she is.

Fiadh knows she's fucked up with Maverick. The day of the rafting trip, he went to check on her and she scorched the earth to push him away. An action she immediately regretted once he left.

"We can call Shea and Amelia when we have a vague idea of how we can make the mill work." She takes the blanket from my hands, wrapping it around herself like the apartment is freezing.

"You're going to sweat to death under that," I say.

She ignores me, further wrapping herself in the blanket for comfort, the popcorn hidden beneath the pink fabric.

"Rule number one stands." I mark the rule in the center of the board. "Rule number two: We acknowledge it's okay when plans change. Maybe they're changing for the better." I swallow at the thickness in my throat, wanting to explain this isn't simply for her but for me, too. A conversation for another day.

She lowers the blanket from the top of her head. "I don't want to teach Fermentation 101 or 201 next year. Not if I can rewind time and flick all the switches that make a revision of the second plan work."

"This is progress. What is most important to you at this point, with all the new variables you have?" I grab for the cup of decaf on the side table. A separate sheet opens in my head to mark my own variables. The first being that I know how much Thad's changed my view of time for the better. That all situations I put her first have been out of love, and it's okay to let more people get closer to me. I've never had to think about dropping everything to rearrange my time for her—this is who we are together. But choosing Thad has shown me that I want meaningful relationships in addition to the two of them, that I'm worth more than being a transactional acquaintance.

"Is the mill important? Is Maverick important? Can one exist for you without the other?" She needs the bluntness right now, the push to answer.

"I want both." The blanket falls behind her, and there's a vulnerability on her face. "Is asking for both too much?"

"No, but in the long run, would you be okay if you had the mill and Maverick but it didn't tie to the university?" I prepare to write on the board to avoid looking at her.

"Did you turn in your syllabi?" Her words come out hesitantly. "I keep worrying they're going to send me an email to teach because they don't have enough people."

I know she heard my question.

"No," I answer softly. Both of us are avoiding topics tonight.

"That's not like you," she says. "How many classes are you teaching this fall?"

"Stop avoiding the question. If you get the mill and Maverick, are you prepared to have it not tied to the university?" I ask.

"In this scenario, do I still get to teach? Because I don't know what I'd do if I don't get to teach in some way," she says. "I don't know that I'm me if I don't have a class."

"We can sketch everything out so you can teach, but it may not tie to the university," I say.

"This wasn't part of the plan," she says. "The plan was we teach together."

She grows quiet. I write "teach" on the board between "cider mill" and Maverick. My hand shakes. Keeping the secrets from her is painful.

"Turn and look at me," she says.

I turn. Looking at the upper swoop in the chair isn't helping. She knows me too well.

"How many classes are you teaching this fall?" she asks.

"None," I whisper.

"None," she says.

"I'm on a recommended sabbatical for the fall." I click the cap on and off the marker.

"You're suspended? There's no way you're suspended." She chews on her lip. "What the hell happened? When did it happen?"

"Sabbatical not suspension. We don't have to talk about this right now. We're working on the mill."

There's a tiny dent in her lower lip from her teeth. "Like hell we're not discussing this right now. When, Piper? When? And why?"

"Lisa and Vera put me on a sabbatical on the last day of classes." My voice shakes. "They think I'm burning out. I have enough research and projects going to substantiate the sabbatical."

"The president of the university and the provost knew you were overwhelmed before I did?" she says, pain tugging at her face. "I'm a shit friend. Like, the worst fucking friend ever. How did I not see that you were stressed? I was crying to you about my ex and a grant, and you immediately came to help me, because of course you did."

"Stop it. You aren't a horrible friend. The timing was unfortunate." I walk over to kneel in front of her chair, not touching her because I know she'll break, and we still need to figure out a plan for her. "I'm fine. I'm me, I promise. But I needed the summer and fall to get out from how much I've taken on. I don't want you to take on too much, so I want to work through the mill with you."

"Are you going to leave the university?" she asks.

I hesitate. The constriction in my throat makes it hard to focus on my thoughts.

"Piper, if you're asking me if I want to let go of the plans for working together at the university, and it will help you, then yes. Let those plans go. We achieved the goal. We beat the idiots who said we'd never land at the same university, and we both got tenure."

"Then I'm going to say the same to you. If you need to let go of the university to have the mill, to have Maverick, please tell me how I can help make that happen." A lightness comes over me with the permission from her to let go of the university. The financial situation of the institution is a different issue, one that still needs more conversations with Vera and Lisa.

"I'm not ready to stop teaching. I'll figure that out with the dean. But I believe in this project with my whole self." She pauses. "Pipes, is there anything else I've been too self-absorbed to see that I also need to know?"

One giant confession per night is enough. I shake my head. We need to plan first, and then I'll tell her. Given the fact that Amelia is Elin's cousin and is tied to this project isn't helping the steady worry that lives beneath my skin every time she's at the adventure center or the farm.

I write across the lower part of the board "Operation Fiadh's Dream."

She sits up, the bowl of popcorn emerging above the fabric. "You're ridiculous."

"Love you, too." I underline Fiadh's name. "Now, I propose we actually split the entire dream from the university. Separately, you revise the courses you want to teach to have a location set at the mill. From there, we draft agreements between the mill and the university, but the university is separate. This keeps pencil-dick exes from interrupting your dreams."

"This protects Shea and Amelia, and Maverick," she says, her voice trailing off.

"We protect the people important to you and figure out everything else," I say.

"Is this how you advise your students?" she asks.

"No. I teach something different. This is more like organizational economics, which focuses on understanding the existence, nature, design, and how we want the organization to perform. I know you, and you have the answers to each of the questions, but what always comes first for you is the people. We need to focus on how this will be successful and what success means for each person involved." My heart flutters. "From there, we'll map out costs and everything else."

"We're going to need more popcorn," she says.

My body is buzzing with ways to make this all work for her.

A green flash blinks on my phone. I click open the message.

Thad: *We won! On a scale from one to five, what is the chance I can get a good night kiss tonight?*

"Thad?" Fiadh wags her eyebrows.

"Is it okay if he joins? He's really good at investments and may have another perspective."

I punch out a response. *Any chance you're up for sleeping in Hoboken tonight? If so, five out of five. I don't know what time we'll be done.*

"If he's coming, can he bring more coffee?" Fiadh asks. "You're out."

Thad: *Last match ends at 11:00. If I fly, I can get there by midnight. Is that too late?*

The time on my phone shows 10:15.

Me: *Not at all. Unless you're too tired.*

Me: *If you do come, the code to the garage is #5552. Can you bring Fiadh coffee? We're in for a long night.*

Him: *Does she know?*

Me: *No.*

Him: *I'll bring lots of coffee.*

"Piper, you're smitten." Fiadh makes kissy faces at me. "Oh, can we go on a double date? Pretty, pretty, pretty please."

"Uh..." I glance at Maverick's name on the board.

She lets out a frustrated groan. "This is all going to work."

"Rule one," I remind her. "We have a little under two hours until he gets here. Let's flood this board with ideas."

I kneel on the floor next to the board, marker ready to plot. I'm better on the left side of the board, the part specific to the business end. The part with Maverick, I don't have nearly enough knowledge to help with, aside from knowing he loves her. The first time they met, I knew. She didn't, but their inter-actions with each other, their dynamic—they complement each other. They push each other to get out of the routines of living.

Neither of us deserves a complacent life. She's got too much in her to give and explore to play life safely.

Fiadh slides down from the chair, making her way to kneel on the other side of the board. She picks up the dark green marker and writes "Wild Apples" on the board under his name.

"I'm lost," I say.

"I have a recipe I've been working on. It incorporates crabbed apples, and there's an essay by Thoreau with this title. He'll understand." She stares dreamily at the board.

"Give me the short version of what the purpose of the mill is." I ready my marker.

"A gathering place for people to learn the craft of cidery, to commune with one another, tell stories, celebrate history, and to share the love of an old pastime both here and in Ireland." She watches as I write her words as fast as I can.

"How will this sustain itself once the initial funding is sourced?" I create a second column under the mill category.

She presses the tip of the marker to her lip, leaving a green dot. "I suppose through a partnership with the university."

"I'm expanding this. You don't want to rely on the university alone." I control my tone to maintain nonchalance. Informing her that the stability she thinks she has outside of this project is in fact unstable isn't necessary right now. There has to be a way to make the mill work. Beyond knowing that this project is her dream, I cannot let the financial situation of the university potentially destroy her.

"I can run mini retreats from the adventure center. A woman from one of the other mills had some fantastic ideas regarding revamping some of the old New Jersey history relating to cidery and bootlegging."

"Bootlegging?" I ask. "Do I need to add bail money to the funds needed?"

She shakes her head. "No. This state was so heavy in the manufacturing of alcohol during prohibition that even the cops were on the take. Those little bits of history are interesting to people. I think it's a draw with the mill."

I write "PERMITS" in giant capital letters on the mill side of the board. "We'll need to budget for these."

She turns to the Maverick side, adding, "family Shea + Amelia" below "Wild Apples." I add a dotted line between their names and the left side of the board. We stare together, adding in suggestions, crossing out areas that are less important to complete immediately. Time whooshes by while we work together, planning for her future in the same excited ways we had as children.

A knock at the door makes me jump. Fiadh stands up, walks to the door, and opens it a crack without removing the chain.

"Password," she says.

"Coffee," Thad answers. "I'm going to sit in the hallway and drink all of your coffee."

She removes the chain from the lock, opening the door for him. He unloads a tray of drinks onto the coffee table, careful to place a coaster under each.

"Those two are decaf, and these two are full caffeine. That one is French vanilla. The other hazelnut. I wasn't sure what you drank." He reaches into his soccer bag, pulling out large packages of ground coffee. "If those aren't right, I have all of these."

"Thad, have I mentioned you're one of my new favorite people?" Fiadh picks up the hazelnut coffee, taking a deep inhale. The sniff alone awakens her energy to fill in more parts of the board.

I grab for the decaf, handing him the other. The buzz of sitting here with both of them is more than enough to keep me alert.

Thad makes himself comfortable on the couch. He squints at the hot mess of our notes on the board.

"Confirm if I'm caught up. You're sketching out running the mill and trying to fix Fiadh's relationship?" he asks.

Fiadh and I nod. He's dressed down from the game, a fresh pair of black soccer shorts with white stripes down the side is paired with a generic green jersey. His eyes are soft, like they're more than ready to sleep, but he's projecting the energy he has at the two of us.

He checks out my left hand. My three bands are scattered across my fingers. A cute smile spreads across his face. I twist the ring on my forefinger.

"I don't think you need to worry about Maverick as much as you think." He takes a sip of his coffee, his gaze settling on me.

"Have you ever had a woman slice your horribly bruised heart open with a sword after you showed up to profess your love?" I ask him.

He sucks in air through his teeth. "I have not."

Fiadh's knee bounces. She takes another inhale of the drink without a sip.

"I have to fix column *a* for column *b* to work," Fiadh says.

"That's *d*, but yeah," I say.

Thad studies the board further. "If you love him—and this is from my outside perspective with little to go on—*a* through *c* are nice-to-haves. But you only need to focus on love, which is *d*. Focus on what makes *d* so special, and then *a* through *c*, if they happen, great. But love comes before everything else."

"I'm stuck on the fact you think I need to focus on the *d*," Fiadh says, a thread of teasing in her voice.

I giggle, watching the hues of his face shift through reds.

Fiadh throws the marker at me. "Focus, Piper. He's not wrong, but *d*..."

"Maverick," I say.

"Maverick's family is the entire world to him," she says.

"From what Piper's shared, if he loves you the way she does, you need to figure out *d*. *D* comes before *a*. Love before everything."

Fiadh's face crinkles.

"I thought I left the twisted comments on the soccer pitch." He slumps into the couch. "What's the ballpark figure to get everything up and running?"

Fiadh shields her face with the cup. "Rough estimates put us at $1.5 million." She turns to me. "He didn't even flinch."

"He's like me with investing. For what you want to do, $1.5 million isn't awful. Is this guess high or low?" I ask.

"High, I think," she says. "This is impossible."

"What's the timeline?" Thad asks, focusing us on *a*.

"The fall semester starts in less than two weeks." Fiadh's excitement falls quiet.

"I'll help with funding. We need a group conversation with Shea and Amelia. Set up a call for everyone in the group text," I say. "If the grant's covering half, we can figure out how to bring the number down."

Thad sips his coffee, eyeing me. He knows what my investments are worth.

"All this money talk is making my head hurt," Fiadh says.

"I'm thinking we all need sleep," I say.

Thad yawns, his eyes drooping further.

"Ugh. I appreciate both of you so much." Fiadh takes a picture of the board, then shuffles to the door.

"Text me when you get home so I know you aren't sleeping on the sidewalk," I say.

Fiadh shifts her feet side to side next to the door.

"Is she all right?" Thad asks. "I can walk her to her apartment if she's nervous."

"I don't know that I could lift you after you pass out on the sidewalk from exhaustion. She's fine. That's her 'I want to hug you, but I suck at hugs' dance." I get up and walk to the door with my arms open.

"Can a person be bad at hugs?" he asks.

Fiadh grumbles under her breath, "I'm appreciative. I don't know what to do with all the emotions flinging themselves through me."

I hug her. Rather than protesting or leaving her arms dangling down, she wraps them around me, squeezing until I cough.

"Do not think we are done talking about how you didn't tell me you aren't working in the fall." Her words come out with a prick of umbrage meant only for my ears.

"The plan will work. Go get some sleep," I say, unable to shake the hot water she's poured on my nerves. "Text me when you get to your apartment."

She gives a wave to Thad and leaves. A rawness takes over my head. I glance over to Thad. If she's this upset about the fall semester, she's going to go nuclear when she finds out we're married.

Chapter Twenty-Two

THE IRRITATING NOISE OF the apartment's front buzzer at the base of the stairs startles me from my early laptop cram session. Once Fiadh texted she was safely in her apartment around 2:00 a.m., Thad passed out immediately, and I snuck in four hours of work to respond to inquiries for interviews, answer a bunch of stressed students, and respond to my chair, who was told not to message me this summer but had a quick question. Or should I say twenty quick questions in separate emails while my body realized my decaf coffee wasn't decaf? Working was a good way to let Thad sleep and control being wide-awake.

Buzz. Buzz. The irritating person holds their finger on longer with each press. I stumble from the desk, doing my best to not disturb a still sleepy Thad, who worked his ass off all day yesterday to then drive while he was exhausted to simply be with me. The clock on the microwave reads 10:00 a.m., and I stumble-step to the intercom. When's the last time I slept this late? My mental calendar pops up, and on my to-do list for today is to finish blasting through all the responses that came in from last night, as well as do a final revision check before I email the author who submitted a revision on their research article to the journal for publication.

My new enemy at the door holds the button down until I cut off the buzzing by pressing the button on my end to talk. I'm going to break their finger if they wake Thad up.

"I think you have the wrong address." No one comes here, and if it were Fiadh, she'd have let herself in.

"I have a delivery for a Dr. Yeats," the visitor says.

"I haven't ordered anything," I say into the silver box on the wall.

None of my colleagues would send me anything this time of year.

"Delivery from a Fiadh O'Cleary. She said to leave it outside if you couldn't give me access to the backyard."

Backyard? What could she possibly have sent? The term "yard" is being used incredibly loosely.

Thad wanders into the living room, rubbing the sleep from his eyes. His hair is mussed from the way he plays with it as he comforts himself to sleep. The soccer jersey is long gone, but he's still sporting the shorts from last night. I check him up and down, and realization slaps me awake.

I press the button on the door again. "Can you deliver it later?"

"Ma'am." The man's voice is tentative. "Please don't make me blow it up in the street."

"Who is blowing what up?" Thad asks, heavily alert at the words.

"Fiadh…" I hesitate. "I'll go handle this."

I walk out the door, down the stairs, and hear Thad's footsteps right behind me.

"You're half-naked," I say.

"You getting blown up would be super hard to explain to my sisters and parents if I'm upstairs. Oh, so my wife was told she had to come downstairs to let a man in or he'd blow something up in the street, and I let her go alone." He stops for a dramatic pause. "Not that I think Fiadh would blow you up."

"That woman doesn't have a malicious bone in her body." I gulp before opening the front door to greet the guest.

"Hello. You can send the package around the corner to this address on Bloomfield." I pull a clipboard from his hands, and scribble Fiadh's address on a receipt.

"I'm under clear instructions to not do so," he says, taking back the clipboard. The man's wearing a full blue jumpsuit with red piping. The logo on his cornflower-blue brimless cap is a giant white outline of a balloon animal dog. "What's the best path to the back?"

I glance up the stairs for the primary option. The crate on the hand cart is nearly as tall as I am.

"We need to go up to the second floor and then take the stairs down," I say.

"Can you tell us what's in it?" Thad blocks the man's entry into the common area.

He's now standing half-naked, half-outside the apartment, and a tickle in my nerves wants to pull him inside so fast. My neighbors are as nosy as anything.

"Have it your way. I'll open it right here and shove it to the sidewalk." The man pulls a crowbar from a belt loop of his pants.

"No, no, no need for that," I say, fearing the contents of the box.

Thad slides into the doorway, following my lead on the guest. He crosses his arms over his chest and fills the space with confidence. An "I'm here and will protect her" manner I didn't know I liked. I take the stairs up two at a time. The delivery man follows, grunting the cart up the first step and then the next. Thad's posture drops with his need to own the space. He jogs past the man, turning to help shove it up the stairs, through the apartment, and then into my yard.

"Shit, this is great. The wife and I don't have nearly this much space." The man wipes his forehead with his sleeve.

I've worked hard on this space. The yard is a brick patio with potted plants of various sizes bordering the outer edge. The first year I owned the place, I tried grass, but grass needs sunlight. Grass also needs mowing, which doesn't seem worth the hassle.

Thad drops his hand to his rumbling stomach. Mine gurgles, but I can't think about food while I strain to see what explodes from the box.

The man grabs the crowbar and motions to Thad for assistance.

"If you hold that, you're officially an accomplice to Fiadh," I say.

"I suppose I am." That's when the slickest grin I've ever seen crosses his face.

No. He did not. They did not. I read him wrong earlier.

"What did you two do?" Blood drains from my face, possibly straight through my feet and out of my body.

"Phoned a friend," he says, helping open the crate and removing a heavy folded plastic inflatable.

They remove a fake bottom on the crate, exposing an electric pump and a filled-to-near-bursting bumpy canvas bag.

I slide down the wall in defeat. The man I shared a bed with last night, assisted my best friend in whatever nonsense is unfolding. "When did you two plan this?"

He muscles the silver plastic inflatable open. "When you were in the bathroom, she mentioned she needed my help this morning for a special delivery."

The delivery man hits the electric pump, and a huge invisible hand packs the air I was exhaling into my lungs. Thad may have been in on the prank to let the delivery man in, but based on the number of times he's fussed with his hair as he stares up at the monstrosity filling my yard, he was not informed she'd sent a glittery bouncy wedding chapel complete with faux stained glass and a cross on top.

"Do you think...? Do you think she knows?" Thad trips on his words.

I shake my head, choosing my response carefully. "We wouldn't have a chapel if she did."

"This is a thing you two do to each other?" he asks.

"Yup," I say.

"This is...impressive." He scrunches his face, the bright sun shielded by the steeple.

My phone buzzes in my pocket. I check the screen, and a picture of Fiadh pops up along with a text message.

Fiadh: *Had I known you were stressed, I'd have sent this sooner. There's a second package on the front steps.*

"Crap. She says there's another package on the steps."

He disappears into the house. How do I explain this to my tenant?

Piper: *Seems too subtle. Next time I want it floating like a blimp.*

Fiadh: *Done. Go get the other package.*

Fiadh: *Can you confirm whether he ran straight from the apartment or if he stayed? I'm hoping he stayed. He seems great.*

That's a positive. The approval isn't necessary, but at the same time, I'm a little lighter knowing she approves of him. Or, she approves of my current happiness and that he showed up not only for me last night but for her.

The man gives up on staking the ropes. Not that the thing can go anywhere with the way it's wedged between the wooden fence and the plants. Seriously, she must have come here to measure the yard to get the exact size.

"Don't clean it with soap. Avoid shoes and bodily fluids." The man's words sound like he's said them thousands of times, and that people ignored the requests ten thousand times. "This is yours for the next twenty-four hours. I'll grab it from you tomorrow." He opens the canvas bag, dumping blue ball pit balls in front of the chapel like a moat.

I hand the man a tip for his efforts with the stairs and the small backyard, but mostly for dealing with the shenanigans of two thirtysomethings. On his way out, the man passes Thad, and I can hear him reiterating the instructions he gave to me a few minutes ago.

"I will do my best to keep bodily fluids out of the chapel." Thad hoists the brown bag in his arms higher. He crosses the small patch of grass left between the door and the entrance to the monstrosity.

I wipe grass off the bottoms of my feet. A brief calculation tells me I'll need to hoist myself up through the entrance. Thad walks past me, sliding the package inside the building. I bolt to the entrance, diving up through the netting and onto the floor of the chapel. Inside is a cozy illustration of stone walls. Thad comes shooting through the entrance, sliding past me and crashing into the blow-up table and chairs in the center of the floor.

He bounces up to his feet in one swift movement like a kangaroo, his strong legs pushing into the floor and flinging his body up. Then, as if the entire situation is an everyday occurrence, the man begins pulling out flips and back tucks.

Fiadh wins this prank round.

Piper: *Go away. We're in the bounce chapel.*

Fiadh: *Pictures please.*

I take a picture of him mid-flip, his body holding in perfect form. I'd bet if he tried, he could do similar on the soccer field.

Fiadh: *This is amazing! He's a real-life superhero!*

Fiadh: *Thank you for everything yesterday. Love you.*

Piper: *Love you.*

I tuck the phone away. Thad bounces next to my leg, sending me forward toward the bag. His chuckle comes through his whole body. There's an effortless smile on his face, and if I didn't know any better, I'd say this might be my favorite prank from Fiadh. Watching his muscles flex each time he lands is...Wait, the bag. I pull the second delivery toward the table, taking a big moon bounce with each step. Inside the bag is fresh fruit, bagels, and a growler. There are paper plates and rubber cups similar to the ones you'd use on the beach, complete with lids to avoid spillage.

Thad takes tiny steps to the table to avoid knocking everything over. "I feel like a king."

"Are you pretending this isn't a glitter chapel on the outside?" I ask.

"Kings go to chapels." He sits in the inflatable chair across from me, his head tilted a little to the right.

When I open the growler, air escapes from the top. I fill each of our cups halfway.

He sniffs the liquid before lifting his cup for a toast. "To friends who love us and infuse our lives with what's important."

I cheers him. My attempts to dissect his words go in too many directions. What's important? Pranks? Silliness? Poking at one another? Physical and mental exhaustion over the past few months of pushing too hard is taking its toll.

"Reminding ourselves that making time for fun is important." His eyes follow me as the room grows fuzzy.

The cup of fresh cider falls from my hand, violating one of the rules for using the equipment. The air is still. The room grows dark. Then black.

"Piper!"

The ground moves beneath me like the ocean.

The heaviness of my eyes is not in the mood for the poking or shaking that's occurring. I peek my right eye open to see three faces inches from my own. The first face is Thad's, his reddened eyes narrow. The second is Fiadh's. Her nose is so close to mine, I'm certain I'm breathing her air. The haze of my memory takes a few minutes to fill in the gaps. To Thad's right is a woman with mousy-blond hair tucked into a messy ponytail, with eyes the same as Thad's. Deep creases on her forehead are identical to his right now.

Lucia? Gianna? No. "Antonia?" I get out with barely a whisper. When I lick my dry lips with my dry tongue, the taste is similar to what I imagine wallpaper to taste like.

"Hey, Piper," Antonia says, shooing the other two for space.

"You gave us a little scare." Her fingers are on my wrist, and there's a cold metal disk on my heart.

I blink my eyes the rest of the way open, the room coming into focus. I'm in my bedroom, and Fiadh's here. Thad's sister is here. I press my hands on either side of my head.

"Yeah, let me do that part, okay, hun?" Antonia drops the stethoscope.

Her fingers move in front of my face, her perfect nails half-painted.

"Don't look at those. I left in a rush when he called. Manicurist was pissed." She giggles. "I should keep to using the stickers—makes it easier to remove the color for work."

"I like the pink ones on you." I push up on the memory foam, fighting for strength. My arms give out, and I crash onto a heap of pillows.

"Hospital time?" Antonia asks.

Thad and Fiadh nod repeatedly behind her.

A trip to the emergency room is not going on my calendar. "No, I'm okay. I need a nap."

"Well, I'm not going to force you to go to the hospital here. I don't have access to this one. I'd need you to come to Morristown if we went." She taps on my arm from my shoulder to my wrist. "Calm down, Thad. I can feel the worry radiating off of you."

Thad jerks his body around, then does a slow squat to sit on the bed without shaking me. I lean on him to prop myself up. Fiadh is rubbing her hands raw.

"Fiadh, I'm fine," I say.

"I gotta say, when Thad called and explained you were passed out in a bouncy castle, I was not expecting a chapel." Antonia folds her hands in her lap. "I still advise the hospital, but everything I'm seeing looks fine. Are you up for answering questions?"

"Absolutely." My attempt to perk up, to push through and be fine, fails.

"Are you under a lot of stress lately? Any major changes in your life impacting your regular routine?" She lifts an eyebrow at her brother.

By the grace of all things, Fiadh speaks first.

"The university pushed her to go on a sabbatical for the fall. She takes on everything she can. She never says no. If she took the sabbatical, knowing her, she's still going full tilt on all the other stuff she does." She rubs at the corner of her eye. "I don't think she sleeps, and I hurt her by getting a stupid bouncy castle and giving her one more thing to add to her schedule." Fiadh bursts into tears.

"No, you sent me the best prank you ever have." I offer her a soft smile. "But yeah, my calendar is a mess, and I've been trying to get everything done. I need to remember to drink more water. I'm all right." That babbling doesn't even convince me.

"Your body is telling you that you are in fact not all right. That you need to clear your calendar and rest before you do end up in the hospital. Or are you like Thad and think you can conquer the world? Do everything for everyone else and forget yourself?" The tone in her voice is loving, with a hint of *pull your shit together or I'll make you.*

Her words thread uncomfortably deep into my skin. Thad has done everything he can for me, including last night when he drove out here at an awful hour to come help. This makes sense, given the current situation, but it's more than that. He's kept our secret even though I imagine he'd rather shout it loudly outside so it echoes across the earth. I feel the same around him, but my shouting remains in my head, echoing throughout my body, lifting me when the world is crushing me from all the yeses. Keeping this in isn't me. I'm the person who shouts with excitement. The one who takes pleasure in being the head of the hype team for good news.

Three sets of eyes are focused on my face, waiting for an answer, while my body wants me to pull the blanket up so I can sleep.

"If I make arrangements to go talk to a doctor, will you all stop?" I ask.

Thad threads his fingers through mine. "Antonia is one of the best doctors around."

"I'm an ER doctor. I'm good in emergencies." She brushes down her crisp white shirt.

"I'm sorry about your nails," I say.

"Eh. This is what family is for." The moment the last word slips out, she mouths, *Fuck*. She pats Thad's elbow. "Isn't that right?"

Thankfully, Fiadh didn't see her face. I have no doubt the slip went over her head, but I now know Antonia is a risk. At the same time, I'm acutely aware she confirmed she sees me as family, which makes my insides doughy and has me granting her instant forgiveness.

"I promise I will see a doctor this week. Will that calm everyone down?" I ask.

"No," Thad says. "Show me your calendar."

Fiadh takes my phone, pressing her finger on the lock screen. I sit up fast to find my head—the room—spinning out of control. There's no way to fight the pull to lie down again so I don't throw up. Hello, vertigo, please go away.

She hands him the phone, helping him to the calendar. The three of them huddle around my screen, their hands on one another as if they're a cheer team getting ready to go do a routine. Or that they've found an amazing artifact and are studying it.

"My calendar isn't super interesting," I protest.

"This is meticulous," Antonia says. "I thought I was anal about scheduling my day, but this is a whole other level."

She flicks her finger across the screen. "Hun, this is not healthy. I want to add myself in here, but there's not an ounce of room. When do you flop to enjoy life?"

"Flop?" I ask.

"Yeah, like have a day when you can sleep all day and aren't running to one thing or another." Antonia flicks the screen to what I'm assuming is the next month.

"She shuffles," Fiadh says, throwing me under a bus so fast. "If her calendar is full, she'll clear time and then pull an all-nighter."

Excuse me, former best friend. That was uncalled for. Painful. And worst of all, true. I bite down on my tongue to keep the tears in.

"Who invited her?" I point at Fiadh with my chin.

"You did. When I pressed the emergency contact in your phone, it rang straight to her," Thad says. "What's not in the planner?"

"Emails. Responding to inquiries for her side work takes up huge chunks of time. She also doesn't schedule check-ins on her properties. Those usually happen on the fly." Fiadh's not done driving the bus over me.

"I'm right here. I can answer for myself." I throw my arms up uselessly to draw their focus. When the room stops shifting in and out of focus, I'm adding a new emergency contact.

"What are these blocks?" Antonia points to the screen.

"Those are class blocks, but she isn't teaching this summer." Fiadh taps on her upper lip, understanding pulling through. "Did your chair send those?"

"Yes," I say, switching my gaze to the ceiling. "I said no."

"You said no to that but then said yes to helping me with the mill and said yes to additional interviews. What else have you said yes to?" she asks.

I refuse to look at Thad, but I can feel his and his sister's blazing stare on my face.

"The additional courses..." There's no point in answering them.

"The additional courses would have sent you over the edge," Antonia finishes for me. "You wouldn't be with my brother..."

I suck in a hard breath through my teeth. She's wrong. She has to be wrong, I'd have made time. I made time to go on the trips with Fiadh. I've made time for everyone. There's not a sound from Thad, not a tap of his foot or even a light touch to check in.

"Deprioritize me," Fiadh says. "I'm the easiest. You rely on everything else to run your business. I'm not going anywhere."

Pain shoots down my spine to my feet. The university might be, and she needs the mill. She needs happiness and Maverick.

"I'm not going anywhere," Thad says.

I reach for him, grabbing at the polyester fabric of his shorts. Clearing the thickness forming in my throat leads to a choked cough. I can't stop doing everything I've taken on. People depend on me. I can't give everything up because my body stalled on me.

"We love you," Thad says. "I promise you, there's a lot more than two of us who want to help you right now."

The words swell in my heart, increasing the flame in me that Thad's helped grow the past few months. I need rest, to not touch my phone, and to recover from my own calendar.

What part of myself is it time to let go of? In my marrow I know Antonia is right; this is stress knocking me down.

This useless sensation is not me. I rally. No one is allowed in here because this is where I come to safely crumble. The privacy of this space, the ability to demask the parts of me pushing to be everyone's cheerleader, to hit all my goals, is infiltrated. Fiadh knows this. I imagine that's why she sent the chapel. A sign she knew I trusted him so much, I invited him into my space not once but twice. Her weird way of showing exactly how much she approves of him.

Thad puts the phone in my hand. Instead of opening the calendar to see whether appointments were added or moved, I drop it onto the bed. I want to sleep, to stay in. After I rally later tonight, I'll call a doctor or two.

CHAPTER TWENTY-THREE

A FTER TWO DAYS OF sleeping at Thad's house—our house—I'm in Hoboken, much to his frustration. Possible frustration? Likely annoyance. When I told him my doctor's appointment was out here, he offered to drive me. When I said "blueberry macaroon," he got quiet, said "Okay," and headed to work. I'm not stopping him from doing his job when the current state my body is in is my own fault. All I can do is keep an eye on him and make sure he's sleeping, eating, taking care of himself, and not fussing over me, which he's done the entirety of the past few days.

I lean against the wood backrest in the rounded booth, letting the cushion of the bench seat press against the base of my skull to relieve pressure. The table is as sticky as ever, and unlike my last visit here, the other tables are packed. Each stool in front of the bar has a patron enjoying the European soccer match being broadcast on television.

"All right, this may be our new permanent meeting spot," Vera says, tapping on the breakfast menu.

"Do I want the Greek omelet or baked eggs?" Lisa bites her thumbnail.

While I'm nearly done with summer break, they're on full-year contracts because of their impressively high positions. One text under the covers to them when I was faking sleeping midafternoon at Thad's, and these two had their assistants clear their schedules for the morning straight through to lunch.

"Get both, plus a plate of extra toast. We can all share," Vera says.

I'm not hungry despite only having had a cup of Irish tea before they arrived. Tea that is now adding an unpleasant ache to my stomach from the acid.

Nico, the bartender, walks over and swaps out my empty cup of tea for a fresh one.

"You've never been here on a match morning," he says. "Who are you rooting for?"

I pull the cup closer to me. "Who should I root for?"

"I'm partial, but I'd say the team from Greece." He plays with the spoon in the white cup. "You've never asked about the matches before; I'll help you out. Don't let any of the guys at the bar bet with you on the outcome. They know the score from watching at about 2:00 a.m. This is a replay match."

"I played when I was younger." Lisa's eyes are glued to the television. Her arm is shaking with tension as one of the Greek players rushes up the field, dancing in and out of the other team's players. The man's gorgeous, thick black hair bounces in a manner I'd assume Nico's would if it weren't tucked under a thin headband.

Thad's done similar at the field house when I've watched his games, always ending with more of a humbleness than many of the other players. But I've caught him glancing at me more than once to confirm that I saw how amazing he plays. The little tilt up of his mouth when he's made an assist or scored is so small, I'm not sure anyone else is catching his full excitement.

The player on the screen scores a goal, runs to his friends, and does a front tuck before being buried in excitement. Never in my academic life have my colleagues ever celebrated in this way. A full-bodied explosion of energy celebrating the joy in doing the jobs they are paid for.

"What position did you play?" I ask.

"Center back," she says, like I have any idea what that means.

Vera sips her mimosa. "I was more of a stopper when I played."

The two of them look at me, waiting like this is some pastime I should have done growing up. Did everyone play soccer as a kid? I didn't. Fiadh didn't.

"I cheered in high school and studied." I let the bitter tea coat my tongue. "What is a stopper?"

"Did you do more studying than cheering?" Lisa asks, her jovial nature coaxing me to relax.

I crinkle my nose. "Equal. There's no way Granny would have okayed more time cheering than studying." Despite having dropped out of high school herself, she knew her shit when it came to ensuring my parents and I were well educated. They were scholars long before I was born. Their misstep was landing in fields where they worked a billion hours either researching or teaching and weren't around much for me.

Oh. I press my hand over the squeeze in my heart. I work nearly the same number of hours they did. Thad's face comes into focus when I close my eyes. My heart beats in painful thumps. I open my eyes, but the outline of his sweet face takes a second to dissipate.

Lisa orders for the table. Nico rolls up the sleeves of his black shirt, disappearing into the kitchen while several of the center tables cheer with their fists raised high.

"Out with it, Yeats. I want an update." Vera twists the chain of her necklace.

"Can't a woman text her two favorite mentors in the entire world to get breakfast for no particular reason?" I ask through my painted-on smile.

Lisa looks me up and down. "Don't bullshit me, Piper. You are pale, which means you aren't getting out as much as you should."

"Sunblock is a wonderful invention to help us prevent skin cancer. I recommend multiple applications to protect ghostly white skin." Proper skin care is a routine worth investing in to avoid the freckles that run in my family. "I've been out with Fiadh on a farm and doing outdoorsy stuff."

Vera squints at me, like she's trying to recall a conversation. "Outdoorsy stuff wasn't specifically on the list, but I'll take the effort. Plus, you've made time for your friendships, which was part of our first conversation."

I've never stopped making time for Fiadh. This is what people do when they care about one another. A feather tickles at the growing ache in my throat. Thad didn't go to work for nearly three days. He's got to be so backed up.

Nico returns with a massive tray of breakfast foods, placing their orders, along with a side of fresh fruit and yogurt, on the table. "Let me know if there's anything else I can get for you." He catches a man standing on a chair with his finger on the television. "I wouldn't change that!"

He leaves us and goes to remove the man from the chair before the other patrons choose alternative means to keep the match on.

I pull my knees together to fight the shake in my legs. There's too much to do to relax into this lazy breakfast.

"Any word on financial updates for the university?" I ask, with no regard for whether it's the right time or place.

Lisa presses her lips together, dropping a spoonful of baked eggs on her plate.

"You don't need to be worrying about that," Vera says. "We need you to rest."

"You must feel so liberated with less on your plate," Lisa says.

Sure, except for getting married and pushing through on other items on my list. I keep my focus on the yogurt I've obligatorily put on my plate alongside the fruit.

"How can I help with the university?" I ask, hoping to divert Lisa.

Lisa drops her fork on her plate. "Vera has assured me there are a number of faculty members working on securing funding, and I'm working on some leads. The university will keep pushing forward for the short term." Lisa's tone is reassuring, but I know the numbers. The knowledge that programs will need to close looms over us.

"I have a network interview coming up. I'll ask that they put the university name under mine so it gets press." I tuck my hands underneath my still-shaking legs.

Vera purses her lips. "What interview? Was this one pre-planned, or is it a new one you're taking on? The instructions were to dial down the work you're taking on."

"We agreed to keep the interviews. This was a shift of medium from radio to live television." The soccer match on the TV above grows obnoxiously loud. "The station has been good to us."

Lisa pinches her chin. Her full focus is on me. "What have you slowed down on this summer?"

"No teaching. I'm not doing the normal level of consulting work I do in the summer." Which they don't need to know I've pushed to the fall.

"You're still answering work emails and doing interviews. And I understand you've been working with Fiadh on her grant," Vera says.

"Yeah, but it's Fiadh. I'd be helping her anyway," I say.

"Yes, but helping her with reworking it is no different from you working with a much larger company for hours on hours of consulting." Vera's obnoxiously right.

"That's one little thing I've added that's fun and makes me happy," I say.

"I know you. Before you even try to say you're doing less, Fiadh texted me yesterday to say you're exhausted." Vera gives a small squeeze to my arm.

I dip my chin down, focusing on the teacup. No wonder their schedules cleared so fast. "How much did she tell you?"

"Don't be mad at her. She's worried," Vera says. "*We're* worried."

"You're leaving out a detail in what else you've taken on this summer." Lisa pulls her mimosa to her chest. "Who's Thad?"

I roll my eyes, pick up my cup, and hide behind my mug. *Thanks, Fiadh.*

"Your cheeks are heated!" Vera's enthusiasm for my discomfort floods me with memories of when we all worked as professors together. Before either of them shot up the ranks. We'd sit in Lisa's office when she was the head of our department, before she was tapped to be the acting chief academic officer and then university president. We spent hours imagining the future, of the department, of ourselves.

I steady the excitement bubbling in my core with my hand. "Thad is...He's the welcome surprise of the summer."

"Is he worth cutting back on work for?" Vera plays with the horn on her necklace. Her eyes are hazy with the gentle memory in her head.

"That's the thing. He hasn't asked me to slow down any-thing." My body is doing that part all on its own.

I shift in my chair. Deep inside me is a piece that wonders whether I've dragged him into me too fast. Most of my life has involved staring up at the future, which is why everything with Thad is so surreal. With him, I exist in the right now. I'm not playing catch-up from having overbooked myself.

In the last two months, I've lived more in the moment than the chess board of life where by twelve I was thinking eight plays ahead with contingency plans. I don't want to miss things with him, but maybe I did act too hastily. Not that I regret being with him. But it's possible we married too quickly, like we should have planned out more of what we wanted instead of doing things day by day.

"When I met my husband, I cut back on things without realizing I was," Vera says.

I stare down at the liquid in my cup. "I've shuffled a lot of projects around, but..."

"You're going to keel over if you keep up your current pace," Lisa says. "What if we extend your break from teaching through the spring semester? Give you a full year to catch up."

A full year is enough time to continue to overbook myself. The mere idea of having to start classes in less than two weeks is a like a vice grip on my lungs.

I'll end up with Antonia in my office alongside her sisters, coming to drag me out or find a way to clear my schedule, because I can't imagine Thad asking for more time. Even if he needs the time. Life wouldn't be awful if he spun me to face him, held me firmly in place, and said, "You need to choose."

My stomach roils. Fine. The moment would be awful. I'd fight, cry, and fume if he made me choose. But the version of Thad in my head where he pushes for what he wants openly and verbally is right. Even though he'd never make me choose, I need to permanently give up parts of my schedule.

"I need time to think. The offer is so generous, but I know you'll need help fundraising, filling classes, and getting the name of the university out there. There are too many students who need the courses to graduate and too many colleagues I can help if I'm on campus."

Lisa grabs my forearms. "Yeats, I'm going to tell you this once. You are not responsible for saving the university by sacrificing yourself. Do not—I repeat—do not put that pressure on yourself."

A bitterness coats my tongue. I need more time in a day to get everything done. I need to protect Thad from this nonsense that lives in me, where I don't know how to relax or let go. I lick my lips before engaging their sympathetic eyes.

Chapter Twenty-Four

T HE FIELD HOUSE IS empty except for Thad and I. He's a worrywart who asked me to come here tonight, defying the instructions from Antonia that I should still be resting. I've rested-ish. I slept, met with doctors, both things in barely a week since the bouncy castle incident.

"Antonia says she texted you twice today to check in and didn't hear back from you. I told her you were fine, but do you understand the risk of not responding to her? They are going to hound you. She's going to go through a whole dramatic stance where messages are passed through my parents and my sisters that she thinks she offended you or that you don't like her." Thad juggles the ball with his feet. "I'm not saying you have to like her, but be prepared for more messages."

"I don't like that she told me I should stay in bed for two weeks straight." There is no planet on which I'd have been able to pull off two weeks straight. "Other than that, she's amazing."

"Yeah, about that, I'm pretty sure part of that was alluding to rest, and part of it was my sister being inappropriate. They're going to compete for attention. This is going to grow into a whole thing. Especially since I only called her and not the others when you were sick." Thad lifts his leg up, sending the ball into the air. He traps it between his shoulder blades and the back of his head.

He shuffle-steps, nearly galloping over to me. When he straightens his spine, the ball rolls down to my feet.

"Are you showing off?" I pick up the ball to inspect the density. There's more cushion to this one than the one that hit me in the woods, so it shouldn't do as much damage if it hits me.

"Depends. Is it working?" He leans over the ball to press a gentle kiss on my cheek.

I drink in his body. "You didn't need to touch the ball; the outfit alone is a ten out of ten. Those shorts make your booty look squeezable."

He turns around, almost daring me to pinch his cheeks.

I chuck the ball up and over his head. As he jogs to go pick it up, the muscles in his calves tense with each strike of his foot on the ground. Oh, yes, this is way better than sitting in a bed or being buried under work.

He picks up the ball, turns, and hurls it across the field to me. I push up with all my might, stretching my arms up to grab the ball. Unlike the day we met, I catch it firmly between my palms like a basketball. No finger injuries.

I eye him, then the net. The dizziness is gone, and I'm clearheaded enough to be playful again. I casually walk to the goal and stand on the line.

His lips curl up. Without his even touching me, my body lights up. My insides grow zoomies, and I want to race from line to line. I only just manage to keep the facade of cool by bouncing in front of the goal.

"Are you sure?" he asks, jogging to the ball I left behind.

I could watch him run away from me all night. My preference is running toward me, so I get a better view of his face, of the way his eyes light up every time he notices me looking at him. The way his pupils turn into saucers when he is ready to kiss me.

"Are you scared of beginner's luck?" I lengthen as wide as possible, a move I saw his goalie do last time he played.

He bites his bottom lip, kicking the ball from side to side, growing closer to me.

Rather than strolling straight past me into the net, he stops at the metal post on the side of the goal. I strongly need to brush up on my soccer lingo. He leans against it in the same way delicious men in romances rest an arm against a doorframe. For a man the Bees said wasn't into romancing the league, he is well aware of how attractive he is right now. The perfectly proportioned muscles, the height over me, the vanilla taking over my senses.

"Are you trying to distract me?" I ask. "Mr. Yeats, you're going down."

Thad drops to his knees, his nose so damn close to the elastic line of my running shorts. Breathless, I lace my fingers through his hair, daring him to make a move.

"Mr. Yeats, huh?" He wraps his arms around my legs, stands, and picks me up over his shoulder.

"Mr. Cosimo," I yell, laughing as he carries me, bounding up the field with the ball at his feet to the far goal.

He places me down gently on the goal line. "You know I'll change my last name to yours. I'm happy to do whatever you want."

The lightness from the run and the playfulness turn heavier. "What about what you want?"

He taps the ball to the goal line. "A happy wife is what I want."

I fidget with my bottom lip.

His demeanor stills. "Have I said something wrong?"

"No. I...I'm thinking about the ball on the hike, that's all." What is wrong with me? Tell him. Tell him what the Bees said and that he deserves more than convenience.

"Where'd the confidence go?" he asks. "I seem to recall you bragging about beginner's luck not two minutes ago."

"Yep." My voice pitches high.

He taps the ball back and forth in front of him. For a man who was joking with me, lifting me, jogging with me, his lightness feels almost pensive.

"Care to make a wager?" he asks, not making eye contact.

"Are we playing strip soccer?" I put my hands on the lower hem of my shirt, ready to pull it up.

"No. It would be unfair to have you completely naked in goal with a ball whizzing at you at twenty miles per hour," he says, finally looking at my—stomach.

"If I block the ball, I get to ask you a question. If you make it in, you get to ask me a question. Is that where you're headed with this?" Strip soccer sounds much too painful with the twenty-miles-an-hour comment. "Can you really kick a ball faster than I can ride a bike?"

He nods slowly. "Yes, but I'd never kick it that hard at you."

"*Pfft.* I could totally stop that."

He raises his eyebrow in question at me.

I pace the line between the posts, trying to figure out how many steps there are from one end of the goal to the other. For the next measurement, I lie on the ground, measuring the space from my fingertips to my toes, including rotations on the floor to get the best estimate.

Thad watches me, his head tilted. "That is a new technique for measuring," he says.

"How else am I going to know how far I have to travel when I hurl my body to either side?" I ask.

His eyelids droop. "Let's do the questions part. I'll stand halfway across the field to make it fair."

"I'm not appreciating your underestimation of my skills here." I feign insult and gesture to either side of the net. "I have a better idea. How about you just ask me the question that you want and not kick any balls at me in the process?"

He musses his hair, transforming its perfectness into a sleepy hotness.

A tilt of his chin to the side, and he's half looking at me but more hiding his face.

"Now you have to tell me the question, or my brain will start filling in whatever it wants." *Does he want to ask if I regret getting married or if we can get an annulment?* My mouth goes dry.

"Is the reason you wanted to elope because of your parents?" he asks.

Nope. This is not at all the question I expected to come out. I hold my hand over my mouth to stop a laugh laced with pain from spilling out.

"Anything else?" I ask.

He starts to walk toward me. I raise a hand in a gesture for him to stop where he is. I need the extra feet of space.

"How did it happen?" His words are tentative, careful.

This shouldn't sting in the way it does. This mix of happiness in understanding how they felt about each other, which I feel every time Thad's name is mentioned or when we're together, mixed with the pure knowledge that they died far too young—for me and for them. That I've used humor and lightness most of my life to cover the random emotional stabs thinking about them brings. When I'm busy, I don't stop and think about the world.

Eloping meant not having to stop to answer people's questions on how big changes the like university failing or getting married will impact me. Elopement from the reality that no matter how much happiness I know Thad and I will have together, there's a part of me I didn't want to let into the present.

Clarity rings through my consciousness, and that clarity contains Fiadh's name spelled out in flashing lights. Avoiding telling her about the wedding and the issues with the university was to avoid talking to the one person who knows all the truths about me. Including the ones in relation to how I cope—or don't cope, as it were, with changes.

I motion for him to kick the ball at me. He pulls the ball back farther and kicks it. I leap forward at the direct shot he's given me and let it knock me to the ground. In no way was the ball hit hard. Hard enough to get it to me, soft enough to do no damage, much like the way he phrased the question.

He rubs at his hair again, mumbling to himself, "I pick the wrong times to ask things."

"No, it's a good question. I should have explained more when your family was interrogating me." Clutching the ball to my chest, I lift myself up from the downward drag of my body before the incoming avalanche of emotions can bury me from being happy. "When I was twelve, they'd gone to London to do research that summer. The university library had acquired a new collection that my parents were itching to get their hands on."

The intense concentration on his face lets me know he's here, fully present, and wants every word. Still clutching the ball, I stand up, facing him with my new comfort ball in my arms.

"The short version is, the ceiling and all the books above them came crashing down in the rare books collection. They found them beneath the collection, my dad's body over my mom's in a failed attempt to shield her."

He rubs at the base of his neck. His eyes are glossy with a wet slick. I roll the ball out to him, instantly crossing my arms over my chest when it hits his feet.

"You and Fiadh decided to become professors when you were twelve," he says, putting together pieces of my past.

"Later that summer. We'd mapped out our lives together so neither of us would ever be alone." My eyes are now slick, and the lights above are blinding. I let the tears fall, not only for my parents but also for Fiadh and all the things she's always given up to make sure I'd never be alone. "Except, she's always done more than we'd agreed upon that day. Like coming home from Ireland on her year away, instead of staying and transferring schools to keep working on her craft. I know she and her nana came home because Granny wasn't well, and they came to help me."

How can I be a good wife to anyone when I'm one of the neediest friends ever? The truth feels like ice, sharp against my heart. This is why I couldn't tell Fiadh. I didn't want her to stop her life again, not for me. At first it was the timing. I wanted to help her, not worry her. And then things got complicated with the university, the cider mill, Maverick, and Thad. "I swear, I don't usually cry this much."

He draws me into him.

"Damn stealthy cat," I say shakily into his chest.

"I needed a hug," he says, squeezing me. "You have a huge family. So does Fiadh. One that's so big, you don't even know how many people already love you before you've met them."

I've had decades to go through the story of my parents over and over, so much so that at times it's hard to remember this is my story. Until I'm asked by someone who matters. And they don't usually get the part about Fiadh and me, because that's a part reserved for those I let in.

Thad drops his grip from me. I wipe tears from his face with my thumb.

"They died together, loving each other and their lives." My voice shakes. "I have always wanted my version of their love…without the tragic ending. One where I'm celebrating fifty years with my love. They died never knowing loneliness."

Thad stands so still, not responding in any manner to my wish.

I wince. "Man, am I a mood killer or what?"

Still no words from him. I've broken him. I've broken Thad.

"I'm going to grab a water from your office." I turn on my heel to leave the field.

We walk in the quiet to his office, my temples pounding. Not being well versed in uncommunicative men, I'm going with the assumption I shared too much.

I need to call Fiadh.

Queasiness takes over my stomach. I can't call her. *I talked too much after being asked a direct question, and I'm fairly certain my husband is weirded out by me. Oh, also, I ran off and got married and didn't tell you.* Yeah, that'll go as well as the Hindenburg.

The university shutting down flashes in my head, the vision nearly choking me. Fiadh is sitting on the steps to her closed building, crying. She can't lose her cidery dream. Not with everything she's given up for me. There's got to be a way to get the funding she needs to rehab the mill.

We pass Thad's desk and sit on the black futon in his office next to a vintage-inspired red mini fridge. He takes out two waters, handing one to me and placing the other on his forehead.

A strong pain grows at the base of my skull. I reach into my bag to pull out my small roller massage ball. I press it against my shoulder blade and push the vibration button.

Thad slides in next to me, our legs ever so lightly touching, and takes the tool from me. He presses it firmly against the space I'd held it, the vibrations attacking the pool of stress forming.

"Is this the official use for this...or is this off-market usage?" Thad asks.

This is his question? Not anything more specific about the information I dumped on him, but whether this is a vibrator. "I would not simply whip out a sex toy after that conversation."

"If you had, I wouldn't blame you." He wraps his warm palm over the tightness in my tendons, positioning his thumb to rub circles. "I'm sorry for pushing you."

I turn to face him, contorting his arms when he doesn't let go.

"You didn't push me. There's really never a good time to bring things up." I stretch forward, exposing more of my neck for him to move up the ball.

A black-and-white print of a woman holding soccer balls over her chest steals my focus. Art. Artwork. "Where are all those pictures from?"

"A local artist did the series." He finishes a sip of water. "If you're looking for art, Ariana is the Bee you want to talk to."

He adds pressure to a stiff spot at the base of my skull, discharging tension. I moan at the freedom it releases in my neck.

"I have one more unrelated question," I say. "Why is there a futon in your office?"

"It's not what you're thinking." His hands stop moving, hovering over a spot yearning for more of his touch.

"I'm not thinking anything. I was already told you don't—didn't—really date from the league, so why the fraternity-guy futon?"

"There's more noise here." His hushed tone is confusing. He begins to rub at the pain, each extra second of touch healing the ache but not erasing it completely.

"You live in the woods. Why not live in the city if you like noise?" I ask.

"The issue isn't the noise. There's people here when I fall asleep. By the time I wake up, there's people again, either cleaning or showing up for super-early-morning practice." He turns my upper body to face the wall. His pressure on the ball changes, and he rolls it slowly up and down either side of my spine, sending a chill straight through me.

Realization bites at me. There's an energy here, unless he eloped to not feel lonely. I tuck my chin down, hiding biting my lip. That can't be the only reason—for either of us.

CHAPTER TWENTY-FIVE

F IADH IS UNCHARACTERISTICALLY LATE tonight. I glance at the auction house doors, impatiently waiting for her to burst through and rush to her seat. The goal tonight is to help with the mill and to lay the foundation for her to give a grand sweeping gesture to Maverick. I can officially confirm, the litany of options keeping her from getting here on time is lengthy, but I'm imagining her throwing the PATH train conductor from the train to take over and blasting through whatever delay she's experiencing to get to Midtown.

"She'll be here," I say softly, for only Thad's ears.

"Why wouldn't she?" Thad asks, matching my tone in the pre-auction buzz of the Heritage Auction space. "Do we bring up Maverick, or do we...?" He gestures a slice mark across his throat.

"Probably better to leave that one alone for a little while." I blow air through my lips, gaining a disapproving glasses-down-the-nose stare from a man two seats over.

Glasses man is within the magic triangle of influence, where we're a few rows behind the triangle. Triangle people—my new name for them—exist in the section where the bigwigs or their representatives have reserved seats. The tip of which is the podium up front and center for the auctioneer. In the case of tonight's festivities, that's Ariana.

I dig my heels into the regal blue carpet, leaving dents in the deep pile. The cream walls are dressed with old oil paintings, throwing off the entertainment and memorabilia vibe of the lots tonight. This room is too formal for what I've brought. Or, maybe the tornado of Ariana coming through in full Bee fashion to help is the part I'm still working on figuring out.

I've barely said words to her, but she's jumped in and taken over everything so I wouldn't have to worry about whether the collection would sell. In less than a week, Ariana and her auction house army managed to get my collection cataloged and up on the Heritage Auction website. She's insistent that there are going to be interested buyers tonight. Now that the day is here, I'm even more convinced this was the right decision. There's nothing in my collection worth keeping if Fiadh can't have her dream. Based on cursory research, pulling together an auction takes a whole lot more time than a week.

"Is there a Bee for every occasion?" I ask, leafing through the catalog of items for tonight's auction.

Thad slides his paddle between his knees, threading his fingers through mine to give a squeeze. "I think you know the answer to that."

Ariana gave me options where I could be live in the auction house and watch my collection go piece by piece, follow the live stream online from the comfort of a hidden room, or she'd call me and give an update afterward. A small part of me wants to see the person taking them home. A tiny goodbye from one collector to another while we raise funds to help offset the up-front costs of the mill rehabilitation. Minus roughly 25 percent of the collection, which is now in the guest room at Thad's—our—place. What's not up for live purchase tonight is up on their website and on online sales sites for special collectors.

I squeeze Thad's fingers between mine, the anticipation building while patrons fill every gray seat cover in the room. The sea of dark blue suits makes my stomach drop. This isn't the right type of crowd. If this doesn't work, I'll sell it off piece by piece on my own to raise the funds.

Thad leans into my side. "I can feel your nerves from here. There's no way she'd have put the items up or as many into the auction as she did if she didn't think they'd sell." He's right. I know he's right. But knowing that doesn't stop the bouncing of my leg.

"I'll cover the gap for anything that doesn't sell," he says.

"Fiadh would never accept the money that way." Plus, this is mine to do for her.

"What can I do to help you right now?" he asks. His whisper slows the energy coursing through my cells.

I check the grandfather clock to the side of the stage. Fiadh's got five minutes. There's no way she's getting here before everything kicks off. Is it possible that selling all of this is one too many changes? I need a sign like the one from the day I met Thad that spelled out for me he's the best.

Thad hands me a small bottle of water. "She'll be here."

A metal door clanks closed, alerting the nosy man with the glasses to turn and look past me. He raises a finger to his lips for a shush, and I turn to check out his latest victim. Rosie-cheeked Fiadh stands with her fingertips on the door behind her, her eyebrows nearly touching, and while I'm glad to see her, I know the cringe on her face is the look of *Let me disappear in peace from sheer embarrassment.*

I wave high at her to come join us. She stays frozen at the door like a deer caught in headlights. I squint for a better look. Skip that. She's a deer whose baggy pants leg of her jeans is caught in the door.

With a short laugh, I get up and walk quickly to her to bail her out of her current situation. Only, where she'd normally chuckle once I'm with her, the blood rushes from her face, switching her typically paper-white skin to a shade of translucency.

"The door ate my jeans," she says. The words stagger on their way out.

I crouch to inspect the situation. This is not good—not for her jeans, or for the fact I'll be lucky if she doesn't pull a full disappearing act.

"How did the door rip your pants so bad?" I ask.

"Oh no. No. No. The first rip was from the subway. The doors shut on my bag when I was almost all the way out. I yanked it and stumbled, but the loose bottoms got caught on a piece of metal sticking out from a sign advertising our damn university. When I tried to pull them free, there was a loud rip!" She draws her hands high.

"Tell me you gave everyone in New York a show on your walk here." How do I help her? We need to get to our seats.

"Do you feel the air-conditioning breeze, or is it simply because my ass cheek is out?" She looks up at the ceiling.

I glance behind me. Everyone is staring at us. They're staring because it's auction time. Not because a woman entered with a gorgeous lipstick-red silk top and ripped jeans that are now keeping her tied to a door.

"I'm going to open the door a crack. Then I'll run behind you to cover your underwear," I say. "Why didn't you go home or get new pants on the way here?"

She scrunches her face in an *are you kidding me* manner, adding an eyeroll for emphasis. "You're selling off your collection to help me with the mill. A collection that you don't have to sell because we can come up with an alternative."

"I'd have understood," I say.

"Pipes, I'd have ridden a damn ostrich to get here if I had to," she says.

Whoa. Fiadh voluntarily—figuratively or literally—offering to be anywhere near a bird is a reinforcement of how deeply rooted the love in our friendship is.

A high-pitched voice comes from the microphone up front. "If everyone could take their seats, we'll be pushing the start out fifteen minutes while we wait for everyone to settle in."

Thank you, Ariana.

"I'll never make you ride an ostrich. As far as the auction, we're auctioning off investments to reinvest." Then I offer, "Do you want my pants?"

"You love those investments," she protests. "I want my own pants. Free my jeans from the little rubber thing down there, and get behind me."

I reach over, unlooping the loose material from the door stopper. Eek, I pull back. The rip is wide and high to the point I can see the white of her panties.

My nervous, attention-loathing best friend channels her inner diva, holding her head high, walking with the flap of her jeans behind her. I rush ahead, putting my hands on her hips, blocking the view of her cold cheek.

Thad does a double-take while Fiadh and I move to take our seats. He rips off his jacket, a move I don't mind thanks to the extra glance at how delicious his biceps look in the button-down, and hands it to my brave friend to put over herself. With her short stature, her ass is now well covered, and the whole ensemble looks like a student's design from the Fashion Institute.

"Did you get mugged?" Thad asks.

"Yes, by a clown and three hamsters," she deadpans.

"There was a clown?" He shudders.

"And three hamsters." She picks up the program and leafs through the schedule.

The bounce returns in my legs, and no matter how many times I cross and uncross my ankles, I'm not able to anchor my extremities to the floor. Fiadh fidgets with her coat. Loose strands of her red waves flow from between the teeth of her silver sunflower clips.

"If you don't chill your legs, the chair's screws are going to come out and you're going to fall down." Fiadh scans the page with her finger.

I wrap each ankle around the legs of my chair. Thad places his hand on my thigh, instantly sending waves of comfort through me. All the pieces need to sell to get through the initial funding stages, and this crowd, full of people with stiff spines, isn't giving me the confidence I want.

Fiadh elbows me, pointing to a painting of an orchard done by a comic book artist that's also up for bid tonight. The sweet piece would be perfect in her future tasting room. Tonight is going to go smoothly. Despite my legs having been tamed, my heart continues in a skip-beat rhythm, inching me closer to the edge of my seat, which unintentionally sends Thad's palm up closer to my hip.

"Thad." Fiadh waves her pamphlet in front of me for his attention.

"If this involves three hamsters, I can't help," he says.

"No rodents. More of an investment question." Fiadh tugs on her fingers.

I squint at her. This woman rarely asks financial questions, and if she needs anything answered, I'm here.

Thad gestures for her to finish her thought.

"How did you know buying the field house was a good investment?" Fiadh asks.

Thad's mouth opens slightly. "I was expecting you to ask my favorite color." He picks up his catalog and fans me with it, cooling down the sweat seeking to peek from my skin.

A spark of excitement blooms in his eyes. "I don't come out looking great in this, but I've never once regretted buying the field house. I'd say it was the most impulsive thing I've ever done."

Most impulsive? We were married quickly. There's a deep comfort in knowing that his decision to marry me wasn't on impulse. Unless he's phrasing it this way to keep our secret. A deep inhale pulls sharp in my lungs.

Thad has our full attention. Screw the auction. What could he possibly have done that could ever make him look bad in anything?

"There's a cocky blond guy that comes in on Thursday nights," he says. "He walks around with a puffed chest at all times."

I nod, picturing the man with the scar down his arm who gives cocky, peaked-in-high-school vibes whenever he walks in. The one who practically ignores Thad unless they're on the field together exchanging aggressive grunts.

"He's Elin's ex-boyfriend, Nate," he says.

"Elin dated that doorknob?" I cover my mouth with my elbow when I realize how loud my response was.

"For far too long." Thad lowers my arm. "He's talented, but the league is built to have fun. If he's not winning, he's kind of a jerk. When he is winning, he's a sore winner. He was always awful to her, and to Hawk. One night I had it with him. We started trash-talking, elbowing each other. Next thing I know, he slides out from the goal, attempting to break my ankle. Literally. No one caught that part but me and the security cameras. He got up, mouthing off in his aggressive way, said an awful thing about Elin, and I knocked him out." He looks down at his feet. "Honestly, I don't know what came over me, but like I'd told Elin, if my sisters were ever with someone who treated them like he did, I'd have it out with them. I went at him like she was one of my sisters. In the dysfunctional family that the league is, she is one of my sisters."

I pull his hand onto my lap, brushing the inside of his wrist with my thumb in comfort. His gaze lands on me. There's a sadness there I've not yet seen.

His chest rises high. "We were called into the owner's office. He did not have the same feelings about the importance of the league and was ready to disband everything. Mainly thanks to Nate, who caused most of the previous owner's headaches and many of mine. My sisters and I already bought the corporate buildings as a family investment but hadn't made a bid on the field house."

"Why didn't you buy the field house with everything else?" I ask. "The investment for the whole property would have made more sense."

"The property was owned by a different person, and the owner held out when the corporate buildings went up. He was like a doughnut hole in the middle of the property. At that point, I was burned out from working a corporate job. I spent all my time scrolling for tips and tricks to find a career that I could be passionate about and wanting to set my laptop on fire every time a spreadsheet came to my inbox." He mindlessly pulls me to sit closer. "The owner knew who I was and made me an offer while Nate sat there with his mouth wide open." He chuckles low. "I went ahead and shook the owner's hand, which meant I bought the place and protected my friends. People there rely on one another. They escape the day jobs they hate and come hang out with me at one I love. My deal was to not tell people, which Nate agreed to if I let him stay in the league. I fake suspended both of us. That secret lasted all of three months before the papers picked up the stories."

His catalyst was his friends. I shift in the dark blue seat, the buckles on my boots banging against the metal leg.

He nods slowly. "If you're asking if you should buy the mill, yes. I think you're going at it from a more levelheaded manner than I did when I bought the field house."

"I don't think you look bad in this story at all. More like a hero," I say. "Was buying it that way honestly the most impulsive thing you've ever done?"

His eyebrows pinch with confusion. Revelation smooths the creases on his face.

"A thousand percent," he confirms.

My heart swoons.

"Had we met before I bought the field house, I don't think you'd have liked me as much. I wasn't so pleased with myself then. I tended to be much quieter. Working in corporate was quickly killing my soul. The field house gives me a sense of purpose and community."

As much as his story was for her, I know it was for me, too. Reinforcement of the importance of living a life that makes me feel fully myself. My loud self who for far too long fell into the comfort of the hug chair night after night to do work.

He takes my hand, shifting it to his lap, refocusing his attention up front. "Everyone deserves joy in their lives. Not everyone is lucky enough to be able to leap at the opportunity when it presents itself. Or has the means or support to make the opportunities happen. I had the means and support. You do, too."

He's talking to Fiadh, but the swell of tears at the ready is nearly impossible for me to fight. He pulls a plain white handkerchief from his front pocket, handing it to me without a word. Because of course he's prepared. I dab at the corner of my eyes, not letting a single tear fall.

Fiadh leans close to me. "Are you okay? Your eyes are leaking."

"I'm proud of you, that's all. These are happy tears." Mixed with stress and the sadness that comes with knowing how much time I've burned over the years. Sitting between the two of them fills me with an indescribable drive to take the leaps they have. To be brave like they are.

Ariana walks out onto the stage, standing behind the podium in a black-on-black pantsuit with a slick neon yellow silk shirt under the jacket. She grabs the gavel, and the quiet woman with the five-foot-one stature, the one who giggles on the bench watching the matches, transforms into a powerhouse with more than five hundred sets of eyes from within this room alone set on her, ready to take in her every word.

"What's your favorite color?" I ask him.

"The deep brown tone of your hair is a close second to the green of your eyes," he says.

A flutter hits my ribs, and I sit taller. The leg bounce is long gone.

"Fuck, that was smooth," Fiadh says. "Keep treating her well. She is long overdue to be treated with kindness."

Ariana smacks a gavel on the front of the podium.

"Let's raise some funds to rehabilitate a piece of New Jersey history with some rare pieces of American pop culture..." She continues. Words fly from her mouth, and numbers fly across the room.

As fast as my brain can do math and process numbers, I'm not keeping up. Thad's got his phone out, and he's punching them in. So is Fiadh. But my mind is elsewhere. I'm at the mill years from now with Thad, having a picnic with Fiadh and Maverick on a random Wednesday morning when I'd normally be teaching before we head to the field house. To grabbing coffee with Fiadh's mom or even Thad's on a Tuesday between interviews.

I shake my head, focusing on the room, the numbers blurring around me. Hours pass in the way seconds usually feel. When Ariana exits the stage, the room is a rumble of people congratulating one another for their purchases. I know the numbers went high, but how high has yet to be announced.

Fiadh sits with her mouth open, tears in her eyes. The numbers on their phones match.

"Take off a cut for the house," I say.

They oblige, punching in the numbers. Air squeezes from my lungs in shock. I knew what the collection was worth, but this exceeded my initial calculations. Could this money help the university? Maybe. But the university isn't either of the people who've invested their everything in me.

"This all goes to the mill," I say, pride blossoming in me.

Thad needs time as his investment, not money. Every imagined scenario of joy I have in the future includes him. My gaze darts between both of their smiles. I gulp down.

CHAPTER TWENTY-SIX

W HY IS IT THAT the older I get, the faster the weeks pass? Fiadh and Mav, from what I can tell, are on the mend. Meanwhile, I've been commandeering Thad's desk at the field each night so I could work while being close to him. We steal kisses between my editing articles and his dealing with the hordes of people who come in and out every day. This man seriously interacts with thousands of people a week in person and treats every single one with kindness. Except for one who gave me bad vibes, also known as Elin's ex. That blond prick was cold to Thad. I wanted to claw the jerk's face—for the arrogance vibes and for what Thad shared about how he treated sweet Elin.

My newest mission is simple. Make sure Thad makes it home each night to our bed and not the futon. Neither of us sleeps alone. Which has worked great until we got out at one o'clock last night and my early call at the television set this morning was seven. He's chilling in the upper booth with the people running the boards that make sound and light work while I'm pounded by the spotlights from above.

I thrive on television interviews. Elation for the day is helping push me ahead, though a little caffeine would make being alert once the cameras are rolling much better.

To kill time, I scroll through a list of numbers on my phone, checking in on my current career standing within my peer group at the university. Academics, much like professional athletes, have stats that mark where we stand among our peers. The projected statistics surrounding my academic life leave few complaints other than the fact that my once rapidly climbing H-index, where an algorithm determines my productivity and citation impact as a researcher, hasn't moved as much as I wanted this year. This is the equivalent of a star soccer player not getting enough playing time to up their stats—their productivity value, as it were, in their field. My stomach sinks. The makeup artist swipes a fluffy powder brush across my forehead to reduce shine.

Without taking my eyes off the stagnant numbers in front of me, I reach over to grab the strategically placed yellow coffee mug filled with iced coffee. The large swig coats my mouth. I take two more long sips and place the drink onto the long white news desk that spans from one side of the set to the other.

After I down roughly a quarter of the mug, my insides race. My heart, given the opportunity, could do a hundred laps around the room without needing to slow down.

I tap my name into the search bar for a general query and watch the number of my social citation stats go up. Too bad these don't count as greatly in my department. Social clout in my department comes with a litany of mixed feelings. On one side, it's great for getting the name of the university out there and helping to add an academic voice to arguments regarding way-too-specific topics. On the other, several people in my own department would like me to stop taking radio and television interviews. They see them as chasing fame rather than adding to the general body of academic knowledge. I happen to like the opportunities I get to teach people on a greater scale. Public television interviews are great, but the university especially likes what happens when I show up to a larger network.

I drag my finger down the screen. Now is not the time to read the comments from under my last interview. I wish a mentor warned me when I started out taking these types of interviews that the comments would eat my confidence. Even if they had, I'd probably have still read them.

The soft brush tickles my nose. I sneeze, sending a mess of powder to rise up into the lights roasting my face. The room is smaller than it looks when I'm at home watching on TV.

"I sneeze every time she brings out that mammoth brush, too." Alexa Letters sits perched high in her chair with a silver plastic cape protecting her outfit.

The makeup artist takes a playful swipe across the bridge of my nose with her softest brush.

"Better to sneeze than to look like I'm sweating buckets." I gently run my fingers across the top of my hair to ensure my ponytail is still smooth.

Alexa's hair is in a straight blond bob. Her gray suit was one of the options I also had to choose from, but rather than opt for the pants, she's wearing orange leggings. Not that anyone can or will see the leggings. I'd feel half-dressed if I'd done similar. Growing up, Granny instilled in me that half of overcoming impostor syndrome is dressing for the part you want people to identify you as. I glance down at the deep gray single-buttoned tailored skirt suit I came in wearing and at my metallic steel-blue nails. Alexa taps her pale pink nails on the long white desk between me and the one and only Brent, my personal academic clout chaser. I should thank him for the hottest date I've ever had. Thanks to him I had that full evening of intellectual foreplay, flirtation, and mouth fucking with Thad. Though there were blips of Brent's overenthusiasm pushing toward uncomfortable during the lecture. He's got to be more chill tonight.

He leans down to fidget with the height of his chair, raising it to be taller than both Alexa and me. This is not starting off well.

"The chairs are preset so we are all the same height," Alexa says.

"Sorry, my knees were hitting a bar under the table," he says. "I'll fix it."

I glance under the table and watch as her feet swing. Maybe Thad is right. Maybe he is a little strange. At least he's reset his chair. I link my heel over the bar near the base of the chair to keep my lower half still.

"Piper, I'm sorry ahead of time," Brent says, his words harried.

A man next to the camera signals a countdown.

"Sorry for what?" I ask.

Five...four...three...two...one. A red light blinks on overhead.

He grimaces and it's too late for an answer. Sorry for what though?

My foot starts tapping, shaking the chair.

"Hello, everyone, and good morning. We have two special guests with us to continue our series on hot topics in the business markets. The topic for debate today was selected and voted on by you, our wonderful viewers." Alexa tilts her chin down, and the monitor on the floor shows she's in a tighter shot.

She drones on, recapping the last few special segments. None of which I was a part of due to scheduling issues. The rule for participating in these segments is that we cannot know the topics ahead of time. There is a forced reliance on what we know. For me this meant prepping each night for hours on end on any and all hot topics that could come up. I concentrated heavily on international trade markets.

"To join our conversation on the market power of education is Professor Piper Yeats on my right and Mr. Brent Gover. For those of you who are new viewers, Dr. Yeats is a professor of economics from right here in New York, and Mr. Gover is a private consultant." Alexa continues to rattle off Brent's accomplishments, forgetting to mention the name of my university.

The topic is a spicy one. I take another gulp of my coffee. I place my hand over the pinch in my heart. My insides speed as if they're on a track going five hundred miles an hour. Every one of my senses sparks awake, and colors are richer despite the bright lights above.

"Please, call me Brent." He folds his hands on the desk and tips a sheepish smile at Alexa.

"Well, Brent," she says while I do my best to not gag.

Should I feel my heartbeat in my tongue? I sip my drink. This isn't nerves. What is this?

"Stop drinking the coffee!" a voice shouts in my earpiece.

I give Alexa a side-eye. She pushes her drink away, and Brent follows suit.

I reach for the cup. Immediately, the voice booms again, "Do not drink the coffee!"

The nearly empty mug's dark liquid looks normal. I take a deep sniff, wrinkling my nose. I place the cup on the table and push it away. That's when my taste buds begin to buzz. My brain switches to hyper-speed, and there's no slowing it down.

"The simple starter question here is about market demand and education. Where do we see the shifts, and what hurdles or advantages do you believe are developing in relation to the current demands relating to obtaining a post-secondary education?" Man, she's talking faster than a direct train to New York.

"There's been a lot of talk lately about higher education and the way it's essentially taken huge portions of the market who would normally go into the trades, which we desperately need, and have created a monetary hurdle..." Brent's speaking very fast, too.

Or my listening skills have sped up everything around me.

"Are you positing that the universities are responsible for this or a shift in the overall mentality on how education itself is viewed?" I ask.

"This is a marketing angle by the universities. They knew there was an untapped market, and they went and created all these majors for students who, rather than going to take on apprenticeships, have opted to get a degree that is driven by the market. The market is creating a surplus, and then people can't get jobs in the field they have a degree in..."

I look around. I'm not engaging in this. I truly cannot. I mean, I can. I know my stuff. I know how all this works. But this is bait and fluff, and I'm not about to be a meme or insult my field.

"Hold on, Brent. I'd really like to know more about why you think the universities are to blame for a shift in market demand. Give me an example." I stifle the rudeness screaming to surface, remaining perfectly pleasant. This is a gentle, happy interview.

"Take the college you work at, for example. You offer courses on ballet, brewing, and cidery. These are not things you have to go to college for," he says. "You can opt to go to college, but it isn't a requirement."

The train whistle explodes in my brain. Why is he acting so different? What happened to gushing Brent? Coming straight for my academic family to throw me off. "The business program

I work under partners with the food sciences program for the brewing and cidery concentrations. We cross-teach chemistry and business to create a well-rounded student, preparing them to create opportunities for themselves. What happens in the food sciences program adds expansion to the general knowledge, where we study things like food safety, the impact of farmers on the production of food on a local, national, and international level. These majors help people."

Brent folds his hands in front of him on the table. His entire attention is on me and not the camera. The third cameraman rushes around the side to get a different angle of us, which flashes on the lower projector.

"You went to college and studied a super-niche field. I'm confused by your hesitation to support the struggling universities who are listening to what their student bodies want," I say.

"Piper, I don't need to disclose my résumé to everyone." Brent's words continue, but they get quiet, thanks to the loud ringing that started when my name came from his lips in a far too saccharine tone. "The fact of the matter is, you and your peers have systematically changed how employment works by leveraging a market shift."

"I'm not completely following," I say with as much sugar as possible despite seeing red from his cloying sweetness or the coffee raging in my system. "My inquiry as to your academic background is to help ground others in the fact that this is a 'do as I say, not as I do' situation you seem to be sharing. If memory serves, you're a Wharton grad. One of the top schools out there for business."

Brent furrows his eyebrows.

"Oh, is that not part of this equation?" I ask. "You go to an elite program, network to enhance your profile, and then tell others they shouldn't?"

"Piper," he says in a manner that's a half step from telling me to calm down.

"I've dedicated most of my life to learning how the market works, writing, publishing, and teaching others."

He shrugs, reaches for the coffee, takes a sip, and spits the hellhound liquid into the cup.

Alexa's smile never leaves her face. I'm not 100 percent sure, but her features look glued in place. "Oh, you two."

Really? That's it? Man, my body could do a full marathon right now in five-inch heels and still manage to run home to Hoboken without needing to get on the subway. What is in the coffee?

"Isn't your life boring if all you've done is dedicate your entire self to books and other people? When do you hang out with friends? Have a life?" Brent's words scream "Asshole," with a capital A. What is this personality he's brought today?

Rage bubbles under my skin, but my practiced classroom *go fuck yourself tone* comes out instead. "Thank you for being so concerned with how I spend my time, Brent." Saying his name sharply is soothing for my head. When I say his name right, it sounds like I'm slapping him with his own name. Brent. Smack. Brent. Smack, smack. "I make time for important people."

He gives me two fast claps. They echo in my ear. Alexa's facade never fades, but Brent's shoulders rise to his ears on each boom. Is Alexa frozen?

The red light goes out. Alexa stands, screams "bathroom," and runs out of the room.

"If either of you two needs to use the bathroom, now's the time. The intern forgot to mix water into the coffee concentrate, so you've each had six to eight cups of coffee in that one cup," the voice from above booms into the room.

"Brent, when did you become a prick?" I ask unapologetically.

"I know. Honestly, we're on the same side on this. But ratings are ratings, and my uncle owns the station. He said I was too excited to be a counter point to you and told me if I wanted to go on air with you I had to go hard in an opposing view. I don't think I'm doing it well." He tugs on his shirtsleeve. "Are you seeing rainbows shooting from the walls?"

"Nope, but I'm certain my insides are doing an Irish jig while I work to sit still." I grip the edge of the table. "Don't ever tell a woman what she's dedicated her life to isn't worthy. If you ever do it to me again, I'll staple your cheap tie to the desk on air."

"Fair." He is staring up at the bright white lights above us. "Do yourself one favor tomorrow. Try not to stare at the numbers on your phone for an entire day. I was watching you before. Not texting friends, not watching silly videos. Staring at your name and a bunch of numbers. I can feel Thad glaring at me from up there."

Caffeine poisoning is worse than having too much of Fiadh's cider. Coffee shouldn't have this power. I peek up and catch Thad's figure in the window high above us, his hands balled into fists at his sides, his intense eyes narrowed on Brent.

"Brad?" I ask. "Can you talk to me in your normal voice and stop coming across as a dick?"

"Brent. And yeah," he says. "There is one commodity we can't get back, no matter how much we track and plan for changes."

"Time," we both say.

Alexa comes back to the desk wearing a set of green leggings. She takes her seat and holds her head.

"Fire the intern," she says. "Or pour the rest of the bottle down their throat. I don't care. I threw up all over my other pants."

Brent shields his eyes. "Is there any chance we can retape this segment?"

Alexa grimaces, stands, and runs from the room again.

"That was live," a producer booms from above us like God.

The man in the booth does a finger countdown, but Alexa's not in her chair yet, leaving me with unpredictable Brent.

"Hello, and thanks for sticking with us tonight. We're continuing our conversation on market shifts as they relate to higher education and the overall impact. I'm Piper Yeats, with Brent, whose last name I can't recall because we've all had way too much caffeine." I wipe sweat from behind my ears.

Alexa comes crashing into the room. Cameras are still rolling, and the air goes dead while she nearly topples from her chair when she goes to sit down.

Brent taps on the desk, and the cameraman swivels the shot to him. He gestures for the camera to go to a wider angle, placing all three of us in the shot.

"Right, where were we?" Alexa shuffles her stack of notes.

"I'd like to reset a bit. I do know firsthand that Piper has friends. That was incredibly rude of me." He gestures to my left hand with my three bands stacked neatly on my ring finger and tilts his head like he's losing himself in thought. "Are you and Thad married?"

Vomit rises in my throat. Dazed, I stare directly into the camera. I grab the coffee from Hades and work to swallow down the remainder in a bad decision to wet my mouth. He outed me on national television. My phone vibrates in my pocket over and over and over. Without needing to take it out, I know what the messages are.

Thad's watching from the upper booth next to the voice from God, his hand over his mouth, his own eyes bugging out behind the giant glass wall separating us. I picture Fiadh smacking my face on the television for an answer.

This isn't how this is supposed to go. "Wow. Yeah, this is not part of the purpose as to why we're here." My heart beats so fast, I can't count the number of times it pounds in fear.

Brent hesitates, his mouth opening and closing. He's caught on that he's fumbled.

"Thad and I are, in fact, married." I will not hurt anyone by lying.

Alexa pukes coffee into the trash can under the desk. The on-air light blinks out.

"Commercials are rolling," the voice from above booms.

"Piper," Thad's voice calls through the same speakers.

I glance up at him, holding in the anger and tears seeking to rip through my eyes.

"Maybe it's better this way? I had to tell her," I say, unsure if the microphone is still hot.

Alexa strokes my hair. "I'd have totally come to the wedding. Was it fantastic?"

"We had a small ceremony in his greenhouse," I say, stunned. This was set to be a simple interview. What happened?

Thad comes through the studio door, heading right to me.

"I'm sorry, man. I saw the rings, and then there was the way you introduced her at the lecture. I've had so much caffeine," Brent says with a whine. "Was it a secret?"

"Yes, and no," Thad says to him. He crouches next to me, cupping my cheeks. "Thank you." He kisses my forehead, and I slump into him for support.

I love you, I say to him in my head, unready to process the words aloud with him. Not wanting to speak them next to a rancid pile of puke.

My throat is sore. Every ounce of me is throbbing with pain. Time slows despite what my heart wants it to do.

"We're friends," Alexa says, a thread of hurt in her voice. "Can I take you two to dinner?"

We both look at her.

"On a night I haven't spent the morning vomiting coffee?" she says. "Piper, you're the best. Seriously, I'm so happy for you."

She wraps her arms around me in a hug. The waft of sick coming toward me unsettles my stomach further. I bend to grab her garbage can and add my own recycled coffee to the bin.

I pull out my phone, scrolling down to see no messages from Fiadh. I blow out a breath of relief. Then comes the dreaded ding. Her name and picture follow.

Fiadh: *You're fucking married.*

Not a question, a statement. A strong statement. I need to get to Fiadh now.

CHAPTER TWENTY-SEVEN

THERE ARE FEW PEOPLE in life I hate with my entire body. Right now, I hate myself for not telling Fiadh about Thad. From the studio to my car is as much of a blur as the day I tried but failed to fully hit the button looking to escape higher ed.

The friend finder app on my phone blinks the route to Fiadh. She's at her apartment in Hoboken. I press my foot down on the gas so the car will travel as fast as my heart.

The phone rings, and her face dances on the screen. I hit ignore.

Her face appears again, smiling, as tan as a pasty redheaded academic who spends most of her life in either the lab or a classroom can be. Only, I know this is not going to be a phone conversation. This is an in-person conversation.

Fiadh's face appears a third time. I hit ignore. This is not how I imagined telling her. I wanted to set up a double date for her and me. To have the conversation with Mav and Thad present. Not anywhere out in public, so it wasn't like I was forcing set manners. If anyone can understand how isolating the rise up in academia can feel, it's her. The pressures, the late nights, the all-consuming burnout trying to hit tenure only to obtain it and immediately face another hurdle to hit the next level of academia. All of which leaves minuscule morsels of time to choose between sleeping and meeting someone.

"Stop staring at me," I say.

Thad bites at his fingernail. "Why won't you answer the phone?"

He is bouncing his leg repeatedly, which is only winding the knot in my sternum tighter. I couldn't leave him at the studio, and I didn't want to lose time by dropping him off, so now I'm headed to Fiadh's apartment while her fuse is fully lit.

Please, please, please let her simply yell at me. Scream. Get all the feelings out. Hell, get my doubts out in the process. I know all the arguments she's going to make. I've had months to compile them in my head in preparation for this exact moment. She has to understand my desire to feel more like I'm living life rather than slowly dying in academia. For goodness' sake, she's got the mill, which takes her half out of academia. Not just half out of academia, but fully with Maverick.

I put her in higher ed. She never needed to work at the university. She followed me there because she's Fiadh, and Fiadh honors her promises. I trapped her in academia, and our little world is near to collapsing, like the damn ceiling in the library. Our agreement was changed by my decisions, and I didn't even talk to her. I didn't give her information or options.

"I need you to stay in the car when we get there. Or you can take my key and go to my apartment." I open the console between us and hand him my spare key. "Fiadh will rain fire on you."

I rest my hand on his leg to stop the bouncing. "Relax. This is my fault. I can handle this. It's not like she and I haven't fought before." Never to this level.

He frowns, like he knows I don't believe myself. Instead of lecturing me or giving me any advice, he pulls my palm to his mouth and presses a kiss of reassurance.

"Your sisters didn't bite off your head," I say. "I can fix this."

"Knowing them, they duked it out with each other before they got to the house." He presses another worried kiss.

We arrive at the apartment. My stupid luck is that there is an open parking spot directly in front of her stoop. I look around, and there's no car coming for me to surrender the spot to so I can buy more time. This city never has parking, yet now, when I need time, there's parking everywhere.

I use her spare key to let myself into the building, then rush up the stairs and right to her apartment. When I go to use the key, the chain is on, and I can't let myself in.

Fiadh is visible through the few inches the door is open, her arms weightless at her sides.

"You're married?" Fiadh doesn't scream or yell. She uses the worst tone in her arsenal, where the words slick out as solid ice forms inside her to protect her heart from an awful bruise.

Only, this time I can't go fight the terrible person who caused this level of hurt for her. I can't distract her with adventure, brunch, or coupon spa days. I've already been fighting that person, and I'm exhausted trying to live in two worlds.

I jiggle the handle, not bothering to hide the tremble of panic on my lips. The fire I want to be in her eyes is gone. Replaced by indifference. We're better if we yell this out, if we argue. I know this version of her. I've seen it before. This is where, rather than fire, she turns everything off.

She walks to the door, shuts it, and slides the chain off. When she opens the door, I'm greeted with the face you'd give a stranger. There's no warmth. My heart cracks.

"In the past few months you've kept secrets from me about your job, and now this? What do you think friendship is? If you aren't going to tell me, the person who knows you more than anyone in the world, that you're struggling from pressure you've put on yourself. Or even better, rushed off to get married, the only person you are trusting is yourself." The flatness of the words is distancing.

"That's not what the wedding was about," I say, stumbling while I combat the sting in my sinuses. "I didn't tell you because you were hurting. You didn't need my hurt."

"We lean on each other. That is how friendships work. There's a back-and-forth of support. But there are times when both friends need each other at the same time. I'd never keep anything so big from you." Fiadh adjusts her jaw. "I don't even care that you ran off and got married! That's romantic and spontaneous. I care that I didn't find out from you. That I found out accidentally from a stranger on national television. You don't want me in your world unless it's to come fix me. To swoop in and—" She cuts herself off. "I'm happy for you and hope you have the most wonderful life ever. But it's clear I'm not the person you need anymore when your world is spinning off-kilter. That's fine. If you let Thad in to take care of you when you need it, even better."

"That's not fair. We all deal with shit differently. I didn't want to burden you with my mess." I give up fighting tears and let them flow.

"Mess?" She touches her heart. "What mess? I'm here for all of it. For celebrating, for crying, for looking at dresses you may or may not want. For being the arm to help you walk up the aisle even though you think the tradition is stupid. I know you don't think it's stupid, but it's easier to not face the emotions it drags up than to see you have people right here ready to help you through the rawness."

The words don't stop flowing from her, one thought colliding into the next. "I cried on my couch. We drunk registered for shit, and the entire time you were hurting. Before I even lost the grant or my ex, you were struggling and said nothing. I'm an awful human who didn't know my best friend was hurting." There's a tremble in her tone, only instead of the fight coming through, the words grow more and more lifeless. "I'd have been the first to shout congratulations. There's never been a hesitation on my part as to the importance of our friendship. I'm not sure what I did to deserve the hesitation from you."

My gut grows pointy spikes that scrape at my skin.

"I saw you happy, and I wanted happiness," I say. "I needed to feel again."

She stares at me, her face softening, but this is her fake politeness. Her clear sign that I'm not currently wanted or tolerated.

"You're willing to end thirty years of friendship over this?" I know the answer.

"We'll still be business partners—that is, until I can repay you for your investment in the mill." That was the last punch she had.

I cross my arms, digging my fingers into my elbows to steady myself. "Let me be clear. In no way would I ever want you to repay me for the mill. I did that out of love, friendship, and faith in my best friend."

"Bullshit," she says. "From where I'm standing, it's more like you felt guilty and spent money on me to make yourself feel better. I'll see the lawyer and have the paperwork sent over."

I was wrong. That was a worse stab. The money for the mill was because she deserves the mill, and why have money if you can't use it to make wonderful things happen for good people? "I care about the mill."

She presses her tongue between her teeth. "I'd have found a way to pay for it."

"Not soon enough." I fling my hand over my mouth, wishing to push the words back in.

"I'm not an idiot. I read the same information on the university as you, but you can't spend your whole life protecting me and not letting me be there for your moments too." She grips her hips until her knuckles turn white. "Do you know what would happen if the university shut down and I couldn't teach?"

I shake my head, knowing this is rhetorical.

She raises her hand at me. "For me, friendship must go two ways, and you mentally shut down when the tables are switched and I try to take care of you. You have to accept help at some point, or you're going to die alone. There were people ready and waiting to lift your ass out of a bouncy chapel, our hearts ripping in pieces until we knew you were going to be okay. I had to wait until you were unconscious to be able to help you. I'm not an obligation to take care of. I'm a person who knows every piece of you."

My body aches, the pain growing worse. This is a much worse reaction than I could have imagined. "Fiadh, you upheld a childhood promise to take care of me. I've only ever wanted to repay that."

"Where's Thad?" she asks, in the first gentle tone she's given me all night.

I swallow at the glass in my throat. "Downstairs."

"Did he offer to come up and talk too?" she asks.

I say nothing.

"You couldn't even let him help you," she says.

"I...I thought it'd be better..." I stumble on the words.

"No. You turned away another person who cares for you deeply and was looking to help you," she says. "Bye, Piper."

She shuts the door, shredding my insides. Heavy sobs pour from me, and in harmony from the other side of her door.

I pull out my phone and stare down through my tears to pull up Thad's name. The heart that'd cracked earlier is now ripped apart, floating inside my body.

Tears drip down on the screen. Being cut off by Fiadh is worse than a breakup. She's stubborn as hell.

Me: *She's done talking to me.*

Thad: *I'll wait here until you're ready.*

So would Fiadh before tonight. How long until I screw things up with him, too? Until I say or do the wrong thing? Until I'm too determined to take care of myself, even when my body has been falling apart from the decisions I've been making.

Me: *I need a minute.*

That ache of seared friendship is nothing compared to the acid in my stomach if Thad leaves, too. Moving hurts. Thinking hurts. I lean against the wall for support. On each step away from Fiadh, I have to pretend, out of respect for her shut door, that she isn't sobbing.

Me: *Raspberry macaroon*

CHAPTER TWENTY-EIGHT

F IADH IS EXCRUCIATINGLY MIA. Ten days of silence is agony after talking every day, even if it's just a few quick texts. I long for the steadiness she brings to my life deep in my bones each time I pick up my phone. Waiting on our bench with my tablet is a cheat in a way. Like, I'm here, waiting for her to see me. To come hug me and watch the people work their sailboats up the Hudson River.

Except it's the second week of the fall semester, and I'd normally be in my office prepping to teach, but I'm not. Worse, it's not clear whether the nagging in my stomach is because I miss being on campus, or if it's Fiadh's texts my body is mourning. Fiadh's probably busy at the mill, leaving my camping out on our bench even more pointless.

I tap the screen of my tablet, clicking open a blank document with my stylus. Pigeons land around my feet, then march over to the next bench when they correctly sense a lack of sharable food. The few trees around give enough shade that I won't turn into a pink lady apple. Early September is the best time of year.

The temperature is warm, but I'm not sweating and gross. A soft breeze pushes small caps on the waves not ten feet away. I love this city and everything it's given me.

I scribble a header on the top center of the screen: Healthy Decisions. "Healthy" isn't the right word. Staring at the page doesn't fill it in any, but then again, I'm not ready to tackle hard decisions.

My phone buzzes. Thad's face glows on the screen.

Thad: *Hey beautiful. I have a few more hours of maintenance to do—how does dinner in the greenhouse tonight sound?*

Perfect. I glance across the street at the Greek restaurant.

Me: *I'll pick up food since you're working.*

Him: *I have ten dollars that says you're working too.*

Me: *I'll put the money toward dinner. Be safe.*

Happiness rains down on me. I write Thad's name in the center of my tablet, circling it twice. I add Fiadh's name and circle hers twice. The computer adjusts my script to text, dropping the swished circles and bolding the names instead. Fiadh's name nearly pulses on my screen. I rub at my eyes to get my brain to stop focusing too much on how mad she is right now.

"Piper?" a woman's deep but familiar voice asks.

I turn around to find Antonia leaning to the right, crouch walking toward me. She squints, stands up straight, and lengthens her stride to close the distance between us.

"What were you going to do if it wasn't me?" I ask, genuinely happy to see her.

"Sit down, pretend I knew you, and chat for so long that you started to think you did know me and got frustrated that you couldn't place where from." Her hands wave with every part of her story. "But it is you, which makes this day better."

Suspicion creeps up my spine. "Did Thad send you?"

She places her hand over her heart. "No, ma'am. I came to see Nico."

"Come again?" I ask. "Nico? Like bartender Nico?"

"Is there any other?" Antonia takes the seat next to me, scooting to sit close.

"If I recall correctly, his father, his nephew, and a bunch of other family members of his share the name." I tap the stylus on the edge of the screen.

She peers down, her eyes scanning the barely filled out attempt to descramble my thoughts. "Yeah...we...he...I..."

"Oh, I love him! Hold on. Did you two go on a date?" I fold the screen face down onto my stomach.

"No. No. I don't have time to date right now. I met him after I left your apartment. I was so hungry after my shift, and once we knew you were okay, I went in and ordered half the menu." She shifts her attention from Nico's bar to the waterfront. "He texted me and let me know I'd left a book there. I figured I'd take a drive out on my day off."

"I call bullshit. You got his number after trying all of his food. You came to see him, not to pick up a book you could replace. I could have gotten you the book." This is nice. Joking, teasing with a friend. Not that she's anything like Fiadh, but I'm adding her to the positives on my list. When she isn't here to see it or ask questions. We could be good friends; I can see this happening.

"How obvious is it? I thought the story was good." She tugs down on the sleeves of her yellow blouse; her white pants have fresh crease marks on the front. She dressed up for this.

"You've been out here how many times since forgetting the book?" I ask.

"Four. I sit at the corner of the bar not bothering anyone, and he comes over to chat during the lulls." She lets out a dreamy sigh.

Her crush is sweet. I point to the growing grin on my face. This is amazing. Nico is a great guy. His parents would throw a parade if they met her.

"Sounds like it's time to go on a date not in the bar," I say.

Her attention shifts from the city up to the puffy clouds. "I'm a little traditional there. I'm making ninety percent of the driving effort, but I want him to ask me. What if he's just being polite, talking to me since I'm there solo?"

"He's not. Nico's pretty up front about who he engages with. I vote try. Worst case, I throw him out and get a new tenant."

She snaps her focus to me. "I know you're kidding, but I love you anyway."

"Yeah, I'm not kicking him out. He's nice. Pays rent on time. And I love their food too much."

She lifts her phone up, the screen facing us. "Get in. I'm sending a picture to Thad."

She slings her arm around me, and at the last second I stick out my tongue. She presses the button on the screen mid huge silent laugh.

"Next time tell me. I look like I'm about to eat your head in this shot," she says.

Only, the picture is perfect. The historical brick architecture behind us, natural light filling in all the right parts of our features making us glow. Her skin glows anyway, but when she smiles—the way I'm smiling here...When did the life come back to my face? I recognize the woman in the photo, a much older version than when I was a kid, but she's still there. Strands of gray I didn't have as a kid, invisible baggage neatly tucked away under the metal bench. I like her, even with all the seriousness life forces down my throat, this is who I am.

"Can you send me that, too?" I ask.

She punches out a text and hits send. I get a ding on my phone. She didn't simply send it to me. She sent it to Thad, to her sisters, to her parents. One huge family group chat that I'm in.

Antonia: *Look at this hottie I found in the park. Told you all I'm the favorite sister.*

My phone explodes with messages.

Thad: *Is today a vitamin D day? Great idea.*

Isabella: *I don't want to hear about your D.*

Isabella: *Piper, how do I get a day with you! I call six Tuesdays from now.*

Thad: *That's so specific. Also, I've already called it.*

Mama-in-Law: *I'm calling six Tuesdays from now family dinner at our house.*

Gianna: *What the hell! Where's my invitation? Where are you?*

Mama-in-Law: *Gianna, don't say hell.*

Gianna: *Sorry, Mama.*

We turn so the city skyline is behind us and snap a less silly picture, the frame of the buildings saying tourist rather than local. She proceeds to send the text.

Gianna: *There, I fixed it.*

A picture comes in from Gianna with her head on Antonia's body.

Lucia: *Dad's grumbling that six weeks is too long, but he won't text it.*

Mama-in-law: *Fine, how about three Tuesdays from now?*

Thad: *Piper and I will take a look tonight at our calendars. Love you all.*

Did he type *love you all*? To everyone? A deep beat hits my heart.

More pings come in on my phone, but I slide it into my bag.

"So, why are you really out here?" Antonia slides closer, showing no signs of leaving anytime soon. Not that I want her to, but I do need to figure out what to keep or cut from my life. She gestures to my tablet.

"I am stuck." I flip the screen up to show her. "I came out here to figure out what I want, what makes me happy, what I need to do in life. Where I'm spending too much time or where I'm letting people down."

"That's heavy business before noon," she says, her tone changing to serious.

"I want to be a good wife," I say.

"You are, and you will be. But what does that mean to you, a good wife? Do you want to be a good *wife* or a good partner to Thad?" she asks.

A dull pulse emanates deep in my bones. "I can't be a good wife if I'm falling down from exhaustion and he has to take care of me."

"Married couples help take care of each other," she says.

"I get that, but when the spring semester comes, I don't know if it's possible to give him what he needs. I don't want him sleeping at the field house." Emotion rips through my words, and I wrestle tears away.

"What's the fear? That he'll leave you because you're busy?" she asks. "He won't."

"That he'll leave me because he's lonely," I say so quietly, I'm not sure if she heard.

She sits there silently. We watch as a sailboat makes its way well past us.

"My brother is many things, and lonely was one of them until he met you," she says. "I'm not trying to put pressure on you in any direction, but know that I can see the difference in him. He's playful again. His head is held higher, and his confidence is back. I attribute all of that to you. That is why I really want us to be friends. Because I don't know how else to show you how grateful I am that you're part of us."

I wipe at the water now leaking down my face.

"Oh no. I shouldn't have said…" She takes her thumb and wipes my tears.

"That's the thing. This summer…despite working less, not once did I feel lonely. Even though my best friend currently hates me and the world is hard because I really do suck in many ways…I can't describe it quite right. It's like my insides are matching the outside more. But I'm still being held down by pressures that want to cuff me to the floor."

I scribble those pressures onto the tablet. The university, my properties, consulting, and every other thing I kept myself busy with to avoid seeing how small my life was. Antonia doesn't ask questions, doesn't add anything to the form. She sits with me, watching the river. She doesn't touch her phone; she doesn't move a muscle other than a quiver on her chin.

I circle Thad's and Fiadh's names, the centers of my universe for different reasons. I circle the interviews, the properties, and when I get to the university and the consulting work, I hesitate. Blood rushes to my ears, and my hearing grows dull.

"What happens if he comes to the conclusion that rushing to marry me was a mistake?" I ask.

"We dump his body in the Hudson," she says without missing a beat.

I tap the end of the stylus against my lip. "Or not."

"I didn't say he was dead, but the water would be a good wake-up call," she says. "I'm telling you, my brother worships you. Where is this doubt coming from? Because doubt is an evil that needs to be kicked out."

I appreciate her sentiment. Truly, I do. But if he left me because he found the person for him, not the quick impulse where we ran off to get married, I'd need to let him. That's what you do when you've fallen for a person. You let them do what makes them happy.

The options on the screen are still to circle everything or figure out what to cut. Antonia's already made a house call when I was pushing too hard. Returning to the classroom for the spring will require having her on speed dial. The bench starts spinning, but I'm not really moving. I close my eyes, gripping the tablet and waiting for the movement to stop. The spinning has to stop.

My phone dings. I take it back out of my bag and click it open, but I can't focus on the words.

Antonia puts her arm around me, holding me up, and reads the message to me.

"It's from Hawk to you and Thad. He wants to know if you two can hang out tomorrow at six, and according to this, it's super important," she reads. "The next message says this cannot wait."

What could be so important?

"Don't reply." I press my hand flat over my eyes to relax my eyelids. "I need to talk to Thad first."

"I'm driving you to the field house," she says.

"I'm fine. Go see Nico." This is the bouncy chapel all over again without the blacking out.

"Come on, give me the tablet. Your head needs a break."

I oblige because I don't have any other choice right now. Antonia is right. This tornado of emotions is my body screaming at me to make decisions. Warning shots from my body on my stress level are simply unfair. More unfair is that this is twice now that she's had to help take care of me. Hawk's message plays through my head again. What could possibly be so important that he can't text us about it?

CHAPTER TWENTY-NINE

THAD PACES BETWEEN HIS door and the couch. Hawk's not late, but the suspense of the vague *we need to talk* message he sent has done nothing but stretch my nerves so thin, they're ready to snap. "Super important" should be immediate, not at six the next day.

I sit crisscross on the couch, a soft pillow in my lap, my knees bouncing. The bouncing hasn't disappeared since the television studio. In fact, it's gotten steadily worse over the past few days. "Knowing Hawk, he could come tell us he bought the house next door."

Thad bites at his nail. "There's no way they snuck into the house next door. We'd have heard him."

"He could have stubbed his toe and wants to show you his nail is falling off," I offer.

"He would have sent a picture." Thad feigns a shiver.

The door swings open without a knock, and Hawk immediately joins Thad's pacing. Elin sinks into the white chair in the corner, studying the artwork from my closet that Thad has hung on the far wall, replacing his oil painting.

The two men wear nearly identical burgundy athletic pants topped with a pale gray undershirt.

My stomach churns.

"You're both going to run a hole in the floor if you keep pacing, and Elin's face is a shade of vomit green." I press my elbows into my knees to fight my nerves. "What is going on?"

Hawk tugs at his ear. "I'm sorry, man. This is my fault." His typical overly confident self is gone.

Elin stands from the chair, joining the weird circle pattern of the other two but in reverse. The standard bounce of her ponytail is gone, replaced with purposeful steps.

"Enough. All of you sit down," I command in my lecture-hall voice.

Hawk and Elin drop down immediately to sit, legs stretched in front of them.

"You're not married!" Hawk shrieks.

The room slows. The punch to my heart comes close to exploding all the emotions I've kept trapped. I'm not relieved or mad. I suddenly feel an awful emptiness on my ring finger. I catch Hawk's gaze. His watery eyes and pale complexion rival Elin's.

"Oh...Oh...I...I...I..." There are too many words crashing against one another to respond.

Thad sits on the edge of the coffee table. Then stands. He finally sits one more time.

My body has forgotten how to function. How to think or swallow. In short, my brain is looking to protect my heart by killing me with the textural equivalent of a mouthful of desert sand.

I cough until tears fill my eyes. The room disappears. Footsteps thunk across the floor in a flurry. A cold glass is handed to me. There's no ridding the grit from my mouth. I'm not married to Thad. As a cherry on top, the coughing and tears are accompanied by snot.

I suck in a huge mouthful of air, choking down sharpness.

Hawk heaves a huge sigh. "You're okay. Please nod that you are okay. I can't fuck up and kill Thad's not-wife but should-be-wife all in the same day. I'm one hundred percent certain that despite how chill he is, Elin would very quickly be a widow should that occur."

"I'm not dying." I am, but not in the literal sense. I grimace and place the cool glass against my heart.

"We're so sorry," Elin says.

"*We* nothing," Hawk says. "Elin had zero to do with this. I did this."

The room comes further into focus. All three of them are hunched in front of me, our faces less than a foot apart each. I settle into the deep couch. Elin plunks herself into the open seat on my right.

Thad's keeping his distance? Why? The ache in my body is excruciating, and breathing makes everything worse. I need to touch his skin to calm my head. I need him.

Hawk gets on his knees between the three of us. "The whole day of your wedding was a blur. I sat and did the online training for three hours. I filled out all the paperwork. I ran and got a certified check. Then I went to the library and signed the document in front of a notary. I put everything in my bag. After the wedding, I took the...I'm so sorry." His words come out faster with each sentence, and he's nearly shrieking like his namesake. The crack in his voice is drenched in apology.

"Finish the story." Thad keeps rubbing his palms from his thighs to his knees.

I cover my mouth with my hand to help hide any facial expressions ready to burst through.

"I gave my intern two envelopes. One had the certification to perform the marriages, and the other had the actual marriage certificate signed and dated." Hawk looks at his wife. His breath steadies. "The documents were switched. The ordination company emailed me to let me know they had the wrong documents. I called the municipality registrar, and they confirmed receiving an envelope without the marriage certificate enclosed."

"If the documents exist"—the words fall slowly from my mouth—"Thad and I are still married."

"There's a catch. There was a time frame to get the documents in for me to be a legal officiant. Too much time has passed." Hawk grabs Thad's hand and then one of mine. "We can redo everything right now. They told me they can approve me as soon as they get the proper paperwork."

The gears in my head thunk with each slow-to-develop thought. "Or, this is the clear sign we weren't supposed to be married."

Thad runs his hand over his mouth.

"That's it, isn't it, Thad? This is like a small horrible gift to the two of us to determine the next step. You married me to fight being lonely, but you deserve more than a pulse in the house. The first time I decide to live and go with my heart, and the universe—"

"Hawk's intern," Elin says.

Hawk throws his arms open. "Please forgive me. I'll name our first kid after Thad. This is all fixable. You two belong together. I realize I sound ridiculous, but, Piper, for you and Thad it was never going to matter how fast or slow you got married. All that matters is that you are together. I've known him for so long. He has always been one of the best people I know. But as soon as you two met, there was this extra spark of life in him. Like the one Elin gives me."

The only spark I'm seeing is the red burst of a warning firework booming in my head. Thad didn't correct the loneliness statement either. A dark hole begins to sit where the orb once did.

"The past few months weren't the standard me. I don't give away myself or my time to people I've barely met. Let alone fall in love with a man the minute he touches my aching finger."

"Piper, you're more than a heartbeat here. You're *the* heartbeat. I'd never marry a person I wasn't sure about." Thad's voice comes out strangled.

"There's a difference between sure about and love." The door to exit grows farther from me. "I need to go home." I need Fiadh—now.

Thad slumps. "You are home." There's no fight in his voice. No stomp or urgency. He must be relieved...which makes me an ass.

I cross the room, but before I can grab for the door handle, Thad rushes past me in the most out-of-character-for-him manner I've seen, blocking the knob.

"Piper, stay. This is a clerical error. We can fix it immediately. Hawk will fix this." He's practically panting out the words like his heart's twisting inside.

"Hawk will fix this," I say. "We did—I did all of this wrong. Running from emotions, filling my time to refuse to acknowledge why I'm a workaholic. Why you're a workaholic. We're two fucking amazing lonely people the universe smashed together at the right time for the right reasons."

Thad's face pales.

"I love you." I place my palm flat on his chest, taking in the raceway his heart is on.

"Look, I don't know what I did right in my life that the universe made me so lucky to bring you to me, or why. But I'm not going to fall back and let you walk away without you knowing how other people see you. How I see you." His lips quiver. "I refuse to be the guy who doesn't seize happiness when it's right in front of him, especially when it involves you. I will forever be struck by the life you breathe into every situation. That you put yourself, your positivity, your soul…everything for everyone around you, until your body cannot give anymore." He presses his lips together, the internal battle he's raging showing in the concentration creases on his forehead. "What I want, what you deserve, is for people to do the same for you. Let me do those things for you. I'd be the happiest man in the world if I could spend forever showing you how amazing you are. Being there to help when you need help and support when you're ready to fall down. To celebrate with you. I want all the pieces and all the emotions with you."

My soul aches in a way I didn't know was possible. This is pain, but a sweet pain. Not hurt or anger, but a rawness like I've been read from the inside out.

"I'm your wife," I say. His chest relaxes against my touch. "Or, I will be in two weeks. You'd better be ready to pick me up when I fall down, because I'm going to throw you over my back and carry you when you do the same. However, I fucked up with Fiadh, and we fucked up by not including our families. Hawk did us a favor."

Thad's voice booms through the whole house. "Hawk did us no favors."

A whimper comes from Hawk. "I'm right here. I'm sorry. Tell me how to fix this."

I turn on my heel, walking to Hawk. I squat like I'm talking to a wounded animal. Cautiously, with a thick sweetness to lower their defenses.

"You have two weeks to put together a wedding. The entire thing—only the wedding needs to be what you think of when you think of Thad and me. This means you and Elin need to work with Fiadh, but I need to get to her first." The synapses in my brain are firing too fast to let doubt creep in. Fiadh will be at my wedding. I will be the bride she and I both know I was avoiding. My real wedding. "From there, you three are in charge of making sure Thad and I have the most amazing wedding possible. No huge crowds of people. I want people who know us, love us, and want to celebrate as lively as possible."

"I can do this." The speed at which Hawk agrees adds to my confidence.

"What can I do?" Thad asks, drawing my attention to his puffed chest.

"Decide whether I am who you truly want. Not in a heated moment or some obligation to the romanticized version of what you thought marriage would be. Or because you don't want to be lonely. You've known me a short while, but think through what being married to me will be like and whether you can do that for forever. In two weeks, we meet here." My heart beats faster with unease.

Thad crosses the room to me, leans down, and scoops me up off the ground in the same manner he brought me into the house the first night we weren't actually married. My feet are no longer touching the ground. His firm chest is distracting me, making everything fuzzy.

"Let me be clear," Thad says. "I want to marry you. Until I met you, I didn't know love at first sight could be a thing. I had no idea how explosive finding the right person could feel."

"You make falling in love sound like diarrhea," Elin says, breaking into the moment perfectly.

"I don't like that she's very right." I shrug, settling lower in his hold.

He walks me to the couch, gently placing me next to Hawk like I'm a porcelain doll he's afraid to crack. Hawk's biting his knuckle. His knees are bouncing away.

"Hawk's going to explode all over himself if he doesn't get to talk," Thad says.

"Give me two weeks. I will plan the ultimate wedding, one that says 'Thad and Piper love the hell out of each other.'" He bites his knuckle again.

"I'll ask again: How can I help other than rein in Hawk?" Thad asks.

"Don't rein him in," I say.

Hawk *squees* as if he's won the largest trophy for soccer in his life, or received a Nobel.

Fiadh will rein him in.

"I'm going to buy a dress and a ring for you. I will also let Fiadh know how much I love her ass and that if she doesn't come, it will be like she's pouring gasoline in my veins and lighting a match." Their faces are painted with horror, but Fiadh will appreciate the drama. "She's not going to light me on fire." I cross my arms over my stomach.

"Thank you for screwing up," I say.

Thad cups my hands. He runs his ring finger up and down mine, settling the drumming in my ears. Fiadh could blatantly tell me to fuck off. She may not be ready in two weeks to talk yet. I wouldn't blame her.

"I'll need to be in my apartment for two weeks, to reverse time to before we got married," I say.

Thad keeps rubbing at the spot where a ring should be. "I will happily do whatever helps you two." He leans close to my ear. "Not touching you for two weeks is going to be sheer torture." His soft touch travels up the raised hairs on my arm.

A surge of my old, more confident self rushes over me. There's time for a quick orgasm if we disappear now. I glance at Hawk and Elin, who do not look like they're going anywhere. I'll need to pick up batteries on the way home if I have to go two weeks without his fingers igniting my body or his mouth on my lips. I shift my legs.

I brush my lips to his cheek, offering only a soft, sweet kiss. If he has half the inner wobbles I do, he'll be enjoying himself tonight. I close my eyes, imagining his strong hand peeling off his chinos, removing his boxers, and lying in his bed while he recalls each of the places he's touched me. I open my eyes quickly to dispel the images.

"I need to find Fiadh." I stand, my legs still wobbly and my chest hot with the desire to drag Thad to our bedroom to make him moan. I shake my head, hoping to find a different train of thought to latch on to.

Thad carries me to the door, he opens it, and we go outside. Once across the threshold, he slams the door behind us and places me down, turning me fast so that my back presses flat against the wood. He kisses my mouth, and I am ravenous.

He lifts me up, carting me to the far side of my car, hidden by the darkness of the trees.

"If we're going two weeks, I want to make you remember what you're coming home to," he says. Mr. Quiet, Mr. Letting Things Happen as They Do, grabs me by my waist to pull me tighter. He runs his fingers up the front of my shirt, over the silk of my bra.

I struggle to keep in a moan. "Are you finally telling me what you want?"

"I told you inside." He dips his mouth against the front of my neck, sucking lightly, sending the energy in me to my center. "I've told you the whole time. But now I feel like you need a demonstration."

He pushes his hands down between the two of us, over my center.

"Tell me, is this a panties or no-panties night?" he asks.

I'm not sure where this version of him came from, but the determination is hot. "I'm completely up for being claimed right now."

He moves my hand over his hardness, inviting me to touch him further. I tug down his pants, freeing his stiffness from the sweatpants. He pushes my ass up higher, unzipping my shorts, encouraging them to fall to the ground. I start to rock toward him, seeking friction of any kind. His tongue traces a line from my ear down the side of my throat, and I grip his cock tight in my hand.

"I need this in me. No extra foreplay, no stalling, I want this."

"I can run in and get a condom." He lifts my right leg high on him, opening me to him.

"I'm on the pill. I'm clean." I need this—him.

His left arm slides under my other leg, pinning me against my car. His hips buck up, finding my wetness, sliding his full length inside me. His swiftness causes my breath to hitch. His eyes lock into mine, and we stay this way through every thrust he gives me. If I move, I'll fall immediately. I'll lose the friction, the pleasure. He'll lose the pleasure, the control.

Sweat pricks my skin. His groan grows heavier. Letting go and trusting him were the best decisions I've made. My wrists tremble against his shoulders, and he pushes me higher, higher. My voice hitches mid-moan. Tonight, the night we talked wrapped up in the net at the soccer field, our secret not-so-secret wedding. What he said inside is true. He's been here the whole time. Only his support has been quiet, letting me figure myself out.

"Piper, you feel better than anything I had in my dreams." His urgency shifts from hunger to a slower rhythm, where each slow push in from him adds an intensity I've never felt before. He's taking his time, slowing down.

"Are you okay?" he asks, his eyes studying mine.

Each movement of his away from filling the void in me leaves me anxious to have him inside me again.

I tip my chin up, and groan, "yes." My insides flash hot. A gradual wave of ecstasy gathers, spreading through me until my body shakes around him, tensing before a final wave of pleasure surges. He pauses, watching my face.

"I'm so lucky," he says.

"Me too," I say, taking his mouth in mine.

He slides out of me and lowers my legs carefully to the ground.

I go to grab for him, to finish him, and he withdraws.

"I already came," he says, so quietly I swear the wind took the words. "I'm sorry. It was so fast, and so hot, and not at all how I imagined we'd do this the first time."

He hides behind his fingers. I kiss each one, helping him slide up his sweatpants so he doesn't go inside with a bare ass.

"I don't know if I'll make it two weeks in a bed alone," I say, a heaviness settling on me while I picture the futon in his office.

"One night," he says. "Two nights. Tonight and the night before the wedding. Otherwise, I'll sleep wherever you want. But two weeks of not being close to you is unnecessary torture."

"Oh, thank you. Two weeks really was an awful idea." I breathe a soft sigh. He's dreamy, and mine.

Two figures walk past the illuminated sheers in his living room. I bury my face in his chest.

"They didn't see anything," he says.

"You're going inside disheveled," I say. "They're going to know."

"Who cares?" He leans his forehead against mine. "I'm going to selfishly keep you here all night if you let me, but you need to get to Fiadh. Call me, text me, or take whatever time you need tonight. But I'm here. For anything."

He walks me around to the driver's door of my car, opens it, and slides me into the seat.

My lungs are sore. Fiadh may not open the door. She may have changed her locks. She may flatly say no to my begging her to forgive me. I need her in my life as much as I need him. Hopefully, she still wants me in hers.

CHAPTER THIRTY

"**F**IADH!" I KNOCK UNTIL my knuckles hurt, then keep knocking. I peek around the front door of Maverick's cabin. She's in there, sitting on the couch, pretending to not hear me. "Bestie, open the door, please."

Gravel crunches behind me. I turn to find Maverick coming up to the door accompanied by his massive Irish wolfhound, Brendan. The dog noses at my leg for a scratch.

"Did you try turning the handle?" Maverick raises his eyebrows at me. "We have an open-door policy for you."

"No, we do not." Fiadh's face is painted with a straight-up unnerving glower at my presence.

This is fair. It's not even six thirty in the morning, I'm unannounced, and she still hates me. Thankfully, she hasn't pushed the door shut in my face. I follow Brendan and Maverick inside. Brendan leads me to the couch, taking a place next to Fiadh.

She kicks her legs across the empty seat. "Sorry. Sitting is reserved for nontraitors."

Throw the feelings out there. This is Fiadh. She will come around.

Inside my chest it's like a stranger's hand is forcing my organs to function. Discomfort travels throughout my body. I sit over her legs, careful not to squash them, but trapping them under mine so she will have to sit and listen.

"How much cider have you made the past few weeks?" I ask with all the confidence I psyched myself up with on the ride here after she wasn't at her apartment. I netted zero sleep in the Hoboken apartment, not wanting to show up here at midnight last night. She smartly had her phone off, which meant I had no way to use the friend finder app until this morning, when she turned her phone back on. Her avatar flashed in invitation, screaming at me to press down on the gas. Maverick wouldn't confirm via text that she was here, making it super obvious she was.

"None," she says. Her glassy eyes aren't making contact with mine.

Maverick gives a soft harrumph. He cuts across the living room to the kitchen, giving us space in the one-room building. I catch him eyeing the door.

"Thad and I aren't married." Tears pour out alongside the words.

Her knees snap up, knocking into me. "I'll kill him." Fiadh's whiplash of emotions went straight to protective. "I'll murder him, bury him on the farm, and everything will be fine."

Maverick drops a cup in the kitchen. The metal hits the floor with a hard clank before rolling about. He pulls three metal camping cups from the cabinet, then proceeds to fill them with water from the sink.

"Shouldn't you find out what happened before you offer to kill off Thad?" Maverick asks.

"No," Fiadh says without hesitation. "Because I know Piper, and she wouldn't do anything stupid in a relationship. Except the bullshit of not telling me she was getting married and that she is essentially on a mental health break from work."

Maverick brings the waters to us, keeping the third one for himself. He sits on his massive desk, close enough to join our conversation but far enough to not be intrusive.

I sip at the water. "Thad didn't screw up anything. I did. I fucked up by not telling you immediately I was getting married and very wrongly inferring what you needed."

"Then you are married?" Her lip twitches.

"No, Thad and I are not married," I say. "Hawk screwed up the paperwork, so the ceremony he performed is not legal."

Fiadh holds the cup in front of her mouth, hiding her typically emotional billboard of a face. "Are you relieved?"

"Yes, but not for the reason you're thinking." I clear my throat. "We're getting married in two weeks. There are some preferences I spelled out I wanted if we were going to get married, get remarried, get married for real...I don't know what to call what's happening."

"I'm not coming," Fiadh says, digging a stake into my heart.

Maverick leans in, but instead of speaking, he takes an exaggerated slurp of water. If he were going to talk, this would have been the right time to help me out here.

"You're mad. I get it, but I need you by my side at the wedding." There has to be a way to fix this. I drum my fingernails on my cup.

"Let her pick out your dress," Maverick says.

Now? Now he wants to chime in? I clench my stomach. Fiadh and I do not have the same style. Never mind that two weeks is nowhere near enough time to pick out a dress.

An evil grin creeps up Fiadh's face, and I do not like one bit of the wickedness spreading. She stretches long under me.

"Let me help you by picking out your dress," she says. "And admit aloud the parts you haven't said yet. The feelings."

I take my own extended drink. "I'm going to wear the same—"

"There is no same here. I wasn't there. There is no same. You deserve a wedding dress. I want to see you as a blushing bride. A wedding isn't a checkbox and move forward to the next piece of your life. A wedding is where you stand with the people who love the snot out of you and then promise yourself to the person you cannot imagine your life without. Then I remind the person I will bury them in a field at the mill if he ever hurts you." There's my determined best friend. "We are going dress shopping, and I will put you in every dress imaginable until we find the one that says I'm tough as nails and deserve the world.

I'm buying the dress, and you will wear it. No matter what shade of puce I find."

Maverick's face twists in disgust. Tears of happiness prick my eyes. I sandwich my best friend in a huge hug between myself and the couch cushions.

"I love you," I say. "You'll be my maid of honor too?"

Fiadh groans in fake pain. "If you'll get off me and let me take care of you for a change, I will be your maid of honor. Our friendship can't be in one direction. What else?" The overenunciation of the word "what" comes out in the full threat she intended.

I pull my body off her. She gives a series of dramatic wheezes. "The feelings, Piper. The ones you hate. You're going to say them, acknowledge them, or this isn't happening."

"I have no idea what you're talking about." I chew my lower lip to hide the quivering.

"Piper Anne Yeats, don't make me say why you did this," she says.

Maverick nearly tips from the desk when he leans in.

I rub at the thickness in my throat. "Will you walk me down the aisle so I don't have to go alone?"

"The feelings—the words with the feelings." She picks up a throw pillow, readying to smack me.

"I didn't want to bother you. That part's true. You had a lot going on." My words shake, matching the tremble in me that I do my best to ignore. "But I couldn't think about a larger ceremony—or the ceremony at all—because if I thought about the ceremony, I'd think about them."

"Their names," she says, pushing me in the way only she's allowed.

"I didn't want to think about not having the picture-perfect moments with Mom planning the wedding and my dad walking me down the aisle. Or this off-balance of one person at my side when the entire groom's side would be filled with people. With a massive number of family and friends." Tears stream down my face. "I didn't want the pain that comes with the loss, and I didn't want you to have to feel obligated to take care of me when it consumed me."

She wipes at her own tears. "I miss them too. I know it's not the same. I'm here. I'm always going to be here. You live for everyone else, and you need to live for yourself. I'm so proud of you. I'm still hurt, but I'm so proud of you for choosing to finally live. You're my platonic life partner, and if this is our tiny family, then we march it loud for everyone to know that this is what they're getting."

I can't stop crying. She pulls my hand, tugging me flat against her on the couch. She rubs her thumb against the base of my skull the same way she did when we were twelve and made all the plans for our future at my parents' celebration of life ceremony so I wouldn't have to think or worry. With heaving sobs, I pour everything I've trapped inside onto Maverick's floor. The extra hours of working to avoid admitting how alone I am, the purchasing of buildings to hold on to Granny, to keep Fiadh safe with a roof over her head no matter what's happening. Making sure the people important to me were taken care of has been my life, but it came at the cost of sleep. At the cost of healing.

"Can I come sit on the bride's side?" Maverick asks, his eyes pools of water.

"That's up to Fiadh. She's in charge with Hawk and Elin," I say. I chuckle softly to offset the embarrassment flowing through me.

"Shea and Amelia will come," Fiadh says, pointlessly trying to wipe tears from my face while more form. "Your side will not be empty. You don't even know how many people love you. I'm going to help show you."

"There's more." I wipe my nose with my wrist.

"How can there possibly be more?" Maverick asks.

Brendan comes and lies at our side. The whole house seems to want to check on me today. I scratch his rough fur, letting the gentle giant ground me.

"I emailed my official resignation to the university last night, and Lisa and Vera accepted it at five a.m., after a very long conversation." Weakness takes hold of me, and I slink further into the couch.

"About time," Fiadh says, her face beaming proudly.

A shot of adrenaline tingles in my body. This is not at all the response I'd been expecting. This is much, much better.

"You were killing yourself," she says.

She waves for Maverick to join us on the couch. He walks over, knuckles over his mouth, tears still in his eyes. The man is verklempt. Extra points to him for not trying to solve the problem, for sitting there supporting both of us. This man is so good for her.

"The day you blacked out, I swear I almost sent an email resigning for you." She balls her fists. "You can't save them from the mess they're in. If anyone could, it would be you. But I looked at the reports, and they have five, maybe ten years tops, unless a miracle happens. You'd drive yourself into a grave, and you're so much more than that job. We both are."

"I accepted a contract job from the television station," I say. "Do you remember that guy Brent?"

"Yup, hate him," Fiadh says with fire in her words.

"Well, to be fair, he didn't know Thad and I being married was a secret. And, he was attempting to play a counter position role for his uncle who owns the station thinking it would help with ratings, and everything slid into a dumpster fire fast. I've met him before and he tends to be overenthusiastic, not whatever the heck that was during the interview." I shrug.

"I still don't like him," Fiadh says. "But I do like when you do the television interviews."

"The contract at the station is just three times a month. Fewer hours, I get a wider audience to teach, and I can do all my research at home. I can still write and do my consulting work, but mostly, I can feel alive again. I do feel alive again."

"Your pain-in-the-ass spark has returned. It's been nice. The way you manhandled Brent was..." She kisses her fingers and pulls them from her mouth. "I've never been prouder."

Fiadh brushes off her leggings, stands, and walks to the door. "Are you coming?" she asks.

I get up and jog to follow her. She opens the heavy log door to find Shea and Amelia with a stack of shirts in their arms. The scrunch of Shea's face and the frozen stance of Amelia are clear tells that they do not know how to react to me being here.

"We're going wedding dress shopping," Fiadh says.

Amelia glances past me to Maverick. "For who?"

"Oh! Oh! Oh!" Shea bounces.

"For Piper," Maverick says.

Shea stops bouncing, confusion settling on her face.

"Come with us." Fiadh takes the shirts from them and tosses the stack on the couch.

Amelia wraps her arm around Shea's waist.

"I thought she was already married?" Shea says.

"She's not," Fiadh says. "We'll fill you in on the car ride."

Amelia stomps her foot. "I have a giant field. No one would ever know."

"Why is everyone jumping to being murdery and protective? Two minutes ago you may have buried me in the field for being here." I close the door behind me, leaving Maverick to the peace of his cabin.

The four of us pile into Fiadh's car. She gives them a brief synopsis of what happened.

Amelia shakes her head. "I love Hawk, but this doesn't sound like him. Not when it comes to anything super important."

"He said it was his intern," I say.

"This makes more sense. He is a cannon of energy," Amelia says. "I wouldn't give him anything huge to take care of beyond paperwork, though. The man loves love and thinks love should be celebrated in big ways."

Blood drains from my face.

"Are you going to puke?" Fiadh asks.

I cover my face with my hands. "Hawk is in charge of the wedding do-over. This is his way of apologizing."

Amelia snort-laughs. "I guarantee your wedding is going to scream love, possibly quite literally."

He couldn't go over the top. He's been given instructions, and he was so distraught thinking he'd messed up or betrayed Thad. The wedding will be fine.

"Besides the dress, is there anything else you need to get?" Shea redirects the subject perfectly.

"I need to get Thad's ring." His size, I need the size, too.

I pull out my phone to text Hawk.

Piper: *What's the theme of the wedding?*

Before I can click off my phone screen, there's a reply.

Hawk: *Thad and Piper in Love. That's the theme you gave me. Can you send Fiadh's cell number to Elin?*

"Fiadh, I'm sharing your cell with Elin," I say.

"No need. I'm setting up a group chat with everyone," Amelia says.

Two phones ding simultaneously in the car. There's no message on my phone.

"I didn't get the text." I show her my phone screen.

"I know," Amelia says. "You're not in the chat."

I can let go of the details. Thad and I get to be married and have everyone who cares about us there to support the ceremony. My finger itches to send another text.

Fiadh takes my phone from my lap and hands it to Amelia.

"This is now mine for the day." Fiadh flips on a turn signal and pulls out onto the parkway. "Now, tell me more about Thad. I need to know more about my future bestie-in-law, other than that he loves you."

"Ooh, Liv's offering to get the cake," Amelia chimes in.

Please don't let it be a penis cake.

CHAPTER THIRTY-ONE

CHIN UP. BOOBS UP. I am stronger than the hurricane of emotions brewing in me. This is the way today is meant to be. I own my future, and I choose Thad as my partner. I take a sip of water in an attempt to calm the ripples of anxiety that are galloping from one shoulder to the other. Not about marrying Thad, but about whatever Hawk's done to prepare for the ceremony. Marrying Thad is the easy part. Today I experience every emotion that arises no matter how much I want to hide. Happiness to a level I can't properly describe? Yes! Enormous adrenaline rush? Yes! Anxiety, I mentioned already. Sure, why not? Not all anxiety is bad.

"How can one be both radiant like an angel and sexy as fuck all at once?" Fiadh finishes pulling my hair up into a slick ponytail like when we were kids, finishing it off with a deep pinkish-purple ribbon. "There was zero reason for me to do your hair."

"I'm the bride," I say.

She walks in front of me, taking my hands in hers. "You are!"

Fiadh gushing only helps my insides soar. This is what was missing at the first chaotic wedding. I never should have tried to hide anything from her. Her eyes are misty.

I dab below my lower lashes. "Stop that. I'm going to cry. This dress cannot have tear marks before the ceremony." I blink up.

"I promise, if you get teardrops on your dress. I will add to them, and the entire dress will look like it is supposed to have all of these amazing little water droplets." Fiadh dabs the corners of my eyes with a tissue. "I will make sure every person has the marks on theirs, too."

I place a hand on her shoulder to tuck her in for a hug. "I love you too."

"Man, you're getting really mushy today." Fiadh stuffs the tissue into the dress pocket of her carnation-pink dress. Her dress is a version of the pearl-white satin number she picked for me. The swoop in the back of mine goes to right below my shoulder blades, with spaghetti straps, whereas hers sits a little higher because she wanted to wear a bra. As a bonus, hers flares at the waist, highlighting her goddess hips, and has pockets, whereas mine fits snugly to my figure. Her rationale was that she was my designated holder for today. My phone goes in her pocket, as does my red lipstick and extra bobby pins.

In short, my best friend made me a slick city bride with a touch of preppy, and the entire dress is perfect.

I link my elbow with hers. When we make it to the green-house in the backyard, Thad will be there. I blow out a long breath. We walk in silence together. The world for us is changing. It has been for a while. We both know this. I know her, though. Those moments when we were kids planning our futures, we never described who we'd be with. We mapped out our futures and made promises to support each other forever. The world is adding people at the right time.

We walk through the house and to the greenhouse. I check her face, and she's focused on the huge circle of people inside the glass and even more crowded around the outside of the glass. Inside are Thad's family, Fiadh's parents, Shea, Amelia, Lisa, and Vera. Outside, I catch a few faces from the university, from the television station, and even Nico. A piano plays from the far corner. Instead of being seated, hundreds of people stand gathered, breaking any type of fire code, leaving a thin aisle to walk up.

"There's no bride side or groom side. Everyone is here for you two together," Fiadh says.

My wrist shakes while I grab for her. To my left there's a different arm. One dressed in a formfitting purple and smashingly stylish suit. Thad's here. He hands me a bouquet of flowers wrapped in a handmade limerick lace handkerchief, the same one my granny and my mother used on their wedding days.

I pull in a shaky breath, letting the moment be real. That we're connected through this simple piece of fabric.

Fiadh gives him a kiss on the cheek. She rushes to the center to stand with Maverick.

"You're here." The frank comment tumbles off my tongue, carrying every affirmation of the world being right.

Thad places his hand on my cheek, pulling me in for a kiss. I wrap my arm over his shoulder to pull him in closer. An *aww* comes from the audience I've forgotten exists.

"Excuse me. No one said to kiss the bride," Fiadh says. "We need you two to process."

I can't tear my eyes off the beaming expression on Thad's face. He walks us through the circle of friends and family to the center. The music stops when we arrive in front of Hawk.

Hawk is sweating so much, his collar is darker than the rest of his shirt. I'm not sure he sweats this much on the soccer field. The room is hot from the sun, but not that hot. He wavers on his feet. Hawk shakes out his arms.

The overly excitable, extroverted, super-confident man set to marry us...a second time...for technically the first time is ready to pass out. Elin rushes to the center from the piano. Hawk's eyes flutter. She loops her arm through his, tugging him to her, keeping him from hitting the floor.

"He was up all night practicing to be perfect." She fans his face. "Hawk, come on, honey. You have one job right now."

Maverick disappears from the circle. He reappears with a piano bench high in the air. When he reaches the center, he places it behind a ghostly Hawk.

"I can do this." Hawk brushes sweat off his forehead. "I owe him everything, and I..."

Thad crouches next to his friend. "You owe me nothing. Be my best man, from there. Don't move from there."

Hawk frowns. "Who is going to marry you two then? I need to get up."

"Can anyone in here perform the ceremony?" Liv's voice cuts through from where the couch should be.

Fiadh elbows Maverick.

Maverick rubs his arm. "We should wait a few minutes while Hawk gets himself together."

Fiadh's short stature rises up. Despite the fact Mav is way taller than her, she's projecting short-girl powers that are best described as *don't mess with her or she'll turn into a fiery tornado.* She then takes a step closer to him and stares up, her eyes wide in a silent plea.

"Mav, do you perform ceremonies at the adventure center?" I ask with a full playful plea. "If so, I need to call in a favor."

Maverick leans down to kiss Fiadh's cheek. Fiadh narrows her eyes on Hawk, inspecting his current state of wooziness. Hawk's jacket is now off and on the bench, and three buttons of his shirt are undone.

"I do them at the adventure center and at the farm." He bites his lip. "I didn't want to say anything, though. I know Hawk wants to do this. I have nothing prepped for making this unique or special."

Hawk holds out a very wet piece of paper. I don't know where he's pulled it from. Maverick takes the disgusting paper, folds it, and returns it to Hawk.

"If everyone could join hands, snaking throughout the room and outside, we can get started," Maverick says.

He's doing it! *You'd better fuck the hell out of him tonight,* I mouth to Fiadh.

She gives me a strong nod. Come to think of it, that really isn't anything I needed to say or picture.

The mass of people around us closes the aisle they formed, leaving a circle around us. As a group, Maverick, Fiadh, Thad, and I shift to stand closer to Hawk so he can rightfully stand at Thad's side. In no way is this what I pictured my wedding day to be. Not that I'd ever pictured what I wanted in full until my first wedding to Thad. Today is different. This feels right. I feel whole.

"Inside this circle, those in the circle itself, and the crowd of people outside the glass are people who've come to join in friendship, love, and support, which serve as a reminder of the importance of unity in marriage. These individuals are your family." Maverick gestures around the greenhouse. "We as a whole are your family. Thad and Piper, please take each other's hands."

I reach my left hand to Thad's left and my right to his right. We allow the weight of the moment to settle over us. I glance over, and Elin and Hawk are connected. Fiadh and Maverick have two fingers locked together.

Maverick places his free hand atop ours. "'Friendship is never established as an understood relation. It is a miracle which requires constant proofs. It is an exercise of the purest imagination and of the rarest faith!' Henry David Thoreau."

Thad's eyebrows rise. He looks as surprised as I feel at the words flowing from Maverick's mouth. I know Fiadh's mentioned his love of literature, but pulling a full quote out without rehearsing is simply impressive as hell.

I love you, Thad mouths.

My heart swells. The gentle pounding in my chest hits a rhythm of joy. We're really doing this.

"Friendship is the strongest basis of any relationship. The two of you are forever each other's first support. But with that bond come more people to lean on. Relationships are never done alone. They require the support of those closest to you. The best friends by your sides, throughout this room, are here to witness and to affirm their own constant proof that they are here for both of you and your marriage."

Fiadh's eyes glimmer when Mav speaks about love.

"The people here to witness your union are here because of the love you have given everyone. We are together to root for your successes and to stand by you through moments of struggle. To remind you that merely being around you makes us strive to improve ourselves and to selflessly spread joy whenever possible."

He continues to talk. Poetic was not the impression I got when I first met Maverick. I wonder if Thad's as lost in what's happening as I am. The angles of his cheeks are so symmetrical. I've never noticed how perfectly aligned they are.

"Piper?" Mav says.

I snap out of my wandering. Thad squeezes my hands to let go.

"Piper, do you want to do vows first?" Maverick asks.

I don't respond in time. We didn't discuss this part of the ceremony. Then again, we discussed nothing of the ceremony at all with Maverick or Hawk. He wants me to talk? I'm not the person who can have Thoreau tumble from my mouth at a moment's notice. That's him or Fiadh.

Thad pulls my hand to his mouth and kisses my ring finger. "William Yeats said, 'Love is created and preserved by intellectual analysis, for we love only that which is unique, and it belongs to contemplation, not to action, for we would not change that which we love.' Piper, from the day you horribly tried to stop the soccer ball with your bare hand to protect your best friend, who didn't know what was happening, I saw someone who gave herself unconditionally to those she loves. A person with energy, intellect—someone I knew I wanted in my life forever. While Yeats would argue I didn't have enough data to know you, I knew myself. When we met, the world slowed down, and my brain flew through every scenario possible of what we could become in ways I've never experienced. There is only one of you, and I vow to honor you as you wish to be. To cherish your uniqueness and remind you it is okay to live out loud. To encourage you to lean on me and others for support when you most need it. I, Thaddeus Angelus Cosimo, do take you, Piper Anne Yeats, to be my forever. To be my wife."

Maverick turns to me. All the eyes of the joined guests are solidly on us, and the room isn't light and airy. The tone is serious. Yeats? Yeats. *Does everyone shove quotes for proper occasions...*I stop the ramble. He prepared for today. To have the words be perfect. To pull from my unconfirmed—likely not, but wouldn't it be cool—relative with whom I share a last name. Shared? Share? We'll need to sort this.

"Yeats? I need to follow up Yeats? Thad, I once had this thing where I thought I could figure people out within minutes of knowing them. To analyze the short data set in front of me and think I knew everything about a person. Before you, my life was often under a pile of books, giving interviews from my apartment, and adventures with Fiadh. My world was good but much smaller." I lick my lips. "My granny taught me that love is the beat of your pulse. The second I met you, my heart found the right rhythm. My favorite parts of you are that you go for life. You are kindness, a heart for everyone who knows you, and quietly generous in ways you can't learn within five minutes of meeting someone. Thad, I'm asking for more minutes. Hours. Days. I'm asking for a lifetime with you. To find ways to have fun and to remember to take chances."

I let out a nervous laugh. I'm not done, but he's got tears in his eyes.

Are you okay? I mouth.

He sniffs and waves for me to continue.

"I'm not as great with these types of words, but I'm amazing at keeping promises. I promise you we will have the best life, no matter what we are faced with. I promise you we'll tackle challenges together. I promise you this is only the beginning of grabbing hands and leaping into the unknown together. When we met, it felt like I'd known you for more lives than this one. That every part of me believed in things that aren't statistically provable. I, Piper Anne Yeats, take you, Thad Angelus Cosimo, to be my husband, my partner in this life and the next."

Hawk stands next to Thad and hands him a box.

"Piper"—Thad takes my hand—"please accept this ring as a reminder of my love, my commitment to our forever."

I stare down. On my finger is the most perfect platinum band with square-cut diamonds flanking rows of sapphires. Had I looked at a thousand stores, I'd never have found a ring more perfect.

Breathing is not keeping the tears from gathering. They're good tears, but I am not ready for them yet.

Fiadh pokes my side with his band. What I picked for him is much less ornate. When I saw this one, it screamed Thad. The flat sides give it the modern edge, but the simplicity of the traditional gold was perfect. I remove my hand from his, feeling the weight of my own ring. Fiadh slides his ring into my other hand.

"May I have your hand?" I run the tip of my ring finger down his long palm to flatten it.

"Thad"—I grin—"please accept this ring as a reminder of our connection, our love, and my commitment to our forever."

Thad's frozen. He's staring at the ring. A swirl builds in my chest. I picked the wrong ring. He hates the choice, or the ring has made every choice we've made too real and he's ready to run. Only we're married now. I think, though Maverick hasn't said that final line. Therefore, Thad could—

"By the power invested in me, by the state of New Jersey, I now pronounce you married," Maverick says. The words echo through my soul.

Married. Fuck yeah we're married.

"I hope you understand, I'm never taking this off," Thad says.

"Kiss her," Hawk says.

"I get to deliver that line," Maverick corrects him. "Please kiss your wife."

In a flash I'm lifted high in the air. Thad's mouth is on mine, his arms wrapped around my waist, holding me tight to him. Tears roll down my cheeks, hitting our smiles. I didn't know I could smile this much when I kiss a person. But when I'm around him, I can't keep from smiling. I follow his lead, opening my mouth slowly for a sweep of our tongues against each other. I don't want him to put me down. I want to keep kissing him. He drags his thumb up the side of my neck, sending a warm desire through me. I want to devour him. He places me down to stand on my own but refuses to let go. Our mouths can no longer touch, which is simply not fair. I protest with a grumble.

He looks around the room. People are whistling and applauding. My cheeks heat. I'd forgotten they were here. But they are here. My worry of rushing into this marriage, of people talking us out of what we both knew at our cores to be right is gone. Maverick is right. We are loved by a huge number of people. None of them would have kept their mouths shut, especially not Fiadh, if they didn't believe in us succeeding.

Our best worst-kept secret was our first wedding. The best decision we've made as a couple was to have this wedding, where we're surrounded by love. By people, by once-strangers gathered together for a common purpose.

A line forms in front of us. Person after person hands me a flower with a card until I cannot hold any more and I'm piling them into the arms of our support team. Fiadh's collecting the flowers as they topple, shoving them into a big bucket. Liv's collecting the cards into a neat pile.

Near the end of the line, a pair of penguins and a delicate woman with long braids and wearing an olive-green zoo uniform nears us. She leans forward and squeezes me. I stare at her, and her dynamic little best-dressed beaked dates.

"We wanted to wish you both congratulations and thank you for everything you've done for the zoo," the woman says.

"Do you normally bring such wonderful guests to a party?" I need to touch the penguin. He's too big to cuddle, but I'm so excited it might be worth risking the mistake.

"We do when you've donated as much as came in for your wedding." She hands Thad an envelope.

He swiftly opens the top and pulls out the paper.

"Total donation number is in the envelope, along with a list of the donations unless someone asked us to remain anonymous."

Anonymous?

"You two have brought in one of the largest non-corporate donations in years, and we thought you might enjoy Pebbles and Harriet. Is it all right if they stay?" she asks, checking over her shoulder.

Outside is a vibration of energy already. Jazz music threads through the air, and laughter, happiness, and friendship fill the yard. Today is the first of many times for this.

"I'd never say no to two party animals," I say.

Thad groans at the joke. "You did that, didn't you?"

The woman wanders out, and Thad turns to me, showing me the total. Faint is an understatement; I stagger to the bench once occupied by Hawk.

"There's no way that's right," I say.

His face scrunches while he reads, "Total donation, $257,618."

This generosity is next level. "Please tell me it wasn't all Fiadh." The mill flashes before my eyes.

"No, it was Brent," he says.

Brent who isn't here. Not that I saw. Brent who acted strange on television and outed us. Per the line on the paper, he donated $100,000 on his own. Brent, who no doubt talked to his uncle after the interview and helped me get the job. Thad was right, but instead of *weird*, I'll say *peculiar*.

Thad holds out his hand to me. "Let's go continue this for-forever thing we started."

I grab his hand, and the two of us join the hundreds of people plus two penguins outside, where they are already dancing, laughing, and sharing in the celebration with us. Tonight we dance until we fall over. Tomorrow I figure out more of what comes next.

CHAPTER THIRTY-TWO

WATCHING THAD PLAY ON the field the Wednesday after our wedding charges me in nearly the same way as him taking me to an academic lecture. The largest difference being that here he's sweating, sexy as hell, and I get to ogle him openly while I half drool on myself. This morning he gifted me a pair of black-and-yellow indoor soccer shoes for when I'm in the field house. They're like the ones the Bees wear, but mine have a tiny pink heart on each of the tongues.

Not teaching in the spring semester doesn't totally feel real yet. There must be a support group of some kind for former academics going through the pressure withdrawal. Learning to live life not by semesters is a big change.

Our marriage is officially confirmed, and we walked into the records area with Hawk on Monday to deliver the paperwork. Wednesdays contain my new favorite night of the week. Watching Thad play is incredible, but the added bonus is the Bees play tonight.

The buzzer sounds for the end of Thad's match. He lifts his shirt, exposing his abs for my eyes. When he drops the front of his jersey down, he gives an eyebrow wag. He turns to head to the handshake line, exposing the muscles in his delicious calves. The ones I will bite later tonight.

Large double doors on the far end of the field bang open. Hawk and Elin snake their way around the outside of the black netting. Elin takes a bag off her shoulder and places it on the bench between us. Hawk tugs at his earlobe on his walk to Thad.

"Fiadh will be here soon. She's been looking forward to seeing you play," I say, not taking my eyes off Thad. His wedding ring catches the light, sending a wave of comfort through me. Wedding rings, I've come to discover, are a way of openly declaring love for a person, and, at the same time, they represent all the secrets held within the bond of marriage.

Thad digs friendly knuckles into Hawk's shoulder, nudging him to the netting. Elin coughs out a laugh. Hawk twists at his black lobe piercing...a move I finally understand is a tell he's nervous. He and Thad step through the netting. Maverick opens one of the large doors, kicking a door stopper in to prop it open before it can slam closed. He walks right behind Fiadh, stretching his long arm out to hold the black netting open, clearing a path for her. When he's behind her, she looks even tinier. His broad shoulders, in combination with jeans and a yellow flannel, are out of place. Her leggings and tank top are at least athletic, showing off her muscles from pressing cider.

I wave wildly at the two of them, like they can't see Hawk or Thad standing with us. Thad slides into the seat next to mine and plants a tender kiss on my lips. The world hazes until the buzzer goes off for the far field. The bleep of the buzzer is enough to snap anyone out of a love trance.

I've never seen the field this empty. There's a green team, suited up across the way, with a line of players ready to go. They walk out onto the field and take their net for practice.

"Shouldn't the Bees be here?" I ask.

Elin pushes herself closer to me, making room on the bench for Hawk to sit, followed by Fiadh and Maverick.

"They're here. Liv texted me when she pulled in." Elin presses her hand against her chest.

In walks Liv, followed by Rose, and a line of other Bees. I squint at an accessory on Liv's wrist. When she gets to us, she grips the net with a braced hand. Rose raises her right hand to show off the brace on her own wrist. Two of them hurt themselves less than a week after our wedding? I look down the line. Both of Margaret's hands are bandaged, as are each of the other players.

Tonight got suspiciously weirder.

Elin dumps her kit onto the bench. A fresh set of shorts and jerseys tumble down.

Fiadh glances up and down the line of players, a smirk painting her mouth. Maverick can't look at me. I focus down at my now super-suspicious shoes.

Elin drops her hand to her lower stomach. "Margaret! I needed you to play tonight. You hurt both wrists?"

I can say with solid conviction, Elin is not a good actress. I scan across the bench to the pile of soccer gear. The shirtsleeves on the jersey that's tumbled out are long.

"Dance injury from the wedding," Margaret says. "Liv hurt hers opening the champagne. Rose slide tackled a poor guy in a pickup match..."

One by one they pout out their lips. All of their eyes stay glued on me. I look down at the fake grass, avoiding eye contact.

"The doctor gave me clear instructions. I can't play goalie while I'm pregnant," Elin says.

My heart grows to burst. "How pregnant?" Tears well in my eyes. Hawk and Elin are going to make the best parents.

"There really isn't an option of partially pregnant." Elin strokes her swollen belly. "Twenty-six weeks. There is zero ability to hide this bump anymore. We didn't want to say anything or make any big announcements until after your wedding."

I put the pieces together of everything that happened since we met. Moving the wedding up earlier. Elin not drinking at our wedding despite talking about Wednesday-night beers after games. The loose dresses. Missing matches, which her teammates said wasn't like her. This explains why Hawk is losing his mind.

"I'm still sorry, man. Twice I screwed things up on you. Twice!" Hawk sinks his fingers into his hair.

"There is zero doubt in my mind that I'd have had the same reaction," Thad says. A gleam like he's gone to a different place than this field in his head. Thad will one day be a great dad.

"She wasn't feeling good, and we peed on sticks," Hawk says.

"We? Were you worrying there was a fetus in you?" I ask, deadpan.

"He got excited about the science end of peeing on the stick." Elin glances up at the time clock. "His was negative, much to his disappointment. Mine was positive. The doctor confirmed the morning of the first ceremony about the pregnancy, and on the day of your actual wedding, he recommended I get my belly off the field until at least ten weeks after the kids are born."

"Kids? There was an *s* on that." I stare at her belly.

"Three. All girls, from what the blood test showed." She gestures to her teammates. "The Bees will continue for generations."

"Three?" I stare over at Hawk.

He nods. "We were making up for lost time, but I did not see three happening at once. It's like she's superhuman. She is superhuman and carrying my girls."

The sweetness of the words, the excitement. No wonder they've been losing their minds. Three babies at once.

"These girls are going to have the fiercest fairy godmothers ever," Liv says.

Margaret points up at the clock. "There are five minutes to go, and there is no one to play goal, which makes us down a player."

"Fiadh?" I ask, knowing the answer is no before it comes from her mouth.

"Jersey doesn't have my name on it," Fiadh says.

Excuse her? She's in on this. I scrunch my toes in my shoes. A Bees jersey drops onto my lap.

I grab the kit. "I'm in."

Hawk leans forward. "League rules state you need permission from the owner to play if you haven't played before. There's also a medical waiver."

Thad hands me a clipboard to sign.

"I'm your wife," I say.

"Does committing to the Bees scare you more than marrying me?" he asks.

I grab the clipboard and sign the form. "I'm half owner." My nerves are half petrified when I hover over the last name. I scribble out Piper Yeats Cosimo.

Elin peeks at the paper, then tugs the jersey out of my arms, replacing it with another jersey.

"Do you have three different jersey options?" I reach for her pile.

"We weren't sure the direction you'd go, but my guess was using both." Fiadh leans against the painted cinder-block wall.

Rose holds up her wrist. "There's two minutes and you're still short a player."

"Your injury is real?" I gasp.

"He had it coming. I will never understand why men underestimate me on the field." Rose takes a seat on the bench.

Fiadh dives for the pile of jerseys next to Elin. She pulls up a blank one. I stand and face Thad, who blocks my chest from full view on the other field while I switch my shirt. I swipe off my shorts, replacing them with Elin's padded ones.

A flush crosses Thad's cheeks. He absently hands the clipboard to Fiadh for her to sign a form.

"You are bringing that home tonight." He pushes me through the net, onto the field.

The clock buzzes. I check out the numbers, and they're going backward. He's buying time before the match starts. The green team either doesn't notice or doesn't care.

Wrist protectors come off Liv, Margaret, and two other Bees. They swarm into the large square in front of the net.

"I know you've been watching our games and Thad's games. If you have any questions, let me know. I'm here to keep the ball away from you. You can pick it up anywhere in the box. Do not under any circumstances pick up the ball outside of the box." Margaret gestures to the different areas of the pitch to pay attention to. "Fiadh, you have one job. Protect the goalie. You keep the ball far from her. I don't care how, as long as you don't knock anyone over or pick it up with your hands."

"I know how to protect Piper." Fiadh ties the strings on her new-to-her yellow shorts.

Fiadh does know how to protect me. She always has, and I know in my gut she will do so forever.

"Piper, if you get the ball, feed it to me," Liv says.

I raise my hand. "I'm going to need clarification on that."

"Roll it, kick it, punt it, drop it, head it, punch it...to me." Liv points up the field.

"There is no way that is happening. New plan, please." Sweat drips down my neck.

"Get the ball to a yellow jersey," Fiadh says. "You keep it out of the net and get it to a yellow jersey."

"Why couldn't Liv just say that?" I ask. "All I can picture is her licking and eating balls."

"I'm good at that too," Liv says.

My eyes fly wide. Margaret punches Liv's arm.

"She'll get used to me," Liv says.

I huff a laugh to center myself. "Fiadh, we are going to suck at this."

"We're going to suck together," Fiadh announces.

Thad gags on his water.

Maverick drops his forehead to his palm. "That's my girlfriend."

"No one is sucking." Margaret holds her composure. "I don't care what anyone does after the game. But right now we need to get ready. Remember, the only important thing—"

"Keep the ball from the net," I say.

"Ha! Wednesdays are for fun and friends," Elin says. "Go stand on the line!"

I oblige. I open my arms wide, mimicking Elin's stance on the side near the net. Coach Elin erupts from the sideline, yelling to each of the players on the field. The majority of the first ten minutes of the game, the ball is at Liv's feet.

When I look to our cheering section, Hawk's busy watching Elin, his chest puffed out, his arms splayed across the top of the bench. Maverick is next to him, wearing that cool look of chill he always has. Like he knows Fiadh's capable as hell, and going to protect me from anyone flying up the field. Then there's Thad. He's leaning forward, his eyes locked on me, a huge smile on his face. His mouth widens, and he yells my name. I turn in time to see the ball coming at me. I raise my arms up in an X. There's a pop, but the impact never got to me. The flash of the blank jersey and wild short red hair is dancing in place.

"Did you see that! I headed the ball!" Fiadh screeches in pleasure. She runs up and down the field three times, expelling energy off the adrenaline high.

"My hero," I say.

Margaret kicks the ball up and over to Liv, who then passes it to another player. Liv sneaks up near their goal and takes the shot. The ball goes in the net! All of the Bees look at one another.

"Hell yeah!" shouts Elin from the side. "Reset and do it again!"

There's an openness here, a celebration of success and encouragement that it's okay to try and fail like I've never experienced before. I'd worried that Thad married me because he was lonely, but I know that's not the case. Deep down, I think we were brought together by the people here and by some cosmic intervention to learn to recognize that it is important to seize the opportunity for happiness. Since I've met him, I've reconfigured my life with a better understanding that I desperately needed to reevaluate when I felt truly alive. Happy.

Happiness is being on this field for the sole purpose of having fun, of connecting, of being part of a larger family. My happiness is on the bench, and I promise I will do everything in my power to make sure he feels nothing but love for the rest of his life.

His touch restarted my pulse the day we met, intertwining us on our unexpected path of forever. Happiness is being with a man I love and who loves me back.

EPILOGUE

Thad

One Year Later

SURPRISING PIPER WITH A trip is one of the hardest things I've ever had to pull off. Second hardest. The hardest was after we agreed to get married, convincing myself she wasn't going to ghost me. Telling myself she was real and that the confidence she exuded when I met her was going to do me in went along with those fears. Learning her gentle side, the parts where she lets me in to see her vulnerabilities, those are the moments where it solidified my first instinct of "she's the one" was bang on.

The week after our official wedding, her schedule filled fast with interviews, guest hosting spots on news channels to be a commentator, magazine article requests, and she had more consulting work than ever. The work offers coming in were suspiciously but unsurprisingly tied to many of the companies the Bees work for. This week was fake booked out with the assistance of Margaret and Rose. As soon as it was time to leave for our flight, they deleted all their meetings for the week and replaced them with the Greek word *agape*. Unconditional love.

I grimace at our shared calendar. Appointment request after appointment request unanswered since we arrived in Milos three days ago. Two more come in while I grab two bottled waters from the beach bag. Resigning from the university freed up her schedule, but that hasn't changed how in demand she is.

The emerald-green waters in front of the sheet Piper's topless and laid out on make her eyes fit perfectly into the scenery. Her skin is no longer ghostly pale, thanks to a soft base-layer tan from the trip. I shouldn't stare at her, but I don't think a living soul would blame me. The curve above her slender hips rests flat on the gray fabric. Her dark hair is pulled tight in a ponytail to keep the breeze from flooding strands into her eyes or mouth.

Ping. Ping. Ping. My phone lights up like the night sky on the Fourth of July.

Ping. Ping. Ping. Ping. Ping. Hers is worse. She slides the phone up, checking the stream of texts. I hold stiller than the marble statues that line the beach house. Studying her face to guess what she's thinking is getting easier. Around me, she has no poker face when she looks at the messages she gets. I am one of the lucky few who get to see her without her mask. The corner of her mouth lifts, and I know it's a friend, not work.

She flicks her gaze over at me. I toss my phone onto the ground. Lowering myself to take my spot on the ground next to her doesn't go as smoothly as I hoped, and I let out a grunt as I land hard on the sand.

"Your goddaughters are too damn cute." Piper turns the phone to me. The redheaded triplets are half gnawing the soccer ball teethers we gifted them while simultaneously falling on one another in the video clip from Elin.

"Where did all that red hair come from?" I ask for the thousandth time, knowing the answer already. Hawk also had red hair when he was little, but by the time he was four, it darkened.

She flicks to the next picture, where Elin is napping, sent courtesy of Hawk. Thumbing back a picture, she takes a deep inhale, peeking at the soccer-ball-gnawing triplets.

The dreamy look in her eyes appears every time she sees the girls and when she sees my sisters' kids. I've even caught her watching the screen when the pre-K kids are taking lessons at the field house.

"We're babysitting when we get home so they can go on a proper date," I say, reveling in the deepening of her smile.

"Does this mean you've forgiven Hawk?" she asks.

"Yes, but don't tell him that until we get home." For the past year he's asked how he can make up for what happened. To me, everything ended up as it should have. But that doesn't stop him from feeling guilty. He's managing the field house while we're here. Fiadh and Amelia are helping out Elin when there are late games, though I've already received several pictures of all of them hanging out at the field house—including one that suspiciously looked like they were setting up the babies to race down the field.

Piper stacks her phone on mine and slides them into the black bag of technology time-out, leaving the two of us to connect without the mass of family and found family swarming us. Given the buzz coming from the bag, they're still trying. My mom and sisters were only quiet last night after I sent photos of the house, of the beach, of Piper relaxed and laughing.

"This beach is unreal," she says. "I don't think I've ever seen pink sand in person before."

The beach is ours for another four days. There's not another visitor in sight.

"Remind me to knock off a month from Nico's rent," she says.

"When he told me his family had a house to rent on the water and we'd be alone, I paid three months' worth of his rent in exchange for this week." I open her water, setting it in her hand.

"He better have tongue kissed you for that." She sits up on her elbows, surveying the glistening water.

"Pretty sure Antonia would have objected," I say, opening my water. "He did kiss my cheek and tried to refuse the check three times."

"I know what you're about to do, and don't you dare." Piper sits up, her breasts moving freely, forming way too great a distraction.

Water pours down my leg from tipping my open bottle. I drop it into the sand and chase her down to the ocean, easily catching her and lifting her up on my side with one arm. She wiggles, laughing, and throws her legs in a huge jerk, knocking the two of us over. The salt water is refreshing, and the need to sit to hide how easily she turns me on is urgent. I crouch, the soft waves rising to my chin.

She slides herself onto me, resting her cheek on my shoulder and wrapping her legs around my waist.

"I'm sorry." I let out a shaky breath.

"For what?" She snuggles in tighter.

She knows for what, and the slipperiness of her skin makes me groan. Think about anything else but friction. I slide my hands under her ass to support her while the waves work to bring us closer together.

She lifts her chin, kissing me softly on the mouth. Once. Twice. Settling into a snuggle on my chest.

"If you keep kissing me like that, I'm never going to be able to get out of this water," I say. "We have a full schedule of pirate coves, rock formations—"

She kisses me again, cutting off my words.

"Dinners," I wheeze out.

She grinds down on my hardness, our swimsuits keeping a barely there barrier between us. I pull at the string on the side of her swimsuit, her eyebrows rising in excitement.

"I've even secured us a walking tour with a local professor. Say the word, and I'll text him to come over." I pinch her nipple between my knuckles, reveling when she grinds down on me to show her appreciation.

I take her breast in my mouth, circling my tongue around her peak, using my teeth in the way she likes when I pull it out. She dips her head, her hand dropping to the other side of her suit. I shoo the hand away.

"Let me take care of you," I say, pulling the last string apart.

She wiggles on me, fabric floating between us, all four blue bikini strings bobbing. I shift my groin, fighting myself from moving too fast. She's given me her greatest commodity, time. I will never lose sight of how precious that is. That's how I figured out she loved me too before she even said it.

I kiss her. Her sweet mouth opens, letting me in. Our tongues glide across each other. We take our time, giving ourselves over to each other. The first time she shuffled her schedule, she was saying how she felt about me without needing words. The more time we spent together, the more I felt guilty. Then I realized I was doing the same. Finding people to cover at the field house. Leaning on my family instead of running everything for them. She helped bring balance to my world. She's brought fun, joy, and an understanding of how it feels to show most of the world one side when you're hiding parts of yourself.

She runs her nails down my sides, sending electricity up my ribs.

"Not fair." I groan, floating breathlessly.

She helps tug off my swim briefs, tossing them but missing the beach. I peek around us to ensure there're no fish.

Piper inspects me like she's trying to memorize my face. "How did I get so lucky to find you?"

My heart hits hard in my chest, and I need to be inside her. "I love you."

I pull her hips over mine, sliding myself inside her, catching my breath from the wave of her softness holding me in her. She rocks on me, waiting for my jaw to open. She then seizes the opportunity to take my mouth in hers. I set my knees down, rocking my hips, pumping in and out of her with care, with determination to make her eyes roll in want of more pressure.

Her fingers slide between us, stroking at her warm clit. Her fingers add pressure across either side of my cock on her downward strokes. When she starts to pulse around me, I nearly fall into the water. I steady myself with one hand and let the waves keep us both up while her moans increase and pressure builds inside me. Her whole body tenses, making me lose control, and I nearly black out from how hard and long I come. She sits high on me, her arms draping over me for balance, and nestles in.

"This is the only thing I want to do today," Piper says. "Today is orgasm day."

"I'd like to remind you that's what you said yesterday and the day before." I slide myself from her, snagging her suit bottoms while lifting her up from the water.

We walk back to the blanket, her glistening wet skin taunting me with every step.

"Every day should be orgasm day." She lies on the blanket.

Fuck. I'm not ready yet, but fuck. My brain does not want to stop touching her. I walk my fingers between her thighs, tickling between them to open.

"Here?" she shrieks, spreading her legs enough to let me run a finger up her slit.

"You said this is orgasm day. I'd be a moron to turn that request down." I place my face close to her center. She wriggles beneath each breath I blow on her. "Where do I start?"

She takes both of her hands and pushes my head down.

Piper laughs so hard as her legs fall open. I spread her lips open, flicking my tongue down from the top to her entry in one swift move. She presses her thighs on either side of my face, holding me in place.

"I take it you liked that?" I ask, laughing at the vise around my face.

"Where did you learn how to do that?" she asks.

"Remember that fascination you had with what I can do with my tongue?" I ask. "Time to learn what it can do for you." I dip a finger inside her. "If you release the vise, this may go better."

"I can't," she says. "I'm scared it'll be too good. Too high a bar to beat next time."

I dart my tongue from the top to the bottom, pushing a finger in. She releases the vise, letting me suck in her sweetness. But it's not sweet. My tongue is an ocean salt lick. If I keep going, I may die of sodium. On the other hand, hell of a way to go.

She stops wriggling. "How awful does the seawater taste?"

"You taste great." I can do this. It's only seawater.

"I want to taste it." She pushes up on her elbows, not buying the answer.

I crawl up her body, taking my time to let her breasts brush against me for as long as possible. Water droplets fall from my hair to her forehead.

"Fine, I taste the ocean." I pout a lip. "But I promised you orgasm day."

"If I were to take you in my mouth right now, would you be upset that I was sucking the ocean dry?" she asks.

There's a strong part of me that wishes there were a shower out here to clean up and keep going. The shower is in the house. If we dry off, we'll still be salty. Not that we weren't turning each other salty from sweat, but this is a different kind of salt.

I dig into the beach bag, pulling out her not-so-shoulder-massager, and turn the buzzer on. "This little thing has come in handy so many times."

She bites her lip, watching as I lower the ball between us, landing it on her arousal.

"That's not what that's for." She shakes under me.

"Let go." Planking over my wife, holding a pleasure toy to her while she discovers ways to submit to the sensations growing inside her, is the hottest thing I've ever done.

Piper lifts her arms over her head, grinding her hips on the ball. Her breath hitches high.

"That's right. Do it for me," I say, my focus purely on seeing how hard I can make her come for me.

A series of pleasure moans ring out of her. She falls, spent, her hair messed over her face.

I tumble to her side, lacing my fingers in hers. Unsure of how we ended up here, understanding better why time after time I stepped away from potential relationships. In my heart I knew from the first moment I saw her, there was no one else, nor would there ever be anyone else as exactly right for me as Piper.

About the Author

Beck Erixson writes about the beautifully awkward world of navigating the journey to true happiness through friendships, love, and family—be it blood, found, or chosen. Her stories enhance the importance of positive interconnection, even when we feel lost or lonely. She lives on the Jersey Shore, and can often be found either writing *by* the river, or *in* it in some way. When she's not writing novels, she can be found at open mic nights with her short stories, cheering her talented author friends on loudly, or encouraging one of her close friends to go for whatever it is that makes them happy.

Like the FMC in *Feeling Lively*, she loves her best friends deeply and surrounds herself with people who unapologetically seek their unique paths to joy.

Connect with Me

Learn about upcoming releases, short stories, and more by visiting her through one of the platforms below.

instagram.com/BeckErixsonAuthor

www.beckerixson.com

If you enjoyed the story, please consider leaving a review on whichever platform best suits your fancy.

Acknowledgments

In full open-hearted honesty, this book could not have happened without learning over time how loved I am by my friends. The ones who have known me my whole life, Erica and Heather. The ones I gained along the way, Kristin and Kristen, Alana, Janine, Katie, Mary, Shannon, Steph, Ann Marie, and so many more I'd fill another twenty pages. The ones I met working in a university, Dr. Lisa Sisler and Prof. Stina Mastroeni. (My friends have been excitedly awaiting the final book in this series. When I was done with this book I realized I essentially wrote a series which is a love story to friendship. Here you all go. I love you forever.)

My writing group, the ones I check messages from daily since #RevPit in 2020, consistently cheered me on to write through this last book in the series while my life was flipped upside down twice in the process. Thanks for not giving up on me; Amelia, Ariana, Janet, Katrina, Kim, Liv, Melisa, and Rose, for your friendship.

My usual suspect writing friends in my WriteAlong group,

Tiffany, Aliya, Christine, Dani, Kali, Kearstie, Nancy, Narjis, Zoe, Sam, Tashi...

Kristen Weber may be stuck with me for a long time as my developmental editor. After several books, years, and kids, I consider her a friend at this point. (A wickedly amazing editor, and a friend.)

Penina Lopez, I cannot thank you enough for picking up on every detail and helping my academic brain understand college sports. I'm admire your skill and am grateful for your agreeing to copyedit this book to help make my writing beautiful.

Elaini Caruso your energy and patience is amazing. I appreciate you for attention to detail as well as your gentleness in letting me know where to make changes to strengthen the writing even further.

No book is complete without a gorgeous cover. This is my fourth cover with the fantastic Melody Jeffries. She is exceptional at taking rough words and ideas and sketching them in wonderful ways.

Chris, Greta and Svea, you hold my heart always.

Thank you, dear reader, for going on this journey of love and friendship with me. Thank you for taking the chance on Piper, Thad, and myself.

Awkwardly,

Beck

If you enjoyed the story, please consider leaving a review on whichever platform best suits your fancy.

BOOKS BY BECK ERIXSON

<u>Love is Awkward Novels</u>

Feeling Ballsy

Feeling Fiery

Feeling Lively

<u>Additional Books</u>

Just a Fika: Coffee, Connection, and a Matchmaking

Ghost Grandmother

www.ingramcontent.com/pod-product-compliance
Lightning Source LLC
Chambersburg PA
CBHW020329010826
48973CB00005B/1190